The Reincarnation of Wind©
By Paul Grandpierre G.F.G.

"Everything that is, is the Spirit, but also conceals the Spirit. Look closely and you may see who you truly are looking back at you."

I0682226

ISBN 978-0-6152-1042-1

Cover by Ruqayyah Ali
Edited by Morgan Quincy Dowe

Contents

Prologue

Plumes of smoke wafted eerily into the air here and there throughout Chamiache like specters with gaping mouths lamenting an ominous day and a dreadful night. The sun had not yet risen the day after to emblazon the sky and to bring new hope to a populace still captivated by the smoldering remains of a madman's dream.

The man called Nausterus had imagined a more auspicious outcome for his bold plan to sack the high city from within. He arrived at the high city with his shadowy Droa-he to terrorize its inhabitants and to overthrow its ruler. Now fatally injured and shaken, the self-assurance and boldness characteristic of men in his Atenarix order abandoned him.

Nausterus' failure was personal and complete. His assault began well enough. Weeks before the assault was attempted, he sent spies to the city to report on its inhabitant's preparedness. The Atenarix captain's detachment of Droa concealed their presence and purpose, entering the city under the guise of merchants and pilgrims just before the Levying festival began. The Droa stealthily blended into a cluttered canvas of citizens and revelers and maneuvered into place. As darkness fell on the chosen day, they sprang and set out to assassinate the city's Vyrdmar regent, Ylarin, and his entire family.

The Vyrdmar dynasty had exerted powerful influence over the political and military landscape of Maspeidon for hundreds of years. Many in Maspeidon believed that the god Yggir favored the Vyrdmar. Yggir led their ancestors to the holy ground upon which they built the temple Irilsflir under the sky dew of the Kuriox. Yet Nausterus was confident that his plan would succeed. The brooding Atenarix captain was quietly buoyed by visions of Vyrdmar desolation as his men began their assault. He wondered if he would have the opportunity to put king Ylarin under the sword himself. After his Ayimar reinforcements swept in from their subterranean catacombs to the south to pacify the entire city, he would climb the city's ramparts and present the king's head on a pike to a raucous throng of Droa and Ayimar.

Nausterus believed that with the Vyrdmar regent dead, all of Maspeidon would be swept up by the tide of Atenarix enlightenment and justice. "Disguised as drones-" Nausterus declared to his Ayimar benefactors, "We will enter the Vyrdmar's nest, and slay its monarch."

"This assault is unexpected. And that is why we will succeed. Walls and ramparts protect the Vyrdmar city against sieging armies. But the Droa is not an army. We will not bombard the city with stones and iron balls or batter down its gates. We will strike a blow from within. After the king is slain and the royal compound is seized, fear and confusion will ensue throughout the city. Then, in those chaotic and precious moments, the Ayimar will sally out from under the mountains to the south and seize the city proper.

Nausterus explained to the Ayimar Lord Secant of the Ayimar that "a full scale war with the Vyrdmar and their allies can only succeed if we first strike a blow against their cohesion and belief in the inviolability of their godlike king. We cannot crush our enemy by force of arms alone. We must shake their confidence. In so doing, we may not have to wage war at all."

The Lord Secant agreed with Nausterus' premise that the power of the Vyrdmar rested on the mythical belief that the Vyrdmar regent was godlike and inviolable. But he questioned the timing of the attack. There were other more immediate objectives to be achieved that could strengthen both the Ayimar's and Atenarix council's position. He worried that an attack on the Vyrdmar would jeopardize one particular objective the leaderless Ayimar had long endeavored to achieve.

"There is something very fragile and yet very consequential to us in the high city." The Lord Secant's words were barely audible.

Nausterus had anticipated the Lord Secant's concern. He did not initially reveal the full scope of his plans for effect. He was silent for a moment. When the Lord Secant sighed and looked as if he would speak again, Nausterus spoke.

"My lord... of course the trees hide the wood. I am certain that my assault will topple the Vyrdmar. But even if it fails, it will serve as a diversion for a far greater objetive. The Great One beneath the city will return among us. But the more likely outcome is that we will sever the roots of the Vyrdmar dynasty so that the roots of the Atenarix dynasty may be revealed."

The Lord Secant reluctantly sanctioned Nausterus' plan and promised an entire Ayimar division in reserve to secure the city if Nausterus was successful, or, to check any Vyrdmar retribution if he was not.

But Nausterus' attack ended badly even after a promising beginning. The cheers of the victorious still bellowing from the city, he and his cohorts were now in full retreat. Many Vyrdmar were initially lost during the siege, but the fabled servants of the Celestial roused themselves to write another awe inspiring chapter in their glorious history. Led by princes Varenhil and Hovin, and the Harfingals, the king's royal guard, the Vyrdmar routed the Droa. The threat to the Vyrdmar receded by the early morning like a murky fog at sunrise.

Even worse for Nausterus, he was gravely wounded. Prince Varenhil hacked off his arm in a fierce melee before the walls of the royal compound. Nausterus's men rescued their captain from Varenhil's attack, but with his ambitious assault unraveling before his eyes, he thought fondly of death.

Shortly after daybreak, after the failed assault, a gaggle of Nausterus' men mustered near a spring not far from the high city. They were soon joined by a trickle of stragglers. Clinging to life and fading in and out of consciousness, Nausterus was among the stragglers.

"Listen to me my faithful Droa-he," he murmured in a conscious moment. "Take me to the upper stratum. There is a saternum there," he insisted. "Only these masterful instruments of our fallen benefactors from the stars can save me now. They know almost everything – even knowledge beyond what is known by the greatest Atenarix physicians. He will surely know how to rescue me from death's icy grip and restore me."

Nausterus was given a potion to drink and after whispering incoherently for a while, he fell into a deep sleep that seemed almost like the death he in one moment wanted to forestall and in another to embrace.

Now mustered, what remained of the Droa host divided into three companies. One company traveled south on horseback with a horse drawn cart carrying their captain Nausterus. Another fled into the nearby wilderness to scout on the Vyrdmar's movements. A third company hurried west to the coast where a ship awaited them.

The company tending to Nausterus rode as fast as they could with their captain in tow. By early afternoon, they arrived at a waterfall concealing the hidden entrance to the Ayimar upper stratum. Behind the fall was a high and narrow cave, wide enough for horses to pass. Inexplicably, only four from the company passed on foot behind the roaring fall – the others continued south. The four Droa carried Nausterus with them deep into the hidden cave. Two carried torches while the others followed more slowly, straining under the weight and displacement of their tall and lanky captain.

The men descended into the dark cave until they came to a wall of smooth rock. The forward Droa passed his hand over the even cave surface and spoke a series of strange coarse words followed by clicking sounds. The men began coughing as smoke from their torches filled the space around them. Then suddenly they heard a continuous clanking sound.

The cave wall slid down to reveal a downward sloping passageway.

"Hurry!" a hushed voice could be heard in the darkness beyond.

The Droa dragged their captain through an emerging round portal.

"We need a saternum!" a Droa cried out. "Our captain is wounded. He does not have much time."

A very small man, perhaps two feet shorter than the average man came forward. He was covered from head to toe with layers of mismatched apparel and a cowl.

"A saternum?" The small man shook his head and shrugged.

"Our captain needs the assistance of a saternum as soon as possible," a Droa remonstrated. "Hurry. He will not last long."

The small man sighed and muttered almost inaudibly. He then motioned to Droa.

"Come quickly. I welcome back you to the upper stratum. We must go deep into this realm to find a saternum. There is one they call Gygus who serves the Ayimar Lord Secant. He is one of the few saternum left – one of the few that is of any use."

Nausterus passed on to the dreaded void shortly after his Droa entered the Ayimar upper stratum. The company of five hurried as fast as they could through tunnels with smooth rock surfaces and illuminated by small glowing fixtures. They finally passed through an ornate portal guarded by two slender Ayimar armed with short swords.

"Speak!" one of the sentries commanded.

The small man cleared his throat and stood very upright before he spoke. "We bring dark tidings. The Vyrdmar repelled our attack. This man here was injured in the assault. He is well known to the Lord Secant and the Lord Secant will want to see him as soon as possible."

The guard motioned to two younger Ayimar crouching in the distance. They came forward walking briskly and took away the visitors' weapons.

"You may pass." The Ayimar sentry said coldly.

The small man led the Droa past the Ayimar sentries to a large node illuminated in the same manner as other places in the Ayimar realm. The din of earth working, digging and grinding and carting could be heard in the distance, broken intermittently by sharp snapping sounds and groans and shrieks. The company passed through an archway leading to a vast and dark node. Beyond the node, a bright red light could be seen.

When the company finally reached the node where the Lord Secant could be found, they were led to antechamber. A small man soon arrived and addressed them. The small man had very large eyes and ears adorning a peculiarly flat face and clean-shaven head.

The small man guiding the company of Droa addressed his counterpart as "Master Gygus."

"These men left us many days ago. Their captain was injured in the high city. Can you help us?"

Gygus approached very calmly the fallen Atenarix captain. Gygus knelt next to Nausterus and passed his hand over his nose and mouth. He placed his index finger over the base of Nausterus' neck and looked up.

"Master Nausterus has expired," he said impassively. The Droa looked down pitiably and covered their faces with their hands.

Nausterus' body was taken deeper into the Ayimar realm. The Droa and now two small guides took the fallen captain to a large node appearing to be a subterranean arboretum. Larger glowing fixtures were all around this large node. Jutting up from a patch of trees was a obsidian tower. Nausterus' body was taken to this tower where the Ayimar Lord Secant of the upper stratum dwelled, surrounded by a small community of Ayimar.

The Lord Secant's face was solemn when looked upon Nausterus' body. For a while, his golden eyes were shut tight. His deep chest expanded and then contracted as he heaved a deep sigh of disappointment and sadness. Touching his old friend's forehead, he spoke.

"He shall be preserved in our mausoleum after he is treated for his voyage."

"Perhaps-" he said. "He will rise again after our great order is restored, and we have recaptured the former glory of our Atenari forebears. Regretfully, we will sorely miss his quality in our time and in the battles to come. The die has been cast and the blood of our bravest, have anointed the battlefield of armies and ideals. Now it is up to those of us who still live to struggle against dogma and darkness and free the world from the tyranny of the Vyrdmar."

The Lord Secant looked up toward the vaulted ceiling of his great hall as he spoke. He looked up from his sunless world toward the surface, a world his kind was cast from long ago. He pondered the fate of his Ayimar charges. He wondered how the Vyrdmar would respond to Nausterus' daring foray. He knew that princes Varenhil and Hovin were formidable warriors and leaders of men. Their response will surely be lethal.

But there were actors hidden even to the Lord Secant. The Lord Secant thought nothing of yet another of king Ylarin's sons. He thought nothing of prince Jaïem – a thoughtful and aloof young Vyrdmar who had, during Nausterus' assault, thrust himself into the great unfolding drama of his time. Jaïem was not renowned as a warrior or as a leader of men. War was not his calling yet. But his time was fast approaching. The Lord Secant could not know, but Jaïem's ascent would be glorious like a great day rising. But even if the Lord Secant did know, perhaps he would counter that even a glorious day falls into darkness.

Chapter 1: Secret of the Hidden

Jaïem had been withdrawn for some time now, a state not uncommon among men his age. He was old enough for grooming, but not yet old enough for to be a Harfingal squire. After the Leyving festival, he would have a few more weeks of study at the academy.

Young as he was, he could be a little too withdrawn. Some would say he was melancholy. And being a young, prince, his disposition and demeanor was cause for concern among for his kin and for others close to him.

Jaïem lived in his dreams. His were not hopeful dreams that consume the flippant young. His dreams were somber and foreboding dreams, narrated by a raspy voice.

The voice seemed familiar to Jaïem, but haunting nonetheless. The voice told Jaïem it had been searching for him for a long time. It told Jaïem that it was sent from the heavens to reveal the world's secrets. He said that together, they would uncover the past and shape the future. The voice probed and prodded Jaiem and uncovered deep longings and desires Jaïem had buried deep within.

"I love your pride," the voice once whispered, and Jaïem smiled in his sleep. One night, weeks before Nausterus' attack, the voice revealed the past to Jaïem. It was an eerie dream – a vivid dream about a conversation. Jaïem dreamed about a dark haired man speaking to a familiar voice from beyond a massive wooden door with a small porthole. The dark-haired man sat on a stool in a dark archway.

"What can be wrong with a conversation?" The familiar voice asked from behind the porthole.

"Of all species, yours are the most curious and expressive. But what is wrong with that? Are your tendencies not simply a banal means to great end? Your inclination to seek bears fruit when you find. Your fondness for expression reveals that you have something to say – does it not? You want to have a conversation because you want to share what you already know, and because you want ask questions so that you may learn what you do not know. Even now, we two lonely souls are bearing out this truth. We are two disconnected pieces of one mind, finding each other again in a conversation."

The dark haired man listened without a word. He sat there by the door with his chin cupped in his hands and his elbows resting on his knees.

"You are reluctant to speak," the voice mused and prodded.

"You come to me half-hearted and timid. You were not so uncertain when you faced me beneath the Pelares. You were fierce and masterful then. You were like the wind indeed. You struck me down and brought me here to this forsaken dungeon. But was that really you? No. I think not. You were merely an instrument. You were spurred on by powers hidden from all but the chosen few. But look at you now. Where is your benefactor? Where is your god?"

"You are wrong," the dark-haired man muttered. "The Celestial has never left me. He gives me power over you still."

The voice scoffed at the dark-haired man.

"You are not hidden from me Vyrdmar king. Your life is laid bare before my eyes. I know that your conversation with your god has ended. Your god has left you all alone. That is the way of the immortals. They seize men and use them for their purposes and then they leave them to death. Who can suffer the pit of merely living when they have experienced the lofty calling of the gods? You have tasted power, but your god will not let you feast. That is how it has always been for your storied people, the Vyrdmar, the exalted servants of the Celestial."

"Tell me what you know about the Celestial and the immortal hidden." The dark-haired man stammered, lifting up his head for a moment. "I know them. They are not vain. They love humanity and they preserve order and peace for our sake."

"Ha! Why do you ask me? I am your vanquished foe. Yet you are here. We are having this conversation. I have an allure for you. Are you not afraid that the Celestial will chastise you for your heresy?"

"The gods love those who have served them," the dark-haired man answered. "Surely they will forgive one transgression-especially if my motives are good."

"To speak to me is forbidden. This is a capital transgression for even kings. The Celestial does not so much deride transgressions of the moment and of the flesh. They mostly eschew those transgressions that are deliberate and that wither away the soul within. They deride the intimate transgressions of the curious, the inventive, and the resourceful mind.

Knowledge is like air to the mind and the soul. The Celestial would find fault with you if you left the aromatic garden they have created for you, to inhale the noxious miasma of the sunless world of heretics."

Now there was laughter coming from behind the door, broken by a bout of coughing.

"You hunger for more than your father's religion provides," the voice began again. "Your father's religion offers you fundamental truths. But what is truth? Whatever you are willing to accept is truth even if it is a lie. I offer you the facts of history and a deeper knowledge of the symphony of life and death. I offer mastery over life and death."

The voice behind the door paused and listened for a moment but the dark-haired man was again silent.

"Have you ever heard of the primordial flame?" the voice behind the door asked.

"No," the dark haired man replied. "W-w-what is the primordial flame?"

"The primordial flame is the boundless creative power of the cosmos. It is a fire burning beneath the cauldron of creation. To some, it is also the light of the world."

"But mighty Yggir is the light and all is realized through him," the dark-haired man interjected.

"That is lore for children," the voice behind the door snapped. "It was not Yggir who brought light unto the world. Indeed, in the beginning there was the primordial flame. The one who wielded it brought light unto the world. You know this is true and you want to know the secrets of the flame. Why else are you here? You want to know the secrets the immortals keep from mortal men, which give them power over you and your world. Why else have you come down here to seek me out in my cell king Nnyreinin?"

The dark-haired man's face became grave but he did not retort.

"Let me tell you a story-not about the primordial flame. I want reveal your past to you. I want to tell the story of your storied people and the immortals they serve. I will reveal the secret of the primordial flame to you at the proper time. But listen for now to a story about your people and reflect on your place in the world. Perhaps by experiencing your traditions and history more objectively, you may better discern your place in history. This is your story Nnyreinin – the wind that swept through the eastern raiders of Nurim. This is the story of the Vyrdmar, whom the gods have forsaken to spiritual death on the banks of mortal yearning.

Your people, the men of Gaalden came from the east some time at the beginning of the seventh age. They were passionate about the sea and the surf that splashed on their rugged coast. They loved the wind that swept their ancestors, the Vyrdmar to the shores of Gaalden, where they founded the high city of Chamiahce beneath the Kuriox that sprayed down into the sacred pool of Yggir. But more than anything, your ancestors were passionate about commerce.

The Vyrdmar were were noted for their voracious appetite for wealth, which they expropriated through commerce and war. They spread like a disease throughout, going as far as Ausremer beyond the sea to the south. They came in fast ships, but unlike the marauding tribes that came to Maspeidon before them and after – they built settlements and colonies. They founded their most prosperous settlement here along the rugged coasts and of western Maspeidon. This settlement grew and expanded over time and became the high city you know as Chamiahce.

Now this propitious settlment was actually founded by some nameless Vyrdmar profiteer. But history tells us that Namreddin, a great craftsman of fast ships, and a captain of the sea, founded the city of

Chamiache proper.   Namreddin was the city's first lawgiver.

Truth be told, Namreddin was a merchant of notable wealth but marginal craft. As with many of his ilk at the time, he cared only acquiring more and more wealth. Yet the Vyrdmar were inexplicably bound to this old merchant's code. This code prescribed with some specificity how commerce was to be conducted. The code required strict observance of agreements and controlled all manner of transactions.

Yet this code only applied to dealings between the Vyrdmar. Surrounded by the region's scattered tribes of Gaalden, the Vyrdmar soon found that their destiny had become interwoven with other destinies of diverse peoples. Conflicts soon erupted and alliances formed. War ensued and the Vyrdmar zeal for wealth found new expression in war.

Yet another nameless man brought an end to these conflicts with an armistice. But by the end of the many battles, Namreddin was chosen by his peers to preside over a provisional body charged to organize and restore trade and commerce. The Vyrdmar and their allies chose Namreddin because they were wary of giving power to already powerful men. In the end however, Namreddin used his position to coalesce a faction beholding to him. Then he utterly destroyed other powerful Vyrdmar factions and established a new a new order.

Namreddin revealed that Yggir, then a tribal diety, had seized him and decreed to to him that the Vyrdmar embrace a new law and way of life. Namreddin decreed that the Vyrdmar swear fealty to Yggir and subordinate all value and all life to Yggir's will.

Characteristic of Vyrdmar subtlety, Namreddin established a monastery of chosen men he called surplicants and a priestess identified by prophecy as the ceremonial arbiter of Yggir's will. As the Vizir of a

Vyrdmar council, Namreddin enforced Yggir's laws. Of course, Namreddin was the sole and actual arbiter of Yggir's law and will. As the saying goes among the Vyrdmar, the sword subjugates in battle, but the law subjugates at home, and into perpetuity.

Namreddin founded the city of Chamiahce as the seat of his new Vyrdmar order. He called this new order, the Hold.

In the end, Namreddin used a tribal religion to immunize himself, his descendants, and his allies from the vicissitudes of the turbulent commerce his people had grown to cherish and extol over life itself."

The man behind the door now began to cough again. He paused as if to catch his breath and then proceeded.

"By your time, king Nnyreinin, the Vyrdmar and the people of Gaalden, have become masters of the continent of Maspeidon. But the wind and the sea have never been far from your hearts. The sea remains the source of your wealth and power. Your heirs, the men of your court, and your nobles, have all been instructed in seamanship, navigation, and the protocols and principles of command at sea at the academies.

When you led the lords of Maspeidon against the eastern raiders of Nurim, you commanded a fleet of fast lupeiders south and then east across the Krheinth Sea. Your ships were carried swiftly and safely ahead of favorable winds to the shores of Kuthgelon. Distinguishing yourself on the seas, you turned your noble genius to field engagements and sieges against cities captured by the Nurimite's invading armies.

Having witnessed your exploits in that hard fought campaign, the lords of Maspeidon evoked your people's seafaring heritage and remarked that you, Nnyreinin, were the 'Wind that swept the eastern raiders before him.'

To this day men call you 'Wind' in honor of your fierceness and genius. So strong were the bonds of friendship and loyalty between you and the lords who fought with you against the men of Nurim, that they swore allegiance to you and your line when you succeeded your brother Tamenor to the throne of Gaalden. Now all monarchical power in Maspeidon is consolidated in the Vyrdmar king in the high city. Now mighty Wind, because of your virtues, the Vyrdmar's power has become hegemonic.

But you know that your people are merely pawns in the immortal's endgame. You know that you serve at the leisure of your gods, whom you have never truly seen. But what they, the gods do not realize is that men are not mindless golems. Men are curious and proud. They are not naturally inclined to blind obedience. That is why you are here. You want to know what your purpose is and why you must obey, if you must obey at all."

The voice behind the door paused again as if to gauge the dark haired man's reaction. But he again kept his silence.

After a brief silence, the voice behind the door began to speak again. "Who am I to challenge your god's truth and reveal your purpose? But among my adherents it is said that the world is nothing more than particle within space engaged in the dance of probability. Everything that is hidden can be revealed and all outcomes can be anticipated. I hearken to this belief now and foresee your house's almost certain decline. Your son, Ylarin, who is merely a boy now, will succeed you and will rule during peaceful times, empowered by your virtues and deeds, but imperiled by the envy of many plotting vassals, and the excesses of his own court. Your son will cling to your ancestors' beliefs in the gods, and become aloof from his vassals and even the guild masters upon whose industry and skill your kingdom relies for its commerce. The harvests will wither along with your descendant's prestige. The crowds at the markets will lessen, and your people will suffer privations. Only then will your people's blind obedience to the gods finally bring your house to ruin."

The voice from behind the door echoed through the years into Jaïem's ears a generation later. He awakened with sweat pouring and struggling to breathe. His dream of the whispering past had greatly alarmed him. He peered into the darkness of his bedchambers, wondering where he was in space and time. Hearing the barking of dogs, sounds familiar to him, he drew a deep breath. He was home. Relieved, he gathered his thick blanket around him, tried to go back to sleep.

With winter now thawing and spring waxing on the wings of warmer winds from the south, the future the voice behind the door prophesied was unfolding. The lords of Maspeidon came to Ylarin's court, Irilsflir, for the Levying festival during difficult times. The Levying festival was the lengthiest, though least attended festival in Gaalden. It was mostly of interest to the king's court and his vassals. The tradition began during king Nnyreinin's reign. He then decreed to his vassals:

> "After the coming of Wind, and during the calm and the peace we have hewn together, return to Irilsflir after idle winter, and look to see that weeds of decadence have not grown to choke out the nobility from my house."

Every third year since, vassals owing fealty to Nnyreinin's line came to Irilsflir just before the spring rains to inquire into the state of the monarchy, by pitting the strength of Maspeidon's finest warriors against Wind's house in Wind's Crucible before Namreddin's Beacon along the city's rugged shores. The tradition also had the purpose of reestablishing the bonds of allegiance between the king and his vassals, as well as to foster camaraderie between the royal princes and their future vassals.

Irilsflir was the holiest site in Maspeidon and it was Gaalden's seat of power. Though, the temple was not actually the royal residence of the monarchy or its ministerial center. Irilsflir was the religious center of the city and the kingdom, and the temple of the Vyrdmar's supreme deity, the god Yggir. But to the Vyrdmar, Irilsflir was the city and the kingdom.

Visitors to Irilsflir were astounded by the skill and artistry of its builders, the Galdic metics from the southern regions of Gaalden. The Galdic metics built many structures and monuments throughout the city, but the temple Irilsflir, the adjoining royal compound and the academies were together their crowning achievement. The temple, the academies, the royal apartments, and the royal garrison, which was called the Hold, were set apart from the rest of the city by strong battlements and great arches.

Looking west from the city's eastern gate, the temple Irilsflir could be seen rising above the city walls. It was a shimmering structure of white stone with two thousand marble columns along its octagonal base. Positioned along the city's northwestern walls, Irilsflir was skillfully blended into the thick walls and covered arcades. The rest of the clerestory structure rose up from a solid stone base into five stories of receding octagonal terraces held up by columns of ever receding diameter. A wood frame dome with fitted polished cerulean alabaster plates topped the uppermost structure.

The walls surrounding the temple and the city were a system of winding bastions with facades positioned on an upward sloping angle. Contained within these bastions were tunnels and inner arcades, passageways, and armories. The city walls were divided into three sectors marked by jutting guard posts above massive archways and guarded by city militia, Harfingal warriors, and strong iron portcullis.

Beyond the walls, sprawling westward was a network of buildings and roads connected by two major thoroughfares, one running east and west from the city's main gate. Running from the eastern gates to the temple and the king's royal court, the main thoroughfare ever bustled with activity. The other major thoroughfare ran south and north, and through the marketplace at Commoners Square.

Along the main thoroughfare, there were nine arches adjoined to elevated arcades, marking major clusters of buildings. These centers were adorned with relief sculptures depicting Gaalden's nine greatest kings in scenes emblematic of their reign. Each king could be seen holding the Vyrdmar rod of power, for unlike other rulers in Maspeidon, the kings of Gaalden did not wear crowns or symbolic headdress. Faithful to their seafaring past, a simple silver rod, wielded by the ancient Vyrdmar sea captains, was the symbol of power for the Vyrdmar kings of Gaalden.

The main thoroughfare wound west to the temple archway adjacent to a tall brick structure called Aufrey's tower. Through the temple arch was a system of narrow enclosed arcades. The arcades were supported by stone columns, and wound north and south to the two academies, which were circular domed structures with strong spandrels. Beyond the system of arcades were wide walkways intersecting across the temple quadrangle, and connecting the academies, the temple and a smaller archway leading to the royal compound. At the center of the quadrangle was a massive black obelisk with an eagle perched atop it clasping a cross-staff. Up overlooking the statue, and perched on a high stone base was Irilsflir with its gleaming dome.

Given the city's political and religious importance, the Levying festival, was a time of great anxiety for the Vyrdmar. This tradition brought both peril and esteem to the monarchy. It gave Namreddin's line and Nnyreinin's heirs an opportunity to display their strength. The tradition also exposed them to the scrutiny of their enemies. In that regard, King Ylarin sent his Harfingals into every sector of the city to ensure tranquility and good order. The king also displayed his strong and gallant sons Varenhil and Hovin for all to see.

Jaïem, Ylarin's youngest son, was hidden away in the catacombs of the temple of Yggir where mounds of dusty neglected scrolls and manuscripts were stored. Jaïem had been in the temple library all morning scouring a cluttered and secluded section with master Owidobel, the librarian of the temple.

"Ah!" Owidobel exclaimed. "There it is. I knew this was here – exactly where I placed it."

"Undoubtedly…" Jaïem snickered.

Producing a bounded manuscript, he blew the dust from off its leather sheath. "The Codex of the Hidden!" he marveled. "This is undoubtedly a compilation of the most provocative, fascinating, and introspective writings in this library. It's not at all the kind of work one would expect a surplicant such as me to compile. But I surmise that a surplicant did indeed compile it.

When I first became the librarian many years ago, I was shown this codex by my predecessor. From the start, my interest in it was piqued. My predecessor explained that it held many bizarre insights into the world. But I was not afraid of it. I wondered how it could have survived the scrutiny and censorship of the Urdar."

The old librarian now thumbed through a few pages and perused a few passages.

"I thought perhaps that the codex was compiled on orders from the king himself, to ensnare the heretical and curious. There is no way to be certain who compiled it. But the Urdar are as cunning as they are steadfast in their search for heretics. It would be perilous to discuss it beyond these catacombs.

Having poured over it, I personally do not believe it is a heretical work. Its contents were not written in the style typical of heretics and Atenarix scholars. Admittedly its contents are intriguing. But this is not the kind of work that generally concerns the Urdar.

The codex is full of fascinating accounts and verses about dreams and longings. The passages are quite endearing and delightful. Heretical works tend to be scholarly and pedagogical. But the passages in this codex are subjective and have a poetic quality. The accounts and verses I have read cannot be attributed to any event or historical actor. In my opinion the passages in this compilation lack any of the typical indices of heretical works."

The librarian paused and then chuckled to himself.

"It sometimes reads like verses uttered by a person wavering on the precipice of reality and a wonderful kind of madness."

Sensing that the young prince was becoming impatient, the old librarian clapped his hands.

"Come my lord," he beckoned, gathering the old dusty manuscript and bringing it over to a small table in an alcove.

Jaïem sighed and remarked with a glint of annoyance, "You have spoken. I have listened. But I have heard nothing of interest."

The old librarian appeared slightly alarmed and his growing apprehension only seemed to stoke Jaïem's displeasure.

"The Codex of the Hidden-" Jaïem sneered. "Old man, why do you bring this manuscript to me? What I need are records detailing my grandfather's reign. Perhaps documents he may have authored himself. I thought you brought me here for that purpose."

"Yes my lord," Owidobel replied meekly. "How many times have you come here asking about your grandfather king Nnyreinin? I cannot begin to count. Yet it was not until recently that I began to understand."

"What I am really after?" The young prince asked tersely.

"Yes – well I meant that I thought since you were dissatisfied with the other manuscripts, which were of a historical nature, that perhaps you were looking for something more introspective, personal or esoteric. Now when I found this manuscript, I was at first reluctant to bring it to your attention. I was not sure if I surmised correctly. But when last we spoke, you intimated to me that you had been having dreams. Your account of your dreams convinced me that this manuscript would be helpful."

Owidobel paused and twirled his wiry gray mustache.

Jaïem nodded and then commented. "Be at ease old man. My displeasure is waning - slightly. What you are saying has the ring of truth. I think that you are right when you say that I have come to you in the last weeks in search of something other than a historian's account of my grandfather's rule. I am aware of your reputation as discerning and knowledgeable. Men say that you are also well versed in matters of tradition and lore. Men from your family have always been a source of knowledge of Vyrdmar traditions. Your father and his father were viziers at court. I suppose you may be just the man to help me decipher my dreams. I will place my trust in you. Please reveal how this manuscript will help."

Seeing that the prince's annoyance was abated and that his eyes were now opened wide with curiosity, Owidobel proceeded.

"From my reading of it, the Codex is a book of dreams. It is a book of many dreams interwoven into a theme or story of a world hidden from most men and revealed to the few."

Owidobel spread the manuscript on the table and began flipping through the pages.

"My lord-" the old librarian continued. "You described one dream in which you experienced a sense that you were descending into darkness. But yet the darkness was eerily soothing, and beyond it there was a golden light. There are passages in this book of men who have had this sort of dream.

This dream suggests that you feel that something in your world is inverted. After all, most perceive darkness below and light above. There are similar accounts in the Codex. Such a dream reveals that the dreamer is searching for truth beyond what is accepted by others. This yearning is a matter of concern for the Urdar. But then you are a prince, and likely exempt from their inquiries.

The authors of the Codex too may well have been princes and even kings. I cannot say for certain. It is not uncommon for great men to explore the dark foreboding sea of knowledge of Yggir Himself. This is a very rare and precious yearning we speak of – but also perilous. The world of the hidden is not a place for lay explorers. The Urdar maintain that not even great men should tread there. They believe that what is hidden is hidden because the gods purposed that they be hidden to protect men from confusion and madness. Who can say for certain?"

The old librarian turned to a couple of passages and pointed some lines out to the young prince. Now he turned the conversation to king Nnyreinin, which was the subject of the prince's inquiry.

"Our historians recorded king Nnyreinin's public actions and life. They have done this for all Vyrdmar regents. However, they have very rarely provided insight into the feelings and motives of these historical actors. These matters have been omitted from history, and, if a king was wise, even from all but his most trusted advisors. Though there have been kings in your father's line who were rumored to be poets and historians themselves, and chose to memorialize their inner joy and turmoil, and the complex motives behind their historical actions."

Owidobel peered at Jaïem. "This manuscript may contain precisely these personal insights expressed in dreamlike verses."

Jaïem listened intently and drew closer to the manuscript.

"This is a good passage!" Owidobel lifted up a loose parchment placed as if to mark a page.

"This is very interesting. While I cannot say for certain, I think that it is a phylactery belonging to king Nnyreinin, your grandfather. Now your godlike ancestor was not known to be a man of many words. Historians say that his speech was slow and belabored. In most accounts, he was depicted as a silent and brooding man; some would say melancholy. Yet, at the time of his death, when all of his personal effects were gathered by the royal vizirs to be bound or burned, it is believed that certain writings were found. The king himself perhaps authored some. At least that was the rumor some of my fellow surplicants espoused. Whoever authored or invoked this phylactery possessed a profound sense and affinity for something very hidden and transcendental.

No one can say for sure if king Nnyreinin authored this or invoked its nebulous power. Whoever authored it or used it, was immersed in an inner struggle to find meaning that was not easily discernible to others. Now while this verse, of royal authorship or not, did not inspire much curiosity in the many years since its likely composition, I think, assuming that it was authored by king Nnyreinin, or someone close to him, it may provide some clues about the nature and meaning of your dreams."

Jaïem raised a nearby lantern above the parchment.

"Be careful my lord." Owidobel brushed away some dust from off the parchment.

Jaïem began to quietly read the document. As he read it, his eyes began to widen and his heart began to race. Owidobel peered at the prince curiously and licked his lips. Jaïem had stopped abruptly, deep furrows disturbing the smooth contours of his youthful face. Anxious, the old librarian held his breath.

"Very bizarre," the prince muttered. "I will have to review this more thoroughly. I will take this parchment with me master librarian. I will return it if I must."

Owidobel reached out to touch Jaïem's cloak. "My lord-" Jaïem's eyes flashed and the old surplicant stumbled back.

"Forgive me lord," Owidobel pleaded. "My actions are inexplicable and unforgivable. My hands should never touch your person for you are a prince in the royal house of Namreddin. I was merely reacting to your apparent distress. I was motivated solely by my love and concern for you."

Jaïem clasped the old parchment, folding it and placing it in a pocket of his plain leather tunic.

"Very well librarian," Jaïem said sternly. "Thank you for your guidance and insight. I will speak to you again. I will return this parchment if I must after I have reviewed it in the solitude of my chambers."

Owidobel watched as Jaïem hurried away. Then as the prince disappeared into the shadows of the catacombs, Owidobel turned to close the manuscript and return it to his leather sheath. Meanwhile Jaïem could be seen marching up a main stairway and through the temple's expansive interior module flanked by marble columns. The lofty interior module of Irilsflir opened up through five levels to the gaping mouth of the temple dome. Torches hanging on ornate sconces bound to the capital of every other column facing the interior module illumined the entire space.

Even after having visited the temple many times, the beauty of the temple's center module slowed Jaïem's pace. He found himself admiring this architectural ideal of the Galdic metics. The structure was a blend of structural simplicity and harmonious proportions, governed by the lofty center module, which was octagonal. As was a consistent theme for all holy places dedicated to Yggir, there were no depictions of men. The entire temple was decorated with striking geometric sculptures wrought from stone and marble and, colorful friezes of bucolic scenery.

Jaïem pried himself away from his visual wandering and walked briskly through the center module past the great pool where the holy dew of the Kuriox collected. He scampered down stone temple stairs and made his way across the temple quadrangle toward the royal garden, the royal compound, and the royal garrison. He slowed and looked back at the towering temple as he approached the stone archway into the garden. Taking a deep breath he disappeared into its narrow walkways, bushes, and lush foliage.

Chapter 2: The melancholy prince

It was late afternoon, around the time when the king's Harfingal guard and squires practiced swordplay and grappling in the grand courtyard of the Hold, the Harfingal barracks. Found among them were Jaïem's brothers Varenhil, prince of Gaalden and lord of Greingspen, and stalwart Hovin, captain of the Harfingal guard. Observing from the elevated terrace of the central structure of the citadel were several Maspeidonian lords and their viziers and captains.

But as usual, Jaïem was not present. Jaïem liked to be alone with his thoughts and his books. On this day, he could be found in the garden, in one of his favorite places, by a little fountain with a stone statue centerpiece depicting a dolphin shooting water through its spout. He lay on his back looking up at the cloud-speckled sky, clasping the parchment he took from Owidobel the librarian.

"Is the royal compound haunted?" he wondered. "I hear voices even when I am awake. I dream about people who do not exist. I dream about my grandfather – but he died long before I was born. There is also this special voice. I hear it and it seems to connect me to my grandfather. I wonder if that was really my grandfather. He did not look like I imagined. He did not look like the metic sculptors depicted. He did not look like me. He stammered. But there is this voice. We have that in common. This voice in my dreams connects us. But I don't think this voice belongs to the Celestial. "

The young prince sighed and then contorted his face.

"It does not matter though. Dreams are not real. And so this connection cannot be real?"

Sighing again he whispered, "I do not want to live in my dreams. I want to live in this world. I want to realize all my desires in this world for all to see. I want my father to see. I want my beautiful sister Ylia to see. I want…"

He paused, hearing the rustling of leaves, and sitting up he looked around to see who or what was nearby.

He scanned his surroundings for a while then he resumed with his precious thoughts.

"I want Besia to see," he lamented. "But she does not see me at all even though I am a prince."

Jaïem thought to himself in this way for quite some time until finally, he heard a sound he recognized in the distance. Rubbing his eyes, he stood up and listened closely and heard someone whistling a tune from an old fable. "Csem," he whispered. As the whistling sound drew nearer, he could hear heavy panting and the clanking of chains.

Jaïem stepped over some bushes to peer down a narrow trail paved in geometrically shaped polished stones. He saw a young man being dragged by two large dogs in the distance.

"My lord-" the young man called out when he saw Jaïem. "The afternoon exercises are nearly over and now the court is retiring for their baths before dinner."

"Tngshaz and Faeut-" Jaïem knelt down on one knee and opened his arms as two massive shorthaired and muscular dogs trotted into his arms, panting and licking. Tngshaz and Faeut were the formidable watchdogs that patrolled the royal compound and even the halls of the king's palatial residence. Their massive shoulders were as high as a man's hip. Excellent hunting dogs as well as guard dogs, they had powerful jaws and short muscular necks. They appeared sluggish and idle when at rest. But they had tremendous stamina and were surprisingly agile. Often the royal hounds accompanied the king and his courtiers on their forays into the plains to hunt because they were adept at tracking and running down wounded game.

Before Jaïem fell into his recent bout of melancholy, these animals were his frequent companions. He seemed to cherish them more than the king, who took them on hunting forays. He loved Tngshaz and Faeut because they were always pleased to see him and never judged him. Jaïem's fondness for Tngshaz and Faeut was almost equaled by his fondness for his boyhood friend Csem, whose father Cerondilus was one of king Ylarin's principal Vizirs. Together, they would often sally out to the hills and fields to the north of the city and spend idle time by the many streams and springs found in that region.

"My lord," Csem said glibly. "Your father asked about you at the afternoon exercises in the courtyard."

Jaïem ignored his friend and continued to stroke and play with Tngshaz and Faeut.

"A prince must lead by example and fulfill his obligations," Csem snickered.

"You have not conducted yourself well of late. You have been aloof ever since the Levying festival began three days ago and your father's vassals began arriving in the city. Your father asks for you all the time and wishes you would accompany him to his assemblies with his vassals."

"Surely you are mistaken," Jaïem replied coldly. "These assemblies are momentous events. My brothers are more suitable for such tasks than I."

Csem knelt before Tngshaz.

"You are mistaken my friend. The court misses your skill at the harpistar and your songs. The court misses Jaïem the beautiful."

Jaïem stood up and snatched the dogs' leashes from Csem. "Jaïem the beautiful-" the prince sneered. "I despise that moniker. You are my friend and you know my mind. Why do you persist in addressing me so? Address me as who I am. I am Jaïem; nothing more and nothing less."

"Of course you are more than your title to those who know you and love you," Csem interrupted. "But you are prince of this court and your father is king. You have duties and obligations to them as they have to you."

"Csem," Jaïem retorted as they began walking toward the gates of the royal compound.

"I have reached that age when a young man, prince or commoner, must choose his path. My eldest brother Varenhil is the crown prince and if I know him well, this suits his prideful, overbearing and egomaniacal temperament. My brother Hovin is like these dogs; he longs to show his strength and skill, but always in the loyal service of others. It is only appropriate that he is the captain of the Harfingal guard. Who am I? I do not know what my calling is. Yet I know that I do not want to be known as some dithering poet or dainty court celebrant. If these are my choices, then let me simply be Jaïem."

"Don't be foolish fair Jaïem," Csem replied.

"You are master Idram's favorite student of philosophy and parlance at the academy. I have heard many say that if you practiced, you would rival your brother in martial skill. My friend, I love you more than my own brothers. Yet I find your interminable aloofness, if not, melancholy, very wearisome."

Csem put his arm around Jaïem's shoulders and shook him. "Let us go to the baths and then make an appearance at the king's great dining hall and eat with lords, and princes and princesses. Besides, I think my sister Besia will be there."

Csem winked and smiled and hastened his pace. "A man should never reveal his heart to others," Jaïem groaned; "especially not to his best friend."

The young prince and his friend walked together through the royal garden and into the courtyard of the royal compound. "Hail prince of the Hold!" The guards shouted as they bowed and parted the gates of the royal compound. Jaïem acknowledged them by raising a hand with palm exposed and walked briskly to the royal bathhouse.

The bathhouse was a large rectangular structure of stone and mortar on the exterior and polished limestone on the interior. It contained an elevated ceramic water basin heated by a furnace attended at all times by servants. The entire system was fed by the royal aqueduct, which supplied water to large siphoning cisterns, which in turn supplied the entire royal compound. The heated water from the upper basin fed the main pool and the successive four individual pools, all of which were emptied twice per day.

The royal bathhouse was a popular place for the men of the Hold, young and old. When Jaïem and Csem entered, warriors of the Harfingal guard were straggling in after their afternoon exercises. They spoke and laughed loudly. Gossip was a favorite pastime in the bathhouse, and especially if it was carnal and descriptive.

The bathhouse was an escape from martial and academic life of the two classes of nobility to be found in the Hold: the Harfingals, who were the royal defenders of the king and the temple; and the royal viziers, who administered the affairs of state. Both the Harfingals and the viziers were instructed at the academies in martial and ministerial disciplines respectively.

Soon the din of young men reveling in the strength and vitality of their youth echoed as they shouted, laughed, and then cheered as their captain, Hovin entered the bathhouse.

"Who is more admired and loved than this prince," remarked a young man bathing near Jaïem. "His skill and quality is awesome and terrifying, and yet his humility and sense of duty to others inspires so much love and admiration."

Another young man nodded. Voices rang out "Hail Hovin, the captain of the guard."

The dark haired prince acknowledged his men, as he walked arm in arm with his lieutenant and friend Macheleion.

"My brother Hovin is truly loved by the Vyrdmar," Jaïem remarked. "Men bow and show respect for rank at court, but I believe that his Harfingals would honor him even if he were not of royal lineage. He is truly a man who lends credit to his office in a court where a man's office prevails on others to an extent far exceeding the quality of the man."

Hovin was more like his father and his sister Ylia, than his brothers Varenhil and Jaïem, who favored queen Feystra, their late mother. Hovin's dark hair, prominent forehead, and broad shoulders were heirlooms from his father, which distinguished him from his brothers. His physical stature and temperament assured his ascendancy to the highest pinnacle of martial life.

Prince Hovin walked to the far end of the bathhouse, which was reserved for those highest in rank, and removed his plain white tunic. He did so without noticing his brother Jaïem and Csem bathing nearby. Servants hustled behind him with a flask of sweet scented oil and a flat wooden instrument. Attendants poured oil over his entire body and thoroughly scoured it before he waded his way into the bath. Every eye was on him, as was usually the case when Hovin was present among a gathering.

The young men of the Hold remained in the bathhouse until servants came to announce that dinner preparations were completed. Then they leapt from their baths grabbing their tunics, talking loudly and jostling, and made their way to the garrison hall where they would sit for their evening meal. It was then that Hovin noticed his younger brother and greeted him with a gesture. The princes of the Hold made their way to their bedchambers to prepare for the feast being prepared to celebrate the first week of the Levying festival. They could barely contain their excitement, for the winter was cold and long.

"Brother-" Hovin called out to Jaïem. "Will you be joining us this evening? Your skill at the harpistar has been dearly missed."

Macheleion and Csem echoed Hovin's sentiment. "Your songs capture the joy of spring and summer and on many dark and cold evenings, during this past winter, you brought a brief thaw."

Jaïem's face flushed. Then he looked sternly.

"I will no longer play the harpistar, or sing, or recite the poems of Rhoesus or any other poet. I have chosen a new path, a path that is more familiar to princes." Hovin walked closer to Jaïem and put his arms around his shoulders.

"Indeed brother, if martial discipline is what you speak of, I wholeheartedly approve. If so, let us train together just as before. If you had not neglected your training these past months, you would now be one of my lieutenants. Yet there are graver experiences than idle winter, which require both the courage and discipline of a warrior and the skill and inspiration of a poet. There are times when a song can inspire as surely as the martial exploits of a stalwart captain. I would therefore plead with you not to abandon your love of the harpistar even as you commit yourself to your martial training."

Jaïem did not answer his brother. He looked away and walked toward the royal apartments. The two young princes parted ways with Macheleion and Csem when they reached the courtyard of the royal apartments. Now Jaïem and Hovin walked alone together.

"I beg your pardon brother." Jaïem stopped and grasped his brother's arm. "I have forgotten an errand. We will see you later at dinner."

Hovin placed his hand on his younger brother's head and stroked his golden hair and nodded. "Very well," he said, I will see you then."

Now the two princes parted ways, and Jaïem walked briskly in the direction of the royal garden as his brother scampered through the portico of the royal apartments and to his bedchambers. Jaïem meanwhile hurriedly went looking for flowers and soon found a cluster of yellow daffodils. He produced a small knife and cut a few stems and wrapped them in a silk handkerchief he kept in a pocket in his tunic. He then rushed to his sister Ylia's chambers, as he always did this time in the day to bring her flowers, which she would wear in her hair at dinner.

Jaïem and gray-eyed Ylia were dearest to each other among the king's children. They loved to walk together in the gardens and take rides out to the countryside to the many groves, springs and brooks near the city. Ylia loved Jaïem's thoughtfulness and gentle heart. Jaïem was drawn to Ylia's thoughtfulness also. Ylia was also warm and charming, and accepting; she fostered and enjoyed levity. She was not at all judgmental. She found everyone's gift and virtue and made that the best thing in the world.

Jaïem knew that Ylia loved beautiful things, beautiful poems and songs, and she loved to adorn her hair with flowers. She always rejoiced when she saw Jaïem the beautiful, who played beautiful songs on the harpistar, and often brought her beautiful flowers before dinner. Jaïem obliged Ylia in these fixations because it made her happy and because it affirmed his sense of normalcy and belonging.

Lately, Jaïem had other motives for bringing her flowers and seeking audience with her, motives other than the satisfaction he felt in seeing her smile and laugh. On many evenings Csem's black-haired sister, Besia accompanied Ylia to dinner. On those evenings, Ylia's handmaidens tended to Ylia and Besia in her bedchambers. Jaïem would ordinarily walk to his sister's chambers after carefully picking out the best stems. But he had tarried so long at the baths that now he hurried though the royal apartments scattering bowing servants after fumbling through a thicket for a disheveled cluster of flowers. As he approached Ylia's chambers, he slowed his pace to catch his breath and wiped some perspiration from off his brow.

Taking a deep breath and clearing his throat, he walked slowly toward the massive wooden double doors leading to an antechamber. He opened the doors slightly and slowly entered into the large and dimly lit antechamber and closed it behind him. He could hear the chatter and giggling of young women beyond the layers of long curtains hanging in the arched entry into Ylia's bedchambers. He nervously drew closer and listened intently in the hopes of entering at an opportune moment.

"For my part, the young men of the Hold are detestable and dim-witted." Ylia said in a stern tone reserved for her commentaries on men at court.

"Yet the more mature men are fractious in public matters and timid in their own houses. This is precisely why so many fair maidens at court take refuge in gatherings such as ours."

She paused for effect as if to underscore a hidden meaning.

"The truth is revealed that we are our own equal in this world. Our creator must have purposed that we subordinate ourselves to our witless brothers out of resentment of His own masterful creation."

Jaïem could hear laughter.

"I have to disagree." Jaïem could hear a melodious voice say.

"Men are flawed. But some wear their flaws better than others. I know at least two such men. One is my own father."

"And the other?" the princess asked. "I agree that there are a few like our king – your father too Besia. My brother Hovin is an honorable man. Of course my brother Jaïem is my favorite because he has a great ear and eye for beauty."

Now Jaïem blushed. Then he heard Besia make a retort.

"Surely there are many more; many that are sisters here regard well. I know that in spite of their unflattering disregard for our divine nature, men adore us more than they can say or show. They are a beleaguered lot, single-mindedly pulling and grasping for tiny morsels of praise from old and even dead men. Yet this is what the world asks of them. All we can do is love them and help them find solace."

Ylia laughed loudly, followed by a chorus of shrill chuckles.

"My divine brethren," she said in a loud and ebullient tone. "This truth is transparent. Our temperate lady Besia of the rosy cheeks and lustrous black hair has found something precious in this murky and desolate pool we call the Hold. My dear, I pray that you are certain of what you have found. Sometimes a heart that is long forlorn may look upon a pebble and see a pearl. Who is this man who has your heart my love?"

Ylia reached out for Besia's hand. Besia flushed and smiled.

"I am too fond of my father to give any man my heart; though I may fancy him and show him compassion. I love only my father and my king. I doubt that I have any room left in my heart for another man."

"Come now," Ylia pried. "Even if you have given your father and my father each a share of your bounty of love and devotion, I am sure you want to give this man a full measure of your flesh."

Besia was startled. "You are profane mistress."
The princess laughed loudly. Jaïem listened closely.

There was a pause and brief silence.

"You are as perceptive as you are profane mistress." Besia sighed. "Yet you do not perceive all. A heart holds mysteries that are hidden to even the immortals. Who can explain love? What justifies devotion? All we can say is that the heart is precious than silver and gold; it adorns the faithful and the wise. I would like to think that love between a man and a woman has its own place in the ethereal of the heart. That is my secret. I can love a man, and love my father and my king, each in kind. I know nothing of matters of the flesh. That, I leave to worldly women."

"Alas," Ylia quipped. "Your words sound like verse. I have lost you my countrywoman. I fear we have lost you."

Besia placed a finger on the princess' lips. "You know my heart. I love you. It is not peculiar then that I would love one whose eyes and countenance mirrors yours my gray-eyed princess. You know well who has my heart. But I dare not speak his name until he has promised his heart to me."

Jaïem grew tense and weary as he listened. His heart sank, his vision grew blurred and his hands cold. The flowers he brought for his sister fell as he retreated, stumbling from the antechamber. He could hear his sister's hushed voice and he could imagine that she spoke the name of Besia's true love: "Hovin?"

Jaïem fled his sister's chambers, again scattering bowing servants here and there. He rushed to his chambers in another wing of the royal apartments. On the way to his chambers, his mind was seized in a paroxysm of emotion and incoherent thoughts. He felt a chill all through his body and a weight, which sank to his stomach. He seemed to gasp for air as he tried to compose himself. By the time he reached his chambers, he was overwhelmed with emotion. He burst in and slammed the double doors behind him. The young prince stumbled over a footstool and slammed headlong into the armrest of a long couch with ornate golden trimmings and strong wooden cabriole. He slid to the ground, lying on furs spread on the ground, and wept. During his brisk and yet seemingly endless walk to his chambers, the young prince had experienced the ebbing tremors of shock, which became sorrow, and then anger, and then sorrow again. He was overwhelmed and weary.

Jaïem sulked in his chambers into the early evening and through the night. Servants shuffled away after knocking on the large double doors of his chambers to call him to dinner. The legend of the melancholy prince was growing all the while. He lay still on the ground and then on his bed bemoaning his solitude and staring into the darkness, which was a perfect reflection of his heart. Then a gentle breeze seemed to pass through his chamber window and parted the curtains. He turned and gazed into the darkness, his mouth gaping open as if he saw a specter. He heard a whispering voice call out his name. Placing his hands over his ears, he clenched his teeth in anticipation and trepidation. Then he sighed and spread his arms.

"Take heart young Vyrdmar," he could hear.

"The world is a strange place. It does not make sense unless you make sense of it. Your elders shape your expectations of it and then you realize that your world, like a wild beast, surprises you and throws you, and mocks your expectations, and resists your will. So now, what are you prepared to do? What is your answer?"

"I don't know," Jaïem answered barely above a whisper.

"I love her. But it was not meant to be. I don't know what to think. I don't know what to do. I just know that I hurt."

I sense your pain," the voice said softly.

After a brief pause the voice began again more firmly.

"Your pain arises from a failure of expectation. Do not shut it out. Let it awaken you to the falsehoods clouding your judgment. Did you believe that your amorous feelings would be requited with love? Is your love even real? Why do you continue to believe in these children's tales? As sweet as they are when you are young, these lies will be bitter as aloe's milk when your mind's eye awakens."

"You are not what I thought," Jaïem interjected aloud and ruefully.

"I thought you were a benevolent spirit. But you are not. You are a bakiren, a wicked spirit dragging me deeper into sorrow and despair. How did you find me in this hallowed city; so close to the Celestial's temple? I will not listen to you. I will not let my pain harden my heart against what my fathers have taught me."

"Sweet words young Vyrdmar. But your conviction is wavering. I sense your doubt and apprehension. I am hidden from you, but you are not hidden from me. If you were certain about your path, you would not be so frightened of me, and you would not treat me with such aversion."

There was a brief pause and then the voice spoke again.

"You have read the parchment given you by the old librarian. What does it say? If you truly believe in the power of the Celestial, you must realize that I cannot harm you here so close Irilsflir. You found this parchment in bowels of Irilsflir. Surely nothing in it can harm you. Therefore, go to your harpistar and place your fingers on its keys and strum a melody. Only then try to remember the words on the phylactery and speak them aloud. If your invocation is evil, the Celestial will not suffer you to speak it."

The young prince thought for a while, recalling the words on the parchment. He reluctantly walked over to a shadowy corner in his chambers and sat at the console of his harpistar. He closed his eyes and began to play and to remember.

"How my eyes pierce," he whispered, "and achieve vision with such clarity and contrast; that I may know what is and what is not."

The voice encouraged Jaïem, saying "Yes. What else."

"There is a place in mind," Jaïem continued. "There is a place in my mind ever full of memories to guide my passage through the darkness, that I may not drift, and to drift is to dwell in the chaos all men fear."

"These are the words of prince Nnyreinin himself," the voice interjected.

"He too could see that there was a world beyond that which was offered him by the priestess of Yggir and the schoolmasters of the academies. He too was…"

"Afraid…" Jaïem finished the voice's sentence.

"He was afraid. 'I am afraid,' he intoned, 'but I am drawn from the certainty and serenity of my path. Now I am lost and now I am found by something existing in cryptic order; that I must seek, and must dare to tread the mire, in search of it.'"

"It-" the voice interjected again, "is power. There is greater exultation and salvation in wielding power than in submitting to power. You can, like the Celestial, wield power if you dare to tread the mire in search of it. But the Celestial does not want you to search and to find. The Celestial does not want you to know who you are; where you come from; and where you are going. He does not want you to know that beneath the surface of your sedate and orderly world are caverns teeming with fire.

I can teach you how to wield this fire and to forge the world into what your heart desires. In the end, you will realize that there is only power and desire, and bitter alienation for those who do not have the courage to wield power, to actualize desire, and master their world."

Chapter 3: The prophecy of seasons

That night, after sleep had swept away the toil and bustle of the day, and Jaïem had succumbed to sleep, an old woman was still stirring. A solemn old woman carried a lantern to light her way into a dark rectangular hall. The wavering light shone eerily across her gentle face and gray hair gathered over her shoulders and bound with silk tassels. A gray shawl was wrapped snugly around her shoulders to ward off of the crisp night air flowing in through a large arched window at the farthest end of the hall.

Now pausing abruptly close to the center of the room, she glanced beyond the light as if looking for some expectant guest. Unsure of whether she was alone, she walked slowly and tentatively toward the center of the room. The heel of her leather slippers smacked against polished stone adorned with a concentric pattern carved with crude rustic scenes.

Strange crosses with loop crests were prominently displayed on the narrow hem of each circle.

The old woman cast her light on a circular formation of twelve stone benches positioned all around a marble dais and paused again. Looking this way and that, and, finally folding her robes around her with care, she sat on a stone bench and placed her lantern on an adjacent bench. Bowing her head for a moment, she gathered her thoughts for a pending engagement.

Her solemnity now seemed appropriate, given the ostensible purpose of the hall. The stone benches revealed that the room was a place for spiritual reflection and communion. Accordingly, the old woman bowed her head to reflect. But it was not long before her head lifted. She was startled by what sounded like a gentle breeze whistling in from beyond the partially opened panel doors of the large window at the far side of the hall. The sound got louder and louder and then suddenly, a gust blew and the panel doors swung back on their hinges. The old woman reached for her lantern and reflexively cupped her hand around its thin metal panes to shield its fragile flame.

For a moment, intermittent darkness passed over the entire hall. A feeble aura shone from behind the old woman's hand, casting a shifting and forbidding shadow. Then the air quieted abruptly and was still, and the silhouette of what could have been a large bird appeared at the window. The creature folded its wings, which were pure white and shimmered like the morning sun on the face of dark waters.

Peering through almond shaped luminous golden eyes the creature scanned the hall and then bowed its head. It then sprung, moving like a dream, effortlessly, gently, and silently. It moved to the center of the hall, spreading its wings momentarily to reveal colorful plumes across its bulging chest. There were striking red, blue, and gold plumes, interlaced from just below its neck to just above its hinds and talons. It moved up onto the dais, and lifting its elongated head, crowned with white plumes, it revealed its subtly simian countenance. It passed its golden eyes over the old woman and smiled. Then the creature folded its wings and crouched. Its face was expressive and purposeful as if it was about to speak; but its mouth never opened to make a sound.

"I have passed over the land," the old woman could hear the creature say gravely, and in a tone that belied its outwardly pleasant expression.

"I have communed with my brethren who dwell in the beacon by the sea, and they say that your flock is hopelessly adrift down the river of time. They say that the Vyrdmar are tangled in a web of apathy, greed, and strife. Their reliance on the adherents of the Atenari increases every day that passes, and their judgment becomes more and more stained with vanity and wickedness."

The creature sighed and jutted its head out slightly and its eyes flickered.

"Perhaps we have been too permitting. Our purpose is to watch over the Vyrdmar to ensure that the specters of their primal nature do not unleash the doom of our world. Our purpose is to teach them compassion so that their fearful and brutal temperament does not consume them and everything around them. You know well that their minds are ever conspiring, scheming to unleash powers beyond their mortal understanding."

"I cannot answer for them," the old woman replied. "I can only bear witness that they are capable of much compassion."

"Does not life in the high city reflect the hearts of its inhabitants?" The creature countered.

"A man's life reflects what he values. That there is so little charity in the city reflects that the most notable among the Vyrdmar lack compassion. Truly, if the greater falter, what hope is there for the lesser?"

The old woman nodded and placed both hands over her face. "O' light of the world, without you we are helpless against this tide. Minds are clouded with fear and rumors of intrigue and war. Divine law is slowly receding and the primal law of species is waxing stronger. I cannot deny this. But there are many still holding fast to your traditions and rites."

"Your flock burns many sacrifices and offers many prayers in my name," the creature interjected. "But they reject my laws. Most obstinate among them are their cousins below the Pelares who are ruthless and persistent still in their pursuit of vengeance and of forbidden knowledge. Even though you teach your flock that these excesses may bar them from the afterlife, they persist. What must I do to save them, and our world?"

The old woman's face turned grave. "Give them your boundless mercy and patience mighty Celestial. Their minds will grow, and so too will their hearts. It is very difficult for them to resist the exhortations of fear and power. You immortals pass through this world unscathed and fearless. They are fragile. For them, the lure to search for solace is strong. The inclination to wrest it from a seemingly uncaring world is compelling."

"Perhaps all will be lost in the end," the creature murmured thoughtfully.

"Our love sustains them, but they seek power and sow enmity and suffering. We shelter them out of love. But perhaps we deny them true understanding. We deny them the bounty of consequences. How will they ever realize their error if we do not let them suffer the moral and spiritual famine of power? Surely they will become haughtier and crueler. Without knowledge of love, the primal heart will prevail. Without love, your flock will never gain divine judgment, and all will be lost."

"But they are innocent," the priestess contended. "The Deceiver is to blame, for it is he who seduces them. He tells them that the expression of power can defeat death, which they fear. Even though the Deceiver has been cast from the world, his words echo through time, and are gathered up by his adherents like precious pearls."

"Though there is always hope," the creature relented. "Another of my brethren, who returns to us from time to time, like a fanciful season, has come to us again. His coming has, in the past, augured great upheavals. But his passing has been like spring rains that restore the garden."

"Shall I prepare for his coming?" the old woman asked.

"There can be no preparation for this eternal messenger. No one will know of him or his purpose. It is all well if you shepherd the Vyrdmar, taking them to graze in the familiar places. Continue to instill my laws in their hearts through the traditions their ancestors have practiced, and hope that they will in time realize their place in the world."

"As you wish," the old woman replied. "The day of the Levying festival draws near. Who will you choose among the Vyrdmar to submit to your test, and face you in the beacon by the sea?"

"I have known my choice for some time. It has been a while since I chose one among the Vyrdmar who was fierce, to stem the tide of savagery and death from the east. But now this is a different season, requiring a different champion. I have chosen one who is constant, selfless and faithful. He will give even more than is given to him. And serving others will be his joy."

"I know of whom you speak. I saw him just today." The old woman paused as if trying to recall.

"An old man who had been away from the high city for many years returned," she said softly.

"There was no telling where his travels took him or why he returned. His clothes were tattered and hung loosely around him for he was frail and sickly. He must have wandered the city for days looking for his kin and for a warm place to rest and eat a good meal. But he must not have found his family or anyone who remembered him or who wanted to care for him in his old age.

I do not so much frown on the Vyrdmar's apathy. The people have been very anxious of late, with the harvests diminishing, and ships from beyond the sea bringing less and less foodstuffs. I suppose this has also made the people less charitable. And so, alas, the future appeared ominous for the old man. But then, he must have recalled, as he searched his muddled mind for solace, that there was a place where the forlorn and hungry could go. He remembered Aufrey's tower where, long ago, the poor and forlorn could gather to eat porridge and take shelter.

But when the old man came to Aufrey's tower, its door was bolted and no one came when he rang the rusty bell hanging by the door. Across from the tower was the archway into your temple, which was guarded by the Harfingal guard. The Harfingals looked on, but dared not leave their posts to help the old man. Many citizens passed by and did not notice the old man who soon began to weep. Then men from the city's militia rode by in a wagon with provisions. They saw the old man weeping and pleading for just some bread and water. But they would not be deterred from their errand. Alas again for the old man, for the people were not swayed by his suffering because they were uncaring and anxious. Their judgment was clouded. Yet while they lacked judgment, they were nonetheless judgmental, for they glowered at him.

Finally, up came the noble Vyrdmar, of whom I know you speak, looking so much like one of his fierce and lordly ancestors. But a gentle heart tempered the fierceness long attributed to his kin. Unlike many of them, he had not been blinded by his power. He had not placed himself on a pedestal, and turned his mind's eye on his own glory. He looked outward and listened, and was not afraid that the world would regard his gentleness as frailty. For, his hand was strong and his stature great, and he was apart from the others and aloof from their judgments. He rested on his inheritance like the wise men of old supported themselves on strong columns and reached out to teach and comfort others.

He saw the old man pleading and whimpering, and like a good shepherd, he rushed down from parapets above the strong archway, and came to him. He held him in his arms and lifted him up and brought him under the shelter of the arch. That is when I came down from a section of the parapet covered by a canopy and passed just beyond the archway. I passed by where he was tending to the old man and heard him saying, 'why did you not call out to the Harfingals to aid you.'

'My lord-' the old man replied, 'I was afraid that the sentries would strike me and send me away harshly.'

'Old man,' the noble Vyrdmar said. 'What virtue is there in the strong, if they do not hold up their brothers when they are weak? Though, I know of the brutality you speak. But this day you have brought glory to the Harfingals because you have given us a chance to serve, and that is our purpose'

The noble Vyrdmar had food and water brought to the old man, who ate heartily and was thankful. Now as I recall his deed, I am certain that this is the man you have chosen."

The creature nodded in agreement and stood up on its hinds, spread its wings and shifted. Folding its wings, it crouched again.

"This noble Vyrdmar is a shining symbol of hope," the creature remarked. "His courage and compassion comforted an old man. Perhaps more will return to Aufrey's tower and find that its legacy still burnishes. Times of plenty may be returning. I have not seen so many caravans lining the roads to your city in over a generation. Surely the bounty of the harvests in the lands beyond the sea was great."

"I will tell my flock of what you say about the winter harvest from the south," the old woman said taking a deep breath.

"A good harvest, a good son, and an eternal traveler returned among us. Perhaps these are good tidings. Perhaps the signs are good for the coming season."

"I will not brood over your raucous and wearisome flock tonight," the creature chimed in.

"I will return to my lofty beacon by the sea so that I may rest. My brethren and I will remain here with the Vyrdmar a while longer and watch over them like good gardeners. Though, we will wonder still what lies beyond the horizon."

Chapter 4: Shadow across the sea

Jaïem awoke even before the farmers in the countryside stirred in anticipation of the new dawn. He was fitted in his leather breastplates and gauntlet in preparation for his morning exercises. Pulling out a large wooden chest with a simple iron lock from a small alcove, he opened it and momentarily closed his eyes as if to savor the moment. Within were several parchments and scrolls. Jaïem carefully set the parchments, scrolls and other of his personal effects aside and clasped an object wrapped in black cloth from the bottom of the chest. He set the object on the ground and carefully unfurled the folds of the cloth to reveal the ivory hilt of a sword and then the length of its scabbard. As if trying to rediscover his sense of the weapon, he ran his fingers along the ornate carvings on the hilt and then wrapped his fingers around the weapon and partially unsheathed the sword to inspect the blade. Then he sprang up, fastened the scabbard to his belt and walked sternly out of his royal chambers leaving his effects scattered.

The morning sun had not yet risen to glisten off the morning dew rolling off the new spring leaves and petals, when Jaïem set out for his early exercises in the royal courtyard. A thick gray mist hovered over the royal compound. While the furnaces for the royal baths, located in the bowels of the royal apartments, were lit, the halls of its three levels were not yet busy with the chatter and movements of servants preparing meals and tending to the needs of the royal household.

Jaïem stopped briefly to gather some fruit from a bowl in the palace's large dining hall on the first level. He nibbled on a few grapes, almost swallowed a pear whole. He placed a second pear in a handkerchief and took a draught of water from a clay urn. Trotting out of the main dining hall, he made his way to a wide corridor speckled with finely embroidered tapestry and rugs, benches with supple and lavish pillows, and colorful shrouds leading into dimly lit alcoves.

A young servant girl peered out of an alcove to see the young prince marching toward the massive double doors leading to the royal palace's rounded portico. Guards stationed in the portico, on each side of the doors, bowed as Jaïem passed. Jaïem hurried down the portico steps and onto the paved path. The path ran through an archway and into a wider causeway leading south past the guard post to the royal garrison, and north through the royal garden. The royal garden was adjacent to both the royal apartments and an archway leading to the temple quadrangle.

The morning air was as cool as his determination, but the young prince was too focused to notice.

"He is right," he thought to himself. "Nothing matters in this world. There is only power. I must train myself to first gain power over my own feelings. I will train my body and mind to bend the will of fortune and tame my fickle passions. I will do this. This will distinguish me from others as a noble's comportment distinguishes him from commoners and slaves. I will throw my lot with the strong and turn my back on the weak. I swear I will do this and he will see me. Everyone will see me as I truly am."

As these thoughts buzzed in Jaïem's mind, his passions began to thaw his icy determination, which then became a raging flood of emotion. His throat constricted and his eyes welled with tears. He saw himself newly set on a profound journey, which would transform who he was into a new being with whom he was presently unfamiliar. Jaïem was anxious. He wondered if he had the moral courage and perseverance to carry out his transformation. Wiping his eyes with a hand, the prince hurried through the narrow walkway leading to the Hold without even hearing nature's symphony of insects and the birds circling above. He did not see the little colorful birds perched on the trees lining the walkway. All he could see were the polished stones under his feet and then the arched guard post before him, leading into the Hold's main courtyard. His entire being crouched, and all his energies were recoiled and held in preparation for his task.

Under the watchful eyes of sentries, and the dark blue sky above him, with its silver moon, its streaks of clouds, and twinkling stars, Jaïem's trials shared a stage with other actors. He could not have known, but there were events unfolding, which would intersect with his own personal trials. There were plans being laid, which would reap great sorrow that would eclipse the torment he now knew. Far away across the sea to the south and east, in the northern province of the kingdom of Cadera, in the city of Tidthra, the sounds of daybreak awakened another royal actor.

Tidthra was a magnificent city encircled by a sprawling ridge many travelers called Kruuma's ramparts. Kruuma the Faithful was the distant ancestor of the noble line that now ruled most of the western coast of the continent of Ausremer, and the scattered islands clinging to its rugged western coasts.

Surrounding the city was a patchwork of clay and brick structures and homes. The inhabitants of the outer city were mostly artisans and traders, living in compounds with traditional clay courtyards surrounded by a main dwelling structure.

Perched high along meandering ridges overlooking the rugged plains leading to the Khreinth Sea was a magnificent citadel with many elaborate and strong polished stone structures. Within its walls as the palace where the kings of Kruuma's line held court in the great hall called the Vizicun. The Kradaken guards, a corps of elite warriors, guarded the citadel.

A day in Tidthra began at dawn when the sentries of the night watch blew their horns to announce the day, and then passed their horns to their relief. On this day, as the sun crept over the eastern horizon, Meno, the Irsei ambassador to the city would leave the city and travel east to make his report to the Elihe council in the Irsei city of Arshis. Meno often climbed to the parapets facing his country to enjoy the sunrise. But as he did so on this day he observed a man hunched on a watchman's stool wrapped in dull gray cloak.

"A good morning brings new hope with a new day," Meno pondered out loud.

"Yes. It is a good morning." the man replied.

"Enjoying the first light before you retire from your watch?" the ambassador said smiling.

The cloaked man stood up and walked to the far side of the lookout and answered solemnly as he scanned the landscape.

"My watch will not end until death has kissed my lips. Then, I pray that the Creator of all things will take my spirit to the paradise promised to the faithful."

"Well-" Meno said walking toward the man, who was actually king Xremede, master of Tidthra.

"I will forgive your momentary slackness. I will pray for you that Eizierh, the Creator, looks favorably on you and your charges, and shelters you from your enemies."

Xremede pulled back the hood of his cloak to reveal his grizzly face and sparse gray plumes on his balding head. Though he was the Caderan king, Xremede looked more like an artisan, or a hardened soldier. His face was haggard, his brown eyes were bulbous, and he was stout. With his strong and corpulent hands revealed, his silver signet ring glistened in the morning sun.

"I was thinking of you Meno son of Arnon," the king said thoughtfully.

"I am pleased that Atilar's son, and king of men, Xremede, has thought of me – I hope favorably. I am humbled and eager to serve whatever purpose your mind has devised."

"My friend-" the king gestured. "Come with me for I am weary and my mind is troubled. I would very much like to share my burden with you. You have been a dear friend for a long time and you have given me good counsel in the past."

"Certainly," the Irsei ambassador replied.

"Very well," the king said smiling.

"I wanted to seek you out earlier, but the affairs of state left barely enough time for grooming. We have been good friends since we were children. I did not know whether I wanted to burden you. What troubles me is a most grave matter of the heart as well as the kingdom..."

The King paused and reached out, placed a hand on Meno's shoulder, and smiled. Meno saw deep sadness and anxiety in the king's eyes.

"My lord-" Meno whispered. "What burdens you?"

Xremede clasped his head in his hands and shook his head.

"The Atenarix-" he began ruefully, "They are my enemy. They are no longer a benign order sworn to the service of kings. They have become usurpers of kings. I fear they are poised to overthrow me."

Meno's face became grave and, rubbing his thick gray beard, he put his arm around the king.

"My friend, we know well the Atenarix's inclination for treachery. Your rule is fraught with danger to be sure. But you have reconstituted your council with my people. Your borders are secure with fortresses manned by vigilant sentries. Loyal vassals and strongholds surround you. Your ships patrol the Khreinth Sea to the north and the Tareian Sea to the west and south."

The king shook his head again.

"No matter how great their knowledge of secret arts," Meno persisted. "No matter how influential they are with the guilds, they do not have an army. You can destroy them with one swift stroke."

"My friend," Xremede cautioned. "You do not know the true extent of the Atenarix's power. Their power over the guilds is absolute and is alone troubling. But even more disconcerting is their power over life and death. Men say that in Cadera, I am inviolable and am master over life and death. Yet to say this does not to make it so. I must have the present and actual power to destroy life though my Kradaken guard and my armies. I must live a cloistered life and live behind walls and sentries and be held aloof from my people. Yet I realize now that I am not beyond the reach of the Atenarix. Therefore, I cannot freely act against them. There will undoubtedly be consequences. They can reach me."

Meno laughed uneasily. "Consequences?" he snorted. "How can this be? This must not be. You are a king. Your power is absolute. You are strong. Your alliance with the Elihe council and the Cirphed in Irsei makes you stronger. Together we can bring these cults of commerce into line with the force of law and the sword."

"You do not know the Atenarix' true power," the king warned. "Recently, a stranger visited my bedchambers just before sunset. While I was resting in my chambers overlooking the city, a veiled man swept in from my balcony like a strong gust. He wore a flowing blue tunic with overlapping layers and a shawl over his head. I would have thought he was a priest if he was not so towering and menacing. He looked into my eyes and spoke to me thus:

> 'Atilar's son, king of men, Xremede, I come to reveal to you the declaration of the Amretar masters. Do not stand between man and those who would deliver freedom and the bounties of life unto him. Do not stand in the way of the hand of providence. Do not provoke us who are humanity's faithful benefactors. If you do, you will bring ruin to your house. You will surely be destroyed.'"

Meno was incredulous. "Where were your guards? You must double your guards. No. Perhaps some of your guards are in league with the enemy. You must purge the treasonous from your Kradaken guards. Then you must take bold action. Round them up-all of them. Seize the guild-masters and their adherents and raze their pyramidal guild halls."

Xremede shook his head and moved away from Meno.

"No," he said. "You do not understand. There is more to this than I have told you. I thought this man's visit was a dream. He knew things about my affairs that I have kept secret from all but my most trusted advisors. I have not told you this. My daughter Eje has been secretly betrothed to Namreddin's house across the sea. This stranger knew this, and warned me not to follow through with my plan. He warned that his sword was not yet unsheathed, but that he would return again, and this time, when he returned, he would slay me. Then like a demon he leapt from my lofty balcony and vanished."

Xremede turned to look at Meno.

"This creature was an agent of the Atenarix. I was well within his reach and I defied him. I sent my daughter away to Chamiahce. I sent her in secret by land to Tehmas. From Tehmas she was to board a galley from Beonon provided by the sea lord Dorias who is king Ylarin's most trusted vassal. As we speak, she must only be days from her destination. Now therefore, that I have rebuffed the commands of this Atenarix agent, I fear that he will return one last time to mete out his justice."

"My lord Xremede-" Meno interjected. "What are you saying? You speak as if the Atenarix are the instruments of immortals. You are a descendant of the Cepheid. The twins were scions of your god Yggir, who slew Nur the cunning beast in the beginning of time. Yggir slew Nur and blew on his hot molten blood to create form and the world. Then in his sorrow at being alone he turned Nur's body into a tree, which bore man as fruit. Dissatisfied with what he had created, Yggir withdrew his being from his body and scattered it into the Four Winds who command the destiny of the living. Now, as you would have it, these immortals favor the Atenarix, who have never sacrificed burnt offerings or built great temples to honor them. That is preposterous. The Atenarix are godless. And those among them, who delve into the existence of the immortals and the unseen, only do so to harness their power for their own selfish purpose. My king, what you suggest is simply not possible."

"I do not know what to think," king Xremede confessed. "Yet I fear that when, and if, you return to this city, I may be dead."

The king sighed and looked even more troubled than before.

"These are perilous times. I have to look to matters of legacy and succession. I will entrust you with my will and testament, which I will seal with my signet ring. If, when you return, my city is in mourning and my house is in disarray, you will convene a council, calling for those who I have secretly given scrolls setting forth my desired line of succession. Those I have who possess these scrolls will come forth. There will be yet another scroll with two seals, one of my house and the other of Irilsflir, which I have sent to Gaalden. That scroll will determine the rights and obligations of my daughter's new lord."

Meno stared at the king blankly and then taking a deep breath turned away. He began walking down stairs leading down from the parapet. Xremede touched his arm and held him a while longer.

Xremede and Meno continued to speak for some time as they made their way to the king's chambers where they tried to eat their morning meal together. Their minds wandered and their eyes peered uneasily at the sentries and servants around them even as they nibbled on fresh fruit and drank warm mead. They whispered together for quite some time and then met with members of Xremede's court until late in the afternoon. Yet even as the king presided over various ministerial matters, he was unfocused and forgetful because his mind was on his precious and beautiful daughter Eje.

Far away across the Khreinth Sea, Eje's mind also troubled. She sat huddled in a thick black cloak draped over her delicate shoulders like moss over a sapling. She sat by a lonely stream littered with shiny white stones, as if listening to the sound of the undulating waters for news about her father and her homeland.

Yet Eje was not listening to the water at all; her mind was humming with incoherent thoughts. She was confounded by her unfamiliar surroundings and numb with fear. Her recent travels were fraught with peril. She looked over her shoulder now and then, like prey fresh from pursuit. Like prince Jaïem, and like her father Xremede, an unseen power hovered over her destiny. Like farmers are mindful of their crops, all three actors were mindful about the future they had sowed, hoping for a good harvest, but wary of a looming pestilence or a savage storm that could imperil everything dear to them.

A young man with a leather herder's cap, walking with a javelin, appeared from some thick brush in the distance, startling several horses bound to a tree nearby. He wore a gray wool tunic, which fit awkwardly about his broad shoulders. His skin was dark like the sediment rich rivers in his homeland, and his limbs lengthy and sinewy. Around his neck he wore black and red beads. He bore a curved sword around his waist and a bow hanging about his shoulder and chest.

"My lady-" he whispered. Eje did not hear and so he came close behind her and picked up a small stone. He looked at it and then flung it into the stream. The princess, Eje, whirled around, seeming somewhat startled.

"Ahktel," she exclaimed, taking a deep breath. "You startled me. Is it considered good manners among the Hekare to startle young women?"

"Forgive me," Ahktel said earnestly.

"No," Eje assured him. "I am sorry. I am glad to see you. I was thinking of home. I should be more mindful of my surroundings in this wilderness."

Ahktel knelt beside her. Eje pulled back the hood of her cloak revealing her thick black hair. Her forehead was high, broad, and prominent, and her face oval and slender. Her eyes were dark and deep and her nose broad. Her full lips were chapped from the chill air, but her sun kissed skin still glowed. She turned to look at Ahktel who peered down and away to avoid her stare.

"Where is your kinsman and the others who brought us here?"

Ahktel turned and gestured. "They are here and there even if you do not see them. They are scouting like the herdsman from my country when they are looking out for bandits and poachers. As for my kinsman Ixhor, he is not far behind."

Then, even as Ahktel spoke his name, tall and broad shouldered Ixhor came lumbering out of the thick brush.

Ixhor's clothing also hung awkwardly over him. He wore a gray cloak like a shawl and the tip of his boots were cut to reveal his toes.

"I found berries just down the trail there." Ixhor opened up a small pouch to show Ahktel.

"Dear friends-" Eje warned. "Be careful! There are things that should not be eaten in this strange wilderness. Eat the provisions master Bojingren has provided. Be mindful also that there are protocols to be followed. We are Bojingren's guests in this land. Here, as in our Austral land, a duty is owed to guests. Let Bojingren provide therefore less you shame him."

Ahktel peered at Ixhor and nodded. "Take care Ixhor. Do not embarrass us. Besides, these berries may be poisonous."

Ixhor reached in his pouch and grabbed a handful of berries.

"I have seen a very swift animal with horns eating these." Ixhor smiled and ate a mouthful of berries.

Ahktel shook his head. Eje frowned and looked intently at the Hekare.

"Listen to your kinsman Ixhor, and be careful. We are strangers in this country and these men of Beonon have guided our passage here. They seem honorable and good. Yet I cannot be certain. I do not trust them as I trust you. You rescued me from those men who held me captive back in Tehmas. You asked for nothing in return. You have earned my unwavering gratitude and trust."

The two Hekare squatted beside Eje. "Do not fret," Ixhor mumbled. "Ahktel can see many things. He can see what is in the distance. When we boarded that great ship from Erebis to come to the shores of Beonon, I was anxious. But he told me not to be afraid. He said we would sail safely across the sea. He said he could feel his feet tramping on Maspeidonian soil even as he spoke with me back then. Sure enough, we were carried by favorable winds all the way here to this foreign land."

Leaning on his javelin, Ahktel cast a stone into the stream nearby. "Those who walk with the Spirit should not fear death or misfortune. For the Hekare, a man who walks with the Spirit is always on the right path. Yet a man who strays from the Spirit is certain to drift into the desert of despair and forgetfulness. I cannot claim that all is revealed to me. But I can feel the Spirit's presence. He is with us."

Eje smiled and then shivered as a cool morning breeze blew.

"Look!" Ixhor interrupted. "Here is the captain of the guard. It must be time to go."

Bojingren appeared around a bend in the stream on horseback, followed by three riders. The horsemen all clad in mail armor with light helmets with a pointy crest approached at a trot. Bojingren, the Red, as he was known for his red hair, dismounted and approached Eje and the Hekare.

"Come quickly. My scouts say that the way ahead is clear. We must try to reach the foot of a range of mountains quite some distance north of here before nightfall. There is an outpost there and we will be able to replenish our provisions as we are traveling very light."

The Hekare helped Eje to her feet, and then Ahktel scampered to bring her horse to her. Eje thanked

Ahktel as Bojingren walked to his horse and mounted. He looked at the Hekare and Eje and thought how peculiar they were together.

"How strange these Ausremen are," he thought. "By their own account, the two young men are herders from a region of Irsei called Eptare. The girl is an envoy from the royal court of Cadera, and even stranger she bears a commission with the seal of the Vyrdmar regent as well as the court of Cadera, obligating any vassal, sentry, or citizen owing fealty to either court to suffer any expense, whether life or limb, to ensure that this girl has safe passage to king Ylarin's court in Chamiahce. What commission would the world's most powerful rulers entrust to such a company? Why not send this commission with emissaries under guard?"

Bojingren lost his train of thought when one of the three warriors in his forward company called out.

"Hurry my captain; we must not fall too far behind."

"Verily Tyeshar," Bojingren answered. "Go forth. We are behind you."

Tyeshar saluted along with the other two warriors, and the forward company rode off. They rode up along the edge of the gentle stream for a while. The water moved more quickly as they rode until they reached a pool of water at the foot of a ridge. The pool was fed by gushing water from a cave gaping at the base of a crag.

The forward company followed a natural trail up along a ridge on the side of the crag and followed the trail to an elevated clearing. Now they could see the peaks of a range of mountains along the horizon. Seeing that the way ahead was clear, they sent word back to the others and then rode at a trotting pace heading north.

Meanwhile in Chamiahce, within the white halls of the academy, master Ceresmin was proceeding on his lecture before dozens of students. His lecture was on the conflict between primal sentiment and morals in an ordered society. Several young men looked very weary as he spoke. As was his habit, he stood sternly with both hands on the knob of his ashen staff rather than sitting in the manner typical of other schoolmasters. Most schoolmasters sat on a massive marble bench placed on a dais at the center of every lyceum hall. However, master Ceresmin was a young man, while the other schoolmasters were advanced in age, and could not bear to stand for long, even while leaning on the ashen staves that symbolized their station.

"During the winter sessions, we learned the fundamental nature of species – that species are endowed with an inclination to perpetuate. Some learned men call this sentiment chonatus or lower sentiment. We more precisely frame this sentiment as a duality – that is domination and submission.

We also learned how law, both moral and civic, interacts to fetter lower sentiment. We agreed that moral law fosters the development of character and higher sentiment. Since the dawn of history, the Vyrdmar have cultivated higher sentiment in the hearts and minds of men, so that together we may achieve excellence in human action and avoid calamity."

The schoolmaster paused and looked around the lyceum hall.

"It is not a foregone conclusion that moral law will hold sway in an ordered society. The Celestial may be the author of life, but men are imperfect and willful.

It is through the Celestial's exercise of power over life and death through the Vyrdmar king that free men are guided toward right thought and action. This view seems pedagogical because men do not see the Celestial. Many industrious men reject our view. Many wonder why the Vyrdmar king, and not the Celestial rules, if the Celestial is the actual source of power over life and death. Many also wonder how conformity with the will of the Celestial promotes survival and prosperity.

For example, the Atenarix ponder such questions. They believe that men do not need the Celestial. They believe that men can reveal all the world's secrets, that we can deconstruct the world, and reshape it in our own image. The Atenarix even say that men can defeat death and become like the immortals.

Those who place their faith in the Atenarix way have always risen to prominence in the world. The Atenarix seem to more aptly answer the existential questions that mystify us. They seem to better solve problems that threaten survival. The Atenarix even seem proficient at enhancing the enjoyment of life.

But even if a man could harness all the world's phenomena and triumph over death, what would he do with that power without the guidance of Celestial's perfect wisdom and purpose. What do men generally do with power? Without moral law and divine guidance mankind will surely destroy the world. Unbridled, man's primal heart would consume everything."

The schoolmaster looked around the hall into many faces with heavy lids. There were many jaded and doleful expressions. There were a few with eyes wide with interest.

"Now having moved on to a full discussion on the apparent conflict between man's primal nature and the Celestial's purpose, can anyone explain why the way of the Celestial is the most perfect path to peace and salvation?"

There were no immediate responses until a portly young man stood up to speak. There were a few groans, but the young man collected himself and spoke clearly.

"Master Ceresmin," he began. "As you have often said, man is a problem solver. But we are inclined to solve problems for ourselves – often without regard to the greater good. We are fundamentally selfish. Our efforts to solve our problems often result in discord and suffering."

"Very well Bairn," Ceresmin said clasping his hands together and smiling. He paced again contemplating his next point.

"We are born with primal values, the fundamental pillars of perception and choice, and even moral judgment. However, the Celestial builds on this foundation and attunes our minds to His divine laws. As master Idram once said, 'this transcendent act is the beginning and the end of our humanity and our genius.'"

The schoolmaster paused briefly again.

"Divine law can be discerned and understood. But discerning and understanding divine law does not necessarily translate to action and consequences. It is not enough that we know what is right. To ensure that knowledge of right and wrong translates into right action, those chosen by the Celestial to teach and lead men, must provide their charges with rigorous mental training, and exert moral and civic authority through civic law and punishment."

Master Ceresmin began pacing again.

"Are we truly free if we must obey divine law?"

To startle a few dozing pupils, the schoolmaster stamped his ashen staff on the ground and smiled awkwardly.

"Yes indeed. What of choice? Where does choice fit in? How can we be free if we are compelled by divine law to be righteous? "

Master Ceresmin looked around the great hall for an answer to his questions.

"Master Ceresmin!" a young man called out. The schoolmaster acknowledged the young man saying, "Oresias, son of Dorelias, you may speak."

"We have the ability to choose," the young cadet replied. "But then my dog chooses my sister over me when she holds out a morsel of food."

Some muffled laughter could now be heard. A cadet near Oresias rose to speak and Ceresmin quickly acknowledged him.

"A bird in the courtyard chose hapless Lepryaus' head for its droppings."

Now laughter burst out in the lyceum hall and Ceresmin had to stamp his staff over and over to regain order.

Another cadet rose to speak as the clamor died down.

"Master Idram distinguishes between the idea of the sovereign individual and what some have called the autonomous individual. Some would say that beasts are freer than men. But that is not the Vyrdmar point of view."

"Indeed," the schoolmaster beamed, stamping his ashen staff.

"Men and beasts are driven by appetite. Men and beasts discern the weight of each choice through the mind's innate calculus of outcomes. The autonomous individual may choose in this regard, but he does not deliberate and does not choose according to knowledge of higher values and divine law. That is the industry of the sovereign individual, and only the sovereign individual is truly free."

The schoolmaster now stared out sternly and pointed toward the youth in the hall.

"Beasts may be inclined toward one thing over another, but they do not deliberate or know right from wrong. Knowledge of right and wrong is fundamentally divine. To be constrained by moral law and the interest of the collective in one's choices is to be sovereign over appetite and desire and chaos. Verily, we should strive to be sovereign and masterful like mighty Yggir. We should strive to evaluate competing values through a moral and divine prism. It may be true that men are autonomous, but few among us are truly sovereign.

Very few have awareness of values that evince higher and even divine outcomes.

Alas though, for those mired in the wilderness - autonomy is an illusion. Men may choose, but men do not determine the choices. That power rests with immortals. Nothing brings this realization to the fore more than misfortune, which brings men's hubristic fantasies crashing down around them. We may be sentient and free to choose, but we are not the original cause or author of our own reality and our purpose. We answer if we are called. We read the signs. We read the purpose authored by immortals and we obey or are flung helplessly into the void.

Always remember therefore, to be humble. Do not exult in your own power over outcomes, even those outcomes, which upon careful consideration, seems totally within your control. Some of you will one day lead men on the battlefield. As leaders, you must gather all there is to know about your enemy and the field and decide on a course of action. But know that divine purpose may lay waste to the most ingenious battle plan, or bring victory in spite of your miscalculations. It is not that men are powerless before the gods. The gods are simply greater than we are, and invoking their wisdom is a surer path to victory and salvation than solely relying on our own ability to perceive."

Ceresmin took a deep breath and stepped down from the schoolmaster's dais.

The schoolmaster walked among his cadets all sitting on stone benches forming a concentric circle around the schoolmaster's dais. A few sighed and drew deep breaths, knowing very well that the schoolmaster was likely on the brink of another long and one-sided colloquy.

"To conclude," Ceresmin began again. "If our forebears did not invoke divine wisdom, society would now be lost. We would live like beasts. In such a world, lower sentiment would predominate. Our world would be devoid of morals, duty, and virtue, and greed and violence would triumph."

The schoolmaster walked back to the dais, keeping his back to the cadets. Taking another deep breath, he turned to face them again, and continued.

"I tell you this with all sincerity and goodwill. For, even at the twilight of days, when the bloody and burning ruin of men comes because they have strayed from the laws of the Celestial, this duty may still bear fruit. And out of despair and churning ashes, this nascent nobility may, like a seed, bring forth new life. I say to you truly that in our duty to each other lie our greatest strength and our greatest hope. Like a spark of fire from heaven, it will light our way in the darkness, if we cling to it."

Jaïem looked on from where he sat on the edge of a row of single benches near an aisle. As he listened, he thought of his morning exercises.

He thought. "Duty... How soon we forget old lessons. How easily we get lost in our despair and stray from the path laid down by those the four Winds have entrusted with higher knowledge. I will follow in the footsteps set down by my fathers. I will seek to be moral and dutiful. I will train my mind and I will train my body to be an instrument of divine purpose."

But as he reflected, he experienced a familiar sensation. He felt a chill and the hairs on his neck stood. His heart began to race and he look almost frantically around the lyceum hall. Jaïem then heard a familiar voice asking: "Why?"

Jaïem clasped his hands together and wrung them.

"Why do you listen to echoes? I offer you something that not even the gods will offer you. I offer you a draught from the cup of knowledge and power. Why do you reject me? I offer you the privileges of heaven and you cower and seek refuge in rhetoric and fables. Take my hand young prince, embrace me and inhale the breath of immortals."

Jaïem clasped his head almost as if he would pull out patches of his golden hair.

"Please," he thought. "Not here for all to see."

Jaïem wanted to stand and flee from the the hall. He could hear his heart beating faster and his stomach churned.

"I come to you now so that you may know that I am real," the voice whispered. "I am not merely a shadow in your bedchamber that haunts your dreams. I am real my prince."

"If you are real," Jaïem thought. "Why do I not see you out here as I see others?"

Jaïem listened for an answer and heard nothing at first. Then, from the portal leading into the lyceum hall, a gust could be felt rustling the tapestry hanging around the hall, and tipping over a cross staff sitting on a wooden table with other navigational equipment displayed on the dais behind the schoolmaster.

"Ah!" the schoolmaster exclaimed, "I hope this is a sign of approval from the Celestial."

The young cadets looked up and around, some chuckling uneasily.

Picking up the cross staff, Ceresmin remarked.

"It is not surprising that the Vyrdmar of Gaalden hold civic virtue and duty in such high esteem."

Placing the instrument over his left eye as if he was a sea captain looking to the horizon, he tried to incorporate the instrument into his lesson.

"Seafaring men must stand together, working cooperatively against the formidable sea."

But Jaïem could barely hear the schoolmaster as he stared blankly toward the dais. "Why do you spurn me?" a voice echoed in Jaïem's mind.

"Come to me and I will embrace you and anoint you with true purpose."

Jaïem put his hands over his ears.

"Why do you torment me? If I turn away from you, it is because you are a mystery to me. I am afraid of you because I do not know you. I am afraid that if I choose to know you, I will change. I am afraid I will lose myself."

The voice grew softer. "I want to shelter you. I want to be of use to you. Tell me your desires and I will grant them. All I ask that I walk with you on your path. Through our bond, I will share your struggles, and you will draw on my strength to triumph over all obstacles."

Jaïem rose abruptly and bowed to the schoolmaster.

"Please excuse me master Ceresmin. There is an urgent matter I must attend to."

The schoolmaster looked at Jaïem and then to the other cadets, and nodded reluctantly.

"By your leave," Jaïem said bowing.

"You have my leave master Jaïem," the schoolmaster replied gesturing.

"The movements of the gods have a most profound effect on the pious," the schoolmaster mused, as Jaïem hurried out of the lyceum hall.

The cadets chuckled. Yet Jaïem did not hear them. The young prince's mind was clouded. He quickly made his way through the corridors of the lower academy, crossing the large assembly hall where a statue of the great sea captain Arhyos stood. There were many statues, tapestries, and honoraria to Gaalden's seafaring heritage in the lower academy since this was where the young cadets of the king's fleet were instructed.

Jaïem ran headlong in the direction of the royal compound. Small crowds of pupils and cadets from both the upper and lower academies parted as he passed. They looked at each other, shrugging, and some smiling. The melancholy prince was often seen hurrying to and fro without extending or acknowledging a greeting.

"He must be the fittest in king Ylarin's court," one young man whispered.

Hushed laughter could be heard, but as always with great care, as they did not want to offend the prince. Jaïem passed through the archway leading to the royal compound and the temple Irilsflir. Walking along a parapet above the archway were two men who paused to peer down at the young prince.

"That is one of the king's sons," a finely garbed man wondered out loud.

"Yes my lord Umalein," the second man replied. "He is Jaïem the youngest."

Lord Umalein, the lord from Parilos, dressed in a long sky blue robe with golden trim, had left the royal apartments to speak with his vizir. Approaching mid afternoon, the sun shone through a few scattered clouds. The spring air was mild and ideal for a brisk walk.

"We have not considered this one they call Jaïem have we?"
The gray-haired vizir rubbed his tailored beard and thought for a moment.

"No one man matters in this game. It is the merit of the stratagem that will win the day."

Lord Umalein, who appeared the younger of the two men by many years, snatched the vizir's ornate staff.

"Alfaisten my friend," lord Umalein retorted. "You and I will have to continue to disagree on this point. As a leader of men, I can appreciate the virtue of deliberation and preparation. Yet these intrigues we speak of can only be realized through the courage and exploits of one and every man. In this regard, care must be taken to appreciate the mettle and courage of each man. Care must also be taken to extricate those men, whom fortune tends to smile on, from our enemy's ranks before that pivotal moment when our stratagem clashes against our formidable opponent's machinations. That is precisely why we are here, in the thicket of the enemy, on the eve of our glorious victory. We must take careful account of each man, and determine whether the signs are with him, and whether the season is right for our plan."

The old vizir Alfaisten placed out a hand gesturing for his staff. "You are very wise my lord. Yet you place too much faith in inscrutable things. We who are adherents of the Atenari masters know of only three gods. We know of particle, of motion, and probability. All other gods and abstractions are merely shadows of the triumvirate of our empirical reality. There is no man who by virtue of his sacrifices to the gods of lore, or by virtue of his lineage, who can shape the future without deliberation, preparation, and of course action. The Vyrdmar king who dwells here has lost his good sense in this regard. He has abdicated his good judgment for the babbling of a witch who reads fortunes from a fountain. Therefore it is clear to me that we are on the right side of nature and history and will prevail."

Umalein handed Alfaisten his staff and smiled.

"Perhaps you are right my old friend. Yet you would not be wise to place all of your faith in particle, motion, and probability. Surely your successes have not blinded you to the limitations of your own ability to observe and understand."

Bowing, Alfaisten took his staff and leaned on it slightly. "All we, as men, can do is observe, deliberate and act."

"Let fortune choose sides and let the die fall where it may. The time is near when particle, motion, and probability will mesh on great battlefields, and victories will toll the merit of gods, the Vyrdmar, and the Atenarix."

Lord Umalein smiled again. "Very well my old friend. Your words pierce me to the core, and I mark well your mental discipline and courage. Indeed, the game is already afoot. Far away, our Atenarix agents have already struck the first blow, and yet the Vyrdmar king does not stir. He crouches like a lion stalking and scanning the landscape for his prey. But he does not know that the landscape is full of predators masquerading as prey. And by the time he is finally ready to strike, he will find himself surrounded. Our masterful benefactor will be loosed, and like predators with fallow eyes, we adherents of the Atlantean creed will pounce and devour him."

Chapter 5: On the plains of Edris

After meandering through the Pelares for three days, the riders from the city of Bonthc, in Beonon, slowly made their way down a winding trail into a valley dotted with green mounds and fields split by a rolling tributary. There were six riders out in front of the company and nine riders, including Eje and the two young Hekare in the rear. Bojingren rode close to Eje, sometimes astride with her when the trail was not so narrow. Looking up at the afternoon sky, and seeing clouds amassing, Bojingren kicked Eje's horse, whistled and urged his horse to a gallop.

"Hurry!" he called out to Ahktel and Ixhor who were not far behind.

"The sky is brooding young Hekare."

The riders galloped north across rolling fields and patches of brush, as the sky grew darker to the east. Along the north and eastern horizon flashes of lightning could be seen. Pressing on for some time the riders could see a patch of trees ahead. A light rain fell, steadily becoming heavier, urging the company forward. They were relieved to reach the trees at the onset of a deluge.

But the rains subsided very quickly and the riders took off again. The company rode late into the afternoon, and soon came to a range of hills encircled by a grove. Rising out of a grove was a great cylindrical tower of gray stone. The company followed a narrow trail surrounded on both sides by large stones leading up to the tower that did not appear to have an entrance or battlements.

The company massed before the great tower and a whistling sound could be heard from within the tower walls. Movement could be seen beyond slits in the walls. A cranking sound could be heard. Then a portion of the tower wall receded slowly into the tower structure and then laterally.

Several sentries came out of the dark bowels of the tower and surrounded the company. A stout man dressed in full mail came marching out of the tower. Bojingren came forward and saluted the man. Bojingren removed his light helmet to reveal his red hair.

"Who is the master of this outpost?"

The stout man looked up at the young captain and saluted.

"I am lord Dorias' man in this outpost. I am Cloedus, captain of this, the last outpost in Beonon."

Bojingren dismounted and saluted again. Cloedus gestured for his sentries to stand down and asked Bojingren to follow him inside the outpost. The rest of the company followed behind taking their horses with them through the tall and narrow portals, and the sentries after them.

The narrow portal led into a passageway separating two stable areas. At the far end of the passageway were two outlets, one leading into supply compartments. Beyond the two outlets was a wooden stair leading up to a guardroom with a table and a few cots and sacks.

The company was led up through the main guardroom, up several levels, and past two levels of living quarters. Exhausted, Eje was thankful when Cloedus assured them that they were almost there.

Finally, the company was led to a narrow room with a long narrow table. The room was plain and lit with only a couple of lanterns. Bojingren and his lieutenant Tyeshar followed Cloedus to yet another smaller room while the others remained behind.

"Welcome again countrymen."

Cloedus gestured for the two men to take seats around a table covered with parchments and maps.

"I was not expecting anyone from the city since the lord of the city passed through here over two weeks ago on his way to the festival in Chamiahce."

The master of the tower walked over to a small wooden cupboard and produced a clay ewer and three wooden cups and placed them around the table before his guests.

"Some water?" Bojingren and Tyeshar nodded and were served.

"Where do your travels take you?" the master of the tower asked.

"We go to the high city." Bojingren replied.

"Lord of the tower, tell us of the way ahead to Chamiahce. What of the cave dwellers, the Ayimar hiding in the mountains? I hear that even after the great purge, they still harass travelers and caravans coming this way. I also hear that many avarathein have left the mountains and have been sighted hunting on the plains."

Sighing, Cloedus sat down and took a draught of water.

"Since the purge two years ago, this sector of Beonon has been mostly quiet. Though there have been some avarathein sightings. But I think something is now stirring in the Pelares. Plumes of smoke can be seen wafting up to the heavens as if from hidden the mountain passes. These happenings may have startled the animals roaming the Pelares valley. A few days after lord Dorias came this way my scouts encountered a particularly vicious avarathein. It swept down from the mountains and carried away one of my men. There is not enough going on to be alarmed. But I can't help but feel that something is afoot."

"Did your men kill the avarathein? It will most certainly strike again, becoming bolder if it is permitted to attack without hindrance."

Cloedus shook his head and his face grew graver. "My men did not kill it. An avarathein is a formidable beast, attacking from the sky with thick leathery skin and sharp talons. It flies high and its descent is accompanied by a thunderous sound that shakes men's courage. Good scouts and archers are our best defenses against them. My scouts travel light and our archers are held in reserve. My scouts were no match for that beast."

Bojingren peered over at Tyeshar and then back over to Cloedus.

"I am sorry," Bojingren sighed. "We too travel light. We will need provisions. Not much. I intended to leave here today and ride hard until dark. But your account unsettles me. I think it will be best if we not travel so close to the mountains so late in the day. We will leave for the high city tomorrow. In light of the avarathein sighting, it would be well if, in addition to some provisions, you provide us with some bows and arrows from your arsenal. As you know my men are with lord Dorias' personal guard, and do not, as a matter of course, use bows."

Cloedus nodded. "We will part with what we can spare. What about the strangers among you? What of them? They appear to be from the austral land across the sea. They carry bows and wear them in the manner of the fierce Irsei. Will they be requiring anything?"

Bojingren poured more water into his cup. "Yes. Well they are-"

Bojingren cleared his throat. "It is just as well. They are with us. We will need bows and arrows for every man if you can spare it."

The entire company filed back down to one of the contiguous spaces where small apertures could be seen. This compartment was one of two archery nodes in the tower. There were two sets of apertures five feet apart, one positioned on a downward slope for archers and one level aperture for spotters. Ahktel and Ixhor placed their bows and quiver of arrows, and their leather satchels, which were slung over their shoulders, on the stone floor next to a set of apertures. The two Hekare leaned their javelins against the wall, and Ahktel removed his cloak revealing his curved sword sheathed in a leather scabbard. Ahktel removed his belt and scabbard and placed it on his lap as he sat on the floor with his back propped on the wall beneath an aperture. Ixhor followed in kind.

"Come here my kinsman," Ahktel gestured. "Sit next to me. There is fresh air over here. It is not like lying under the stars on the plains like the Xedun warriors who watch over the flocks. Yet we must rejoice in what we have."

Meanwhile, Bojingren and his men gathered around him and Eje, who sat quietly on a bench brought in by the tower sentries. They brought dried meats, bread and wine in clay ewers from vats in the subterranean catacombs of the tower. Eje whispered in Bojingren's ear and he nodded.

"My friends," Eje called out in the Irsei tongue. "I suspect that the view may be better where you are. But there is food here. Come. Do not be aloof. I need you close to me now more than ever."

Ixhor peered at Ahktel, and shrugging, they stood up and joined those gathered near the center of the compartment. The company ate and tried to speak together, Ahktel and Ixhor, struggling to understand the common tongue of the Maspeidonians and sharing some basic expressions in Irsei.

Night fell as the company ate and spoke together. Wine was mixed with water and consumed until all were jovial and at peace. Gradually one after the other, each man bade the gathering the tranquility of sleep and blessed dreams. After all in the company had gone to sleep, Eje huddled nearby Bojingren and Tyeshar. She could not sleep however. Her mind was burdened by thoughts of home and of her destination, and the new life she would begin there.

She tried to be optimistic about the promise of her new life. But she could not help wondering if she would be happy, if she would have new friends, and if her new family would cherish her like her father. Tears welled up in her eyes as she thought of her father and how much she adored him and how much he loved her. She dried the tears from her cheek with a handkerchief, which she wore under her cloak, and strained her eyes to see if anyone was awake. Then her thoughts wandered back to her father. She could see his oft-haggard face, and his large brown eyes, which were often hidden behind huge lids and eyelashes, as he mulled his terrible burdens. Eje wondered what he was thinking and feeling. She wondered if he was thinking of her.

Indeed, king Xremede thought of his precious daughter every day since she was sent away in the middle of the night. After Eje left, he awaited news of her safe arrival in Tehmas and then in Chamiahce. No news came however. As the days passed, and anxiety and then chagrin weighed on him, he fell ill with a fever. Unable to eat, his physicians brought him mead and mulled wine. A man of great vigor, he now slept for hours during the day, or held court in his bedchambers. Yet the day before, feeling stronger, he held audience in the great Vizicun with his vizirs and greeted emissaries and distinguished visitors.

On the fateful day Eje entered into the valley within sight of the Pelares, king Xremede returned to his bedchamber, from a walk in his garden with his chief vizir just before nightfall. He sat on a large and luxurious couch facing his bed with his back to his balcony. He could hear the melody of birds perched on trees as he reviewed some documents his vizirs submitted to him. Then he felt a breeze that made him shudder and then the flutter of the thick curtains, which were shut for the night. His eyes and his mind paused. Feeling a sense of foreboding, he thought to call the guard posted outside of his door. The king eyed the double doors leading to his balcony warily. Sighing, he put down the parchments and reached for an ornate staff leaning on the arm of the couch.

Yet before the king could stand, he heard a whisper pierce the silence in the room.

"Ye Atilar Lije, Xremede," the voice whispered scornfully in an ancient language.

The king felt a chill that made the hairs on his neck stand. Then turning around slowly, he saw a tall veiled man in flowing black robes standing at the balcony entrance to his bedchamber. King Xremede gathered his breath and began to speak in a hushed tone.

"You have come for me?" The king turned to face his visitor.

"I have come to cast you into oblivion," the veiled man said in an Ausremen dialect.

"All in your decadent house will follow and be purged from the memory of men. Know then, before you die, that your line has come to an end. This mockery, which the men of Ausremer call the kingdom of Cadera, will soon fall before the redoubtable surge of progress."

The tall veiled figure, beckoned for the king to approach him. Xremede, leaning on his staff, drew breath to call his guards. As he did so, the veiled visitor's eyes flashed and the king was frozen with fear.

"Come before me and take the poison I have brought for you, or else your royal person will be bruised and bloodied. Then your subjects will say that you were struck down, and will know how weak and decadent is your house."

Xremede gathered his courage and stepped forward, clasping his staff with both hands as if to strike the visitor.

"Who are you?" the king whispered through clenched teeth.

"I am the hand of the Atenarix," the man replied tersely. "I am of the Vehe-ta. I am a masterful achievement of Atlantis. I am an instrument of progress, come to cleanse the world of kings and false gods."

The veiled visitor beckoned again. "Come and drink this poison or your death will be brutal and painful."

Although weakened from his illness, Xremede stumbled forward to attack. A capable soldier, he lurched forward and swiped at the veiled man with his staff. Suddenly two flesh-colored tentacles thrust from under the veiled visitor's robes to wrap around the crown of king Xremede's staff. The tentacles wrested the staff from the king and he fell forward.

No sooner than king Xremede fell to the ground, the tentacles seized him, one by a sinewy arm, and another around his stout neck. The king could not breathe much less call out for his guards. But they had heard the commotion and were struggling to break down the locked double doors into the king's bedchamber.

Now the king reached with his free arm and struggled to free himself from his assailant's powerful grip. Yet the tentacles clung to him like massive constrictors, crushing his larynx. His bloodshot eyes bulged out, blood oozed from his nostrils, but he could not gasp.

"Do not resist Xremede," the veiled man mocked. "This is the law of heaven and earth; that the strong will devour the weak. You are weak, your kingdom is weak, and the weak must be cleansed from the world, so that the saplings of higher species may rise and breathe free. Behold! Only the strong will survive the coming purge of the Atenarix. Now relinquish your soul to whatever idol you cherish, and die."

The son of Atilar, king of Cadera, Xremede writhed on the floor of his bedchamber, with darkness veiling his eyes, and a sense of weightlessness seizing him. With one last clasp of a hand that was once strong in battle, that had caressed his beloved, and comforted his children, and had gestured the wisdom and assurance of a regent to his court and his people, he fell lifelessly.

With the king having passed into the void, the veiled man feigned to speak the king's epitaph. "If only you could taste this last bitter irony Xremede. The ebbing strength of your line, Kruuma's line, will die before this season brings the bounty of a harvest to the markets. Your house will die, just as the world is renewed."

The veiled man towered over Xremede's body.

"Your furtive attempt to strengthen your hand has failed. Your scheme to ally yourself with Wind's line has been foiled. Now that you are dead, your kingdom will fracture as your petty lords and governors grab for power like paupers. Your children will fall to intrigue, toxins, and the sword. Then the Atenarix will sweep across Cadera and the world and hail a new day when men who rule by right of lineage will be no more."

The doors to Xremede's bedchamber were finally flung open. Two Kradaken guards rushed to their king's side with swords drawn. Sadly, the king was already dead. One guard shouted and another wept as a son weeps for a father. Yet his tears did not flow from a well as deep as Eje's. Her love was as deep as the oceans. She was weeping just then at the mere thought of the distance that separated her from her father.

But Eje could not know that her father was now staring blankly from beyond time. If she knew, her tears would rage like a torrent and her heart would cry out in agony. Her mortal prescience gave her great solace in that for all she knew, he was as she left him when last they embraced. She remembered how grave his face was when he sent her away with his most trusted sentries.

It was a cool and murky morning. The patter of a steady rain could be heard falling on the leaves of trees from the grove encircling the tower. Yet the company set off north and east for the banks of the Yeire River, which bordered Gaalden.

That gloomy morning, a somber Eje appeared particularly frail and somber. She was soaked and cold, her face clammy, and her eyes dark. She was too tired and weak to even think of her bright and warm country. Her travels had drained her. Her memories were fading, and even the last few vivid memories only mocked her and made her numb. All she could do was cling to the reins of her horse with her cold hands and peer ahead at the riders before her. She struggled to smile when Bojingren the Red urged her on every now and then.

By mid-afternoon, the company had followed a narrow trail north to a major caravan road meandering north and west along range of hills. Had the weather been fairer, the company would have seen the open plains on the horizon after passing some rolling hills to the east. On this day however, the sky was overcast all morning and on into the afternoon. Light rains fell and subsided throughout the day. But soon fairer skies outlined the western horizon. Looking west, Eje's heart lifted.

By late afternoon when the sun began to pierce through the gray clouds, the company rested briefly on a mound crested with several large stone landmarks hewn in strange cylindrical shapes. The company of fifteen now gathered around briefly to eat the provisions of dried meats and bread they brought from the tower along the border.

Ahktel and Ixhor sat close to Eje now, and seeing that she was worn from the long journey, Ahktel handed her some dried leaves from a pouch he kept in his satchel. "Here place this along the side of your mouth." Eje gathered the leaves in a cupped hand and looked at the Hekare curiously. He nodded to encourage her. Eje carefully placed the leaves in her mouth and grimaced. Not long after chewing on the bitter leaves, color began to return to her prominent cheek.

"You did not tell me you had any menti leaves left." Ixhor remarked.

Ahktel tied the mouth of his pouch and placed it back in his satchel.

"I kept some for Eje. I hope I have enough left for the rest of her journey."

The company had been eating and resting for only a short while, when their horses began to whinny and stir. Alarmed, they looked around. They heard a terrifying shriek in the distance to the north. Bojingren rose quickly and hurried to the edge of the mound and looked to the northern sky.

"Avarathein swarming in the distance," he gasped.

He turned around and began giving the company its orders in a hushed voice.

"Gather ouor provisions and place them securely in your sacks and satchels. Move down from the mound and get behind the rocks. Hold the horses close."

The company hid behind large stones around the mound as Bojingren and Tyeshar crawled out along an incline to get a good look at the activity to the north down on the plains.

"Look!" Tyeshar gestured. "There must be a kill ahead. An arctodus, several wolves, and two avarathein have converged on a kill. We should keep out of sight until they have disbanded."

The company lost most of the daylight waiting for the predators and scavengers of the plains to disperse. With a few hours of sunlight left in the day, the company rode north, trying to reach a grove adjacent to a tributary of the Yeire. They passed the carnage left behind by both predators and scavengers.

"A herd of shrub oxen passed through here headed east." Tyeshar remarked.

Bojingren nodded. "We must reach the outpost by the river before dark."

The air buzzed with tension and fear. Like prey, the company's awareness was peaked. They sped across the plains faster than they had before. Lashing their horses to a gallop, their hope of reaching their destination by nightfall was fading. Soon the sun disappeared beyond the western horizon and the company had still not reached their destination. The Yeire tributary and the next outpost were still in the distance.

The sky was clear, moonlit and starry. But nightfall brought a strong and cold wind from the sea to the west. The chill air burdened Eje's breathing and bit down to her bones. The Hekare behind her shuddered and were miserable too. All three strangers from the austral lands looked up hopefully as the company came to an abrupt halt to hear a report from a forward rider.

"There is an encampment ahead." Bojingren and Tyeshar rode forward to take a look.

"Look Bojingren. It looks like a caravan."
Bojingren nodded.

"Look how they have positioned their wagons."
Tyeshar gestured. "They have established a good
perimeter and have posted torches all around it."

Bojingren shook his head. "I have only traveled
this way twice before." he whispered.

"But I would not think to see a caravan this way.
It is also strange to see them set up camp in this way
unless they have livestock, which they do not appear to
have. Finally, I wonder why they have not made their
way to the protection of the outpost to the north. Were
they waylaid like us, or are they rogues? Unfurl the
banner of the city and light torches to alert them of our
approach. If I must choose between facing wolves and
arctodi in the wild or camp with rogues, I would choose
rogues. We will see if we can make camp with these
strangers."

The company approached the caravan
encampment slowly with torches lit and with a rider in
front holding up the standard of lord Dorias' house. As
they passed the perimeter of the encampment where
urns of burning herbs were positioned, they saw several
men armed with spears huddled together. More men
came out of the darkness, some with bows, and others
with barking dogs.

"Welcome men of Beonon. Please follow us to
our master. He is a most gracious host."

The company dismounted and followed several
heavily cloaked men to a cluster of tents and tethered
their horses. Along the way, the company could see the
wards of the camp, crouched before fires, staring at the
company as they passed.

"Who is leading this company?" One of the men
from the caravan asked.

Bojingren nodded. The company was then led to
a large tent at the center of the encampment. Bojingren
followed a man inside the large tent while the others
huddled around small fires outside.

When Bojingren entered the tent, he saw two men sitting on furs spread on the bare ground. They sat with their legs crossed around and around lantern dining on an assortment of dried meats and bread on wooden platters. There was a clay ewer and a couple of cups spread across a wooden plank. The men looked up to see Bojingren and blithely motioned for him to sit down.

"Come in and sit," said a man dressed in a finely woven blue tunic. With a gesture, the man sitting next to him, rose and hurried away.

"Welcome stranger. My name is Nausterus. I am a merchant from the east. Please tell me who you are and what brings you to my camp."

Bojingren bowed and sat across from his host.

"I am Bojingren from the city of Bonthc by the sea. Though you are not from my country, I come to your camp as a supplicant and ask for the courtesies of a host. I hope that your ways are as ours."

Nausterus, a lanky, dark haired man reached with a very long arm and nimble fingers for a cup and filled it with wine.

"What I have is yours man of Beonon. But I think that it is I, who am a guest. This is your country. Please accept the hospitality of my tent as I have accepted the hospitality of your country. Have a drink with me."

Bojingren graciously took the cup from Nausterus and took a draught of wine and winced.

"Master Nausterus, I have a party of fifteen including myself. I do not wish to burden you more than necessary. All we would need is to build some fires and huddle near them until the morning. We must ride at daybreak."

Nausterus broke some bread and handed a piece to Bojingren, who thanked him.

"You should not drink with an empty stomach. As my guest you are free make your way around camp.

As you may well know, this is a merchant caravan. Our provisions and supplies are sparse, yet we will provide for you as well as we can."

Bojingren nodded and took another draught of wine. "You are headed to the high city of Chamiahce no doubt."

Nausterus stared blankly for a while, making Bojingren wonder if he had somehow offended his host. It was not proper protocol for a guest to inquire into the affairs of his host. He didn't want to convey that he was pretentious or mistrustful. But hunger and fatigue strained his judgment. Or perhaps Bojingren could not overcome his inexplicable sense of unease.

"Yes," Nausterus answered. "We bring pottery and wine from Tarpedon to the east."

Bojingren nodded. "Tarpedi wine." he exclaimed with delight. "I should have realized."

Nausterus smiled. "What you are drinking is not the Tarpedi wine men from your country would recognize. What you have there, is what men of Tarpedon drink. In Tarpedon, we do not drink what you call Tarpedi wine. We drink a more aromatic wine of greater intensity and flavor than the blend we bring to the western markets. The wines consumed in the west are subtler. Ours is older but yet fuller of life."

The two men spoke for quite some time about wine and other matters. Then the two men parted ways, Nausterus rising up and towering over Bojingren as he led the captain of the guard out. Meanwhile Eje and the Hekare huddled together around a warm fire.

"Tell us Ahktel," Ixhor whispered. "Why does this caravan worry you so? Is it because of our ordeal in Cerulon?"

Eje peered at the Hekare curiously. "What happened in Cerulon?"

Ahktel looked as if he was piercing through the fabric of the present into the past.

"Before we encountered your captors, Eje, Ixhor too was held captive for a while. We had left my father Tilon's herd and traveled west to the games at a city called Cerulon. While there, we were guests at the compound of a wealthy man named Pfraloas, who was known to my father. We participated in the games and performed well. Both of us won Csufas. I won for hurling the javelin and Ixhor for archery.

We did not realize, but our exploits were noticed by a greedy merchant called Didoras. Didoras had amassed great wealth by trading in spices, wool, and textiles. But I think his most lucrative trade was in captives which he sold to miners from a rugged region of Cadera called Udthkun. To repay a debt he owed to Didoras, my host Pfraloas agreed to deceive me and help Didoras take Ixhor captive.

After a night of drinking and frolicking with young women, as Ixhor is wont to do, he was captured and taken west in a caravan. Once I learned of this from Pfraloas, who confessed this to me in a fit of guilt, I set out after Ixhor, as he is like a brother to me. I was able to rescue Ixhor. But by then we were very far away from home and lost. It was during that time that we found you bound in an encampment and rescued you."

Eje sighed and thought for a moment. "Your story is very riveting." she finally said with a thoughtful glance. "I can see why you are wary of this caravan. Yet this caravan is not from our region of the world. This is a Maspeidonian caravan and these men are not the men who held Ixhor captive."

Ixhor shook his head. "Eje, Ahktel is very perceptive. He has a gift. That is what his mother, Cimaji, an elder in our village, said. She was a Hekare elder and a diviner. Hekare diviners know how to read the Durgon stones and the stars as well. The Hekare diviners are masters of dreams and Ahktel's mother is foremost among them.

It was rumored that not long ago, she dreamed that Ahktel's face appeared on all the stones. This was interpreted to be a sign that Ahktel, like his mother received the inspiration of the Spirit, and could traverse the world of dreams. If he says that there is danger, then he has seen it. His warnings should be given due weight. For as I learned in that fateful city called Cerulon, ignoring his counsels can be perilous."

Eje looked at Ahktel and touched his hand. "What did you see my Hekare protector? I have heard of your gift. It is said that this gift is common among the Hekare tribe of Irsei."

Ahktel looked away from Eje's gaze. He seemed to think for a while and then turned his gaze back to Ixhor and Eje.

"I have seen merchants in a caravan with long slender swords hidden under robes and cloaks. They were assembled together just as we are around this fire. Yet they were not talking about harvests, textiles, spices, or wines, or of gold, silver and copper cances. They spoke of intrigue and death. In Hekare lands, merchants are not well regarded because they often trade dishonestly. But these merchants were not concerned about trade at all. They only appeared to be merchants. They spoke like mercenaries and conspirators on the eve of an assault."

Eje and the Hekare sat silently for a while, looking around from time to time. They spoke again in hushed voices for a while more and then Ahktel and Eje retired, leaving Ixhor to serve as watchman, so that Bojingren's men could get some much needed rest.

Meanwhile, in Chamiahce, the renowned son of Wind was troubled and could not sleep. King Ylarin drew a thick cloak over his robes and made his way from his bedchambers with his guards trailing behind him. The gray haired king walked briskly, making his way to the catacombs of the royal apartments. His face dark and grave, he hurried through a hidden passageway leading to the temple Irilsflir.

The guard in the lead held up a lantern revealing arching walls laden with luminescent crystals. One guard followed the king and another stood behind the lead guard. All passed one after the other through the narrow passageway, which wound a long way, leading to a widening entrance with smooth stone walls. The entrance opened into a circular alcove with an elevated center platform. Resting on the platform was a tall and narrow iron cage with a large winch adjacent to it. Walking alone to the cage, the king opened the cage door and stepped into it. Then two guards followed and positioned themselves on both sides of the winch.

After the king entered the iron cage and sat on a bench bolted to the deck of the cage, a third guard came forward and shut the metal door and the king locked it from within. The third guard signaled the others and then the guards at the large winch began to turn it. The metal cage was pulled up slowly, making a loud cranking sound. When the cage had gone up several stories into a dimly let alcove above, the first guard pulled a heavy metal lever and a loud clanking sound was heard, and the cage was held fast.

King Ylarin unlatched the door of the cage and made his way out of the upper alcove illumined by several torches and luminisecent crystals. The king strode up several stone steps leading to large bronze double doors which opened into a dark chamber. The king entered the chamber, which was furnished with two ornate chairs placed across from each other and separated by a small wooden table. The king took a seat on one of the chairs and waited.

The king did not wait long.

"What brings you to the house of Yggir?" A woman's voice pierced the silence.

King Ylarin saw the silhouette of a woman dressed in heavy robes. It was the priestess of Yggir herself who came to speak with the king.

"What weighs so heavily on your mind that you would come here so late into the evening?"

The priestess approached slowly and took a seat in the chair across from the king.

"I have need of your counsel this evening on some urgent matters." The king leaned toward the priestess.

"For many years, my vizirs have warned me about my vassal lords from the continent. Reach out to your allies across the sea some have said. Leverage your foreign alliances against them. Others have urged me to set them against each other by lavishing only some with honors, believing that I could sow discord among them."

The mistress of Irilsflir listened intently. Her graying hair was gathered over her shoulders and she wore no adornment.

"I have agreed to ally my house with King Xremede's from across the sea," the king continued. "This plan has not been consummated yet. But I fear that while an alliance with Cadera will strengthen my hand, rumors of this alliance will only increase tensions on this continent. My spies from the east have reported that the foundries in Tarpedon and Kuthgelon have been blowing out plumes of smoke for weeks. I wonder if lord Umalein has anticipated my maneuver. Is lord Umalein preparing for war against the Vyrdmar and if so when will he strike?"

The priestess paused and seemed to be looking beyond the king sitting before her.

"Men of war," she replied. "They are always making preparations for war. Peace for them is a biding time for war. There is no knowing what their real interests are. What is certain is that your intrigues will cultivate future conflict, even as your hand may seem to be strengthened. These manipulations will ultimately fuel your enemies' antipathy for your house.

Son of Wind, you must learn to trust in mighty Yggir. It was he who inspired Namreddin to build this shining city. It was Yggir who empowered your father against the men of Nurim. Be faithful and all will be well for your house."

"All will unfold as mighty Yggir wills," the king agreed. "But the Celestial's great purpose unfolds across an eternity. I have but a day. Help me save this day. Help me sow seeds of hope and prosperity for my children and my people now. Help us defend our future against our enemies."

The priestess of Yggir touched the king's hand. "Let me know your mind my king. Perhaps if you tell me more about your dilemma, I may be more useful."

"I have betrothed Varenhil to an Ausremen princess," the king began, placing his hand over the priestess' hand. "She should have arrived at lord Dorias' court in Bonthc days ago. She did not. I fear that she has fallen into my enemy's hands. She never even reached Dorias' ships in Tehmas. What do you know of the princess' fate? Is she lost? Has a disloyal vassal captured her, and if so which vassal is responsible?"

"The great Father Yggir passes over the land like a winged shepherd," the priestess replied in a steady and soft voice. She looked as if she was recalling a distant memory.

"Often, I go with him, tucked under a silvery wing. Last I did so, I saw the plains of Yarlpirel, the Aeisus Mountains to the east, and the plains of Edris and the Pelares that gird your lands to the south, and I saw no armies. Your spies have correctly warned you that lord Umalein has fired his foundries. His armies however, are in their barracks and in camps far away to the east and near a city called Ursol.

I have known of your plan to ally yourself with the king of Cadera. I have beseeched mighty Yggir to shelter the young princess against your enemies. Your enemies are many and lord Umalein is foremost among them. Their immediate intentions are diffuse, as if they are of many minds. Only their antipathy for the Vyrdmar and their lust for power unite them. They have taken steps to waylay the princess, but mighty Yggir has delivered her into the hands of honorable and good men. They have brought her to Maspeidon and into the care of sentries from Dorias' city. Yet the danger has not passed and it is not certain if she will survive the perils to come."

The king looked intently into the priestess' eyes. "Can you give me more insight into lord Umalein's mind?"

"Lord Umalein is a pawn and he is not a lone actor. There are many agents acting in concert here and there. There is no telling what shape their treachery will take, and there is no way of telling when they will strike.

Yet know for certain that lord Umalein contemplates your overthrow. His is not a heart churning with hatred however – his heart smolders with ambition. For years he has actively culled the faithless among your vassals into a cadre of malcontents. He has united them around a belief that threatens to destroy the unity and order your fathers have sown. Umalein envisions a godless world. He envisions a world bound together by the forces of a constellation of men and ideas. Irilsflir and everything that you cherish is abhorrent to him."

The king sighed and rubbed his thick gray beard.

"You speak of the way of the Atenarix. Indeed, if I know that wretched Kuthgelonian, he only pretends to extol high ideals. He cares nothing of the Atenarix point of view beyond the pretext it may provide for his own rise to power. Verily, if my house were to fall tomorrow, Umalein would cast aside his beliefs and make himself a god.

Yet he is not a god and he cannot hope to overthrow the seat of mighty Yggir Himself. The Vyrdmar are faithful. We have the Celestial's favor. How can Umalein hope to defeat us? My house has been built on the bones of the faithful. Did not Wind, cupped in the hand of Yggir, defeat the dread Ayimar under the Pelares? Now tell me, high priestess of Yggir, have we lost favor with the Celestial? What has changed? Have we not followed the Celestial's laws? If we have fallen out of favor with Him, tell me what we must do regain our hallowed place."

"Listen to me," whispered the high priestess. "I assure you that the Celestial continues to favor the Vyrdmar. I hesitate to reveal this truth to you even though you are king and the sworn defender of this temple. But there are limits to even the Celestial's power to protect. Simply, there are limits to the Celestial's power as there are limits to all things. There are imperceptible places; places that are beyond the Celestial's sight and dominion. There are immortal powers hidden even to the Celestial. The power of the hidden is diffuse but great. Men like Umalein have been used by the hidden in the past, and some have even mastered the hidden and harnessed their power.

Once upon a time there were masterful beings who bound themselves with the hidden and stood against mighty Yggir and his godlings. These beings possessed great knowledge. They shaped alien ores into powerful instruments and machines. They had preternatural abilities, and used them against the living gods of that time.

Such was their power that Yggir and his godlings left their lofty places and came down to destroy them lest they imposed their tyranny on the entire world. But not all of them perished and not all of their knowledge has been purged from the memories of men. Therefore, be careful Vyrdmar king. Know that Yggir sees all among the living. Know that he will, in time reveal all your enemies' machinations to you. But whereas Yggir sees all, Yggir does not see all at once. And there, within the shadow of time across the breadth of the world, your enemies may move against you and your allies, and bring your world crashing down around you."

Chapter 6: Of love, duty, and piety

After a raucous breakfast together in the royal dining hall, the Vyrdmar king's vassals walked together to the temple. They gathered in the temple's lofty center module in rows before the king's courtiers, the temple surplicants, and mighty Yggir's priestesses. All present bowed their heads awaiting the appearance of the king and high priestess.

Two surplicants flanking a great archway leading into the hall struck the ground with ashen staves, signaling the entrance of the king dressed in the traditional raiment of Vyrdmar warrior kings. The king wore a gleaming bronze breastplate with an engraved emblem of the Vyrdmar, the two headed black eagle clasping a sword and a cross staff in its talons. Under his armor, he wore a plain white tunic. He filed out with the Vyrdmar rod of power clasped in his right hand. Behind him were two priestesses, and together they proceeded and then stood on the right side of a stone chair on a marble dais. After three more strikes of the surplicants' staves were heard, the high priestess of Yggir entered the hall, dressed in a flowing white robe and her head covered in a white shawl.

The small procession filed out before the ranks of courtiers, lords, and priestesses standing around the great pool where the holy dew of the Kuriox collected. The sound of the trickling Kuriox dew echoed not just in the hall but also in the depths of minds. As the principal celebrant among the gathering, the priestess of Yggir took her place on the stone seat on the dais. She held out her hand and the king took her hand in his. The moment was as serene as it was powerful.

"Faithful Vyrdmar," the high priestess spoke with a steady and gentle but commanding voice.

"Your fathers have always walked in the path set before them by the author of life and of the mysteries of the heavens. You know as they knew that the Celestial is the source of the Vyrdmar's power and genius. Continue to be faithful therefore, honor your traditions, your oaths, and your creed, and rejoice in your divine inheritance.

The Levying festival is a new tradition, yet it is one, which the all-father Yggir finds much favor with, as he did with Wind who established it. This tradition, more than any other tradition calls for more than gathering and reflection. This tradition calls for valor and suffering, to cleanse the Vyrdmar of the decay attending the passage of time, that Wind's house may not tarnish, but burnish brightly in the eyes of men. Therefore, you vassals who have been chosen to conduct this inquiry should not be slack or afraid. The king will not look upon your inquiry as faithlessness. The Celestial commands you to make this inquiry. Now who among the king's vassal lords will uphold this duty and stand forth and elect seven of the mighty warriors to face the champion of the Hold in Wind's Crucible?"

There was a brief pause and then lord Elesias came forward with his head bowed and brought a parchment wrapped in golden tassels.

"The lords of Maspeidon have chosen my house. I come before you as the Celestial commands through Wind who swept through the hosts of Nurim, and submit these champions, whose names have been inscribed on this parchment. I pray that the passing of time has not weakened Wind's line and tarnished the Celestial's mighty sword."

King Ylarin stepped forward and took the parchment from lord Elesias and unfurled it.

"I accept this inquiry of the lords of Maspeidon and praise your courage and faithfulness to your duty. The lords of Maspeidon have spoken and the Vyrdmar will answer."

The king saluted the attendees, striking his breastplate with a closed fist. "Go forth, lords of Maspeidon and take account of the city. In three days, present your champions before mighty Yggir's beacon by the sea."

The king took a deep breath and called out the seven names on the parchment. "The lords of Maspeidon have chosen Mishar son of Udthrom, Taldeion son of Clydeion, Wilia son of Prentaur, Tharugaad son of Alberon, Frehil son of Hugiir, Smerdus son of Heryaus, and Scepedis son of Chylus."

The seven young men came forward from the crowd and knelt solemnly before the king with heads bowed.

"I command you champions of the Levying. Take the Levying oath and discharge this onerous duty. I pray that your exploits will echo through time. Now rejoice that even after your passing, your faithful discharge of this duty will be rewarded in Yieryos, the house of souls."

The young men stood before the king who looked down on them from the dais and spoke the oath.

"We accept this, the Levying oath and duty. We honor the love given, and the dominion entrusted to us by mighty Yggir through the Vyrdmar. We commit our strength and our courage to this inquiry so that the Wind that swept the eastern raiders before him may blow strong until the end of time."

"I charge you!" King Ylarin reached out with his scepter, the Vyrdmar rod of power and touched each of the seven young champions on the right shoulder.

The crowd uttered in unison:

"May the Wind that swept the eastern raiders before him blow strong until the end of time!"

When the gathering passed through the great double doors of the temple into the quadrangle leading west into the city and south into the royal compound and the royal apartments, prince Hovin, several Harfingals, and a throng of courtiers and nobles cheered them. First to come out of the temple was the king, with his armor glistening in the morning sun.

The throng cheered, "Hail Vyrdmar king!"

The king saluted the crowd and motioned for the young champions to gather around him so as to be introduced to the crowd. In spite of the grave challenge they would face in three days, the young men smiled and basked in the moment. They knew that, for the next three days, they would be honored and that they would eat the best meats and drink the best wines from the Tarpedi and Caolchean wineries. But first a strong bull would be sacrificed at the royal garrison.

The king gestured for the young men to proceed into the crowd. "Here are your Champions. Honor them for they have taken up Wind's charge."

The crowd cheered again as the young men made their way down the temple steps. The young champions looked on with pride but were nonetheless humbled as the crowd cheered them and carried them away to the royal compound. Several Harfingals, led by king Ylarin's beloved son Hovin, closed ranks around the king and walked with him down a paved walkway leading to the king's entrance to the royal compound.

The king gestured for his son to walk with him and whispered in his ear.

"Captain of the Harfingals," the king said, "I must speak with you. Will you join me in chambers briefly before you join your men at the Harfingal barracks?"

Hovin saluted and gestured to his guards.

"Go to the garrison courtyard and inform my lieutenant Macheleion that I will join him shortly."

Hovin walked with his father to the king's chambers in the royal apartments. When they reached the king's gilded bedchamber, and king Ylarin removed his armor, the father and his son walked out to the king's balcony overlooking his private garden. The two men sat together on a stone bench and listened to the birds singing for a while. King Ylarin looked at his son and smiled.

"Do you still find wonderment in this world my son?"

Hovin looked curiously at his father. "I do not know?" Hovin shook his head. "When I was young I played in the royal garden and wondered about nature's secrets. Yet no sooner did I develop a meaningful interest in nature, I was sent to the academies. As a cadet, I was instructed in duty and piety, and martial discipline, and since then I have not given much thought to anything else."

The king sighed. "You are a dutiful son Hovin. I remember holding you up in your first moments of life and praying to the Celestial that you grow close to Him and exceed me in all ways. You remind me so much of myself in both bearing and sentiment. Yet in many ways you exceed me – especially in your devotion to duty."

Hovin smiled. "How can this be? How can the son exceed the father? How can the pupil exceed the master?"

The king now smiled. "The father may be greater than the son in prestige. Our forebears exceed us all in this respect. But they were not perfect and could not benefit from the experiences we now assiduously recount and examine. We who live today are not perfect, and nor do we exceed our fathers in foresight and judgment. Our fathers who walked before us, erred, and their errors have been recorded. Therefore, the greatness of the son lies in his observance and perfection of his father's example. In this way he may exceed the father by perfecting his enterprises and finishing what he has left undone."

"Indeed," the young prince nodded. "I can see the truth in what you say. I hope one day to honor you in this way."

"You already have," the king replied. Now let me tell you of one peculiar moral lapse, which has plagued your fathers. My father, your grandfather, Nnyreinin had many sons by his concubines. Yet before he died he warned me to shun this practice as it sowed much discord at court. I heeded his warning for many years."

King Ylarin paused and sighed.

"Yet whereas wisdom in matters of governance may attend age for a king, a king struggles mightily against the indulgences of court, and his resistance grows weaker with age. Your mother was beautiful and radiant as the stars in heaven. My strength was overborne; I fell deeply in love, and made her my queen. But I have wavered from my bonds many times. In time I recalled my own father's words to me, and I learned to cherish love over petty passions.

When I look at you I see the ripe fruit of wisdom. You are faithful and the love you give to the woman you love will be undying and unwavering. Indeed, I see in you, what I could have been. I know that your strength exceeds mine my son. Even in your youth, you have the temperance I did not obtain until much later in life. For this, I am glad. I behold you with deep pride and satisfaction. When my time on this earth is ended, and I join my fathers in Yggir's hearth, I will not fear for my house. I know that my sons are strong and wise, and you foremost among them."

Hovin took the king's hand and held it tight.

"After many years," Hovin said softly. "When you are ready to leave this world, I hope to look into your eyes and comfort you in your passing father. I know my place in the world and embrace it so long as I have your love. I am your son. I am your sword, as you are the sword of mighty Yggir. I will strike or remain sheathed according to your will. Tell me what I must do and I will do it."

King Ylarin began to weep. "Hovin my son," he faltered.

"You are peerless among men in martial skill and moral virtue. But the world is no haven for men like you. The world is a wicked place; a wilderness. The order you see around you is a cloistered illusion veiling an orgy of blood and fire. You know of what I speak. You know also that your fierce brother Varenhil will inherit my titles and this roiling and contentious dominion. He is your elder and his bearing and sternness will serve him well at court and with my cunning vassals. My viziers, captains of armies, and lords of Maspeidon will follow him because they will fear him.

Yet the Vyrdmar regent is not only a king of men and armies, he is also a guardian of the temple of Yggir, and the custodian of Vyrdmar traditions. This charge, which will also pass to him, does not suit your warlike brother, and he knows this. This is why I have devised a maneuver to bring you closer to the secrets of the temple, and to increase your prestige and authority in matters of tradition.

Since knowledge of, and favor with Yggir, is revealed in signs, the signs will, over time, anoint you as a custodian of traditions. Your brother Varenhil will recognize the prestige and favor the signs have conferred upon you as a custodian of traditions and will look to you for counsel. Now therefore, when in three days, the champions of the Levying have presented themselves before mighty Yggir's beacon by the sea for Wind's Crucible, a great eagle will circle above, sweep down, and, perch itself on your shoulder. My viziers, my captains, and my vassals will see this, and my chief vizir will announce that Yggir himself has chosen you as the champion of the Vyrdmar for Wind's Crucible. This will be the first sign, and from that day, your prestige will grow if you take care to foster it."

The king stood up and brought his son with him to the edge of the balcony.

"I know you welcome this charge because you are faithful. Before you discharge this duty, let me tell you the secret of the Crucible. During the rule of Yladril, my grandfather, an ancient darkness returned to the land. A disloyal vassal, lord Saareus, who ruled the Ayimar along the southern fringes of Gaalden below the peaks of the Pelares, allied himself with the raiders of Nurim, from the east beyond the gates of Taldur. Saareus was an Atenarix sage who delved into dark knowledge and disciplines. Some said that not only was he a master of metic disciplines, but he could also command fallen spirits we know as the bakiren. But there was more to Saareus. He was a host to a malevolent and deceitful bakiren known as Promothos.

Saareus wanted war with the Vyrdmar and dominon over all of Maspeidon. He ordered his foundries deep within the bowels of the Pelares be fired, to produce weapons of war to arm the Ayimar against Maspeidon.

The Kuthgelonians were the first to be assaulted by the Ayimar-Nurimite alliance. When the eastern raiders rallied their forces and breached Kuthgelon, the Kuthgelonians turned to the other kings and princes of Maspeidon for help.

King Yladril called his council together and the king mustered his armies calling on lord Saareus to honor his oath of fealty to the Vyrdmar king and to repudiate his alliance with the raiders from Nurim. Lord Saareus refused, and confident in the winding ballistas, iron turtles, and canons devised by the Atenarix loyal to him, the king took his army south to punish his disloyal vassal.

When king Yladril faced lord Saareus' army on the plains of Edris, he was not prepared for the Ayimar's own terrifying Atenarix machines of war, and was defeated. The king was slain and his eldest son prince Rowenor, with his brother Uler, led the king's vanquished army's slow retreat. In Chamiahce, princes Tamenor and Nnyreinin learned of the king's defeat and looked to the vizir council for guidance. The council urged prince Tamenor, who was Nnyreinin's elder, to prepare the city for a siege. Prince Nnyreinin rejected this view, but was overruled.

But Nnyreinin was not deterred. He went to the temple to seek the high priestess' counsel. The high priestess told the prince to ride out to Namreddin's beacon and sacrifice a strong bull and appeal to mighty Yggir, who was displeased with Yladril's reliance on the Atenarix. Nnyreinin did as the high priestess counseled, and after he sacrificed the bull, he entered the beacon and remained there for three days.

When the young prince left the beacon, he was resplendent with the purity and power of the Celestial. Prince Nnyreinin rode back to the city and rallied three hundred men and led them south on a campaign to reinforce what was left of the Vyrdmar army.

With Nnyreinin's help, the retreating Vyrdmar army rallied and fell again on lord Saareus and the Ayimar. Prince Nnyreinin shone like a light and was a beacon of hope and power. His exploits on the field of battle inspired the Vyrdmar to victory after victory. The Vyrdmar looked upon him and remarked that he was like a mighty northwesterly wind blowing through the field.

But sadly, many Vyrdmar were lost. Foremost among them were Nnyreinin's brothers Rowenor and Uler, who fell on the fields of Banfyrd. In the end, the Ayimar were routed, lord Saareus was grievously wounded and captured, and was said to later succumb to death. Those among his people who were captured were made slaves in the high city and throughout Maspeidon. Nnyreinin, with a heavy heart, made a triumphant return to the high city.

Soon, king Yladril and his sons were buried in the catacombs beneath the temple in the traditional manner. Prince Tamenor was crowned the new Vyrdmar king. Rather than receiving the honors due him, Nnyreinin was beleaguered by his brother's intrigue at court.

Nnyreinin was not disheartened though. He left the city and traveled east and mustered thousands of men across Maspeidon in a seaside town called Eramos. From that town, he set sail for Kuthgelon with a great army, making port in the city of Cheduz. From this city, he waged war on the eastern raiders, falling on them as they made their way west across Maspeidon.

The legend of Nnyreinin, or Wind as he was called, grew with every victory. He routed the eastern raiders wherever he found them and swept them out of Maspeidon. He pursued them beyond the gates of Taldur and did not return to Maspeidon until his men grew weary and his wounds brought him near death.

Nnyreinin returned home and found his brother Tamenor near death from illness. When Tamenor died,

Wind became king and the people rejoiced. When Wind ascended to the Vyrdmar throne, the lords and princes of Maspeidon came to his city to honor him. They were so fond of him and his legend that they swore allegiance to his line until the end of time.

When Wind heard them, he said to them: 'I accept your fealty, which is freely given and shall cherish it forever.'

Wind's first command to his vassals, was for them to return to the high city every three years to conduct an inquiry of his house, which we now call the Levying and Wind's Crucible. Wind intended that only a champion from his bloodline should stand as the Vyrdmar champion. Yet his councilors persuaded him to transfer the authority to choose the Vyrdmar champion to the vizir council. And so, since that time, the champion of the Vyrdmar has been selected from among the Harfingals and among the nobility.

Now the time has come for a champion from my house to defend the Hold's honor and prestige. The treats are graver than ever before and so the Vyrdmar must restore their prestige. A Vyrdmar prince must answer this Levying inquiry into the quality of Wind's line. This duty I have chosen for you because you possess the character and ability to dispatch it. I am certain that you will uphold the standard set forth by those who preceded you. I am certain that you will prevail over the seven champions you must face.

After you kneel before the high priestess and she receives you as the Amaroi of the Vyrdmar, you will be left before the beacon to answer mighty Yggir's own challenge. The door to the beacon will open. You will know in your heart if you should enter the beacon and face the mysteries within. Listen to your heart my son, for this challenge will not merely test your strength and martial skill. Reflect well on your inner quality and prepare yourself, for while mighty Yggir's embrace is the path to honor and glory, his rebuke is death."

Celebration of the Levying spread throughout the city like wildfire. Cheers could be heard when great horn blasts were sounded as the sun reached its apex. Caravans coming in from the east were greeted with flowers and branches from trees. Citizens and strangers to the city gathered in large numbers at the arched gates of the royal compound to review the champions of the Levying. In mid afternoon, the young men were gathered at the compound's western bastions to hear the cheers. Then they were taken back into the Harfingal garrison to drink the brine of heaven's sea in the garrison courtyard. This mulled concoction was a mixture of wine, pomegranate juice, and an assortment of spices from the wagons of the newly arriving caravans from the east. The young champions drank heartily and were cheered by the Harfingals and the courtiers who had gathered. Then they were given the traditional white tunics worn by the Harfingals by the captain of the Harfingals, Hovin himself, and were taken to their lodgings in the royal apartments.

The cheering crowd of citizens who had seen the champions paraded before an ever-growing crowd of people lining the road to the city plaza. At the city plaza the crowds erupted into a celebration below a great obelisk raised long ago by metic guilds of the city. Though celebrations had erupted in the city and in the Hold, the captain of the Harfingals did not take part in the merriment. The vigilant prince could be found with his Harfingals perched along the city bastions or riding out along the city's main thoroughfare surveying the crush of activity. Where the prince and his Harfingals passed in ranks, with their shining bronze breastplates and round shields, the people bowed and looked on in awe of their bearing and stature.

During a brief lull in his survey of the Hold and the city's main thoroughfare, Hovin, accompanied by his lieutenant Macheleion, made his way through the royal garden. There, he saw a young woman sitting alone on a stone bench. He recognized the young woman's flowing black hair and gestured for his lieutenant to proceed without him. Taking a deep breath he approached the young woman, his eyes surveying her supple curves. He walked behind her somewhat apprehensively and reached for her.

To Hovin's surprise, the young woman spoke even before he could touch her.

"Why are you so fearful and aloof my prince?" the young woman quipped. "Am I terrifying?"

Sighing, the young prince took a seat next to the young woman.

"I am glad to see you Besia."

"Your eyes do not say as much," she said coyly. "You look anxious and burdened."

Hovin sighed and rested his elbows on his thighs and peered down at his feet. "When we are together, our love shelters us like a warm firmament. Yet our paradise is not all encompassing. The power of our love is only a delicate veil encircling the posts of our bed. We forget that there is a cold world out there because the fire within our beating hearts bathes us in the warmth of Ausremen summers. But here we are now in this cool dispassionate air with the will of men ever on the brink of uncertain and ominous times."

"My beloved," Besia replied. "Men are always on the brink of misfortune and ruin. That has been so since the dawn of time. But love has persevered."

Hovin smiled and then sighed. "Indeed, the shadow of the world does not eclipse cherished love. My heart does yearn for you, but my duties beckon me away to ever more difficult labors."

Besia took Hovin's hand. "My sweet prince-what are you saying to me? I am not as naïve as you think. I am not brittle. I know who you are and I know what our love must endure. I know of your responsibilities. Be at ease, for the hearth of love does not need constant tending."

Besia moved closer to look into Hovin's gray eyes, yet Hovin did not turn to meet her gaze.

"My duties will increase in the next few days and my courage will be tested. I do not know how the same heart that loves a woman can also inspire the courage I will need to break my enemies. I suppose this mystery will be revealed to both of our satisfaction in time. I will come to you four nights hence. Then we will know how wondrous a thing the heart is, and how strong is our love."

Besia touched Hovin's face and pulled him closer. "I love you. Tell me that you love me, and I will wait for you to come back to me."

As birds chirped on the branches of budding trees around them, Hovin looked into Besia's blue eyes, gleaming like a jewel, and kissed her cheek and then her lips as softly as a wispy rain. Then the birds scattered out of the trees and startled Besia. Hovin held her closer. The prince looked around him but saw no one. He did not see his brother Jaïem across the clearing, crouched in a thicket observing their embrace. Jaïem's eyes were at first transfixed. Then his eyes began to sting and his vision became blurred. His heart became heavy and his thoughts darkened. Overwhelmed with anguish, Jaïem retreated from the thicket and hurried away.

The city was still in rapture deep into the night. Bonfires roared in courtyards and public squares, and cooking fires burned in stone hearths. Pyrotechnics filled the evening sky with colorful flashes and embers. Feasts were hosted and the bustle of large gatherings could be heard throughout the city. Many in king Ylarin's court, who were young and full of youthful vigor, gathered in the courtyard of the Hold and feasted at large tables out in the open air or under pitched tents. All around, young men were caressing, pulling and jostling young maidens, and some were writhing in tents with them.

Prince Varenhil looked down frostily into the throng. "Haldar-" he commanded, gesturing to his squire. "Go down among this seething horde. Swoop down like a bird of prey and clasp a few maidens from these vultures with your talons and bring them to my chambers. For even the scions of immortals must eat."

Haldar nodded and hurried away to his task and prince Varenhil returned to his bedchambers in the royal apartments.

As Varenhil made his way back to his royal apartments, lord Umalein, who was speaking with a group of merchants from Kuthgelon where he was lord, saw fair-haired Varenhil and excused himself from their company. He intercepted the prince as he reached the steps leading up to the portico.

"Hail Vyrdmar prince Varenhil, lord of Greingspen, and son of Ylarin." The prince turned to acknowledge the Kuthgelonian lord.

"You are too gracious," the prince replied tepidly. "As your host, I am at your service. Please tell me how I may serve you."

Lord Umalein, dressed in fine garments from his own land, smiled. "Lord of armies, I beg your pardon, but I have need of your counsel on a matter of some interest to the lords of Maspeidon."

Already there was a glint of impatience in the prince's eyes. Feigning interest, he nodded.

"Many at court wonder where the king's council actually stands on a certain issue. The rumor is that the king's council has shifted its position on whether the king's heirs should represent the Vyrdmar in Wind's Crucible. Will your father's council select a prince of the Hold as the Vyrdmar champion this festival? What is your sense on this matter? If I knew the council's mind, I could make a small fortune in my wager with the others."

The Vyrdmar prince responded calmly. "I do not know the council's mind lord Umalein. I do not spend much time in the high city. I pine away in my own city looking to the king's defenses in that region. Though, if a prince were to be chosen as champion of the Vyrdmar, it would be one who is highest in the esteem of the council and the king."

Umalein clasped his hands together. "Then I have your answer, which wholly supports my conjecture."

"I bid you good night then, lord of Kuthgelon."

"My lord," Umalein bowed."

The two men parted ways and Varenhil made his way to his bedchambers. He soon came to his chambers. The spaces were sparsely decorated since he was often away in his own sea beaten city on the coasts to the north and east.

That night, cool winds swept in from the sea and dispersed the straggling revelers. The next day was overcast and ominous as high clouds followed the winds and sprinkled the city with flurries and then rain. The spasm of activity that seized the city on the previous day when the Levying festival was consecrated was stifled by frost and then freezing rains. The rains lasted for two days, but Hovin continued to tend to his duties as captain of the Harfingals and prepared himself for his ordeal before the beacon by the sea.

The rains ended on the third day at daybreak. There were still menacing clouds spread across the western horizon. On that fateful morning a procession, most on horses, slowly made their way to Namreddin's Beacon overlooking the sea to the west. Leading them was a detachment of the Harfingals with white surcoats decorated with the emblem of the Vyrdmar flowing over their mail armor. Directly behind the Harfingals were the king, the high priestess, the viziers of the king's council, and the seven young champions whose faces were painted red. Many in the king's court, Varenhil among them, trailed the procession meandering west to the beacon on the rugged overlook by the sea, which was cordoned into four sectors.

When the procession arrived at the beacon, they dismounted and spread out before the towering structure with its glistening spire. A great pyre was erected before the slightly elevating path that veered to the left of the beacon onto a crag overlooking a narrow sliver of beach. Not far away, several mock targets made of bushels of hay with cloth tethered to them were set up.

The Maspeidonian lords serving as judges gathered together to discuss the rules of the competition that would ensue. As the wind whistled and the sea splashed on the rocky banks of the crags and the overlook, the high priestess walked hand in hand with the king to the tower's great portal. Harfingal warriors bearing great horns filed out into two ranks after them. They carried with them the unfurled Vyrdmar ensign with its two headed black eagle clasping a sword and a cross staff in its talons. After the Harfingal warriors, came two surplicants bringing forth a bull to be sacrificed and burned on a pyre.

The Harfingal heralds sounded a great blast with their horns, which was attended by a great gust of wind from the sea, to command the attention of the gathering. The gathering, most wrapped in thick cloaks, grew more solemn.

"Noble Vyrdmar, lords and princes of Maspeidon, esteemed members of the court and citizens of Chamiahce," the king greeted the gathering with a steady voice.

"Not so long ago, the Wind that swept through the eastern raiders decreed that his vassals should bear the obligation of this inquiry called the Levying. The Vyrdmar king spoke thus: 'After the coming of Wind, and during the calm and the peace we have hewn together, return to Irilsflir after idle winter, and look to see that weeds of decadence have not grown to choke out the nobility from my house.'

Since that time the lords of Maspeidon have come to the high city to honor their obligations and conduct their inquiry. Today the champions, whom the lords have selected, stand now before the tower of the eternal light, ready to test the mettle on one who has been chosen by the vizir council. This Vyrdmar champion will endure seven challenges against the seven champions of Maspeidon. The lords of Maspeidon will judge this champion. Should the Vyrdmar champion display the valor and defeat his opponents in four of the seven challenges, the lords of Maspeidon shall render their tributes and return to their own lands. Should the Vyrdmar champion not meet the standard of the inquiry, the king's council shall be sacked, and a new council wholly constituted of the lords themselves, or their envoys shall remain in the high city for three years under a commission of inquiry. Now that the challenge has been set, let us honor the Celestial, who is the author of life, and our benefactor, with burnt offerings."

Surplicants brought forth the bull, which was anointed by the high priestess.

"O' father of the silvery wings, take up this burnt offering from your faithful children."

The gathering bowed their heads as the king and the high priestess walked from the pyre. With their backs turned away from the crowd and facing the beacon, the surplicants felled the sacrificial bull with a great blow from a heavy wooden mallet. After placing the carcass on the pyre, the surplicants set it ablaze, sending plumes of gray and then black smoke up to the heavens. After a collective prayer was sent up to Yggir, the Harfingals blew their horns again and the crowd dispersed, some going to sit under trees at a nearby grove, while others pitched tents.

Soon the lords gathered with the competitors before three members of the king's council adjacent to a large tent pitched around a tall post on which the king's ensign was hoisted. A crowd had also gathered there to hear the council announce the Vyrdmar champion. Cerondilus, the king's principal vizir came forth and addressed the crowd.

"In the name of the Vyrdmar king, the council calls forth Haldar, son of Arunhur."

Varenhil's heart rose and then sank, when he realized that it was not his squire who was selected. Haldar the greater, a Harfingal, sprinted forward with his eyes flashing and his brown hair whipping menacingly. The crowd cheered and news of his selection was whispered and shouted throughout the open field and even to those sitting under trees and on tree branches at the nearby grove.

The lords came forth and stood beside the representatives of the council. Lord Elesias came forward and addressed the gathering.

"Now then, the hour is at hand. Honor has been given to the Celestial. The champions have been selected and charged with their duty. The masters of the Crucible are gathered. The field is ready for the seven challenges. First, the race to Namreddin's spring and back to the beacon of eternal light. Second, the javelin throw; third, the Vyrdmar champion will face the archery challenge. Fourth, the Vyrdmar champion will face the grappling challenge. Fifth, the Vyrdmar champion will cross staves with the Maspeidonian champion, and then the light sword combat. The last challenge will be the full sword duel. Then, if the Vyrdmar champion is successful in meeting the standard of the king's vassals, he will be left to the solitude of the beacon and await the Celestial's judgment."

Chatter began to spread among the gathering of onlookers as Hovin strode up with a detachment of Harfingals to escort the competitors to their places. Lord Elesias spoke again.

"Now for the first competition, the champions of Maspeidon have chosen Smerdus to challenge the

Vyrdmar champion in the race to Namreddin's spring and back again to the beacon."

Suddenly, a piercing squawk was heard that made the blood of those present curdle. The gathering turned to look up to the beacon's spire and saw a great eagle with an ashen crest, a bright yellow bill, and a white tail. The eagle spread its wings and circled the gathering. The eagle then swept down and reeled up near Hovin, and landed on his right shoulder and squawked again as it seemed to nod.

Many could be heard saying in hushed voices that the bird was Yggir himself taking the form of an eagle. The king's principal vizir Cerondilus and many others in the crowd fell to their knees. Then lord Umalein came forward and spoke as the eagle squawked and took to the air.

"We must hear from the king. Surely he will know what this sign means."

Cerondilus scrambled to his feet. "Surely this is a sign. Behold a sign from Yggir himself. He has chosen prince Hovin to face the champions of Maspeidon."

Another vizir, old Bereion stumbled forward. "Listen to me for I have seen this sign before. The young prince has been chosen. He must stand against the champions of Maspeidon, or the future will be clouded, uncertain, and perilous."

Umalein strode up to wise old Bereion and touched his shoulder. "We must give due weight to master Bereion's counsel for he is among the wisest of the king's vizirs. Let him speak for the king, for the impartiality of the king must also be maintained. If master Bereion says that this is a sign from mighty Yggir we must defer to his judgment. Therefore, let the king's stalwart son Hovin stand against the Maspeidonian champions. This is surely the will of Yggir."

Approval could be heard from some in the crowd. Others looked on with visible apprehension. The chatter of approval grew louder and soon rose to a tumult.

The gathering began to say: "The immortals have chosen Hovin, captain of the Harfingals."

"Lord Umalein and wise Bereion-" Haldar interrupted. "May I speak?" The two men nodded.

"Although it would be a great honor for me to stand as the Vyrdmar champion, I will gladly accede to the judgment of the wise men here today. What we have seen is a remarkable expression of Yggir's will. I am humbled and my spirit is gladdened, that the Celestial has graced this tradition and has made it an instrument of his will."

"Mighty son of Arunhur-" Bereion answered. "Your father's virtues prevail in you. The council was wise in selecting you for Wind's Crucible, which is not merely a test of a warrior's strength and skill, but also of his virtues and his piety. Be assured that I do not offer my counsel in disregard of your quality. Yet those who turn a blind eye to signs from above, even in observance of etiquette, choose courtesy over piety to his detriment. Now therefore, take your honored place with your faithful Harfingals. It is mighty Yggir's will that Hovin, captain of the Harfingal guard, should stand against the champions of Maspeidon."

The gathering approved of wise Bereion's counsel and began to cheer Hovin's name. In the distance, prince Varenhil could hear the uproar. He sent his squire Haldar the lesser to inquire about the commotion.

"Your brother has been chosen as the Vyrdmar champion," the young squire reported.

Prince Varenhil glowered. "Is there no honor reserved for the eldest among the king's sons? Is my pedigree not beyond reproach?"

The fair-haired prince strode off, leapt on his horse and rode away with his squire following behind.

Meanwhile Jaïem, who like his brother Varenhil, favored Feystra, their golden-haired mother, had concluded his morning exercises. Jaïem had for many days been fastidiously practicing his swordsmanship and other martial disciplines. As was his habit, he went to the baths after his exercises. He often encountered his good friend Csem at the baths. On this day, not seeing Csem, he did not tarry long at the baths. After a brief layover at the baths, he made his way to the temple library. As he hurried to the temple he recalled his conversation he had with Csem the day before as they parted ways after.

"Why do you spend so much time in the temple's dark catacombs?" Csem asked the prince. "Searching!" the prince snapped.

Ignoring his retort, Csem persisted-"there is so much more to see now that the Levying festival has formally begun."

Jaïem did not answer his good friend.

"Why do we not join the young courtiers? These days we have away from our studies are precious. Let us enjoy them."

Jaïem sighed.

"Why do you not find Besia and tell her how you feel? If you delay, someone else at court will sow the seeds of love in her heart."

Jaïem stopped abruptly with eyes flashing and startled his friend Csem. "Someone already has."

Jaïem made his way to the temple with thoughts thoughts of Besia haunting him. His head throbbing, he tried to clear his mind. Feeling disoriented he stumbled a little while rushing up the stairs leading to the temple entrance.

Jaïem visited the temple catacombs the day before during a brief pause in the rains. While there he saw the librarian Owidobel hurry into a dark and secluded passageway. The young prince followed as quietly as he could. He saw the librarian enter a hidden outlet in an alcove. Now that most in the royal compound were participating Levying ceremony, he decided to go see where the secret outlet led.

"There may be books and secret codices," he thought. There may be writings that have not been seen in generations."

The young prince hurried into the temple, passing several Harfingals. He proceeded down to the temple library and then down dark steps into the temple catacombs. Holding aloft a lantern, Jaïem followed a passageway leading past several archways opening into alcoves.

"He came down this narrow passageway." Jaïem retraced the old librarian's path. He breathed heavily with excitement and his pace quickened. Soon Jaïem slowed down, and entering an alcove, he scanned its walls for a hidden outlet.

He could hear a voice whisper to him.

"Here!" The young prince exclaimed to himself. "He entered here through a hidden outlet."

Jaïem searched for a serration on the wall, passing a hand over the smooth stone bricks and grainy mortar. Jaïem struggled to control his sense of excitement. "Push here," he could hear a familiar voice whisper.

"He pushed here." Jaïem pushed a brick revealing a latch within an adjacent brick. He turned the latched clockwise several revolutions.

"Nothing-" the prince sighed. He then pushed a segment of the wall and to his surprise it moved smoothly back several feet revealing a narrow passageway running parallel to the wall and then cutting perpendicular into a dark alcove. Jaïem made his way slowly into the narrow passageway. As he did so, the young Vyrdmar heard a recurring metal clanking; the movable slab slid back into place.

"No!" The darkness and the thick walls swallowed the prince's voice.

With only one way open to him, the young prince positioned himself to one side and edged his way carefully down a narrow tunnel. He made his way slowly into impenetrable darkness beyond the arc emanating from the lantern he held up before him. Jaïem's heart beat wildly with anticipation of what was at the end of the tunnel and yet he could not help wondering if he was going to be able to make his way back out. Finally, he stumbled forward and the tunnel opened into a circular landing, leading to a narrow stairway. The young prince took careful steps down the narrow stairway, which spiraled down and into an archway flanked on one side by a massive iron reinforced wooded door with a lever bolted to a dial.

Jaïem lifted his lantern high and looked around the octagonal outlet, feeling for more hidden passages.

"There is nothing else; only this door."

Jaïem peered into the door's barred porthole but his eyes could not pierce the darkness. He gently pulled the lever and then on the door's massive iron handle.

"It is locked."

He looked around for a key but the archway was desolate save for a lonely stool. Then he heard the sound of something sliding on the ground within the cell. His heart paused and he grew faint. Gathering his courage, he drew closer to the door and stopped when he heard the sound of bare footfalls on the cold stone floor echoing from the dark cell. Jaïem was frozen with fear. Mustering his courage, he drew a deep breath.

"Who is there?" The footsteps stopped and then began again.

"A Vyrdmar prince commands that you speak. Tell me who you are?"

A deep and frightening voice bellowed a reply.

"You may call me Promothos the historian."

"The historian-" Jaïem remarked, trying to regain his composure. "Yet you dwell here in darkness while history unfolds above."

A gaunt face with a large jagged scar stretching from temple to chin appeared beyond the porthole. Golden eyes within round sockets glowed with a dull luster.

"Yes, my cell is dark. Yet much is revealed to me, and much can be deduced from what is already known. The past is shrouded in lore; it is hidden from you. Yet the past is revealed to me because it is woven into the fabric of my mind. The future is also revealed to me. I can know much of the future to come because I know the past and know the nature of men."

Jaïem drew closer to the door.

"Please enlighten me," the young prince said sardonically. "For example, why did the surpliant Owidobel come down here yesterday?"

Promothos' eyes flashed. "What will you reveal to me in exchange young prince?"

"Hold your tongue," Jaïem snapped. "There are worse punishments than imprisonment."

"An interesting approach," Promothos remarked. "Perhaps you know a little more about the nature of men than I assumed. I will answer your question. Yet all I ask is a couple of indulgences. I ask that you keep our dialogue secret and that whenever you should have need to learn about the secrets of species, life, and death that you return here alone, bringing me sweets from the royal pantries. I love sweets. They ease my pain and sorrow."

Promothos slid down to the ground within his cell. "Now if you would? Draw as close to the door as you can young Vyrdmar."

Jaïem obliged apprehensively.

"The surpliant and librarian of the temple, Owidobel, came to me with many questions. Many librarians before him have come down here to ask me questions. I am always glad to see a visitor, so long as he is inclined to be discreet. It had been quite some time since I had a visitor. And so, I was more than willing to speak with him. It was a wonderful surprise. I thought that the world had forgotten me. Then he came one day or night. It is all the same down here. He came and returns every now and then to make more inquiries."

"What does he want?" the young prince asked impatiently.

"Well at first, he wanted to know who I was. He asked other questions…"

"What other questions," the young prince queried tersely.

"There is one question that men always ask. Men are curious in a peculiar way. They bring their own predispositions and predilection to the inquiry. They also prefer sensational lies over unremarkable truths. As for the old librarian, he asked quite clumsily, if I knew how the world began. He also asked if it was true that men were created by the gods as is commonly believed…"

"What was your answer?" Jaïem asked.

"I told him as I will tell you," Promothos replied. "I told him that in the beginning, there was particle and motion within the void, and that all was ruled by probability. In the primordial beginning, all particles were the same. All particles had equal potential and drifted in the void. Then there was a disturbance. A sleeping consciousness awoke and thought, and then spoke, and that word echoed across the void, and particles were swept up by the sound as in a whirlwind. Particles were then fused together from the centrifugal force of this cosmic expression. Soon complex particles were bound together to create newer and more manifold particles until worlds and then species were formed."

Jaïem became slightly bewildered and was silent for a while.

"What else did he ask you?" Jaïem persisted.

"The librarian recalled that he had heard this story before. He asked how all of this was connected to the primordial flame that the Ayimar below the Pelares speak of. I told him that the primordial flame was nothing more than the power to return manifold particles, such as those that make up a stone or a man, to its original and malleable form. That act, is presumably a predicate step to the ancient practice of recombination. That was presumably how the so-called Beyonders or Atenari began to reconfigure manifold particle into other desirable forms or expressions. Some say that the Ayimar themselves were created from this practice.

The Ayimar also refer to the void as the primordial flame since all particles were once in their original form within the void. There, they imagine, particles are resplendent and alight."

Jaïem paused for a while and then sighed.

"What possible use is such a power unless one has the wisdom of the immortals? But then it does not matter. The cosmology you describe seems unlikely. What else did the librarian ask?"

Promothos did not answer right away, as if he was trying to jar his recollection.

"He did ask me another very interesting question once. He asked me if it was possible for a man to become like an immortal. I puzzled over his question for a while. I asked him to restate his question. Not because I did not know what he was after. I wanted him to be aware of how lax he was with his expression. He thought to himself and remarked that he had asked the question the only way he knew how. I then pointed out to him that what he actually wanted to know was whether I knew the human body's true limits. Nothing can exceed its limits. But I explained what I knew. I told him that no man can exceed is limitations. Yet men scarcely reach their potential.

The old librarian became noticeably excited. He asked me if I knew anything about a certain flower of lore rumored to enhance vitality and enhance cognition and other latent mental powers. He wanted to know if this flower existed and if I knew a certain recipe utilizing its nectar."

Jaïem interjected. "Is there such a flower and is there such a recipe?"

"Yes," Promothos replied. "There is such a flower. As for the recipe, I learned it long ago. The recipe does not however enhance human abilities. It actually cures the occasional sore throat and fatigue. But I wondered if the old librarian would ever return if I told him the truth.

I decided to reveal what I knew in segments to conceal the true purpose of the recipe for as long as I could. I wanted him to continue to bring me sweets."

Now suddenly the young prince could not clearly hear Promothos' voice. Promothos laughed wryly.

"Do you like my ruse?"

Jaïem stood up.

"No I do not."

"That is not surprising. You are a serious young man. You are also very perceptive."

Jaïem began to hear Promothos' voice echo dully in his mind. The young prince spoke as if trying to shake out of a stupor.

"You were not truthful about the flower and the recipe?"

Promothos laughed again.

"Perhaps there is a flower that yields a certain powder, which if mixed with the proper ingredients, in the proper quantities, unleashes dormant potential in men. But I would never have been told or shown this secret if I was inclined to disclose it to all who asked.

I gave the old librarian a recipe. He wanted a way to unlock his potential. I gave him a recipe for a stimulant and intoxicant. He returned and said he felt that he had experienced a metamorphosis, but that the effect was quite brief. I told him that his measurements were wrong.

Unlike you, the old librarian could not uncover my ruse. He lacked the faculty to truly commune with me. That ability is not found in many. Yet you... You were able to hear my whispers above, even as I pined down here in the catacombs."

"I do not understand," the prince lamented.

"My prince, do not bury what your mind has revealed to you. Do not deny your true purpose."

The prince felt a chill and the hairs on his neck stood. "You... You have been haunting me."

"I am not a ghost my prince. I am the lonely breath that once stoked the fire that brought the blessing of light and the warmth of hearths to men. Yet now I am cast away in this abysmal cage, while a beast with silvery wings inspires awe and fealty in men."

Jaïem could hear Promothos in his mind and could feel his anguish and despair and it frightened him.

"What do you want from me?"

"Free me from this cage," Promothos pleaded.

"If you are so wise," the prince asked. "Why do you not free yourself?"

Promothos was silent for a while.

"I need you. I have needed this spent form you see staring at you with forlorn eyes. Yet the power that binds me to this once majestic man is spent. My dying gives birth to a need. This need reveals the purpose of all things. This need and its object, which is to complete the whole from its scattered elements, compel me to seek you out."

Jaïem shrank away from the cell.

"Do not forsake me my prince," Promothos pleaded.

"I do not know you," Jaïem snapped.

"I am nothing to know and no one," Promothos remarked. "I was once Promothos the wise and bearer of knowledge. I was also known as Saareus the great. All that I was is in the past. I traversed this world gathering the experiences of men and cherishing them like dearest keepsakes. I wanted to compile a true history and unite what was scattered since the dawn of time. Yet I made many enemies. I could not understand why so many were resentful of my enterprise, and why my quest for knowledge was regarded as hubris. And so I was reviled and cursed with the mark of the faithless. I was imprisoned in the bowels of Irilsflir never to be seen again."

"Very well then," the young prince murmured. "Here you will stay for it is beyond my authority to release you. I will leave you to your solitude and return no more."

Promothos rose and pressed his gaunt and scarred face against the metal bars of the porthole.

"Will you not grant me a favor and bring me sweets my prince?"

Prince Jaïem turned and walked away turning his mind into finding his way out of the catacombs.

"Come back to me my prince… You will see. Even in the light of day as you try to embrace the comforts of palatial life, you will yearn for my words, which are like honey. You will not spurn me for long. This path is chosen for you."

Jaïem hurried away walking back up the spiraling stairs. "Do not call out to me again. I will not answer you."

Chapter 7: Wind's Crucible

After enjoying the hospitality of the merchant Nausterus, the company of fifteen traveled north and west toward the coasts following the caravan trail. All the while, Ahktel was unsettled by dark dreams. He saw men with dark cloaks brandishing long slender swords moving deftly. He saw fires blazing and heard strange thunderous sounds.

By nightfall the company could see a small village called Anjur nestled among a range of grassy hills and meadows where flocks of sheep grazed. Towering mills dotted the landscape. The evening fires were crackling in the hearths and smoke billowed from chimneys along rows of small homes. The mills awed Eje and the other Ausremen. They had never seen such structures in Ausremer. Neither were there so many rolling hills and glens as before them.

They gathered together under a patch of trees to wait out a bout of rain before entering the village.

While they were waylaid, Bojingren spoke well of Anjur, talking fondly of warm fires, delectable stews, sweet breads, golden butter, aromatic cheeses, and golden mead.

"The people of Anjur are renowned hosts," he said. "They will greet us warmly and delight our senses with the best food and drink in Maspeidon."

But after the rainfall eased to a drizzle, and the companions rode past the village posts they saw weary villagers looking on with uneasiness. A few dogs chased after them followed by a gang of adventurous boys. The companions passed through the village and up over round hills to a large stone residence at the northern outskirts of the town. There, the village prefect, a woman named Eursria, met them at the residence's heavy wooden doors.

Eursria greeted Bojingren warmly. The large red-haired woman embraced Bojingren and held him tight.

"Bojingren the Red!" she exclaimed. "I am so glad to see you again." She held him beside her for a while, peering at the companions and smiling.

"Now what has my son from Beonon brought with him?" She rattled on.

"You must be on a grave errand to come this far. Now you must know that lord Dorias came this way not too long ago. And who are these folk? Ausremen no doubt... I must inquire with them about spices and recipes from the austral lands."

The town prefect embraced every guest and then paused to catch her breath.

"Haven't had so many guests all at once in a long time."

Later in the evening, the companions, the prefect, and several other guests who happened by, spoke together in a large dining hall with a blazing hearth. When Bojingren asked about the caravans and the winter harvests from the south and east, and the flocks, the prefect's face became grave.

"There have been a great many wagons passing through the town with many needed provisions. Now the story with our flocks has been a cause for concern. We have had peace since the purge of the Ayimar two years ago until this winter. As you know, these cave dwellers, with their fallow eyes and golden skin, are tamers of cave beasts and avarathein that dwell on the peaks and perches of the Pelares. Poaching and raiding diminished after the last purge. But there has been an increase of late. We had hoped that the Ayimar were all routed. Now though, we realize that most of them escaped to their caves biding their time. They are back on the surface to sow mischief and sorrow."

The town prefect paused and took a draught of mead as her guests looked on intently. Wiping her mouth, she continued.

"From their abyss, the Ayimar have again loosed their winged plague on us. Avarathein have swooped down snatching up sheep and even the young."

The gathering was silent for a while. Some had troubled faces and others shook their heads and muttered to themselves. Then up sprang a guest who was proficient with the harpistar.

"Mistress may I play a score on your harpistar for our guests from Beonon and Ausremer?"

The village prefect nodded and the man sat at the square wooden console and began to skillfully play. Listening to the resonant intonations of the harpistar, the gathering turned their minds to fond memories of vibrant springs and golden summers. Soon their eyelids grew heavy and they bid their host good night.

The company left at daybreak during a brief pause in the persistent rains. Bojingren decided to stray off the open and well-beaten caravan trail and make their way into the wilderness. He reasoned that the companions would be less likely to encounter avarathein in the dense wilderness to the east, and if they did there would be more cover.

They wound down a muddy and treacherous path leading down into a gorge, and then crossed a shallow stream west. The companions followed the stream, which flowed into a large pond gathering at the base of a steep ridge. The dismounted their horses to make their way up a steep trail. When they had reached a crest, they saw a grove a short distance away. As they approached the grove, the horses suddenly became startled.

The company was trying to calm their horses when suddenly the sound of arrows could be heard whistling through the air around them. Before the company could rein in their horses, three forward riders were struck. An arrow pierced the neck of one forward rider perforating the jugular vein. Another rider was struck in the chest though his mail armor and his arm, and the third was felled by arrows though the chest and upper thigh.

By the time a second volley came, the three remaining forward riders had dismounted and placed their horses between them and their assailants.

"Take her away and go back down the ridge." Bojingren ordered.

Tyeshar obeyed, kicking Eje's horse and then riding away with her. Drawing his sword, Bojingren rallied his four remaining riders forward into the melee. Bojingren gave his men a sign, and they split into two columns, and passed into the grove from two parallel points.

Meanwhile, the forward riders drew their bows and arrows and loosed a volley into the trees. They listened for the sounds of rustling branches but heard nothing. They fired into the grove again and waited. Still there was a dreadful silence. Then dark riders came charging out of the grove firing their light crossbows. Their missiles struck down two more of the remaining forward riders who were leading their horses back toward their rear guard.

Bojingren took two of his warriors with him to aid the remaining forward riders. The dark host fell on the company like a swarm of bees with slender swords. The men from Bonthc unsheathed their swords and faced the dark host with a shout.

The hosts clashed in a frenzy of blows. When the din subsided, the dark riders lay dead or writhing on the ground. But so too were Bojingren's companions; only he was left standing.

Meanwhile, Tyeshar led Eje and the two Hekare north along a ridge and around the grove. Four more horsemen came out of the grove and sped past Bojingren and rode after them. Ixhor came about and Tyeshar followed after gesturing for Ahktel to push on with their precious charge. In the manner of the Irsei, Ixhor pulled the flap of his leather cap over his face.

Ixhor looked menacing as he rode out against the oncoming riders. When Ixhor got within range of the enemy, he hurled his javelin, bringing an enemy down with a groan. He quickly unsheathed his curved sword and drew his horse to the unarmed side of another charging horseman. The enemy deftly evaded Ixhor however, and came about to make another pass.

On the second pass, the horseman parried Ixhor's blow, but fell from his horse. Letting the disoriented lie, Tyeshar dismounted and fired a volley with his bow that struck down a second rider.

Turning his attention now to the first rider, who was now standing, he fired a volley and took him down, just as the last rider thought to leap on him. Ixhor could see this rider from his peripheral vision, and rolled to one side. The rider cleared him and fell to the ground rolling several times. The last rider sprang up quickly. Yet an arrow from Tyeshar's bow sent him crumpling to the ground.

Back at the perimeter of the grove, Bojingren secured his horse, and left his fallen companions to come to the aid of his lieutenant Tyeshar. Realizing that they had dispatched the enemy, the five remaining companions came together and returned to the grove to tend to their companions.

Their hearts sank when they realized that the ambush had quickly felled ten among them. Soon the remaining companions gathered together at a cave, bringing the dead with them. Bojingren whispered a prayer to mighty Yggir and purified the corpses by passing a torch over them. Cremation was not a Vyrdmar burial rite. Men from the east, beyond the gates of Taldur burned their dead. But, according to Vyrdmar tradition, the dead had to be purified and prepared for burial soon after death.

Bojingren imagined that the smoke from his torch spiritually cleansed the bodies. The cave was to be a crypt. Satisfied he did all he could, he set his fallen companion's horses free, and, along with the remaining companions, rode north and west to Chamiahce with a heavy heart.

Eje was hunched over in grief, shock and fear as she thought of how persistent and ferocious her pursuers were. She startled at every strange sound. Others were anxious as well, but they endured and rode along the northern perimeter of the grove west. Soon they found a trail and passed into the grove heading south and west until they emerged from it. Riding down an embankment and they followed a stream back north. That night, the companions made camp by a lonely stream flowing out of a cove. They built a small fire and made a savory stew with their provisions. After they ate they stared quietly at each other.

Bojingren broke the silence.

"These men we faced were disciplined. They were not mere bandits. I drew close to one of them to survey his corpse and saw the mark of the red sun on his palm. These men were Ayimar."

Ahktel had seen this mark before and so had Ixhor, but the Hekare said nothing. They had seen the mark of the red sun on the plains near Tarpis where they first encountered Eje. The men who held her wore this mark. Now the young Hekare wondered if these men had followed them from Ausremer. They wondered why these men were so determined to reclaim Eje.

Meanwhile, in Chamiahce, the first day of Wind's Crucible had concluded. The competitors were encamped outside of Namreddin's Beacon overlooking the sea. They sat around fires, listening to the surf splash against the strong base of the crags and the overlook. Some played a board game called chugrz, others played flutes, and still others told stories.

Hovin lay in his tent listening to the melodies of the camp and the sea, recounting the deeds of the day. Earlier, Hovin ran the race to Namreddin's spring and back to the beacon against Scepedis. It was well known that Chylus' son Scepedis was fleet of foot, yet Hovin outlasted him, as the race was of a great distance. After defeating Scepedis, Hovin matched his skill at the javelin throw against Wilia, Prentaur's son. Hovin threw the javelin farther and truer than Wilia, even though Wilia was known to be highly proficient at this martial skill. Hovin also struck truer and at greater distances than his opponent Smerdus in the archery challenge. By the end of the day, the judges were unanimous that Hovin had carried the day against the champions of Maspeidon.

Before sleep veiled his eyes, Hovin realized how momentous his victories were. He had succeeded in all three challenges; all he would need to assure success in the Crucible was to win one more challenge. He tried to recall what he knew of his next opponents and wondered what was beyond the Beacon's strong doors. He was not anxious though; he wondered about these things as one passing through a dream. He swept from thoughts of the foregoing day to thoughts of the following day. He could see himself grappling with Tharugaad, clashing against Mishar with the staff, and crossing swords with Frehil. He saw his challenges with clarity and depth and could feel his own inner calm, and sensed his opponent's courage wilt into trepidation.

"A warrior's greatest opponent is the fear of outcomes," he thought. "I care nothing for outcomes and I have no desire. I rejoice in the peace I feel, which rests on the certainty that I will not shirk my duty. I will conform to the requirements of my discipline and will strike when the time has come to strike. Let outcomes cloud my enemy's senses and judgment, then, as he quivers with anxiety and anticipation, I will strike true, and my victory will be at hand."

The prince's eldest brother Varenhil spent the night brooding in his chambers. He had with him several young women he found wandering around in the royal garrison, whom he had bound to his bed with silk sashes after he had imbibed much wine and lain with them all. Yet he could not be satisfied because his heart was stung by the betrayal and dishonor he perceived in Hovin's selection as the Vyrdmar champion. Though he had no interest in being the Vyrdmar champion, his ego was chafed nonetheless. Now the young women were pleading to be freed and permitted to return to their homes, yet Varenhil refused.

"I will keep you here and mock your frailty. I will look upon you with scorn and revile, and you will rue your own licentiousness, which you veil with the etiquette and title of maidens."

The young women wept and pleaded, but were wary not to say anything to enrage the prince further for fear of unleashing greater cruelty and abuse.

The second day of Wind's crucible began with the glorious ascent of the sun over the eastern horizon, which dissolved a thick gray mist. On that day, the city's streets and thoroughfares were choked with the traffic of caravans and pilgrims. The procession of courtiers and Harfingals were cheered and showered with flower petals as the crowd parted. The procession rode out to the pitched tents of Wind's Crucible before Namreddin's beacon to commemorate the second day. On the way they passed many glistening brooks and falls nestled in clusters of green trees and under majestic overlooks where stragglers made brief stops. The procession arrived to the applause of the pilgrims and onlookers encamped before the beacon and the king and the high priestess conducted their convocation again, followed by the slaughter and sacrifice of another strong bull.

The first challenge of the day pitted the king's stalwart son against Alberon's son Tharugaad. Now Tharugaad was a stout man from lord Elesias' country. Tharugaad came forth garbed in a loincloth in spite of the chill air. Hovin appeared in a plain white tunic over leather trousers and leather boots rising up to just under the knees. Among the crowd gathered to view this spectacle were many whispering that if mighty Tharugaad grappled with a boulder, it would crack and beg for mercy. Such was Tharugaad's strength, some whispered, that he once throttled a long fanged lion.

The two men circled each other for a while looking for a point of attack and for leverage. Tharugaad was first to attack, growling like a lion with his thick brown hair bristling like a mane. Tharugaad lunged to grasp Hovin's sinewy legs. As he did so, his foot stubbed a small stone, and he fell awkwardly on his round belly. Hovin was cautious, declining to take advantage of his opponent's misfortune or to fall for his ruse.

In grappling, a man had to subdue his opponent until he raised a hand or a thumb in submission, and Hovin knew that he was not strong enough to achieve this outright. Hovin thought to engage Tharugaad for some time until his opponent's knees grew weary and his breath grew heavy from a relentless and extended engagement. It was not long before Tharugaad began to breathe heavily. Then fortune smiled on him when he lunged forward and caught Hovin by an arm. He coiled around the Vyrdmar prince like a constrictor. However, Tharugaad could not secure both of Hovin's arms, and the prince used his free arm and positioned it under his opponent's armpit and hurled Tharugaad over his shoulder.

After much grunting and groaning, and jostling and tossing, and much cheering and gasping by the crowd, Tharugaad was nearly spent. He lumbered this way and that way after Hovin who deftly eluded him and then engaged him when it was most advantageous. Hovin was careful with his opponent. Perspiration and dirt had mixed in the cold air and coated his skin with a sticky film that made it easy for his powerful opponent to grab and secure him. This condition should have been a great boon to Tharugaad. Hovin was however able to use this condition to his advantage also, beating his opponent to every open attack and hold.

Finally, the two grapplers clung to each other by the shoulders and struggled for a while. Then they circled around as if trying to find an opening. Tharugaad was breathing heavily. Hovin cunningly feigned weariness. The opponents grappled again. This time Hovin slipped under Tharugaad's arm and maneuvered into a tight hold behind him. Then when Tharugaad moved to snatch Hovin by his wrists, Hovin deftly dragged the stout warrior down to the ground. Hovin quickly wrapped his arms around Tharugaad's throat and crossed his legs around his torso. Tharugaad struggled to breathe and darkness began to veil his eyes. Then he reluctantly waved a hand to signal his submission.

The second competition of the day pitted Hovin against Mishar in the staff play. Hovin took some time to splash water on his face and drink a refreshing mixture of water, herbs and honey. Refreshed he then he clashed stout staves with Mishar. Again the cheers erupted. Many shouted out to encourage the combatants, and gasped when a blow came close to its mark. Now and then a combatant swung wildly and the other parried or leapt back. Mishar was very skilled in this often neglected martial discipline. Had his opponent been any other than Hovin, Mishar would have been victorious.

The king's sons were very well instructed in all martial disciplines. Hovin practiced every day and was fastidious in his attention to all aspects of martial life. He did not excel in all disciplines, but he was more than competent in them all. And so this competition was going to be as contentious as the last.

Many a day's journey south and near the Pelares, there was no Levying festival. But there was a swell of activity here and there in narrow gorges and lonely groves. Now, a towering figure clad in dark flowing raiment and cloak, stood on a crag overlooking a gorge. A smaller man approached bowing.

"My lord, I have men at the ready. Should we pursue them?"
The man, Nausterus, who had claimed he was from Tarpedon, and ate and drank with Bojingren the Red not so long ago, replied sternly.

"No. I will deal with them another way. I will follow them until nightfall. When they are weary and make camp, I will loose a howling pestilence upon them. Now make sure our scouts keep me informed of their movements."

The five companions from Bonthc passed wearily along a low ridge overlooking a gorge. Bojingren was relieved at having made it through this juncture of the journey since the gorge was a likely place for another ambush.

Bojingren regretted his decision to leave the caravan road for a shorter route through the wilderness. He wondered now if he should abandon the wilderness trail and turn back toward the caravan route. But he could not be sure if the enemy was not still on the companions' trail. If they turned back, they could be turning into the pursuit with only fraction of their original number remaining.

Bojingren wondered why the Ayimar would risk the retribution of lord Dorias and the Vyrdmar by attacking travelers under the lord Dorias' banner. He wondered whether they were after his Ausrmen charges. He surmised that perhaps Eje was a noblewoman from her country. But Bojingren could not imagine why the Ayimar would want to capture or kill her. He wanted to question Eje, but thought better of it. After all, she presented a commission with the seal of Irilsflir commanding any man at arms of Maspeidon to secure her safe passage. A soldier only needed to know his master's command and to faithfully obey.

The companions were wary and uneasy throughout the rest of the journey. Their movements were tentative and slower than usual. Bojingren was traveling blind. He could not spare any of his men to scout the territory ahead, and he did not want move too slow for fear of being overtaken.

But there was opportunity in his predicament. With all but Tyeshar remaining from his detachment, Bojingren wondered about the two Hekare. He appreciated Ixhor's exploits at the grove and was astonished at the lumbering Hekare's display of tenacity and skill.

Bojingren asked the two Hekare to give an account of their martial skill and experience. It was then that Bojingren learned that Ixhor was a Xedun warrior among the Hekare and that both Hekare were proficient in horsemanship and archery. The Hekare shared stories about their adventures since they left their village Sephtu, through Eje who spoke the common tongue of Maspeidon very well.

Bojingren led the company north and east, believing the enemy was in pursuit from the south. Besides, having interpreted urgency in Eje's commission, taking the shorter path through the wilderness trail seemed the only choice. He knew that there were dangers in the wilderness. But he held out hope that they would encounter Gaaldenian sentries along another caravan route to the east. In the meantime, Bojingren scanned the thickets, bushes, and canopies, but the moved the companions along quickly. He was certain they could not survive another ambush.

During the early afternoon the company made a brief layover to rest their horses, during which they ate some dried meats and bread. They ate very quickly and quietly and drank water from their water flasks until they heard a familiar sound.

Emerging from a bend in the trail ahead, they saw what appeared to be a man striding toward them. The man whistled loudly and startled a flock of birds pecking at something in a patch of tall grass. Bojingren leapt up and motioned for Tyeshar and the Hekare to take cover with Eje behind some bushes. But it very soon became clear that the strange man was likely an unarmed traveler.

The pure white robes the man wore shone brightly in the sun, and the closer the man came, the more at ease the companions began to feel. Surprisingly, the man was no man at all; it was a woman of great physical stature with flowing black hair. She wore an enameled silver necklace strung with seed pearl beads and a large pendant.

"Greetings countrymen and friends," she said to the company.

They approached her cautiously. The woman looked at the companions very casually and smiled.

"I am very glad to have encountered you all – especially if you are traveling to the high city. I was on my way there to follow the procession to the beacon by the sea when I had to dream that I would encounter five travelers on the way, and that one of them would have red hair. The Celestial spoke to me and said that I should guide these travelers to the high city. I have found you – the ones traveling with the man with red hair. Follow me. You will be safe with me."

The companions looked at the woman curiously and at each other. Bojingren approached her with both hands clasped together.

"Red haired one," the woman said. "You look upon me as if you think I am a specter. Her gaze was piercing as if to warn Bojingren not to come too close.

When Bojingren paused and stared around at the companions, her expression softened.

"I am Ligia," she said. "I serve the Celestial. It is no accident that our paths have crossed. You are lost and in despair. I am here to help you."

Bojingren knelt before the dark haired woman.

"Mistress of Irilsflir, I can see that the radiance of divinity surrounds you. This brings comfort to us. We are thankful that the Celestial has sent you to look after us. Lead us through the perils before us and we will follow."

Tyeshar followed Bojingren's example and came forward and knelt before Ligia. Eje and the Hekare followed Tyeshar, honoring their hosts' customs.

"Friends, to your horses; follow me, and let us make haste, for there are enemies close behind."

Bojingren rose and gestured for the others to gather the horses.

"Priestess, we do not have a horse for you. With whom will you ride?"

Ligia smiled. "I will ride with the woman. Now we must ride as fast as your horses will carry us. We must take refuge in the caravan routes. Fear not for the Celestial will protect us."

The company now rode north and east with more urgency than before toward the caravan route, which was over a day's ride away. Ligia rode at the head of the company with Eje cradled in front of her like a child. Eje was at first uneasy, but she was soon overborne with a sense of calm. Coming in and out of a light sleep, she felt as if she was riding on a cloud being pushed along by a gentle breeze even though Ligia kept the horse at a gallop. A cool air swept in from the sea to the west and chilled their faces. The air seemed to soothe them and ease their sense of loss and disquiet. Bojingren struggled to maintain his sense of guardedness. He fell back to the rear of the company and then rode to the front, looking this way and that way whenever there was cover nearby. When the company was passing through a glade and a branch from an old tree covered with ivy and lichen fell, his hands moved reflexively for his sword.

When night fell, Nausterus found a high place to look down on the company's position. He saw the flickering light of one fire observable from among a patch of trees. A man approached and looked out with him.

"They have settled in for the night master. What is your will?"

"Go back to your camp and await my return," Nausterus ordered.

"Yes master," the man replied. The man moved away, and mounting a horse, rode away.

After the man rode away, Nausterus produced a small glass flask from the folds of his flowing robes. The flask contained what appeared to be a luminescent insect fluttering within. He opened the flask and released the thing, which now glowed golden and bright. Then he sat on the ground and crossed his legs. Placing his hands together, he began to whisper almost inaudibly.

"Hear me O' breath of the hidden and echo of the inscrutable mind!"

The luminescent thing buzzed around and then came close to him as if examining his gaunt features and peering into his mind.

"I summon you Vashein to whisper my purpose into the doleful hearts of howling hordes bound to the flesh. Whisper now and gather your wrath in them and bind them to your exhortations and my very will."

Then Nausterus whispered words in a tongue long forgotten in the world, and the luminescent being darted away as the air swirled around him whipping up leaves.

Driven by Nausterus' incantation, the being he called Vashein darted out and streaked through nearby fields, caves, and thickets. Leaves whipped up where it passed. It found a pack of wolves and hovered over them. As it buzzed around them, the wolves' eyes flashed yellow and they gathered closely together and set out as if incited by fervor of the hunt.

The Vashein sought out other packs, and soon several packs had converged, growling, with their mouths gaping and their yellow eyes glaring. The Vashein now bound disparate packs together to Nausterus' lethal malice and purpose and formed a great menacing host.

After the great pack had gathered, Nausterus loosed them on the companions. They were just settling in for much needed rest. Bojingren was standing watch. He was perched on a huge stone, reflecting on the events of the day. The horses were suddenly startled. They were the first to hear the marauding wolves approaching from the distance.

Bojingren leapt down from where he was perched and called out to Tyeshar. He noticed that

Ligia was up staring into the southern sky. The others leapt up and looked around frantically.

"There is nothing to fear," Bojingren urged. "Gather up your things."

Ligia was still looking out very intently. Then she turned to face the company.

"Friends, get to your horses. We will not have any rest this night."

Bojingren rushed toward Ligia to look out from her vantage point.

"What do you see priestess?"

Ligia looked deeply into Bojingren's eyes, and he was suddenly filled with dread.

Turning to the company he cried out "To your horses!" He urged them, "Light torches!"

Pale eyes could now be seen in the darkness. Coming in waves, growling and snarling, the great pack was surrounding the companions. Bojingren and Tyeshar pulled back their bowstrings and sent a volley of arrows whistling through the air. To their dismay, their arrows disappeared into the dark mass of growling and snarling pestilence without any apparent effect.

Ligia gathered the companions around her.

"They are upon us too thick my friends. Your weapons are of no use. Draw near me and be still."

The companions did as Ligia asked and gathered around her with weapons drawn. The Hekare waved torches and shouted. But the wolves' advance was purposeful and unrelenting.

The companions looked on with hearts pounding, anticipating a precipitous charge. The pack seemed to be waiting for the hunter's moment, deliberately gathering their numbers and tightly coiling around the companions. Then out leapt a massive gray wolf with yellow eyes flashing and teeth and claws the size of daggers. It sauntered around the company, sniffing and growling. It looked away and then snapped its head back toward the companions, bearing its massive fangs as if it was taunting them.

"Shut your eyes and listen for my voice," Ligia shouted above the wolves' malevolent symphony. She held out her arms and a cluster of small lights appeared over the company, swirling like fireflies. The lights streaked through the air with increasing intensity and radiance until they became so bright that the companions looked away and shut their eyes.

"Follow my voice," Ligia shouted.

The companions followed closely behind Ligia, following her voice. Ligia called out to them again, "Follow me. Be not afraid."

The streaking lights became more and more intense, burning their eyes through their eyelids. The companions stumbled forward, following Ligia' voice and then her melodious whistling, seemingly through brush and then a clearing until the intensity of the light diminished and they could open their eyes. The journey did not seem very long.

How far could they have wandered so blindly and so quickly Bojingren thought? The companions looked back and saw rays of light permeating through the thicket they fled from. They were awed at Ligia' display of arcane power, and were incredulous at how far they had blindly stumbled in so little time. They now stood on a mound overlooking a thicket. But the danger had not passed and there was no time to waste.

The company sped off through the night wondering if they had seen the last of the wolves. Now on foot, the company crossed a fast moving stream without stopping to replenish their leather flasks. Now they passed through dense underbrush sloping down into a gully and out to a misty marsh where they waded and plodded their way through with contorted faces until blessed daybreak.

Back in Chamiahce, a throng much larger than had assembled the two previous days, huddled together before Namreddin's beacon some time after daybreak. The crowd encircled the competitors, looking on with anticipation. Hovin had defeated Tharugaad, Frehil, and Heryaus the day before in the grappling, staff play, and light sword play respectively. Now he was set to cross swords with one of Maspeidon's greatest warriors in the full sword duel.

Clydeion's son Taldeion was lord Elesias' captain of the guard. Taldeion distinguished himself at the ruins of Apryos, which was once a fledgling Ayimar trading post nestled in the valley of the Pelares. Apryos was raided and set afire by king Nnyreinin long ago. Its inhabitants were sent fleeing into the mountains. However, small bands of Ayimar always returned, using the ruins as a camp for raids on towns like Anjur. Now and then warriors from Gaalden and Beonon led campaigns to destroy the Ayimar camps. In recent times, none were as successful as the one led by Taldeion's father a few years before. Taldeion accompanied his father and it was said that he had slain an Ayimar chieftain in hand-to-hand combat. After his father fell in the ensuing pursuit of the fleeing Ayimar host, Taldeion rallied his men, entering the caves and following the Ayimar down to the bowels of the earth where many Ayimar were slain.

The raids against the Ayimar were not all reprisal for attacks against Maspeidonian townsfolk. Although the raid that Taldeion participated in was for that noble purpose, some raids were led by men looking to follow the fleeing Ayimar to their caches of silver and gems. Some were even after their secret scrolls and bounded books written by their scribes, historians, and sages. Others wanted to find their underground city, which was rumored to exist deep under the Pelares around an underground lake.

Yet no one dared to venture too deep into their caves because they were full of traps and beasts tamed by the Ayimar long ago. The Ayimar were the original inhabitants of the continent, and they had always been resentful of the Vyrdmar.

The subterranean world of the Ayimar was steeped in mystery. They were utterly frightening to others on the continent. Their presence in the Pelares was a rallying cry for many, and purges against them were brutal. The Pelares became a proving ground for warlike men and a destination for adventurers. Taldeion was himself an adventurer and he had faced and slain many Ayimar.

Now Taldeion, Maspeidon's newest hero from the frontiers of Maspeidon's ongoing war against the Ayimar, stood against the noble Vyrdmar prince Hovin. The two armor clad combatants clashed swords. The first to strike his opponent five times or three consecutive times with their ceremonial sword would be the victor.

After that exchange, the combatants would continue with three passes without armor with the winner striking the loser twice or striking the most critical blows with his ceremonial sword. To be victorious, a combatant had to either win the full armor segment of the challenge and the final passes without armor, or win at least one of the segments and demonstrate to the judges that he generally acquitted himself better than the other combatant.

Hovin won the full armor segment, landing two consecutive blows, and then matching each subsequent strike by Taldeion, until he had accumulated five strikes. Although they wore bronze cuirasses and helmets, the two combatants were bloodied from wounds on their extremities; in one pass, Taldeion suffered a laceration on his shoulder and Hovin a gash on his left thigh.

After the first segment was concluded, the combatants were allowed to rest briefly and have their wounds bound. After their wounds were bound, and they had drained cups of an herbal mixture, the combatants struggled back to the circle and waited for the signal to begin the last segment of the challenge. Both men were exhausted. Their movements were not as crisp and precise, as their limbs were now heavy from their exertions and the stinging pain of their wounds. Hovin drew a deep breath and looked up at the now overcast sky and then down at his enemy. He gathered his strength and directed his focus on his opponent, rejecting his body's protestations.

The two men made several passes and the clashes of swords rang out loudly over and over. The crowd looked on, too enthralled to utter more than hushed sounds. No one wanted to reveal which champion they favored, for both men were very well regarded, not to mention that one was a Vyrdmar prince.

The two men attacked again, this time with dreadful speed and violence. A thrall foreboding and a hush fell over the crowd as these two men of remarkable courage, skill and reflexes fell on each other in what had to be the final throes of their struggle. Yet, evenly matched, their skillful attacks were parried or evaded again and again. The crowd gasped and then sighed.

Now and again the combatants paused, breathing heavily, hunkering and glaring at each other. Blood soaked their bandages and was oozing through. Then, even as his lungs felt as if they would explode, Hovin experienced a surge of breath and strength. He felt the early morning vigor return to his sinewy arms and legs. His wounds still throbbed, but now the pain only heightened his awareness and spurred him forward. He could clearly see in his mind that his victory was at hand.

He could see himself stand poised with his sword held high and his enemy attack, trying to seize the advantage he perceived from Hovin's wounded leg. He saw himself cutting down with a fierce blow to parry Taldeion's attack. The blow was so fierce that it made a frightening clang and flung Taldeion's guard open to a counter-attack. As if in a walking dream, Hovin could see himself crouching, and then springing, and slashing against his opponent's momentum with incredible speed, and tearing a gash through his leather belt. As Hovin saw the exchange, so did it unfold, and Hovin, son of Ylarin, defeated mighty Taldeion in the last challenge of Wind's crucible.

Chapter 8: Yggir's first law

Mighty Taldeion was hurried back to the city under the care of Qurgin, the great physician from Tarpedon. If it were not for the bluntness of the ceremonial blades and the thickness of Taldeion's belt, the physician remarked, Hovin's blow would have mortally wounded the young warrior. Hovin rushed to him and cupped his head in his arms, calling out for aid. However, Taldeion's wound appeared graver than it actually was. Qurgin examined the wound and dug through his leather satchel for a jar and poured some of its content on a clean cloth. He then placed the cloth on the wound and bound it. Then he looked up and nodded, assuring the concerned onlookers before Taldeion was carted away on a horse-drawn wagon.

The crowd cheered the combatants, shouting their names. Hovin was swept away by his Harfingals who lifted him up and carried him to the doors of the beacon. The Harfingals put Hovin down before the king and the high priestess, who were seated on chairs overlooking the field.

"Your courage and skill has carried the day Vyrdmar prince."

The priestess stood before the prince and motioned for him to rise. The king went to his son and lifted him up. Now the king spoke.

"Let the judges come forth and give their account."

The judges came forth and Elesias addressed the crowd.

"King Ylarin, son of Wind, and lord of the Vyrdmar, the judges declare that the Vyrdmar champion has met and exceeded the standard of the Levying inquiry. Now therefore, let the people behold the champion of Wind's Crucible, and the great standard of the redoubtable strength of the house of Wind."

The crowd cheered, "Hail the Vyrdmar king of the high city" and "May the light of the world shine unto the end of the time."

The priestess gestured and several surplicants came forth and took Hovin to a large tent where he was undressed, bathed and purified. In a sudden and anticlimactic conclusion, the crowd began to slowly disperse, following a procession led by the king and the high priestess back to the city. They sang songs, but not happy songs. They even sang the song of the Cepheid, the song of the twins, Breix and Bruix, who almost destroyed the world after freeing it from the tyranny of the scions of Nur.

Yet the Levying was not over for Hovin; one more challenge remained. None had dared to face this last challenge since Wind proclaimed the Crucible tradition. The champions since that time had not been of royal lineage, but Hovin was Wind's descendant. He felt compelled to face that challenge. As the tradition of the Levying required therefore, Hovin was left in a tent after he was purified by surplicants. He was dressed in a pure white tunic and left to face the mystery of the beacon after nightfall.

Back in the city Jaïem sought out master Idram who taught in the academy. Jaïem found the schoolmaster at his apartment located near the royal compound. The schoolmaster's wife met the prince at the door and led him through the schoolmaster's study into a terrace. Master Idram was painting an image on a very large vase. The image was barely discernable as a stag in a grove of tall firs.

Master Idram seemed very glad to see the young the prince.

"My lord," the schoolmaster exclaimed when he saw Jaïem approaching. "How good it is to see you."

The schoolmaster urged the prince to sit on a soft couch and drew closer, himself sitting on the stool he brought over from where he had been working. The schoolmaster's wife brought the young prince and the schoolmaster some fruit, bread and fresh water.

"What brings you away from the royal compound and to my house?"

"You know many things and are wisest among the schoolmasters at the academy. I thought you would be the right person to answer a question that has been gnawing at me. Quite simply I want to know who Promothos the Wise was?"

The schoolmaster raised a brow. He cleared his throat, took a draught of water, and nibbled on some bread. Then he appeared to give the young prince's question some thought.

Jaïem interjected.

"You do not know of this man?"

The schoolmaster smiled uneasily.

"There is not much in the archives at the academy about this man. There are a few obscure writings detailing his misdeeds."

A glint of impatience could be seen in Jaïem's eyes.

"Why do you ask me about this man my prince? If he ever existed at all, he has been dead since before your time or perhaps even your father's time."

"The academy is steeped in dead things," Jaïem answered wryly. "We often delve into the past and the dead at the academies. How many times have you lectured on dead Atemin kings and sages, their deeds, and their wise counsel? How often have you spoken of Namreddin as if he had just passed into the void a season ago? Yet no one even knows for certain if he actually existed at all – if he was purified, preserved, and buried in the traditional manner, or who interred his body in the temple, or if not, where his mound is. Now that I ask about this man Promothos, who like mighty Namreddin, is dead, you answer is terse."

"Namreddin was a great man." The old man was expressionless.

"Why would men call Promothos wise if he was not great himself?"

"Men say many things."

The young prince sighed.

"All that really interest me is veiled from me. I want you to reveal something of the world to me that I actually want to know, and not what you or other old men want me to know. For once, I want you to put down your paintbrush, with which you skillfully paint idyllic portraits of the world for the sons of nobles and princes, and reveal the world to me as it really is."

The schoolmaster cleared his throat and called out to his young wife to bring wine.

"Water does not quench all manner of thirst," the old man quipped. "I for one will need some wine to warm my blood and stimulate my memory. For as I have said, this Promothos was a very obscure figure. He may not have existed at all, as you have wrongly said of your ancestor Namreddin."

The schoolmaster's wife brought a carafe and two small silver cups. She poured wine into the cups and mixed them with water. After the schoolmaster's wife left the study, the schoolmaster took a draught of wine and then drew close to the edge of his chair.

"The past is dead, but it is also useful. The limestone, upon which strong houses are built are dead, but useful. There are those who build houses and there are those who live in them. Many who live in strong and fine houses are thankful and secure in the knowledge that their houses are structurally sound. Yet there are always those who ask, how was this house built and with what materials. Many who ask want to build their own houses, and not rely on the genius of others such as our metics; or perhaps they aspire to be metics themselves. But if all who desire to build houses were allowed to build them, no one would be secure in the knowledge that their house was built well."

"I agree," Jaïem replied. "But why should not a man be able to choose his vocation? Why should he not be permitted to pursue his chosen vocation for his own purposes? Besides, I doubt that our metics conceal their art and skill for the benefit of others. They conceal their knowledge because it enhances their prestige and power. They would not be as powerful if their knowledge were not so exclusive."

Master Idram smiled again.

"Very well then Vyrdmar prince. But I caution you that knowledge is best left to those who have the wisdom and moral training and courage to make proper use of it. The sages of old have said that Promothos brought fire, but men were burned as much as they benefited from its light and warmth."

Jaïem now looked darkly at the old man.

"That saying is familiar to me," he mumbled almost inaudibly.

"Then you must realize," the schoolmaster added, "that even a little knowledge in the hands of the young and lesser men can result in much mischief. Consider again my axiom. When a man wants to have a good house built, he commissions a metic, and in so doing, is assured that his house will last many winters. Yet if metic arts were revealed to all, many lesser men would dabble in it and confer upon themselves the title of metic. Any man could hold himself out to be a metic, and no man could ever be assured that his house was expertly built. Alas, many faulty houses would be built and would crumble upon many innocents. Then, men would say that metic art is not exalted. It is better that this is not the way of the world. The way that prevails is the better way even if many remain ignorant and subservient to the few. This result may not appear to be useful to all, but the alternative portends chaos and lesser value for all."

"Very well then master Idram," Jaïem agreed. "I cannot gainsay you in these matters. But my request remains. Will you reveal to me who Promothos was?"

The schoolmaster smiled wryly and took another draught of wine.

"The deeds of Promothos the wise present an opportunity to learn that virtue which is most endearing to mighty Yggir, and conversely, the sin which the Celestial most abhors. Promothos the Wise, as he is known among the Ayimar, was the Atenari lord of the Ayimar underworld. He yearned to overthrow the Vyrdmar dynasty and to break the power of the Celestial. He believed that men should be free to pursue knowledge of power over life and death for their own purposes. An utterly absurd idea perhaps, and yet he conceived it. He thought to create a new world. A world he called Atlantis. He envisioned Atlantis to be a lathe of superior men fettered only by their desire and their daring."

"He dared to defy mighty Yggir and the Vyrdmar?" the young prince whispered. "Power over life and death; how provocative."

"Promothos was above all a deceiver. Men cannot have power over life and death."

"What else do you know about this man?"

"As I said, there is not much to know. It was written that Promothos was not merely a man. He was said to be a piece of the broken spirit of Nur, the evil god Yggir destroyed in a primordial age. And so, Promothos is immortal. He is a bakiren. He continues to exist somewhere.

Not so long ago, Promothos inspired the Ayimar lord Saareus to rally the Ayimar against the Vyrdmar. Promothos promised lord Saareus immortality and preternatural power and made the hapless lord his host. Blinded by his newfound power, lord Saareus waged war against the Vyrdmar. He was defeated, along with his Nurimite allies. It is said that Wind slew lord Saareus and cast Promothos into endless wandering. Some say that mighty Yggir himself slew lord Saareus and banished Promothos to the primordial pool in the depths of the world.

Yet how this being was disposed of is not important. What is important is that Promothos wanted to reveal forbidden knowledge. He rejected the Celestial's laws and threatened the order the He had established.

Yggir is all knowing and wise, but chooses not to reveal all knowledge to men for a greater good, which is not always perceptible to men. However, men, in their inferior wisdom, desire to have forbidden knowledge, and fall into the web of deceit set out by Promothos and his wicked adherents. As a prince, you will come to know many things because of your high station. Yet there is knowledge that Yggir conceals from even kings and princes. A wise prince should rejoice in the house Yggir has built for him and the Vyrdmar out of love. If a prince rejects these gifts, and engrosses himself in vain pursuits, he will undoubtedly suffer the Celestial's repulsion and wrath."

Jaïem now sipped a little wine.

"Very well master Idram. Yet it is one thing for the Celestial to conceal knowledge as a father conceals knowledge from his children because they lack the judgment to make good use of it. However, it is another thing entirely for mighty Yggir to conceal Himself. I do not know mighty Yggir and I do not know Promothos. I do not even know my forefathers. I will never those who are dead. But should not those who are hidden, but living, reveal themselves if they require men to obey them?"

The schoolmaster nodded and rubbed his shaven chin.

"Yggir reveals Himself in many ways. Perhaps not to the satisfaction of most, but I urge you to seek him out. Open your eyes and your heart to Him. Become familiar with your unfamiliar faculties because knowledge of the nature of the hidden is certainly not familiar.

It is universally believed that the hidden exist. Even the Atenarix know and fear the Celestial. They believe that the Celestial is the primordial essence of all things living expressed through ideas, which to them is the light of the world. They believe that the Celestial is like a firmament of sparkling desire, ambition, and ideas continuously ebbing and flowing and yearning to be expressed. This God field as they call it, experiences itself and the world we see as reflections off of the sensorial prism of species. The Atenarix believe that species experience this connection with the God field, and the experience is assimilated into thought, giving us a general sense that we are autonomous and have a transcendent soul.

The Atenarix believe that species life is merely animation, and species consciousness an illusion. The adherents of the Celestial also believe that species life is subordinate to transcendent life. Those faithful to Yggir believe that the soul is eternal, and through the Celestial can find its path to Yieryos, the house of souls.

Drawing from both schools of thought, I would surmise that perhaps the the hidden or the bakiren, and the souls of men, are broken pieces from the God field or the Celestial. The bakiren however cause harmful impulses that turn us away from the light of the Celestial, and away from reason and temperateness. And so, you are right to say that the Celestial should reveal Himself if men are to obey Him. The Celestial is hidden, but He can be revealed. He reveals Himself to all who are truly looking for Him and the path to salvation in Yieryos."

Jaïem spoke with Idram the schoolmaster for quite some time. He left the schoolmaster's house just before the revelers and crowds from the crucible returned to the city. After a brisk walk back to the royal compound, he stopped to look at the temple jutting over the compound's inner wall and the trees of the royal garden. At that moment Jaïem thought nothing of what the schoolmaster said of Yggir. Rather, he wondered about the mystery of Promothos. He fought the lure of what he knew was hidden beneath the temple. He very much desired to speak with Promothos again. The compulsion won him over finally, and he detoured and again made his way to the temple.

Meanwhile the prince's brother Varenhil ate a midday meal with his squire Haldar in the dining hall of the royal apartments. Since anger had set on him, he had not eaten a good meal. Now he was devouring roast fowl, bread, and gulping down copious amounts of mead.

"I will request an audience with my father tonight," prince Varenhil said with a mouth full of food. "I want to know his mind before I leave the city and return to Greingspen."

Haldar reached for a piece of the roast fowl. Varenhil smacked his hand away and glared at him.

"My lord-" Haldar said pulling his hand back. "May I speak freely?"

Varenhil called out to some servants and they hustled to him bowing. Varenhil ordered that they bring another roast fowl for Haldar and some more mead, and they left the hall bowing.

"Speak," Varenhil said coldly.

"You have told me yourself that it is best not to reveal your heart to others. It is assumed that a crown prince desires to succeed his king. But you should heed your own counsel, and withdraw from this display of sentiment over the honors fate has bestowed on your brother. Some will say that your actions expose your desire for the throne? "

"Brave Haldar," Varenhil replied. "I am a petulant lord. Yet you give me counsel when I am most prickly. You are brave indeed-or perhaps imprudent. However, I will not chastise you because I know you speak out of love. I will tell you why I am angry and why I will seek an audience with my father. Then you will understand my mind. A prince must know who loves him, as well as who hates him. A prince must be aloof and ruthless with those who hate him. And yet with those who love him, he must be strong, constant, but also inclined to express those sentiments that reveal his attachment to them.

A prince must exhibit strength and moral fortitude with those he loves, because these virtues inspire continued admiration and respect. If however, the prince is all too strong and constant, those who love him will wonder if the prince protects them and holds their counsel because they are dear to him, or rather because the prince is simply morally upright, judicious, or astute. It goes without saying that the former reason is more satisfying to those who love the prince than the latter. I know that my father knows my mettle and quality. But he must also know that his eldest son suffers the pangs of jealousy because he perceives that his father has vouchsafed a lesser son an honor that should rightly be given to him who is the eldest. Then my father will know that his love and favor is dear to me and he will be forthcoming with it in the future."

"That sounds like a familiar homily." Haldar smiled. "You remember master Idram's teachings well."

Varenhil frowned, and yet Haldar was not deterred.

"Why are you stung by the honor bestowed on your brother?" Haldar prodded. "You deride the Levying tradition and scarcely want to partake in it. In fact, you agree with those among the vizir council who say that it is folly to permit vassals to question the fitness of their regent."

Varenhil stopped eating and wiped his hands. "Perhaps I will chastise you."

The prince paused and licked his lips.

"But later... You are my squire and friend and so I will continue to reveal my mind so that you may benefit from my wisdom. You are right Haldar. I do not wish to partake in this barbaric ritual. I find it utterly absurd that a king should have to prove to his vassals that he and his heirs are fit to rule. This practice is reckless and foolish. Future Vyrdmar champions will not likely escape this onerous duty unscathed and neither will my father's house. The Vyrdmar will not continue to thrive if we are to be under constant and sanctioned attack from our own vassals.

I cannot say for sure whether king Nnyreinin was mad or cunning in instituting this tradition. On the one hand, he could have been mad and have sowed the seed of the Vyrdmar's destruction. I still find it hard to fathom a king would do such a thing – to make it lawful for his vassals to challenge him and his heirs. On the other hand, this tradition may have been a noble gesture that so endeared his vassals to him that they at once swore fealty to him and his heirs until the end of time. I can see what many might interpret as the wisdom of this tradition. For men always wonder whether those who rule do so by might or by right, or whether they should rule at all.

But if it was all a ruse, I think the time has come for our vassals to realize the Vyrdmar king's power is absolute and inviolable. Some believe that a king's position is stronger if his subjects consent to be ruled and if his subjects believe that he is deserving of his lofty status. I disagree. I am of the view that right is illusory. All that one needs to rule is power over life and death. Kings do not rule by right. Kings rule by the present ablity to protect and to destroy life. Kings may occasionally bestow their vassals and nobles with titles and honors to soothe their pride. Yet these gestures are not the source of a king's authority. Power is the source of a king's rule. For kings and princes, there is only power. Those who have power rule because rule emanates from power and is an expression of power.

Let men accept how things are and say that divine providence has given power to those whom it chooses. Men should not dare to question this outcome with their inferior wisdom or try to give power to those who providence has denied it.

I reject all claims to right and frown on all traditions and titles. I would brutally remind my vassals who is lord. I would show more love to my dog than to those wretches. I know them as they truly are. They covet power and would use it less providently because they were not chosen by the Celestial."

Varenhil paused and then sighed.

"But I am not king. I must therefore obey and show reverence to my fathers' traditions."

An air of solemnity was with the procession of revelers when they returned to the city. That night, citizens and pilgrims lit torches and candles and lanterns and converged on the temple quadrangle. There they were led in a night of prayer at the moment they imagined Yggir was purifying their champion in the beacon by the sea.

The king spent the early evening eating supper at the royal dining hall with his family and a few courtiers. Even the melancholy prince, Jaïem was present, though he did not eat much or say much. He liked that the hall was silent. But then Ylia began to coddle the king. She fed him from off of her plate and ate off of his. A buzz rose now about matters of court.

Several courtiers remarked how well prince Hovin acquitted himself against mighty Taldeion. Talk began about how outstanding the king's children were in temperament and conduct. Having had more than a few draughts of wine to ease his worries, the king spoke more freely than Jaïem would have liked.

"Jaïem-" the king said, "Why have you, one of the most beautiful flowers in my flourishing garden wilted so? I hear that the frost of winter has not thawed for you as of yet."

"My lord-" Jaïem replied. "I am surprised that the king, my father, gives ear to idle gossip. The court's gossipers have merely misconstrued my newfound commitment to martial training for melancholy. I am sure that the king would agree that a prince should leave frolicking and music making for fools and performers, and resign himself to nobler pursuits."

The king smiled, and shifting in his chair, he lifted a crystal goblet ensconced in silver and gulped down another draught of wine.

"I urge you not to shun those gentler pursuits that make men of your breeding bearable to others. Develop as many aspects of yourself as may please those who love you."

The king paused and looked around the large dining table and smiled again.

"Never has a father looked upon his children and felt as much satisfaction. My son, you said that I have given ear to idle gossip. If that is so, it is only to soothe my longing for my children's audience, who are the stars that illumine the darkening skies of my waning years. I delight in your virtues more than ever now that I am nearing the twilight of my life. Now that you are strong, and your will even stronger, you exult in your youth and venture out on your own and never bother to inquire about your father. You leave him to strain his ear and listen to the chatter of servants and courtiers to learn of your comings and goings."

Smiling, Ylia rose up from her seat, which was closest to her father and embraced him. The king smiled and his face flushed, and those present smiled with him.

"Come now father," Ylia purred. "Your children are not as aloof and callous as you say. Your bedchambers are adorned with fresh flowers from your garden and burning incense, which I have placed for your enjoyment. How often have I seen you taking walks with young Jaïem and Hovin? And before you sent your masterly son Varenhil to Greingspen to secure that region, he was ever in tow and at your disposal."

The king and his audience finished their meal and spoke for a little while longer, and drank fresh water mixed with honey and mint leaves. Gentle laughter could be heard around the great wooden table. The king motioned for his guards after a while, and rose to leave the dining hall. His guests followed behind into a beautifully adorned antechamber where they sat on plush couches and spoke long into the early evening.

Jaïem was too weary of the chatter to remain and withdrew without anyone seeing him. He returned to his bedchamber and pondered on his last conversation with Promothos, who seemed to be getting stronger. The young prince had returned to him even though he said he would not. Now even in the solitude of his bedchambers, he could hear Promothos' thoughts, and sense his anguish, which was growing more and more vivid and intense.

Jaïem wondered if the mysterious sage was getting stronger. Then it occurred to him that Owidobel the librarian could hold the answer to this and other questions. He determined to go to see Owidobel and question him about Promothos.

Jaïem threw on a dark cloak and left his bedchamber on that moonlit night. Jaïem wandered out of the royal compound and out to the temple to find Owidobel. He did not go far before he saw the old librarian shuffling off toward the temple's arched gates leading out into the city. Jaïem resolved to follow him to his destination.

Jaïem followed the old librarian out of the temple quadrangle and watched as he waited for and then boarded a horse drawn carriage. The carriage rode off and Jaïem ran out after it. The young prince looked around frantically for a horse. He was relieved to see saw a young boy leading a mule with several sacks slung across its back in the opposite direction.

Jaïem scampered toward the young boy as the temple guards patrolling the causeway above the arch looked on curiously. He overtook the young boy and his mule and pulled back the hood of his cloak.

"Citizen-" he said panting. "A prince of Chamiahce has need of your service."

The young boy looked up and stared blankly at the prince.

"Here!" Jaïem said in exasperation. "Take this silver necklace and buy two mules with it."

Suddenly the prince felt a strong hand on his shoulder. Turning around abruptly the prince's eyes flashed with anger.

"My lord," the Harfingal guard said hesitantly. "Please forgive my impudence. If there is anything I can do, I would be glad to assist you."

Jaïem took a deep breath and checked his anger.

"Give me your short sword and your belt," he said. The young boy hid behind the mule. Jaïem threw the sacks off of the animal and mounted it, holding on to a rope around its neck.

"My lord, please allow me to get you a good horse…"

Jaïem kicked the mule and hustled off after the carriage, which was quite some distance away heading east on the city's major thoroughfare.

Hunched over, Jaïem rode on the mule with his legs dangling. He was able to keep the carriage within view, as it was traveling rather leisurely toward the center of the city. Soon the carriage turned off of the major thoroughfare and rode south to the merchant sector where the metic guilds built many great halls and obelisks.

The carriage passed by many strong brick houses with high gates and a large stepped tower rising up almost as high as the temple. It proceeded into a roundabout and then headed east along a narrow cobblestone road. Finally, the carriage stopped adjacent to a building site flanked by a small quarry.

The carriage remained stationary for a while and so Jaïem positioned himself and his mule beside a pile of stone blocks. Soon a second carriage arrived behind the old librarian's carriage. A hooded man dismounted the second carriage holding what appeared to Jaïem to be a small clay ewer. The hooded man entered the old librarian's carriage.

The hooded man sat beside the old librarian and handed him the small ewer.

"Here is the instaureum," the hooded man said, handing the small ewer to Owidobel.

"I will take it to him tonight when the priestesses and the other surplicants are gathered around the Kuriox for their evening prayers. Are you certain that you used the proper ingredients and that you brewed it under a blue flame?"

Hidden in the shadows, a cloaked man sitting next to the old librarian placed a hand on his arm.

"Are you sure that the flasks you brought us contained water from the primordial pool beneath the temple?"

The old librarian nodded. "Yes of course, and it was a perilous descent beyond the depths of the catacombs. Your master seemed to know the way very well."

The cloaked man grabbed Owidobel's arm tightly and the old librarian winced.

"Be certain not to let your curiosity get the best of you. Do not take the instaureum for yourself. Do not drink it. It will kill you. Only the master can drink it."

The two men suddenly noticed that the horses were startled. The hooded man leapt from the old librarian's carriage and the old librarian's carriage abruptly sped away.

The hooded man remained behind looking around frantically. He inspected the building site where great wooden cranes and hoists and piles of wood and blocks of stone were kept. Walking around to look into the shadows, he thought he heard the sound of heavy breathing.

The hooded man reached into the folds of his cloak and drew out a long dagger. The sound led him to piles of stone blocks along the street stacked higher than the height of a tall man. Just as the hooded man came around the street side of the stone blocks, he was struck by a mule and fell flat on his back.

The mule hurried away as the hooded man struggled to his feet. Sighing, he sheathed his dagger and continued around the perimeter of the stone blocks. Satisfied that the mule was a rampant work animal left at the building site, the hooded man turned to board his carriage. From just below a pile of stone blocks he looked out to the street and gasped. He blinked and strained to see his coachman lying in the street in a pool of blood.

Short sword in hand, Jaïem now glared down at the hooded man from atop a pile of stone blocks. He felt an uncontrollable urge to pounce. He could see the hooded man's lifeless body before him. A familiar voice whispered to him.

"He is yours…"

Jaïem leapt from his vantage point just as the hooded man whirled around and evaded him. Sensing that his enemy was startled, the young prince at once unleashed a ferocious attack with his short sword. The hooded man skillfully evaded, drew his dagger again, and countered with a few deft thrusts. Jaïem stumbled back. Quickly regaining his composure, he looked for a decisive strike.

The opportunity came sooner than Jaïem could have hoped. Jaïem evaded an enemy thrust and his enemy stumbled. Jaïem seized his opponent's arm and simultaneously disjointed the arm from its shoulder socket. Groaning, the hooded man fell to his knees. Without hesitation, Jaïem finished his enemy with thrust to the base of his neck.

Prince Jaïem returned to the royal compound as the evening celebrations were winding down. He was physically weary but strangely excited. He returned the short sword, wiped clean from his encounter, to a Harfingal now standing guard above the archway.

Making his way to the royal compound and to his bedchamber, the young prince thought contentedly about his dispatch of the hooded man at the building site. He had never slain a man before, but the act seemed eerily familiar. He felt at ease and relieved. As he reached his bedchamber, his thoughts shifted seamlessly to the librarian, and then to his qualms about Besia and Hovin.

"You fool!" he thought.

"Your resentment of Hovin is revealed. Adventure will not mend your heart. I fear nothing can ease my resentment and pain. I will never be as loved and admired as my dark-haired brother. Besia belongs to him.

I am hopelessly bound to my fate. But I must continue to try to find something that brings me satisfaction. I will pursue to this Promothos mystery and uncover what else is hidden in the temple's dungeons. For tonight I will sleep and hope that her face does not haunt me again... So many thoughts haunt me."

Jaïem slept as well as he could that night. There would be no sleep however for Jaïem's brother Hovin. Under the cool light of the moon cast over the eastern sky, Hovin sat motionless before the beacon, huddled in a thick blanket. He calmly awaited the judgment of the mysterious inhabitants of the beacon. Now and then, his thoughts wandered to his father's words to him. He thought also of Besia and how beautiful and temperate she was. He tried to keep his thoughts in the present moment, but many soothing thoughts passed through his mind like a cool breeze from the sea.

His body seemed replenished from his duel with mighty Taldeion earlier in the day, as the court's best physicians had tended to him long after the crowds had moved on and returned to the city. He still felt some pain, especially on his left thigh where he had sustained a deep gash from one of Taldeion's attacks. This wound was now wrapped and treated with herbs and honey. Now rising to his feet, he looked up at what he thought was the sparkling tail of a shooting star.

Hovin stood back from the beacon to get a better view of the night sky. The phenomenon seemed to pass so quickly though. Just as he brought his gaze back down to earth, the great double doors into the Namreddin's beacon opened slowly, revealing an impenetrable blackness within.

A cool gust blew out from the bowels of the beacon and made Hovin shudder. He was suddenly afflicted with a sense of loneliness and smallness. His thoughts of his father, his brothers, and his beloved Besia left him like happy children fleeing a shadow. He looked around as if looking for a sign. Should he enter into the beacon? Or should he flee along with his thoughts back to the high city.

The trees were silent and all living things seemed to suspend their transient works. Hovin was alone, and the blackness within the beacon neither beckoned him nor repelled him. As he stared at the open doors, he heard a whispering voice in his mind, reminding him to listen to his heart. But my heart says nothing he thought as he felt himself being absorbed by the unfathomable silence. Only the courage instilled in him through his disciplined life as a king's son and as the captain of the Harfingals kept him from looking away to the comforting routine and simplicity of his life in the Hold. Back in the city, everyone loved him. His strength and skill were equal to every challenge. However this was a new and unfamiliar challenge. He could not know what the beacon held in store for him. If he left then, he could return to those who loved him and he was sure that no one would fault him for not entering the beacon. He had already proven his mettle many times. He had triumphed over the challenges of Wind's Crucible.

There was no turning back though; this was his destiny. Wind's blood ran through his veins. He had to take his rightful place in the pantheon of the Vyrdmar. As a prince, Nnyreinin was said to have entered the beacon and returned to his people with the aura of the Celestial all around him. But Nnyreinin took the beacon's secrets with him to the dark banks of the netherworld. There at the beacon, Hovin could not find solace in the shadow of his mighty ancestor's prestige. There was no promise in the past. There was only the present, and that present was impenetrable shadow unless he could find a way to bring forth light.

There was however a glint of hope and strength. Hovin could feel his father's eyes; he could hear his voice. He could not dishonor him with weakness and failure. His sense of duty and honor spurred him forward. His father was saying that to be a Vyrdmar prince is to walk an uncommon and difficult path. You must know in your heart that your courage will be a light unto the world, and it shall his father once said. When doors open walk through them and within will be the hospitality reserved for princes. And so, with his heritage and his courage coursing through his very being, Ylarin's son, prince Hovin, captain of the Harfingal, entered Namreddin's beacon, and into the unknown.

The doors shut soundlessly behind him. As suddenly as Hovin entered the beacon, a small space became illumined with a dim light a short distance from him. Now Hovin could see three red balls bobbing beyond the arc of light. He could hear what sounded like sharp metal cutting through stone. The sound made him cringe. Then, straining his eyes, Hovin saw a figure rise from behind the corona of light. He saw the silhouette of a winged creature with red eyes.

"Come forth!" the creature commanded with a piercing voice. "You see me now in the light of the beacon. Not the benevolent Celestial with silvery wings of your fathers. You may call me Acerefon. I am the scourge of men. My fangs and my claws are stained with blood. My purpose is simple and brutal. I yearn always to cleave, break, and gnaw on flesh and bone."

Acerefon, as he called himself, paused as if to savor the memories of all the flesh he had devoured. Hovin felt his strength ebbing from his body.

"You are sinewy and succulent," Acerefon remarked. I will dice you into fine morsels. No. No. No. I will let your blood flow slowly. I will lick your blood until you are faint. Then I will devour your flesh when it is cold, firm, and gristly,"

When Hovin's eyes adjusted to the light, he could clearly see a tall figure with a hard gleaming outer skeleton with sharp serrated barbs. Its elongated head featured three round eyes that were now black, three curved horns and barbs jutting out from the crown of its angular head. Its mouth opened to reveal a cluster of protruding fangs powered by bulging jaws and cartilage lining its strong neck. A long forked tongue wagged every now and then between its menacing fangs. Its armored appendages were of equal length and protruded from its short armored core. Almost every contour of Acerefon's body was sharp and purposed to shed blood and inflict pain.

Acerefon snapped its tongue and lumbered forward to seize Hovin. Yet just as it reached out for Hovin, it disappeared. A gust of wind blew past the prince. He felt a sharp pain as claws tore through his thick cloak and tunic, shredding his shoulder. Hovin groaned and fell to the ground.

"Delightful!" Acerefon mused. "Your contortions fill me with great joy my sweet prince. Show me all the ways in which men can writhe and bend and moan and cry out."

Acerefon returned to the shadows to stalk Hovin again. Hovin rose and turned round and round, but he could not detect his stalker. The prince felt another gust. Now serrated barbs cut him across the back of his leg. He fell again, groaning in pain.

"You fall so easily," Acerefon sneered. "Rise Vyrdmar prince for I have not had my fill of amusement with you. As I told you, I thirst for more than your flesh and your blood. I want you to suffer and to cry out in agony. I want you to cry for mercy, even though you will have none."

Hovin slowly rose to his feet and swung wildly from side to side, with his arms flailing. His mind too was flailing for a tactic against this inhuman foe. He could see its red eyes here and there, as if disappearing and reappearing throughout the unfathomable shadow of the beacon.

"Enough pricking," Acerefon hissed. "Even now you dare to hope that you will withstand me. You are arrogant and stupid. You gaze upon the judgment of immortals and dare to contemplate victory. Do not dare to cling to hope. You will die because your death brings me satisfaction. Perhaps if you satisfy in another way, you may save your life. Perhaps if you plead to me for mercy, like you plead to your gods or to the Celestial, I will relent. If you do not plead for mercy, I will mete out the scourge of many battles upon you."

Hovin was struck again and again with barbs and claws and fangs until rivulets of blood ran from wounds on every inch of his body. He whirled this way and that way. He fell and rose many times. No single wound was deep or fatal. The pain was unbearable, but the taunts and his sense of utter powerlessness were worse.

"Cry out for mercy and your scourge will end."

Hovin did not cry out. All he had now was his courage and his dignity and he was determined to hold on to these until death veiled his eyes. And so, Hovin kept his silence and fell slowly into darkness. But the darkness would be brief.

Hovin was awakened to the sound of a gentle voice calling out from the distance.

He now found himself in a dark pit. He could hear a voice coming from above saying "Your fathers and the immortals they submit to have betrayed you. They have turned their backs to the fealty and love you have freely given. Surely you want to come up out of this pit. Renounce your fear of the dogma of your fathers and embrace the wonderful and cathartic apostasy calling out to you. Reject them all, and let me bring you up from this pit before death claims you."

There was a brief silence and then the voice echoed again.

"Good prince, listen to me. Your life is too precious to cast aside for these old men. Hovin then heard a chorus of beautiful voices chanting:

Forsake these old men with walking sticks
Huffing and puffing and clamoring against old
foes
And clasping with trembling hands at
Old parchments decreeing venerated truths
As their vision and strength ebb and
Matters of legacy sap their courage
As they cower in houses built of
The ashen bones of giants with their eyes
Tearing in the glare of a new day waxing
That hour of their waning
Which young princes with their noble
Powers extinguished
Will never see because their hearts were
Endeared to the industry of death
Just so that old men with walking sticks
Huffing and puffing may have their last
Hurrah.

"Beautiful prince," Hovin heard the first voice
whisper. "Your body is now wracked with pain from an
awful scourge. Death draws near to steal you away
from us. Call out now and say only, I renounce you O'
Irilsflir. Become an apostate and embrace a new life.
Renounce Irilsflir and I will give you my hand and save
you."

Yet the gentle voices had no lure for prince
Hovin. He was resigned to his fate for he thought it
justice that he should perish. Awful horns and barbs
and claws and fangs had overwhelmed him and he was
vanquished. Now, with his life force ebbing, and unable
to stand and fight, he thought only of his dishonor,
wishing that he could rise again and battle death itself.
And since Hovin replied only with groans of anguish
and then resignation, the voices became more distant
and went away, leaving the Vyrdmar prince to the void;
but again only briefly.

The prince awakened again as if death was now
taunting him, permitting him to linger and dangle from a

weak thread of life. Now his eyes opened and he seemed to be lying in a hall engulfed in white mist. A frail old woman calling herself Faena was kneeling over him sprinkling water over his body. When Hovin opened his mouth to speak, she gestured for him to be silent.

"You are restored," she whispered. "Someone who loved you was taken in your stead."

Hovin's eyes glared. Who would have done such a thing he wondered, and why? He tried to speak but the woman placed a hand over his mouth.

"I know you are wondering who could have done such a thing. He was lord Acerefon's servant, and when he witnessed your courage, he pleaded with his lord to spare your life. Acerefon turned to him, eyes flashing with malice and said: 'since you dare to reproach your master, I will slay you and spare this Vyrdmar prince."

The old woman arose and walked away toward a crystal stair spiraling up into a hall of polished white stone encrusted with stalagmite. Hovin struggled to his feet and looked down to discover that his white tunic and his entire body seemed untouched by the scourge he thought he had suffered. He followed the old woman up the spiraling stair and looked up to see a shimmering hall. It was circular and wide and candles were lit all around.

The hall was aglow with a soft candent light. Now Hovin walked on a pure white polished stone cut into large squares. He looked around him and saw that columns of white stone supported arches overlooking the sea on one side. Stalagmite and clusters of white crystal jutted liberally from the walls and out of the ground. In the center of the hall lay a small child with dark hair, covered up to his shoulders in a linen cloth, which was soiled with blood. The old woman walked closer to the child but not close enough to touch him. She knelt before the child and prostrated herself.

"I honor your compassion and courage little one. Perhaps in your passing your spirit will rise above the shadow of death. For in forfeiting your life, you saved a life. Surely you will be given in equal measure, that which was freely given."

Hovin suddenly shuddered uncontrollably as he saw the boy lying there still and bloodied for his sake. He tried to compose himself, but the vaunted stoicism of the Vyrdmar forsook him, and he wept. He walked slowly toward where the old woman was kneeling with her head bowed low so that her chest almost touched the ground.

"I too will honor you little one," Hovin whispered. "I will suffer that my knees touch the ground for your sake and in remembrance of you. For not even the spirits of my fathers came to me in the shadowy pit I was lifted from."

Hovin knelt beside the old woman and asked "What was his name so that I may address him and honor him as you are?"

The old woman looked up and gazed into Hovin's gray eyes. "This little servant did not have a name; dread Acerefon only called him servant."

Hovin prostrated himself before the boy with no name and thanked him with all of his heart. In that moment his heart ached for the nameless boy. He wished he could fall back into the void, if only that could restore the little innocent's life.

"I had never imagined that there was so much power in compassion," he thought. "Only now are my eyes opened to the hidden strength of even children."

Hovin could feel the wavering power of scattered hopes ebbing in dark and barren places in nearby and distant lands. His heart warmed to the small and voiceless innocents who suffered brutal alienation from the light of hope, wonder, and peace. Then he heard a hollow voice echo in his mind.

"Rise Vyrdmar prince and look upon the master of hosts."

Hovin looked up and saw a soft ethereal and silvery flame where the boy's body once was. The arc of the flame spread and drenched the room in its silvery luminescence.

"You have triumphed over your fear and your pride. You have opened your heart to the anguish and pain of the powerless. You have bent your strong back before the gentle healer and submitted to your heart's counsel. You have given that which you were given.

Now you are awakened and can see. Behold! There in your heart is where the Celestial sows the seed of transcendent life, which draws all to it. This seed will not grow in a heart quivering with fear, hardened by pride, and bereft of compassion. Where this seed is sown and grows, that host will be seized with power over the sentiments that cast a shadow over his time.

Rise now, for your strong and compassionate heart has overcome the fear of the shadow of the unknown, of pain, of death, and of submission. You have seen the light of the Celestial, and have seen His mercy, and have been restored. Go forth and stand as a beacon to your people, that the Vyrdmar may not fear what is to come, whether it is the greatest scourge, or death itself. Go to them, and those who are pure of heart will follow you because you reflect the light of the Celestial."

Chapter 9: Encounters on the caravan road

The wagon rode north and then west all through the night. Ahktel could not sleep where he lay huddled in the covered rear cab. It was not that he could not sleep through the creaking and cracking sounds or the jostling and shaking. He was exhausted, as were the others, who were sleeping soundly around him. Ahktel's mind simply would not rest. He thought of home and of his adventures. Then after just a little sleep, he awoke again from a dream.

He was quite familiar with these dreams by now. He'd had them since he was a child. These dreams were not the normal sort that one forgets after one awakens. Ahktel called these dreams walking dreams because when he had them he felt as if he was not asleep at all, but awake and walking and experiencing events.

No matter his perspective, his experience was very vivid and actual. What he saw seemed real and often, but not always, the events in dreams unfolded right before his very eyes later while he was certainly awake.

Ahktel realized that he had seen the men who attacked the company back at the grove in a dream. He also saw men like them gathering for what appeared to be a momentous undertaking. Perhaps they were planning another attack on the company while they slept in the wagon given to them by a kind and generous merchant they encountered on the caravan trail.

Lately, Ahktel began hearing thoughts too. He was a fly on the wall of their inner being as well as their surroundings. Beginning with dull crackling sound he would appear in places and not know where he was or what he was doing there. He could walk, or drift in his dreams. He did not know if he could speak because he never tried. He did not seem to think that speaking would be a practical thing to do.

The Agon Xri from Ahktel's village Sephtu in the Eptare region of Irsei used to say that there were people born into the world who were neither here nor there, real or incorporeal; they were both. He wondered if he was one of these people whom the Agon Xri, the diviners of his country, called Etas-pael whisperers.

The diviners rarely spoke of the whisperers, and when they did, their expression was terse. They come and go, they would say. They warn us of dark times and lead us to the light. Look for them in the children. Look for the signs. Call the child before a gathering of the Agon Xri. Beat the drums and his spirit nature will be revealed.

Ahktel had memories of standing in the center of a large gathering surrounding him like trees encircling an oasis. Ahktel was poised and at peace even when he heard the sound of drums and the wails of the gathering tramping around him. His heartbeat and the ebb and flow of his consciousness were synchronized with the drumbeat. His mind was a steady stream.

Ahktel startled up from a dream and looked around. Ixhor, who was huddled next to him yawned and shifted away. Eje was sound asleep nearby. He pulled aside the flap opening into the coachman's bench and peered up at Bojingren, and Tyeshar who steered the wagon.

"How much longer," he asked awkwardly, trying to use some of the phrases he learned in the common tongue of Maspeidon.

Bojingren thought for a while. "Two days," Bojingren replied, putting up two fingers.

Ahktel nodded and closed the flaps and tried to go back to sleep. He rested his back against a beam along the covered cab and shut his eyes. He wondered where Ligia was now, and where she came from to begin with. She was the most remarkable woman he had ever seen; more remarkable even than his own mother, who was a village elder.

"A sorceress no doubt," he decided.

Thoughts of Ligia and the adventures of the recent days occupied Ahktel's mind for awhile until he finally fell into a deep sleep.

The clear and radiant dawn came too soon. Ahktel awoke to the sound of his companions talking in hushed voices.

Ixhor looked at Ahktel and smiled.

"You are the only pastoral man I know who does not spring up in the morning."

Ahktel mumbled something and closed his eyes. The horse drawn wagon had stopped by a gentle stream and the companions filled their water flasks. They built a fire and poured water into small pots and made a stew, which they ate with bread as hard as rocks. They dipped pieces of bread into the stew, which they ate in wooden bowls. After they had eaten their morning meal, the companions resumed their push west to the high city of Chamiahce.

By midday the company could see the snowy peaks of the Aeisus Mountains to the north. Bojingren peered back through the flaps saying, "We are now passing into the plains of Yarlpirel."

The mostly paved caravan trail was now flanked on both sides with an embankment, which was sometimes very steep. Patches of thick underbrush dotted the mostly grassy landscape to the horizon. Now that Bojingren steered the wagon alone, Eje crawled through the flap into the coachman's bench and spoke with him.

"You should rest," a haggard Bojingren's said.

"Yet you have barely rested at all since we began," she replied somberly. "My lord Bojingren, I am truly thankful to you. I will never forget your strength and courage."

Bojingren smiled wearily. He was still lamenting his judgment to take the company off of the caravan trail and into the wild.

"Mistress, I am a soldier. I have always wanted to be a soldier. I have always wanted to serve the lord I now serve. It is a difficult life. It is difficult to mourn those who have fallen. But this life also brings me fulfillment."

Eje sat with Bojingren long into the afternoon. She asked him about the high city. Bojingren described the city reverently and spoke of its king and his mighty sons, foremost of among them was the crown prince Varenhil, who was also lord of Greingspen, a stronghold farther north. When she asked what these men looked like, Bojingren smiled.

"The men of Gaalden are varied," he began. "But the Vyrdmar are the noblest among them. The Vyrdmar, it is said, are descended from Breix, twin brother of Bruix. Both were godlike. Their limbs are long and lithe and their eyes bright and full of the light of Yggir. They are masterful and just. Their minds are keen, and yet their hearts are filled with goodwill."

Having met Hovin, Bojingren could very well have been describing that noble Vyrdmar prince. That prince had returned to the high city since late in the morning. He was weary and despondent as he was cheered and mobbed by a large throng following him all the way to the arched gates of the temple quadrangle. Many Harfingals saluted and fell in around him and followed him into the temple. Hovin remained there kneeling before Yggir's pool. Priestesses in white robes and surplicants looked on as he remained motionless and solemn for quite some time. Then suddenly, he rose up, and walked out of the temple. Outside, many of his Harfingals had gathered. When they saw him, they surrounded him, looking on solemnly. Macheleion, Hovin's lieutenant waded through the throng and embraced his captain. Then as the two men walked arm in arm to the royal compound, the weary prince collapsed.

Prince Hovin was taken to his bedchamber and laid to rest comfortably on his bed. News of his return had spread and there was a buzz throughout the royal compound. Ylia ran to announce the good news to Jaïem and Varenhil. When she arrived at the king's bedchambers, and shuffled past the two Harfingals standing guard before the large wooden double doors, she heard the short incisive notes of plucked strings of the harpistar. She ran to her father's study and saw him sitting at his ornate wooden harpistar console.

"Father," she called out. "Your son has returned victorious from the beacon."

The king paused and turned to look upon her and smiled. Then he continued playing. Sighing, she approached him and sat on a wooden bench next to him.

"Come and look upon your son." The king paused again.

"Go to him in my stead my beautiful daughter. There will be time enough for me to see him. There will be a more appropriate time. Tell me though. Have you seen him?"

"No," Ylia answered. "But the servants say though he is weary, he looks as if he had spent the last days bathing in the springs of Galasur."

"Very well," the king said softly. The king paused for a while and then held Ylia's hand and kissed her cheek. "Go to him Ylia."

Meanwhile Varenhil and Jaïem stood with many Harfingals holding an early vigil at Hovin's bedside. Hovin was now sleeping peacefully. His face was serene and breathing gentle and steady.

"Faithful Harfingal," Varenhil finally said to them. "Mind your duties. Your prince would find fault with you if he knew that you had abandoned your watches and posts on his account. He is safe now in the royal apartments. Physicians have been summoned and servants are at the ready with food and drink. Therefore, be at ease. Our brother is in the fold now, and when he has recouped his strength we will all celebrate his triumph together."

The Harfingals bowed and left Hovin with his brothers who along with Ylia, the king's personal physician Sadrek, and several servants tended to the exhausted prince throughout the day. By early evening, after his brothers had left, Hovin awoke and looked around him. Seeing his sister Ylia, he sat up and smiled.

There were however those within the walls of the royal compound and temple, who thought nothing of the Harfingal prince's ordeal. The old librarian was one such person. Owidobel could now be found hunched forward in a plain wooden chair in a large alcove in the catacombs. A thick curtain was drawn to provide him with some appreciable solitude because he was above all a private man even in his work. This room was where the old librarian worked on, and bound his own accounts and observations.

The priestesses did not at all condone this practice, but the librarians tended to do this notwithstanding. Since all written accounts and folios of even a personal nature had to remain in the temple, some writing was casually permitted. However, the old librarian was not writing his memoirs. He was mulling over the nature of the Instaureum. He drew close to a wooden workbench and placed a small pouch down on it. He unbound it and removed its content, a small clay jar. He then produced a small flask, which he had already thoroughly cleaned and poured some of the liquid contents of the jar into it through a small funnel. The old librarian paused after he had done this, and he peered over at yet another flask he had prepared, and biting his lip, he thought for a while.

The Instaureum he now possessed was an elixir of lore. The sages among the Ayimar wrote that the Instaureum was the secret elixir of immortality and now he had it in his grasp. The elixir greatly extended life and accelerated cognition. It was said that the Atenari masters used the Instaureum. However, very few men knew its secrets. Even if they had discovered its secrets, no man would dare drink it because it was said to cause immediate death to mortals. Only the Atenari masters, who were mostly annihilated by the Cepheid, Breix and Bruix, knew the ingredients used to make it and used it. Some historians believed that the Ayimar lord Promothos, the last of the Atenari masters, had shared the secret of the Instaureum with his most trusted adherents, who used it in diluted and small quantities.

Owidobel wondered if Promothos was actually the Atenari lord spoken of by the Vyrdmar sages. He was said to have been the great benefactor of the Atenarix and the most powerful figure in the world. When the last winter was drawing near, men from that order who knew of Promothos asked Owidobel if he had ever heard of him. The old librarian said he had not. They said that this Promothos was real and that, long ago, he was in fact imprisoned in the catacombs for composing heretical works. Worse, he had inspired a revolt by the Ayimar below the Pelares and was turning the Atenarix against their royal patrons in Maspeidon.

Owidobel however, was convinced that if there was a Promothos, he had perished long ago, and was not held in the catacombs. As the temple librarian, he thought he would have discovered where Promothos was kept because he was familiar with every inch of that dark labyrinth. Furthermore, Promothos and his Ayimar followers were annihilated long ago. If Promothos was held in the catacombs, it would now be his tomb. Yet the Atenarix knew something of the catacomb's layout. Owidobel was curious about this, and also about any secret knowledge these men could impart. Therefore, he met with the Atenarix at their pyramidal hall out in the city now and then to exchange information and also for purposes not revealed to his hosts.

The old librarian thought he was cunning and duplicitous. He reported to the high priestess that the Atenarix had approached him. The high priestess instructed him to continue to meet with the Atenarix and to report to her. He did this, but never told her of their plot to restore the mysterious Promothos, who was purported to be wasting away in the catacombs. The old librarian gave the priestess information he insisted the Atenarix begrudgingly shared. For example, he said they revealed a recipe to remedy the incessant coughing and sneezing commonly suffered by surplicants who administered the temple library. Owidobel told the priestess that the Atenarix gave him a remedy for the surplicant germ as it was called and in return the Atenarix required him to search for specific manuscripts of interest from the piles in the catacombs.

Owidobel's reports were mostly fabricated. He harbored a secret antipathy for the Vyrdmar and priestess. His life in the temple library was at the root of his interest in the Atenarix and his diminished fealty to Irilsflir. Manuscripts were not placed in the temple library for others to read, but to be concealed and hidden from others who may have wanted to read them. His life's work was antithetical to his creed as a librarian.

Owidobel often mused over his new role in the deception between Irilsflir and the Atenarix. But as he saw it, he was engaged in a heroic endeavor. Irilsflir, the temple and institution he was bound to serve, censored all written manuscripts not approved by the Urdar and the king. Illicit manuscripts were either hidden away in the library or destroyed. Owidobel found the practice of hoarding and destroying manuscripts and other written expression irrational and excessive. All written expression was composed in the ancient Vyrdmar tongue, and yet none, except the most skilled and trusted scribes and viziers, were literate in that tongue. Why hoard and destroy books most would never read.

The common tongue was a phonetic language never expressed in writing. There were of course many who learned to write in the ancient tongue, and yet others who formulated varying versions of an illicit system of symbols and expression. And so many secretly wrote manuscripts, which, once discovered by the Urdar, were confiscated and taken to the temple catacombs, and their authors imprisoned or put to death.

Owidobel reasoned that the Vyrdmar were depriving thoughtful men of life after death through expression. He believed that denying men of the experiences of inspired authors doomed men to ignorance and oblivion.

Yet he appreciated the advantages being the librarian presented. He had access to manuscripts that even the most learned schoolmasters in the academies, did not. His tenure as temple librarian was therefore a hidden boon and a time of discovery. However, his interest in heretical works was not singularly peaked until he spoke with agents of the Atenarix. They revealed a new world of useful knowledge he never knew existed, and which was not fully explored by the manuscripts he reviewed in the temple library.

As a surplicant, he was supposed to be inclined to believe that knowledge was an instrument of mischief to be hoarded and hidden away. The Atenarix opened his eyes to the written word's hidden purpose. They explained the development of ideas and their spoken and written exegesis and expression, as a conversation or a discussion of problems. According to the Atenarix, if problems are not discussed, and the ensuing dialogue recorded, men would not effectively solve their problems. They opined that reliance on the magnanimity of the immortals had its limits, and was itself a grave problem. Consider, they pointed out, if a child was never weaned off of his parent's care? Such a child would never mature and would quickly follow his parents in death because he does not know how to solve his own problems and survive.

Now Owidobel too was absorbed by a conversation about an existential dilemma. His was a dilemma that filled him both with great anticipation and apprehension. He was told of a world he never knew. He was shown a door leading into that world, and given a key, but told that he dare not use it on the pain of death. Was this merely Atenarix hypocrisy and deceit? Were they keeping him from the apotheosis they told him should be man's destiny, and which he now longed for? The Atenarix were accusatory of the high priestess of Yggir. They said she hid away knowledge beneath the catacombs of Irilsflir and stood between man and his purpose. Perhaps however, the Atenarix too did not want him to taste the power the Vyrdmar regime kept from him. Perhaps they merely wanted him to know that this transcendence existed only so that he would distrust Irilsflir and reject their laws. Then the Atenarix could manipulate his distrust and use him as a paw to strengthen their hand.

Owidobel poured the last content of the ewer into the second flask. The flasks, which were small enough to pass through the small porthole into Promothos' cell, were ready. He was instructed to take one to Promothos and he was to keep one in a safe place on the eventuality that one flask was destroyed or Promothos requested a second dose. Yet was that the second flask's actual purpose? Owidobel placed one of the flasks in a pocket and went to his small bedchamber and hid the other in a strong wooden chest bound with a chain wrapped around it many times and secured with several small locks. Owidobel then made his way back down to Promothos' cell.

He made his way down deep into the catacombs with a lantern to light his way through the impenetrable darkness. He passed through a tunnel and followed it to a circular landing leading to a narrow stairway. Owidobel followed his normal route to an octagonal outlet, and through a hidden passage leading to Promothos' cell. He descended down some narrow stairs that spiraled down and down into an archway flanked on one side by a massive iron reinforced wooded door with a lever bolted to a dial. He looked through the cell's barred porthole and called out to its prisoner.

"Master Promothos," he called out in a hushed voice. "I have returned with your sweets."

Owidobel heard the sliding of feet and belabored breathing. Then Promothos' scared and gaunt face appeared beyond the porthole with his eyes glowing yellow.

"Wise librarian," Promothos answered. "I have been eagerly anticipating your return. Your reward will be great. Now bring the Instaureum to me. Soon I will recover much of my knowledge and power. Surely my imprisonment will be much more bearable then, and in return I will reveal my knowledge to you."

The old librarian looked into Promothos' eyes, and hesitatingly, lifted the flask of Instaureum up to the porthole. Long bony fingers slid up and wrapped around the flask, and it was gone.

"You have done well. Go in peace for now, and return in a few days. I will be restored by then and will be eager to begin restoring to you and those who have sent you, that which was taken away."

On the plains of Yarlpirel, Bojingren was beginning to feel a sense of ease he had not felt since he left Bonthc. He was now certain that the danger had passed. The company passed a post manned by a detachment of Gaaldenian sentries earlier in the day. Now the caravan trail was lined by evergreens and stone posts. At posts manned by sentries were great arches connecting small barrack houses on each sides of the road. At a second of such posts where fresh horses were kept, the company left behind their wagon and proceeded on horseback. By early evening the company reached yet another post where they rested for the night.

The companions awoke early the next morning and continued their journey in earnest, riding west with the sun at their backs. They passed yet another post and stopped briefly. The afternoon sun was glaring and intense, but the companions pressed on through the afternoon.

Much later, as the day waned, a threat was unfolding not far from the companions. From a peak overlooking the plains, three avarathein pushed off with their two powerful scaly appendages and caught a warm current with their leathery wings and flew into the darkening sky. They set off from a lonely crag and master Nausterus, remaining behind, urged them forward, his eyes flashing and his mouth uttering incantations. The avarathein uttered blood-curdling squawks and screeches and sped away with their master Nausterus exhorting them all the while. Down on the plains of Yarlpirel, the unsuspecting companions galloped with renewed purpose and speed. They could see the ridges guarding Chamiahce's eastern ramparts, and Bojingren was determined to reach the city before nightfall of the following day. Now on the caravan road, which was patrolled by Gaaldenian sentries, Bojingren shed his anxieties about journeying at night.

The way to Chamiahce was now charmed with clear moonlit skies, and cool mountain breezes from the Aeisus'. If only there were more ominous signs, like foreboding clouds had sweeping in from the sea. Perhaps then the companions would have been more vigilant. No one, not even Bojingren thought to look back at the eastern sky. Ahktel did not dream of these three specks in the sky that soon loomed large and dreadful with great leathery wings and sharp talons.

Yet as the avarathein began their rise from which they would make their freefall and snatch their prey, Ahktel felt a breeze passing behind his ear and up into his nostrils. Almost instantly, the watchful herder brought his horse about and turned to face the oncoming scourge. He sounded the herders' cry used alert the Xedun patrols on the plains when poachers and wild beasts threatened the herd. Ixhor came about to answer Ahktel's call with his javelin held shoulder high.

Reaching the apex of their steep climb, the avarathein came about and began to plummet down to earth. Bojingren shouted, "Dismount and scatter into a circle and aim true with your arrows for the first avarathein."

Bojingren's men began to maneuver form a crude circle. Ahktel and Ixhor followed in kind with Eje staying close to Ahktel. As the avarathein plummeted, the companions heard loud dull sounds and saw plumes of smoke. The air cracked with energy and filled the companion's hearts with dread; but they held their positions. With twangs coming one after the other, arrows cut through the air whistling, almost all missing their mark. Yet one arrow pierced the forward

avarathein through its gaping mouth and it fell to the
ground with a great din of smashing bone, scattering the
companions. The horses galloped away and some of the
companions threw themselves to the ground and
covered their heads. The fallen avarathein's carcass
bounced and cut a swathe through the company's
position, crushing one of Bojingren's men, and casting
Ahktel to one side.

The two remaining avarathein flapped their
leathery wings and pulled up to hover over the
company. One and then the other darted down to snatch
up Bojingren and one of his men. Ixhor pulled down
the flap of his cap and sprung into action, hurling his
javelin at the avarathein lifting off with Bojingren in its
talons. Ixhor's javelin pieced the base of the scaly
beast's long neck and it swerved to one side unclasping
Bojingren, who fell a short distance to the ground. The
second remaining avarathein seized one of Bojingren's
men and tore him into pieces so swiftly that he did not
utter a sound.

Bojingren rose first to his knees and then
struggled to his feet, and scanned his surroundings.
Wincing, he picked up his bow and placed an arrow and
fired a volley at the second remaining avarathein, which
now turned to lunge in Eje's direction. Eje lay on her
stomach with her hands over her face. Fear coursed
through her and she flinched at every sound. Yet her
thoughts were with her defenders, and she knew that
they would prevail. Bojingren's arrow struck the
second remaining avarathein in the fleshy joint of its
leathery wing. Its shriek seemingly brought the first to
its aid. Now the melee was gathering around Eje, and
both Bojingren and Ixhor leapt into action with renewed
vigor and violence.

Before Bojingren could loose another volley, a
leathery wing struck him. Having anticipated the blow
he rolled to the ground and was unhurt. Ixhor too was
struck in the same manner, and Bojingren's last

remaining man at arms, his lieutenant Tyeshar, rushed forward bravely and plunged his sword into a sinewy thigh to draw the beast away. The avarathein swept Tyeshar away reflexively and fell violently to the ground. The second leapt on Tyeshar, piercing his mail armor and lifting him up. Bojingren saw this and unsheathed his sword and leapt on the avarathein's horned back, and pivoting on it, he lunged forward and plunged his sword through its spine. The beast shrieked and convulsed, releasing Tyeshar and brushing Bojingren aside with a wing. Bojingren quickly recovered and leapt back into the fray and swung wildly with his sword and rolled to the side with one motion, and the beast fell, writhing and wailing until it passed into the void.

The last avarathein leapt into the air, snapping its jaws and whipping its tail menacingly. The companions hurled javelins and shot arrows at it, yet it would not retreat. It squawked and shrieked in fury and snapped a tail in Ixhor's direction, and then it lunged at Bojingren and Tyeshar. This last avarathein was fiercer than the other two, and it would not retreat until it had slain and devoured the remaining companions. Its master's exhortations still echoed in its reptilian mind. Ordinarily, avarathein were cautious hunters and scavengers, and would retreat in the face of formidable prey. However, Nausterus had suppressed their natural instincts and emboldened them with his own purpose and malice. The beast would not retreat unless to the void. And so the companions obliged it with a flurry of arrows, javelins, and the sword.

As the companions hurried along the caravan road, and the night wore on, they heard and then saw riders coming eastward under the starry night. When the riders came into full view, the companions could see that they rode with the standard of the Vyrdmar and Chamiahce unfurled. Bojingren hailed them and as they approached, one among them named Tharuin who recognized Bojingren the Red, saluted him.

"We could hear the descent of the avarathein as we scouted nearby," Tharuin said.

"It is good of you to come to our aid good friend."

"Verily," the scout replied. "Let us tarry here a while longer. There are others in my party about gathering the dead and the fleeing horses."

The companions did as Tharuin said and soon they were reunited with their rampant steeds. Together with the scout detachment, the companions rode to a nearby post where their dead were hurriedly buried under a nearby mound. After that brief interment, the weary and shaken companions retired for the night.

Chapter 10: The temple of love

Lord Umalein awoke a little before the dawn to meet with his host. Since the final day of the Crucible, he and his vizir Alfaisten had traveled to the villa of a wealthy merchant named Turias along the Gaaldenian coast of the Western Sea. It was common for visiting lords to be hosted by merchants who, being mindful of the vanity of powerful men, would eagerly host leaders of foreign municipalities and kingdoms to foster profitable relationships. Especially with a lord as powerful and wealthy as Umalein, master Turias spared no words or expense to endear himself to the Kuthgelonian lord.

Merchants knew that Kuthgelon rivaled the Pelares in reserves of ores, gems and precious metals. Moreover, lord Umalein was noted for his vanity and rewarded good hosts with great generosity. He was said to have given a merchant subject a governorship to a small province along Kuthgelon's northwestern border.

Soon after the merchant arrived, a spout erupted near his villa, and out came nuggets of gold. The merchant scoured the small stream supplied by the spout and amassed five hundred cances of gold, of which he sent a sizeable tribute to the kuthgelonian lord.

The day was drawing near for the lords and princes of Maspeidon to return to their own cities and principalities. First however, there was the harvester's feast to attend. In two days, all the lords and princes were to convene on the royal compound for this momentous feast of wine soaked excess where bonds of loyalty were to be renewed through frivolity and dance. And then, with the Levying having been completed, and the inquiry into the administration of the kingdom and the mettle of the king's house having been adjudged strong by the Levying council, the lords and princes would begin to leave the city in earnest.

Lord Umalein's mind was burdened with thoughts of that day. He and his allies had convened for their own assessment of the monarchy in Chamiahce and determined that it was decadent and tyrannical. Many lords, Umalein foremost among them, hearkened to a time immemorial. They had poured over volumes of accounts of historians describing great monuments and spectacles and an orderly society. An Atenari council convened with the Atlantean assembly to govern an age when men lived free of hunger, disease, and suffering. Immortality was within reach, and the firmament of human potential rose beyond the clouds. Mankind flourished under the guidance of benevolent beings from beyond the stars that nurtured mankind's deep yearning to be master over the world and not slaves to nature. These beings, the Atenari strove, hand in hand with their adherents to sow the seeds of higher civilization in the image of their long lost world across the stars.

Then the Cepheid, Breix and Bruix came, and fell upon the Atenari and their adherents. Mankind's benefactors fought a great war against the Cepheid but were ultimately vanquished, at the pinnacle of their power. The monuments of that age were destroyed along with the manuscripts tolling their knowledge and disciplines. The age of scourging ensued and the Atenarix adherents of the Atenari way were hunted. Yet, through the ages, the Atenari's adherents, survived under the Pelares with the dread Ayimar. They later resurfaced after the power of the Cepheid had waned. After the Cepheid became more legend than reality, Atenari knowledge resurfaced. Soon the adherents of the Atenari way became a boon to the rulers in Maspeidon and Cadera. However, the Cepheid rulers were ever fearful of the Atenarix. They were fearful of the secret knowledge the Atenari adherents possessed. They were afraid that the Atenarix would supplant them. And so, the Vyrdmar had since before Wind's time, looked to suppress the Atenarix and their expression through censorship and control over the metic guilds and the academies.

The Vyrdmar's constraints on the Atenarix and the metic guilds were harsh- too harsh some thought. Some thought that these constraints stunted commerce and caused misery and deprivation among the people of Maspeidon. Soon the guilds and their Atenarix masters could look among the Vyrdmar king's own vassals to find support for the usurpation of their proud line. In the shadows, some of Maspeidon's lords and princes harbored a deep resentment and a profound desire to herald a new age of Atlantis, wrought from the blood of the Vyrdmar.

Still contemplating the details of the Atenarix's plan, lord Umalein threw a heavy cloak over his shoulders and walked out into the enclosed courtyard of Turias' villa, which was perched on a ridge overlooking the sea. He could hear the sea splashing on the shores and shuddered as a cool wind blew. Squinting he saw his vizir Alfaisten hunched over on a stone bench.

Umalein took a seat next to his vizir who acknowledged his lord.

"This is beautiful country my lord." Umalein took a deep breath and shut his eyes.

I agree," the vizir said.

"It is a country for seafaring people," Umalein continued. "The sea shapes the character of the landscape as well as its people. The sea to the west is vast, fierce, and temperamental. The strongest among us have aspired to tame it. Therefore, here, the strong are stronger. But the weak cower before it. That is why the weak here cling most to their gods."

"Indeed, you strike at the heart of the problem we hope to solve," the old vizir muttered. "Ours is the highest of callings my lord. Why do some men fear the unknown? Worse, some men foster this fear in others, and strive to hold a cloud of dread and stupor over others. They fashion themselves benevolent herders of the blind, dumb, and weak. They spin tales of wolves stalking in the darkness and their herd shudders. Meanwhile, the virtue and power inherent to species atrophy and dies without its potential ever being realized through masterful expression. That is why we contemplate, and certainly not pray, that new life will spring from the withering foliage of the Vyrdmar."

Umalein nodded his head. "Indeed. Soon our mightiest benefactor will be returned to us, and will lead the restoration of the Atlantean creed. The age of the Vyrdmar will not end soon enough. True nobility will be returned to the world. Let us not dwell on this further today. The time for action is near and I am certain that our cohorts share our conviction. Now let us enjoy a few more days of rest and tranquility."

The two men from Kuthgelon spoke for a little while longer until finally, Turias made his appearance. He was bright eyed and cheerful for many reasons. He was wealthy, his wife was young and beautiful, and he was in favor with his king. He could not now know that he was giving comfort to vipers that were contemplating the overthrow of his king.

Hovin shook his head, musing over how much he had slept. He fell asleep the night before after speaking with his sister Ylia and eating a wholesome meal of no less than would make a pig's stomach burst; or so Ylia said. He slept soundly through the night and had been asleep since early evening the previous day. Hovin had not dreamed since he was a child. But this night he had long and comforting dreams. He dreamed of Ylia and heard the sound of her laughter. He heard the soothing sound of gentle waters and could feel water passing through his fingers like finely woven silk. He did not see her face, but he heard Besia's voice and felt her embrace.

Now, as a new day began he called out for servants to bring his first meal of the day. At first, servants brought him fruit and water from a nearby spring mixed with honey and coriander, prepared by one of the king's physicians. The prince drank the mixture. He pushed away the fruit and asked for roast meats, bread, pastries and butter. The servants hurried along and returned with the prince's desired fare, and he gulped down an entire tray of food before the servants could return with the mead he subsequently requested.

As Hovin was gulping down one of many portions of food and goblets of mead, his dark haired sister Ylia entered his bedchamber. She came in with flowing robes bringing him a sealed parchment, which he immediately opened and began to peruse.

"Prince of the Hold," Ylia announced smiling. "You are so welcomed in my sight. Eat and drink and regain your strength. When you are done you must come with me, for I have an errand from our beloved father. Be at ease, for this commission will not require your renowned strength and skill. It is, as he put it, ceremonial in nature, but no less urgent."

"What is it?" Hovin asked wiping his mouth and springing to his feet.

He sent the servants tending him away. Once they were gone he removed his night robes and began putting on the white tunic typical of the Harfingals. From a shelf by his bed, he pulled down his mail armor, which made a clink sound, which Hovin loved from. He put his armor on over his tunic and his sister helped him put a white surcoat on over it. He then put on his sword belt and presented himself to his sister, who smiled.

"You are beautiful in all ways. Your virtue is comforting, yet grave, for when you are called, those who love you know that you will come. Your virtue makes a woman feel light and at ease because she knows that if she is dear to you that you will bring the world to account on her behalf. Yet this virtue has sent too many brave young Vyrdmar to the void in far away battlefields. I suppose that this is the way of the world. But now come with me so that I may tell you our father's mind. You know that he is fond of you. Be not anxious then because what you must do now is neither perilous nor laborious."

Ylia led Hovin out of the royal apartments, through its rounded portico and through its guarded gates. Standing at the gates were two Harfingals holding onto a striking black mare, with eyes glaring and nostrils flaring, and its muscles flinching. It snorted and snapped its head and seemed to examine Hovin as he approached. The Harfingals bowed as their captain walked slowly to the horse and lifted his hand to stroke its tailored mane. The horse's ears sprang up and pointed sharply forward. The prince whispered gently into the horse's ear, and taking the reins, stood at the horse's front legs facing its shoulders and ran his hands up and down the horse's strong chest. Now the horse raised its head high and neighed and Hovin patted it on its chest.

"This horse is called Feizol," Ylia said looking at Hovin with fondness. "He is from master Cerondilus' stable. And as you know, his are Ausremen mares, brought across the Ausremen plains to Cadera from the plainsmen there, and then on ships to Maspeidon. They are courageous and swift, and beautiful and prized among nobles in Maspeidon. Cerondilus gave this horse to our father not too long ago, and now he has given it to you so long as you can ride it to the springs of Galasur and back."

Hovin looked curiously at Ylia. "This mare is strong and vigorous, but it has been broken and seems to have very good temperament. Surely our father does not believe that this horse requires further breaking. I am certain that even years from now, when his plumes have turned white, that our father will aptly ride a wild musk ox, not to mention this good steed. Yet I will do as he asks. The king, our father has many more burdens than any man should have. And besides, a strong mare such as this one can have moments of wildness even after being broken. I will learn more of its temperament. It would please me to take him as my own and become more acclimated with its temperament.

Hovin smiled and patted the horse on its muscular neck and chest. He effortlessly mounted the horse and steadied himself on it saddle.

"This is a magnificent steed. It would please me well indeed to ride it, even if not all the way to the springs of Galasur to our north. Yet if this is the price to pay for it, I will ride it to the springs. It should not be more than a brisk midmorning ride. Look into my midday meal while I am gone. When I return I will be hungry, and will have to return to my duties."

With that the prince bent down and leaned to kiss to his older sister. He saluted the two Harfingals who bowed, and he galloped away.

Prince Hovin rode out of the remote northern city gates passing by many bowing and saluting citizens.

Some handed scraps from their morning fare; some bread, confiture, and a flask of water. He courteously declined the offers and smiled or waved. With an entourage of young children in tow, Hovin left the city in good spirits. He followed a cobblestone road past several rounded brick structures with furnaces where refuse was burnt. He then took a trail, which led steadily uphill and then around low-lying ridge. He could see the strong walls of the city's three aqueducts winding up and down along the way.

Hovin rode down into a meadow with scattered fir trees. The sun shone through smatterings of clouds and the canopy of fir trees. Now he could see the aqueduct wind its way up to the east toward the highland fresh water lakes and rivers. The way to the spring was speckled with trees and brush and hills. Every now and then he passed herders and with their sheep and goats looking for green fields now recovering much of their lushness. Hovin stopped several times along the way to look back down on the city, which was now bustling with activity. He could see the temple dome, the pyramidal guild halls all the way to the south of the city, and plumes of smoke wafting up from the city's foundries.

Hovin whispered to the horse, Feizol, with surprising familiarity. Hovin would rather have taken the horse east into the flatter plains to more fully gauge its temperament, speed and stamina. Now he walked with the horse, allowing it to graze on some short grass before the trail veered down and north and east into a glade. Soon he saw what he thought were revelers gathered together. The revelers comprised of men of varying ages, some young and some old. No one could distinguish their craft or industry in life from their clothes. They were all dressed quite simply with worn trousers and tunics, some wearing boots while others sandals. The old among them where wrapped in thick cloaks to ward off the morning chill and mist, and any unforeseen rain. The revelers sat around a gray old man, who was crouched on a large stone. Just off the trail, the revelers saw prince Hovin walking toward them, and a hush fell over them. Almost concertedly they all turned to observe as the Vyrdmar prince approach.

When the prince was close enough to hear, greetings were shouted, and Hovin graciously acknowledged them.

"Please do not let my passing disturb you," Hovin said.

"No," the old man insisted and the gathering echoed him with much grinning and uneasy whispers.

"We welcome you young master. We are pleased to have you among us. Please feel free to share a moment with us."

The young prince tethered his horse nearby, looked over the gathering, and then hunched over with one leg bent and resting on a ridge on a mound which the old man was sitting.

"I cannot stay long citizens, for I am on an important errand."

"That is all well," the old man replied. "Stay for as long as you can."

Hovin looked around at the gathering, wondering who they were. They looked like beggars. He had heard about an old man in the city who traveled about with a troupe of beggars upbraiding citizens about their lack of charity.

"Why have you gathered here and not in the city?" Hovin asked.

"We," the old man began, "are known as world watchers. We come out here, away from the clutter and din of the city, to watch the world."

"What is there to see out here?"

"Everything that is undefiled and pure."

"I see," the young prince replied. "But surely you believe that the sacred temple of Yggir is undefiled?"

"You misunderstand my meaning," The old man quickly added.

"It is not merely the birds and the trees that are undefiled, but also the observer. Out here, in this solitude, we who observe nature find a calmness and purity that allows us to see the world as it was meant to be seen."

"What have you observed about the world?" Hovin asked.

"The world..." he began. "If you clear your mind, you will see that the world is everything indivisible."

"The world is many things," the young prince retorted.

"Perhaps you are right. Perhaps the world is every idea and every word that has been contemplated and spoken. The world is every idea and every word that will never be contemplated or spoken, if we, its children are not better gardeners. If we are not better gardeners, the world will despair and die."

Hovin interrupted. "The Vyrdmar are faithful to the Celestial and He demands that we are good stewards."

"Indeed, the Vyrdmar are a noble creed. But there are others who are less than noble. These take everything and give little, or worse, take everything and give nothing."

"There is not and has never been a place in time where there was not evil and despair."

The young prince drew closer to the old man. "There has always been evil and despair because there are always faithless men who choose not to walk with the Celestial. The Celestial teaches us the secrets of the seasons and how to cull the earth's bounty. Yet there are always those who suffer privations because they do not sow during the sowing season. There are always those who choose not to walk with the Celestial."

The old man smiled. "You are wise. You are so young though. The world has one spirit. The spirit of the world does not despair because men are not sufficiently enterprising. The spirit of the world does not despair because men do not reap good harvests. The spirit despairs because men are not good gardeners. In fact, the world spirit grows weary of our enterprises because our enterprises stem not from need but from fear and boundless greed.

Many reap good harvests. But the world spirit too requires nourishment. The world spirit requires sharing, temperateness and moderation. Its wrath is provoked when fear and greed make men scar more earth than is needed to adorn our pride."

The old man's face grew grave.

"The world spirit's wrath is utterly terrifying. It can erupt and split the foundations of the strongest cities and destroy civilizations. Already, tremors have been heard and felt in many places throughout Maspeidon and even Ausremer. How can the Vyrdmar save us from this?"

Hovin looked intently into the old man's eyes, recalling news of tremors and earthquakes from the plains and the eastern fringes of the continent.

"Why now?" he asked.

The old man looked at the prince and then out to the gathering.

"No one can know why the world spirit chooses its time for retribution. But why ask this? Why not ask why we are so intemperate? Why not recognize our place in our world?"

"You speak as if the world truly has a spirit," Hovin said thoughtfully. "Where does it dwell? What will quell its anger?"

The old man leaned on a crooked wooden stick. "Where do all transcendent things exist?" the old man asked. "We come out here to listen because men are easily distracted by the din of commerce. But transcendent things permeate all and are everywhere. The spirit surrounds you and passes through you. Look and listen closely to it ebb and flow. Listen to its soft whispers and you may find your place in it. Only when you perceive without fear and without wanting, will you truly see. Only when you have achieved inner calm will you hear."

Hovin looked sternly at the old man.

"Your views are confusing and disconcerting. There are many spirits in the world, but mighty Yggir, whom the Vyrdmar honor with burnt sacrifices and monuments, rules over them all. We have nothing to fear."

The gathering stirred in apparent unease. Mumblings could be heard.

"I recognize him," someone whispered.

"Yes-he is a Vyrdmar prince."

"Be at ease," the old man said to the gathering.

"Who are you?" he then asked Hovin. "Are you a prince as they say?"

Hovin nodded.

"I am Hovin, son of Ylarin, king of the Vyrdmar and the united kingdoms and principalities of Maspeidon."

The old man's face grew graver than before.

"Forgive me my lord. I did not realize who you were. I am only fit to teach common men, whose wit are burdened by the vagaries of their station. Like the bitter brew we drink in our gatherings, our beliefs merely ease our passage through this life. We take comfort together and assemble in peace."

Hovin could see that the gathering was growing troubled by his presence. "You have not broken any laws. A man's belief is his own affair; so long as he does not write them down. For only the word of Yggir may be written. Only words inspired by Him may be written. I listen to your words and am saddened for you. I am saddened over your lack of faith in mighty Yggir's power to shelter men against misfortune. The faithless will surely suffer the forgetful death."

The old man nodded. "Surely we would do well to heed your counsel. But we do not question mighty Yggir's laws. We do not harbor any thought of dissent or division. We only kindle thoughts of temperateness and restoration."

"Very well," the prince replied. "I do not see the harm in what you say if you know and honor the Celestial. I do not fully understand these precepts you express. Yet, virtue, no matter how it is expressed cannot be vice. Be at ease therefore and fear not, for I will leave you as I found you."

"I should have recognized your proud bearing and raiment." The old man then said. "The Vyrdmar may walk among us for a time, but they hail from heaven. Surely nothing is hidden from you. But even if a kernel of truth is hidden from you now, in due time, or maybe even just around the bend, what is hidden will be revealed to you."

Prince Hovin did not stay long with the world watchers. He rode the rest of the way to the spring, hoping to make it back to the city in time to eat his midday meal before returning to his duties. He rode up a ridge winding up alongside of an overlook. Across the overlook he saw below him a large basin overflowing with water spouting from the side from a series of grottoes. Steam rose from the basin as the cool air passed over the warm water. He could see someone standing at the mouth of a grotto. Curious and seeing that the person was veiled by the steam, Hovin tethered his horse and made his way down to the banks of the basin.

He made his way down the side of the overlook, keeping an eye out for the stranger beyond. The way down was not easy and near the bottom of the overlook he slipped on a mossy rock jutting out from the embankment. He rolled sideways all the way down and came to rest flat on his back. He heard a woman's voice distorted from the sound of flowing water and the strange acoustics of the cavernous spring of Galasur. She snickered at the prince's abrupt and undignified descent.

"Who are you to speak so imprudently to a Vyrdmar prince?"

The woman strode out of the mist toward the young prince – and his eyes clung to them longingly. She was stunning. Her striking figure was accentuated with flowing soft lines here and there as if from the strokes of a master painter. Her long black hair flowed like black silk over her shoulders, which were white and iridescent as porcelain, but soft and sensual like flowers speckled with early morning dew. Her sumptuous curves were revealed through her damp dress, which she held up around her supple thighs.

Hovin's heart beat wildly in his chest and his eyes opened wide. He looked as if he was going to speak her name but she ran to him suddenly and dashed into his arms. Their hearts so yearned for each other that their few days apart seemed like an age. Yet the breath and the flames of passion are inevitably drawn together. The breath longs for a mode of expression. It blows into barren caverns, blusters through the fields, and sweeps all things to a place of fulfillment.

If breath could speak now, it would say, "Besia my love, you are beautiful. You are a perfect place for me to dwell. Without you, I am unbridled and without purpose; a ghost with a gaping mouth saying nothing. But in you I am given form, purpose and fulfillment until the end of time."

They held each other tightly. Hovin could feel her shudder and then sigh. Hovin and Besia did not want to let each other go for fear that they would lose this perfect moment and never be able to recapture it.

Chapter 11: Promothos unleashed

Promothos stirred deep in the catacombs of Irilsflir. His blood flowed in places long bereft of life, causing great pain. The effect of the Instaureum was setting in, but his feeble body was too near death to be fully restored. His essence however was still stirring within his host mind. He retained much of his awareness and potency during his imprisonment, and now that the elixir was flowing through him, his mind moved with great nimbleness. Promothos' awareness scoured the catacombs for the old librarian. It was not long before he found him contemplating. Owidobel's mind was weighing the delectable promise of the Instaureum.

"Of course," Promothos sneered. Finding a good place to survey the old librarian's inner conflict and contortions, he laughed heartily.

Promothos could not whisper to the surplicant and suggest or cajole him to drink. The surplicant's mind was too densely cluttered with conflict and layers of primordial thickets.

"Monkey-" Promothos exclaimed. "It is inevitable that you will drink the Instaureum and die. It is forbidden to you, but that only makes the temptation more irresistible. You cannot know that the Instaureum is the nectar of immortals. If mere mortals consume it, it causes a surge throughout their feeble veins and muscles causing their organs to expand and burst. But even if you knew its secret, your curiosity would have the best of you – you would drink it nonetheless. I am certain that you would and that you will drink it momentarily. Perhaps you will drink it because your belief in your capacity and purpose far exceeds your place in the world. Or perhaps you will drink it to ease the monotony of your inglorious existence."

The old librarian held the second flask of Instaureum in his hand. Sitting on his bed he recalled the duties he performed during the day. He had performed them almost every day for the last eight years. He gathered with his assistants to discuss the tasks he had set out for them. He and the surplicants in his charge spent their days binding and caring for books no one was permitted to read. In fact they were not permitted to read them even though, as surplicants, they were literate in the ancient Vyrdmar tongue. The surplicants were the custodians of the temple and served at the leisure of the priestess. The librarian of the temple was a surplicant, selected by the priestess to seek out censored manuscripts and to bring them down to the temple catacombs to review. To perform this task, the librarian was required to work with the king's Council of morals and the secret Harfingal order of the Urdar.

The temple librarian's tireless work to purge the kingdom of censored manuscripts began with a visit from an Urdar spy, who would bring him the work after its composer had been taken to the morals council for interrogation. Once it was determined that the manuscript expressed censored ideas, the author was imprisoned or executed and the manuscript taken to the librarian. The old librarian was weary of this work. He was weary of the long days in the dark catacombs hunched over small tables in alcoves pouring over manuscripts by the light of lanterns. Could this flask transform his life?

With a deep sigh, the old librarian unsealed the flask and tilting his head back, and squinting, he drank its content. The taste of the Instaureum was surprisingly sweet and pleasant. He licked his lips and then paused to ascertain its effect. He waited for a while and lay back on his bed and crossed his arms. He quickly placed his arms to his sides, thinking that he was not preparing for death, but for a new life. He did not feel any effect for some time, and so he shut his eyes, wondering if he would feel different in the morning. Then his breathing became labored and he began to feel discomfort near his temple. It was not long before he felt slight convulsions over his body. He began to sweat profusely and his heart throbbed in his chest as if it would burst. He opened his eyes, which throbbed, and saw an impenetrable shroud of dark crimson.

Promothos could feel the old librarian's distress and he knew that he had imbibed the Instaureum.

He laughed warmly. "Fool-" he thought. "You relented sooner than I expected. The Instaureum is too powerful for the fragile human body. It stimulates the Atenari host to receive the symbiote that traverse the world unseen. Once the symbiote implants itself into the core of the Atenari host's skull, it and the Atenari become a new being just as the one known as Saareus and I became Promothos. This transcendence was one of many secrets the Atenari discovered in this world. They had already found for themselves, the secret to immortality. But the symbiote promised a connection with an untapped source of primordial power to attend their vision of higher civilization for humanity.

However, the Cepheid have long since broken the Atenari's power. My bid to restore the Atenari's vision has failed many times before. When last I tasted bitter failure I was made to rest sedately in a sarcophagus deep under Irilsflir. Yet my power was not fully broken. I had not fallen into the void. I escaped from my sarcophagus and from my cell whispered until I was heard. Soon my release was secured, but my body had wasted away in captivity. Now therefore, I, Promothos, must detach my being from this body and find another host for not even the Instaureum can fully restore Saareus. I, Promothos, must find another host soon or return to the primordial pool."

That night, a pentad of riders rode into the city with two Gaaldenian sentries at their head. The entourage made its way quickly west through the city. The five remaining companions from Bonthc had finally made it to the city. They were looked at with wide-eyed amazement; especially Ahktel, Ixhor, and Eje.

The two Hekare met the onlookers' eyes and tried to examine their new environment. Her mind clouded with feelings of both relief and dread, Eje did not raise her head. Her clothes tattered and filthy from her long journey, Eje wondered what her new patrons would think of her when they first laid eyes on her. Her face and her hands were caked with dirt and muck; she was barely distinguishable from her warrior companions. But soon her relief at returning to civilization from the wild, prevailed over her anxieties.

With the exception of Eje, who presented her call to order and was taken to the royal compound, the companions were taken to the Harfingal barracks adjacent to the royal compound. They were taken into a large muster hall where they were required to turn over their weapons. The men were taken into small rooms where stern sentries with cold eyes and stern faces individually questioned them.

"Where do you come from?"

"What brings you to the high city?"

"To what guild do you belong?"

Even Bojingren the Red, loved among his countrymen and well known among the Gaaldenians was questioned in this manner. Bojingren smiled wryly as he was questioned.

"Why do you know so little of me," he snickered. "All notable men among the Vyrdmar know me well."

Bojingren was not held long in the barracks, but the Hekare, who were strange men in Maspeidon, were held there long into the night. Meanwhile, Eje was taken to the royal apartments and placed in a guest room where she was tended by servants and handmaidens. Fruit, bread, and wine were taken to her and she ate after washing her face and hands in a small basin. After a light meal, the servants brought Eje night robes and led her to bath chamber wrought in marble with a round window overlooking a courtyard. The servants pulled a lever and warm water came flowing out of the brass faucet above a marble tub. They poured oils and sprinkled jasmine petals into the water and prepared Eje for her bath.

After her bath, Eje put on her night robes and went to bed. She was vaguely aware that there were guards posted outside of her door. Exhausted, she fell right to sleep without even a thought of her companions. She simply thought or hoped that they were as well tended as she was. However, poor Ahktel and Ixhor were not as fortunate as their charge. They too fell wearily to sleep, but they were lodged in small rooms in the Harfingal barracks with guards posted outside their doors to keep them in rather than to keep others out.

Early in the morning Jaïem awoke recalling the small commotion he had heard shortly before retiring to his bedchambers. His sleep that night was troubled as Promothos' voice haunted him throughout. Promothos' voice was now stronger than ever and his presence seemed to have a renewed power. Then sometime

during the night his voice went silent and Jaïem fell
asleep. Jaïem now decided to return to the catacombs to
visit the shadowy prisoner. Yet when he returned to
Promothos' cell, he was astonished to find that the door
had been unlocked. He opened the cell door and
pointed a lantern into the cell and saw a dais with an
opened stone sarcophagus.

Startled, the young prince bolted from the cell
and made his way from the catacombs. Along the way,
as he looked around frantically, he saw a small
gathering of dark robed surplicants. When they saw the
young prince approaching they bowed and parted for
him to pass. Jaïem looked and saw pale and somber
faces, and more dark robed men gathering around into
small groups.

"Promothos," Jaïem thought aloud, but inaudibly.

"Why are you so distressed?" Jaïem asked.

"He is dead," he could hear them say.

"Who is dead?" He asked.

"Master Owidobel is dead," one surplicant
exclaimed with horror.

The young prince was led to the old librarian's
small quarters. There he looked around the room and
saw the old librarian's covered body on the floor next to
his small bed. A surplicant kneeling next to him looked
up and saw the young prince and pulled the wool
blanket covering the body to reveal Owidobel's
contorted face.

"He did not pass well," the surplicant said
shaking his head. The old librarian's head had swelled
to twice its size and blood had caked around his ears,
nose and mouth. Jaïem was sickened by the gruesome
sight and turned away and left the room.

The young prince scampered back to the royal
apartments and sought out the king. As he queried
servants and courtiers, they shrugged and shook their
heads. And when he walked away they shook their
heads again, some wondering what the melancholy

prince was up to now. Jaïem rushed into his sister's chambers and found her dictating to a portly scribe in a small study off a wing of the room's large antechamber. When she saw her brother blow into the study she gestured for the scribe to leave.

"What is it?" she asked.

"I must speak with our father. Surely you know where he may be found."

"Our father is meeting with his vizir council. What do you want with him so early in the day?"

Jaïem came close to his sister, who was sitting on a slender chair with sweeping arms.

"There was a murder at the temple," he whispered. "The temple librarian was slain. I think he was smothered in his sleep by a certain fugitive, long held in the temple catacombs."

Ylia could not suppress the sudden thought that her brother might very well be mad.

"A murder-"

"Yes!" Jaïem insisted. "Master Owidobel, the librarian is dead, and I am fairly certain that an escaped fugitive, who is likely a great threat to the Vyrdmar, killed him and is loose in the city or even in the royal compound."

Ylia stood up from her chair and walked deliberately around Jaïem, eyeing him intently.

"What are you saying brother? Prisoners in the temple... Murder-"

"Sister," Jaïem interjected. "Take me to our father if you know where he may be found."

Ylia touched her brother on the shoulder.

"I do not doubt you Jaïem. But these are strange happenings you speak of."

"I suspect," Jaïem interjected, "that there is a worse calamity yet to come. But I have not solved all what I have seen hidden in this city and in this very compound. I can sense a grave danger creeping and stalking, but I do not know its shape and the hour of its coming."

Ylia led her brother out into the halls and the two of them hurried out of the royal apartments into a center courtyard. Crossing a large courtyard, they were met by two guards.

"Where is the king?" Ylia asked with a commanding voice.

"The king is coming this way. Make way." The king could be seen walking with master Cerondilus. Ylia rushed passed the guards and Jaïem followed. The king could now see Ylia coming toward him and he touched his chief vizir, who seemed to be making an important point, on the arm.

The king held out his arm and embraced Ylia.

"What is it my child? What good fortune I am having today master Cerondilus. Two of my children have sought me out and the day has barely begun."

Taking Ylia by the hand and then Jaïem, the king walked with them to a stone bench flanked by golden elms.

"What is it my children-you seem distressed."
Jaïem turned to look at his father, and placing a hand on his thigh, recounted his dealings with the old librarian and his discovery of Promothos in the catacombs. Ylia looked on with astonishment. The king listened intently, nodding and sighing at times.

"It is well of you to bring this matter to my attention," the king said after listening to his son's account. "Your attentiveness and careful inquiry into this matter will prove to be of great service to your king. This man Promothos was a godless and treasonous malefactor, thrown into a secret pit below the temple many years ago. Yet if what you say is true, then Promothos' web of treason was not broken as was believed. In fact, our master librarian may have been entangled in it."

The king sent his children to their chambers and ordered Harfingal companies mustered in the temple quadrangle and in the great courtyard of the royal compound.

Then the king rushed to the temple, using his secret passages to meet with the priestess of Yggir. Lantern in hand, the king made his way up the stone steps leading to the large bronze doors opening into the dark chamber where it was customary for him to meet with the priestess. As always, the king entered the chamber, which was furnished with two ornate chairs placed adjacently and separated by a small wooden table and took a seat on one of the chairs and placed the lantern down on the table and waited. Then he heard the priestess' voice.

"What brings you to the house of Yggir?" she asked in the usual manner. The priestess walked out from the shadow and took a seat in the chair adjacent to the king.

"Promothos, the heretic Ayimar, who my father vanquished below the Pelares has escaped."

The priestess' face was unusually pale and her eyes were weary.

"Indeed he has. But Promothos is no mere heretic my king. Promothos is an immortal. He cannot be destroyed, and when he is at his strongest, he cannot be contained. Long ago, your father Nnyreinin dealt him a great blow and weakened him. Then he brought him to the temple where, weakened as he was, he was bound as if he was dead in a sarcophagus. However, wounds that are fatal to ordinary men cannot destroy Promothos. His body is a host carrying a powerful living essence, which, unlike the human spirit, retains its identity, prescience and power beyond the death of its species host, which contained him. To destroy his flesh is to release him into the world where he preys on the vanity of men to win over a suitable new host. If a new host is not found, Promothos must return from whence he came. But there his power becomes even more nebulous and his power to' corrupt minds and hearts does not lose any of its potency.

The king's face grew dark and his shoulders slumped.

"This is a vexing quandary. We cannot kill him and yet we cannot suffer him to roam free."

The priestess drew closer to the king.

"Son of Wind," she said. "Mortal men do not dwell long in this world. Mortality breeds a certain pathology, which leads to a false belief that a man may redeem his world before the twilight of his day. So many men have hurried to their destruction while trying to will the world to account for their expectations. You are already thinking of achieving what your father could not, and what even immortals have been unable to achieve. Promothos is like death; he is an enduring and immortal dissembler who preys on the frailty, vanity and greed of men. Like all immortals, he has his place in our world.

Promothos' purpose is certainly to cull the disloyal from mighty Yggir's flock. But in spite of his daring upheavals, all even mighty Yggir can do is restore abide him. Therefore, neither you, nor any other king will have final victory over Promothos. Do not rue that you will not redeem the timeless ills you see in your life. It would be folly to turn your mind now to Promothos' undoing."

The king nodded uneasily and then stared thoughtfully into the darkness surrounding the room.

"Very well... What of the guilds and their Atenarix benefactors? Promothos will return to them and he will use them to foment treason as he did when my father was a young prince."

"You are the shepherd of your people and the defender of Irilsflir. I am sure that I do not have to tell you what you must do with your enemies. Promothos is the unfathomable will of chaos, but the Atenarix and the guilds are mere subjects. If they endeavor to commit treason against their king, their king must act accordingly. Punish the Atenarix and the guilds, but Promothos' name will be spoken even until the last twilight. His name will surely be whispered in the shadows, but his power can be circumscribed if his adherents are made to see fealty to him as a path to ruin. When given a choice, most men are wont to obey even tyrants and shun their most cherished hopes and ideals, so as to avoid certain and unflinching death."

Adjacent to the pyramidal tower of the metic guild in the merchant sector of the city, there was a brick and mortar building, with a dome supported by a stone pendentive. The building had a strong bronze door with triangular stone pediment above it. No one ever saw anyone enter it and the door did not have a handle, knob, or hinges. Yet there were rumors that strange sounds could be heard from within it at times. As the afternoon waxed, and the din of commerce rose loudly in that sector of the city, activity also stirred within the white building. A gathering of men with ashen staves, some dressed in sky blue robes and others in black robes, sat on wooden benches situated around a rectangular dais. Sitting on a large stone seat was none other than Promothos, resplendent in sky blue vestments, and his large and elongated head was adorned with a white headdress.

"I have returned to you," Promothos said opening his arms, revealing long bony fingers. His gaunt face was scarred and his yellow eyes, now dimmed in the ample light, panned all around the room. Many of the benches around the arched hall were empty.

"I have returned to fulfill the creative purpose that brought our masterful benefactors here from their far-flung world of origin. The creation of the greatest of species is but one aspect of that purpose. I am the first of the Amretar masters, once created by the Atenari as the apogee of species being, and host of the primordial power of the hidden. But their creative journey will not end with me. You too who are their creations will continue this march to excellence and perfection."

Promothos struggled to rise to his feet and a shadowy figure swept in behind him to hold him steady.

"We adherents of the Atenari way, we Atlanteans, are the vanguard of a great future-a future without the common man. The common man is weak. He looks beyond himself for purpose. He looks to an author of life and wants to be subservient to Him. He wants religion. If he wants religion, let him have it. But let the truth be told; he can no more fathom divine purpose than a mouse can fathom metic disciplines. Alas, let men know how things really are. Their salvation lies with us. And we shall harness their potential and make them useful.

There was a brief pause as many looked on with wide-eyed wonder at the Atenari master and listened intently.

"But enough of high ideals; let us now speak about action. I am pleased to hear that master Nausterus and master Umalein, have not only secured my deliverance, but have also conceived a bold strike against Wind's house. As you all should know, I am fond of boldness. Boldness cultivates achievement and favorable outcomes. But we must also be wary as to not overplay our hand. I am not yet fully restored and so I was looking forward to an immediate withdrawal to the Pelares with my children, the dread Ayimar. Yet master Nausterus and Master Umalein's boldness has roused me and has whetted my appetite for vengeance. Therefore, I will remain with you as you make your bid for the city. Now that my mind is poised for that undertaking, let us speak together so that I may know your mind."

None other than master Idram, the schoolmaster now rose to speak.

"Master Promothos," he began. "Your adherents rejoice in your return to us, and we cautiously anticipate the restoration of a new Atlantis. Yet your adherents are divided as to the means and the hour of our resurgence. I speak for those among us who urge a little more restraint and less boldness. The Atenarix order has painfully and methodically regained much of our power in the world. We may not have anticipated this fragile harmony, but we should be circumspect about disturbing it."

The schoolmaster walked into an isle and came closer to the dais.

"Indeed, the Vyrdmar are unwavering in their devotion to the gods and continue to espouse an unfathomable dogma that has left the people adrift in pastoral shadow and stupor. They are also ruthless in their censorship of ideas. But they have shown signs of reformation. They have relented in their meddling in the guild's affairs and have increasingly embraced metic craft, industry, and commerce. Therefore, I question the wisdom of lord Umalein's strike against the city. The king would glean that the Atenarix were behind the attack. If it fails, the king would in the least, scrutinize our affairs and strip us of our exalted place in society. But worse, the king would likely put many to the sword and raze our halls."

Another man among the Atenarix gathering rose to counter master Idram's argument.

"Master Idram," the man began. "We all respect your insight on these matters. You are very close to the monarchy and know their temperament. Yet perhaps your proximity to the Vyrdmar has clouded your judgment. The king is surely biding his time. He is strengthening his position and waiting for the most propitious time to move on the enemies of Irilsflir. As long as the Vyrdmar king perceives that Irilsflir is the backbone of his power, we are in peril. And so, rather than survive at our enemy's whim, relying on his magnanimity and goodwill, or his slackness, we should strike him down when he is weak and seize power."

Outbreaks of approval could be heard around the hall.

"Master Idram," Promothos declared. "I was imprisoned in the bowels of Irilsflir for over a generation. The Atenarix have suffered much since then. But for the vanity and curiosity of one young king, this order may very well have been utterly purged in that time. It was king Nnyreinin who kept me alive and ignored the warnings of his councilors and the priestess of Yggir, and permitted the Atenarix order to exist and even to flourish. This order must never again dangle so precipitously close to utter annihilation. Our cause is too great to be so slack in our dealings with our enemy."

Promothos paused to change the tone of the discussion. "I do not recognize any of you before me today. But, the idea of Atlantis has bound you all to me even across the many years. That however does not matter. I know we all share a bond of ideals even as a schism of experience and knowledge strains our dialogue and our association. But do not hesitate to look to me no matter how estranged you are to me. I never betrayed those who came before you. Look to me therefore and rely on my judgment. Listen closely and learn why the Atenarix must prevail, Atlantis restored, and the Vyrdmar brutally usurped.

Long ago, the Atenari masters found man's progenitors writhing in darkness, transformed them into a new masterful species, and lifted them to the pinnacle of civilization. This history has long been hidden from the world. The Vyrdmar and their gods offer their own cacophonous cosmology and history, and they say that Cepheid rescued the world from tyranny. This is furthest from the truth. The Atenari masters found the very gods the Vyrdmar worship writhing in a dark primordial pool. The Atenari reached out to them and bridged the cosmic gap that separates species from the bakiren symbiotes dispersed in the world and united specie with energy. The Atenari created men and the Amretar, and the flickering bakiren symbiotes, which you call the hidden, found their species expression and host. When the gods saw this, they were resentful. Having made the fedir, the so-called gods, masterful, they began to cull dissent among lesser species against their own Atenari benefactors.

The world thrived under the Atenari and their Atlantean regime. The Atenari transformed the world. They brought order to the primordial chaos they found and conceived civilization. But unsatisfied, they also created the Ayimar using their secret knowledge to fuse the best virtues of disparate species into a new species even more masterful than men and the Amretar. And still they were unsatisfied, and they sought more remarkable expression.

But many men grew envious of the Ayimar and were weary of the constant rigors of Atlantis. They found a vehicle for their displeasure under the banner of the Cepheid, the twin godlings, the architects of Irilsflir, who together fomented and conceived the Atenari's brutal usurpation. It is certain that now, after over an age of Cepheid hegemony, that we will not be able to simply restore Atlantis by attrition. The rebirth of Atlantis must be achieved by disciplined action and anointed with blood, whether tomorrow or in the distant future. This irony endears itself to me and to the spirit of history.

Now therefore, go forth like soldiers with unwavering determination and cold resolve, and destroy our age-old enemies. Let caution be the industry of the cowards who give counsel to our decadent enemy. Listen well to your master and bend completely to my will. Hear me now. Atlantis was the past, and is the glorious and peaceful future. If the unfathomable logic of this bold stroke eludes you, then demonstrate your devotion to me and go forth to avenge my suffering and anguish, which can only be quenched with blood."

The Harfingals were positioned all around the royal compound and many city sentries mustered outside the archway leading into the temple quadrangle. The old librarian's corpse was kept in the temple and the king's physicians were sent to examine his body. After the examination, embalmers took his body and placed it on a stone slab and washed it and performed their metic craft. Later, the king met with his vizir council and summoned his son Varenhil to be in attendance.

The men met in the council hall and sat around a large rectangular table of polished stone. The issue the king brought before them was the death of the old librarian who was known to be their spy among the Atenarix and the guilds. Specifically, the council discussed whether the old librarian was murdered for his intrusion on Atenarix secrecy, and if so, whether the king should punish the Atenarix and the guilds. In case a finding in the affirmative was made, a determination was to be made as to what measure would be appropriate. Many of the king's vizirs questioned that even if the surplicant was murdered, if such a matter should have any bearing on affairs of state. The king interjected that he was the protector of Irilslflir and master of life and death in his own city. The king stated firmly that the murder of a surplicant by a faction in his city necessarily had a corrosive effect on his power.

The vizirs then all agreed that a response would be required and that punishment should be meted out. But some still cautioned that a better approach would be to frame the incident as an accident. Those vizirs pointed out that the king's vassals were still in the city and that they had to be convinced that the librarian's death was an accident and not a murder. And since, as it was conceded, that the librarian's role in the affairs of state was secret, treating his death as an accident was the best approach, and would further diminish the stain on the monarchy.

The king now seemed swayed by the argument advanced by the latter view. Even master Cerondilus reluctantly agreed that the king should treat the incident as an accident.

"My lord," he said. "I agree that restraint is required in this matter. Here, your response will determine the scope of the problem as your vassals see it, if it is assumed that the librarian's mission was shrouded in complete secrecy. But while I do not believe that this assumption is ironclad, I also cannot believe that the Atenarix would risk your wrath for the sake of exacting retribution against a spy.

All things considered, I am not convinced that the librarian was murdered at all. Indeed, I urge you all to reconsider whether the librarian was in fact murdered. If he was murdered, we must identify a malefactor and ascribe a motive. If he was not murdered, then we are faced with a mystery. Both murders and mysteries are anathema to good order and require measured responses at the proper time. But first we must proceed on a correct understanding of what actually occurred and why."

Cerondilus' words were met with nods of approval. But the king was not fully persuaded.

"Master Cerondilus," the king said. "Your words have merit. But my own physicians have reported that the librarian was poisoned. The librarian may very well have taken his own life for reasons that are now unknown. But from what I know of this man from others, I have to doubt that he would have taken his own life. There was no motive. He was of sound mind and body. Furthermore, even though he was a surplicant, he was vain. Murder and perhaps error are the only credible explanations.

Notwithstanding, I think that there is consensus among all of you here, that this matter should be treated as an accident. I have determined that this view should prevail for the sake of order and peace during the festival season. The official finding we will reveal to all who inquire and have the privilege, is that the old librarian mistook a flask of binding wax, for ordinary scribe's wax. Licking his fingers after he used it, he ingested the poisonous mixture, and died painfully of apoplexy in his sleep."

After the king concluded his meeting with his viziers, and they left the large hall, he called his son Varenhil close to him and spoke with him for a short while.

"Lord of Greingspen?" he began. "This matter of the librarian will resolve itself, but a greater threat has resurfaced. How strong are my defenses to the north in Greingspen? Are you ready to come to my aid should I call on you in the coming months?"

Prince Varenhil looked into his father's eyes and spoke sternly.

"I have two battalions of infantry and one battalion of cavalry at your disposal my lord. I have also conscripted metics and artisans into three battle ready metic companies. I have wood and metal parts at the ready to hoist all manner of siege weapons in short order, which can decimate enemy ranks or bring a strong city down to rubble."

King Ylarin nodded. "Very well; I will look to you in due time to support our friends in Beonon to our south on yet another purge against the Ayimar. I know, even though you have incorporated metics into your army, that you greatly distrust the Atenarix and the guilds who are their benefactors. But before we can break them, we must weaken them and we must foster the support of other powers in Maspeidon. As you are very well aware, not all of my vassals can be trusted. Some are in league with a united Atenarix council with reach beyond Maspeidon. There are many uncertain outcomes. Civil war is a possibility. If conflict erupts into war, I cannot be certain who will stand with the Vyrdmar."

"Why wait?' Varenhil asked. "Why play this game my king? You will only provide our enemies with more time to strengthen their position, to harden their resolve, and conjecture as to the reasons for our inaction. They may interpret our inaction as weakness. I am ready to do your bidding my liege. But, if you ask for my opinion; I say move against our enemies now. You know we have lord Dorias' support, as he is our kin and your most loyal vassal. With his sea galleons and fast lupeiders attacking from the south, and our armies marching from the west, we can overwhelm our enemies even before they can gather their strength and resolve. Attacking just after the Levying, when our enemies least expect an attack, would be advantageous. If we attack now, we will likely avoid greater losses."

The king shook his head. "I cannot know for sure who my enemies are. I cannot distinguish between those who are ambitious or disloyal, envious or vengeful. We cannot act indiscriminately and without judgment, or else we will turn many who are not resentful of the Vyrdmar against us. Do not misconstrue subtleness with inaction. The continent's landscape is cluttered with the faithful as well as covetous, the wicked, and the faithless. The Vyrdmar must not only show strength, but also good judgment. Good judgment projects strength and rashness weakness. A king must gather his strength like dark clouds before the storm and strike quickly and precisely and destroy utterly.

Besides, I have been as furtive as my enemies. After much deliberation about my vassals' strained and capricious loyalties, I have made overtures to the Austral lands to strengthen my position in Maspeidon. I sought to reunite the houses of the Cepheid, which was fractured long ago. My son, I have taken steps to bind my house with that of king Xremede in Cadera. He has sent his daughter to me, and her rights to Ceptra, a key principality from that vast country. I have betrothed you to Xremede's house to strengthen my hand and the hand the Vyrdmar's future king. What say you? Are you prepared to do your duty for king and country?" The king smiled uneasily. Varenhil was stern and unflinching. "I will obey."

Night fell on the high city with rumors spreading that there was a death in the royal compound. Some in the city were saying that an old courtier had died from too much drink, while others said that an old drunken surplicant fell to his death in the temple. These rumors even buzzed in the king's court and among the king's vassals. That night, the king called his children together and ate his dinner with them. He also invited a beautiful young princess from the austral land to eat with them. At the princess' insistence, she was escorted, all glowing and beautiful, by Bojingren the red and Tyeshar of Beonon, and Ahktel and Ixhor from the little village of Sephtu.

All throughout the meal, prince Varenhil looked upon the princess' countenance, tracing the contours of her slender face, her prominent cheekbones and her almond shaped eyes with his eyes. Mostly demure, she smiled liberally, and knew well the common tongue of the Maspeidonians. She enthralled them with her rendition of her adventure. Her companions were still in disbelief after realizing that their courage saved the life of a Caderan princess. That night, Eje opened Jaïem's mind to the vast world beyond the city he had known all of his life. He had never seen the avarathein, or the arctodi. He had never seen an Ausremen or an Eptarean for that matter.

Shortly after the royal hosts and guests had eaten their dinner and drank their fill of wine, they took their leave from the king and left him in the company of the Vyrdmar and Caderan princesses. The king walked arm in arm with the two princesses out into a balcony adjoining the royal dining hall. He sat on a bench with them and enjoyed the clear but mild night air.

"Some say that beauty adorns the wise," he thought out loud. The two princesses smiled.

"I am very fortunate to have so many beautiful children. I have thoroughly enjoyed this evening with you and my other children. Yet, Eje my newest jewel, my heart is heavy for you. I want you to cling to Ylia who is as strong as she is beautiful. She is also wise and compassionate. I may not know how to hold you when you are heartbroken. I have much to learn about you yet. I do not know when the right time would be to tell you. And so I tell you now that it has been many days since your father, king Xremede, has returned to the house of souls."

The shadow of the Atenarix was then gathering even as Eje's hearts sank to the depths of grief and despair. Tears welled in her eyes. Her mouth gaped open and yet not a sound came out. Her strength shattered like delicate crystal. She fell into the king's arms gasping. The princess was forlorn beyond consoling. She could not have conceived and could not fathom how or why so much tragedy had befallen her and her family. It was as if the gods themselves wanted to shatter her dreams and consume all that was dear to her. A dark power, a malevolent hand, unseen and unfamiliar to her was devouring her dreams piece by piece. Her life had been threatened and her father had been slain. But why - what had she done wrong? What transgression had she committed?

In a dark room within the domed hall of the Atenarix order of the Vehe-ta, Promothos, who could answer all of Eje's questions, held audience with Nausterus. As he did so, his mind buzzed with anticipation of the Atenarix strike on the Vyrdmar. The two men spoke at length about their plans, and the boldness and craftiness of his adherents' scheme made Promothos laugh wryly. His laugh rasped on until he coughed uncontrollably. Master Nausterus knelt before him and wiped his mouth with the cuff of his dark robes. In the shadows, an intermittent presence looked down upon them and listened unseen.

"I am not sorry that you failed in your attempts on the Caderan king's daughter," Promothos gasped. "The story that is now unfolding is delectable still. They will all be gathered together rejoicing in the culmination of one of the Vyrdmar's ridiculous festivals."

Promothos stopped to draw a deep breath. "As they gather, men from your dread order of the Droa, who have entered the city in caravans like merchants will spring into action. In three waves they will attack. One force will set fire to tar and hay at the major thoroughfares leading up to the royal compound and the temple, and a second will obliterate the guard posts at the temple archway and the main gate into the royal compound with awesome pyrotechnics. The third force will attack from the northern gate. In the confusion lord Umalein will leap up to defend the king. Calling out to the lords to follow him, he will lead them through the royal gardens where they will be ambushed by your shadowy Droa. Your Droa will run them through and the ground will feast on their blood. Then I will appear in the banquet hall, having been reunited with my anurium blade, the blade emanating the primordial flame, which you have kept safe for me. I will unleash its primordial aura upon the king and his defenders and its fire will break the bonds that fused particle into expressions of life and reduce them to primordial dust."

Promothos gestured and Nausterus walked to a corner of the room where a sword sheathed in a black scabbard lay on a marble stand. Nausterus brought the sword to Promothos, who was holding out a gnarled hand.

"When the hand of the Atenarix is poised to strike down the Vyrdmar king, his subjects will ask, where are the gods, where is mighty Yggir. But mighty Yggir will not come. Yggir of the silvery wings dares not stand against the anurium blade, for he is a living god who draws breath. I am however, the creation of the Atenari. I was created from their own flesh, which thrives in the fire of the blade. Therefore, when I am so armed with this firebrand, who will stand against me? Who will stand against the culmination of Atenari disciplines, which propelled them across the stars, and made species more perfect?

Promothos laughed, at first softly, and then louder and louder.

"The power of the Vyrdmar will be broken, their flesh burned and their smoldering ashes will be scattered by the winds that swept their fathers here to the coasts of Gaalden."

Nausterus watched quietly as Promothos rejoiced. The Amretar master's laughter was coarse and hollow and made Nausterus' mind numb. This experience was shared by another who was listening. As if witnessing Promothos' ecstasy firsthand, Ahktel awoke where he lay in his guest quarters in the royal apartments with a startle. Gathering his breath, he reached for a cup of water on a nearby nightstand to moisten his parched lips.

Chapter 12: The Atenarix strike

The morning rain was an ominous sign for a day of feasting and revelry. Rain was good for the harvest, but calamitous for a day of feasting and merrymaking. At least that was Tharguld's opinion; he was the quartermaster of the Golden Hearth. The Golden Hearth was a fine public quarters in the city's center plaza. Sitting at a table in the vestibule adjoining the noisy main hall, he explained to a stranger from the east that the harvester's feast was, ostensibly, a celebration of the harvest. He explained that this feast was actually not a feast in the common sense of the word. There were no roast mutton, swine, or fowl. When the feast first began, farmers came from the countryside and brought what was left from their winter stores and granaries. There was plenty of grain, confections, and dried meats. But in more recent times, with stores having lessened as a consequence of poorer summer harvests, it became a celebration of wine and a spectacle of wine soaked courtiers dancing and frolicking.

"While it is not my personal observation," he said. "There has been much feasting and merrymaking in the royal compound. Yet the last few years have been difficult for the citizens of the high city, and especially trying for the hardy farmers in the countryside. For many years, the winter harvests from the austral lands across the Khreinth Sea have not been good and our summer harvests have been worse. Yet from the look of things in the markets, things may be looking better."

The clean-shaven man, calling himself Mardis and claiming to be a merchant, seemed very interested in what the stout old man had to say, which was not surprising to the quartermaster. He fashioned himself the great conversationalist. With his health now fading, he was fonder of the simpler things in life, like having a good conversation. His wife said of him, that his reputation for loquaciousness would have preceded him to the house of souls. Such was his reputation that the unhappy souls of the dead petitioned the gods to keep him with the living as long as possible, to forestall his boisterous arrival, and the present conclusion of their peaceful rest.

Now the quartermaster waved to a group of patrons passing through his doors. Greetings were exchanged, and clearly knowing his habits, the patrons feigned to see a few good friends at a distant table.

"What then is the real purpose of this feast you call the harvester's feast?" The stranger interrupted. "There will be no harvest for months in this region."

The quartermaster rubbed his haggard face and took a puff from his wooden pipe.

"Well, this feast gives thanks for harvests from other regions. After the long winter, all that is left in terms of stored goods are grains, which are scarce these days, are consumed in anticipation of the arrival of the caravans.

Thankfully, in the spring, merchants like you bring fruit, wine, spices, roots, and other bounty from abroad in caravans haling from far away places."

The quartermaster peered back into the crowded hall. "Thankfully, there has been a crush of travelers, pilgrims, and merchants in the city. The markets are full and everyone hopes there will at least be plenty of ale and mead for the harvester's feast. Maybe the king will be able to spare some provisions from his stores for public quarters such as this one."

Gesturing for a servant girl to come to him, he threw his feet on the table before him.

"Bring this man a chair and bring two goblets of ale," he ordered smacking the girl on her rear.

"Now you have not told me what manner of trade brings you to our city. Is this your first time here? You look very young."

The merchant began to speak and then paused as the young girl returned with a chair. Sitting down he continued to answer the quartermaster.

"I deal in textiles," he said.

"I should have been able to tell by your fine garments," the quartermaster remarked.

"I deal exclusively in mixed fabrics and only with guild traders. I do not spend much time at the open market. And yes this is my first journey to the high city. I had heard so much about it from my home in the east."

"Very well," the old quartermaster replied nodding. "This is a good season to visit the city. This is a good time for merchants and pilgrims. As I have said, we have seen better days. The summer harvests have not been bountiful and the winters have been bitter and long. But by all accounts, we are enjoying one of the most vibrant Levying pilgrimages in years. This is good news both for me personally as the proprietor of this lodging, and as a citizen of a city long suffering from shortages and hardships. I will do very well this Levying with so many pilgrims overflowing available accommodations in the city. Patrons here are willing to pay a full quarter's rate to sleep in a corner in the main hall, in the upper passages, or even in the stables. It is the strangest and most fortunate series of events."

The merchant nodded, adding, "-and especially profitable for quartermasters like you who offer lodgings in the town's main plaza."

The old quartermaster laughed. After the servant girl brought over the two goblets of ale, the two men drank together for a while longer.

"Now tell me where you are lodged?" the old quartermaster queried.

"I have slept among my men in tents we pitched in the southern part of the city."

"I do have one room I keep in reserve," the quartermaster said thoughtfully. "It can accommodate three or four of your men. If this rain holds up, you may be in for a difficult night in your tents. You seem like an honorable man and I was planning on making this room available for tonight anyway. You may have use of it for the going rate. Tonight I will serve fresh bread, mead, and many commoners will make merry here. If, as it seems clear from your comportment, that your palette is more refined and you prefer wine made from the fruit of the vine, I can offer flagon from my little cellar below for a good price."

"Indeed," the merchant said wearily. "I suffered many rainy days in my tent and would welcome a reprieve."

The quartermaster agreed saying, "this is a good establishment. We have good food and better service. It is a good location. You are at the center of the city and within a brisk walk of any sector."

"Indeed," the merchant agreed. "I will go for now and return later with three or four guests."

The merchant handed the quartermaster a gold coin.

"Ah," the quartermaster said. "A full gold feranx will be more than enough for a night's lodgings. Rest assured all preparations will be made for your return."

At the royal apartments, Eje lay huddled in her quarters throughout the night and into the morning. At times she was restless, and then falling into a deep sleep, she would awake again from a haunting dream. Staring blankly into the dark room, she was enthralled by specters of her father passing across the room with forlorn eyes peering back at her. She wept bitterly at times knowing that her past was forever lost to her. But then, always mocking her was the thought that all that had happened to her since she saw her father last was a dream and that her life was as it always had been. But some time during the night, she could vividly hear the patter of rain falling on the ceramic roof of the royal apartments and on the leaves of trees. Then she could hear the wind lashing and howling. Her sorrow seemed too real and her reality too vivid to be dream.

By morning, the rain had passed, but it was overcast. Eje still lay huddled and giving no thought of getting out of bed. She was afraid to face the world and to find that her sadness was real. At times, she hoped that eternal sleep would take her if she remained still long enough and kept her eyes shut. But then the bustle of servants could be heard and then the parade of visitors came. She was cordial to the courtiers and to Jaïem who brought her a small pouch of crystals. Every visitor offered condolences and tried to ease the pain of her loss. Ylia came to her bedside to bring her a cup of mulled wine, honey, and mint leaves. The Caderan princess thanked her and took a few sips. Ylia ordered servants to bring bread and fruit and to place candles around the room. Then she kissed Eje on her forehead and left the room.

Instinctively realizing what could lift Eje's malaise, Ylia left and hurried to the southern wing of the royal apartments to the guest quarters and sought out

Eje's companions. She found Bojingren and Tyeshar, and Ahktel and an Ixhor, speaking together and approached them.

"Come," she said. "Your charge needs you now more than ever."

They followed Ylia back to Eje's room. Stopping at her door, Ylia gave them a thoughtful look.

"I think that she has developed a stronger bond with you who came here with her than anyone in the king's court. Go to her now and try as best you can to lift her spirit, or else we may lose her."

Bojingren knocked and a servant girl sitting in an antechamber opened the door and let the visitors in. The companions walked tentatively toward Eje and hearing them approach, she sat up rubbing her eyes. Seeing her friends again she smiled wearily and bowed her head.

"I have not seen any of you for what seems like many days," she murmured. "But that may be all well. I don't know if I would have wanted you to see me this way."

Bojingren sat on the bed next to Eje and held her hand.

"You are a very remarkable woman," he said. "You are noble and beautiful, but you also possess remarkable strength and wisdom. You have been through so much and you know so much more of the world than your years. I would have wished better experiences for you – experiences that you could gladly share with your loved ones. I wish you could have been spared from so much sorrow. But I know that you will prevail over your pain and loss. Just remember that you are not alone. The bond you have with us is strong. Lean on us and we will carry you. Weep and we will dry your tears. We are here for you. Do not be afraid to share your sorrow with us. Our suffering together has awakened our hearts to each other forever."

Bojingren's sincere words were comforting to Eje. She looked into his eyes and smiled. The others gathered around and chimed in, and the companions spoke a little about the future. Eje told Ahktel and Ixhor that she would very much welcome it if they postponed their return to Hekare lands for as long as they could. She told them that it saddened her to know that they were all going to leave her alone in a strange city. It would not be long before Bojingren returned with his lord, Dorias, to Bonthc, taking the Hekare with them.

Weeping she recalled when she first learned of her mission to Chamiahce. She explained that she was betrothed to the king's eldest son, crown prince Varenhil. Her journey and purpose was shrouded in secrecy, but days after she left Tidthra for the coastal city of Tehmas to board a ship to Chamiahce, she was abducted, and her bodyguards slain by shadowy men. Her abductors bound her and traveled to an unknown destination until Ahktel and Ixhor rescued her during a moonlit night.

"I could not have known," she intimated to Bojingren and the rest, alternating from the common tongue to Irsei. "But there were wicked men who swore not to allow my father's house to unite with the Vyrdmar. They were more effective than my father could have ever known. They have hunted me since I left Tidthra and have slain nine of the fifteen of us who left Bonthc over a week ago. They may have also slain my dear father.

Only now do I know how fortunate I was to have such excellent protectors and dear friends. If only my father had men such as you by his side, he may have triumphed over those who slew him. Now though, I must suffer this life, knowing that he is waiting for me in the house of souls. But I suppose that while I am here, I must remember the commission my father entrusted to me. I am here in this foreign land to establish a bond between his house and that of king

Ylarin. Since this was his wish for me and for his people, I will do this for him and for my people. If I can have your friendship all throughout, I may yet recapture my passion for this world. "

Servants came and brought a tray heaped with pastries, honey wine, and water, and the companions paused to eat and drink from what was brought to them. Ixhor stood back, and at first, Eje did not eat. But then she ate little and then, remarking how sweet the pastries were she ate more heartily. Soon there were a few smiles.

At first, no one noticed that Ixhor was standing aloof. But then they noticed him, towering, with his arms crossed looking this way and that.

"What are you looking for?" Bojingren asked. Eje translated and Ahktel laughed.

"He is not familiar with these sweets," Ahktel said brokenly in the common tongue.

"What?" Bojingren asked.

"These sweets are not familiar to him," Ahktel replied. Eje translated and Bojingren and Tyeshar looked at Ixhor curiously.

"Please," Eje remarked, "try some. I am certain you will like it."

Ixhor nodded and Eje handed him a few morsels.

The companions spoke into the late morning. They did not notice the rains receding or the clouds parting at first.

"Listen," Tyeshar whispered. "The rain has passed and the birds are singing."

The sun peeked through the parting clouds and the citizens of Chamiahce looked out with hope for a day of gatherings, reflection, and merrymaking. The old quartermaster, Tharguld called for his son Farwuld and sent him to the market to purchase provisions for the gathering later that evening. He took several servant boys with him wheeling two carts through paved roads and sloshing through muddy alleys. In just such an

alley, Farwuld encountered a young vagrant he
befriended. The long limbed boy, Modi, leapt from a
small atrium and surprised Farwuld.

Startled at first, Farwuld grasped for a dagger he
wore under his cloak.

"Where are you going Tharguld's son?"

"Do you not have some vocation other than
gamboling about like a fool?" Farwuld exclaimed with a
sigh.

"What's a vocation?" Modi asked tugging at a
wooden whistle tethered around his neck by a leather
strap. "If I don't have it, I don't need it. I am lord of
the Skaggs. I romp freely about the city without a care,
while you work like an ass for your father."

"I pity you," Farwuld snorted. "You are a
vagrant. You have no place among honest folk. Now
why don't you come with me and put in a good day's
work for once?"
Modi smiled and trotted behind Farwuld mimicking
Farwuld's gait and the pitiable gloom on the faces of the
servant boys trailing him.

"I suppose I have some time to dally with you
today good citizen." He curtsied.

"My Skaggs are still in their holes waiting out the
foul weather. Later, we will meet at the city roundabout
across from the Golden Hearth."

He leapt in front of the servant boys. "Now you
boys should come and see how the Skaggs live. You
work for scraps. We Skaggs are commoner nobles and
princes. Come and see us tonight. When night falls, we
will spring into action. There will be plenty of drunken
fools about, all very eager to part ways with their
precious things. When we are done we will carouse
about through the night and feast."

"Indeed," Farwuld said without looking back. "I
will get you to appreciate a good day's work yet. Leave
my charges alone and come with me to the market to get
some provisions. There will be roast fowl, bread, ale,

and honey wine at the Golden Hearth tonight. If you strain your back as eagerly as your fingers and your mouth, you may earn a good meal."

"Food and drink," Modi remarked, licking his lips. "What of my Skaggs?" he asked.

Farwuld did not answer. The young troupe soon dragged their wagons to the open market, which was fast becoming choked with citizens; mostly women. The sky was clearing, but there was no telling what the late afternoon would bring.

Mostly anxious women scoured the rows of carts and kiosks picking vegetables and meats and loading sacks with grain. The young troupe joined them, drawing curious looks. But people recognized Farwuld. He ran this errand for his father many times. His father relied on his skill at tabulating and keeping records. As with all commoners, he could not read. But his memory was remarkably reliable and his ability to visualize all matter of abstract problems exceptional.

Some women acknowledged Farwuld as he gathered the produce and supplies his father instructed him to purchase, committing to memory the exact amounts and prices. It was not long before Farwuld returned to the Golden Hearth with his troupe in tow. He had Modi and the servant boys unload the supplies into baskets and bins while he tabulated the new supplies in his inventory.

Fires and hearths were lit throughout the city, sweet breads were baking, cauldrons were full of stews and confecture, and spits were heaped with all assortments of meats. Modi sat in a corner of the dining hall of the Golden Hearth talking with Farwuld and playing a board game called cathres. They played and spoke throughout the afternoon and until the sun began to recede beyond western skyline of the city, which was dominated by the shining temple dome. While there was still a little light out, four strange men carrying clay ewers entered the Golden Hearth and asked for Tharguld the quartermaster.

Mardis, the merchant who spoke with Tharguld earlier, had returned with three men, and to the old quartermaster's delight, he brought Tarpedi wine. Tharguld was gleeful and welcomed the merchant and his small entourage with slightly more than his usual warmth frivolity. Tharguld sat the four men down at a table in the far corner of the main hall, which was starting to fill with patrons. Modi leered as the merchant crossed the hall.

"I have seen this man before," Modi whispered to Farwuld.

"My father says that this man is a merchant," Farwuld replied. "It is not surprising that you would have seen him. Especially since you and your Skaggs filch so heavily in the merchant sector of the city."

Modi scoffed. "The merchants do not like common folk. They look down their noses at us. They especially hate my Skaggs. But that's fine with us. We've been wetting our beaks on their goods since we were old enough to walk and wield a dagger. We take what we need. They have so much and we have so little. We Skaggs take the king's tax for the poor and the orphans. How many of my Skaggs have been orphaned because our fathers and even our mothers work for merchants and nobles and die in mines from the black dust? Are we to die too? We are right to take some of the spoils our fathers and mothers have died for."

"There are laws in our city," Farwuld interjected. "No one has a right to intrude on another's rights simply to square a general wrong. You can't get justice from one merchant to atone for the injustice of another merchant. Go to the merchant who is responsible for your loss and ask him to atone."

Modi laughed wryly and then scoffed again. "I'll do that tomorrow. I will simply find the merchant my father worked for and ask him for some food. I will explain that he should share to ease my suffering."

Modi paused and contorted his face in a clear expression of derision.

"Why should my Skaggs and I suffer when others have so much? What kinds of laws say that the few should have more than they can eat while others have nothing?"

Modi paused again as if trying to recall something. Astonished at hearing Modi utter so many words, Farwuld looked on with particular interest.

"I once heard a wise man say," Modi began again, "that laws should protect the weak. I am not weak. But I think he meant those who are poor. I think he is right. He was wise. I know because he had a thick gray beard like those men who walk with ashen staves. He said something I didn't really understand at first. But now I think I know what he meant. He said, and I remember every word because I have a good memory – 'the full measure of our virtue is realized by the greater good and the expression of charity, compassion and, and understanding among men.' That's exactly what he said. I think I understand what he meant. He meant that the people of the high city should care about each other. I can honestly say that we don't. No one cares about the orphans and the Skaggs. Why should we suffer because people don't care? That's their fault. That's why the Skaggs filch – because nobody cares about us so we have to take care of ourselves."

"Then," Farwuld replied. "You and your Skaggs will feel the stick across your backs. I can't dispute that hard times have fallen on the city. Many have gone to work in the mines to the south and have lost their freedom and their lives. But what are common folk to do? If the city falls into lawlessness we will be worse off."

"If you say so," Modi replied. "But you know that the Skaggs' quarrel is not with the good citizens of the high city. You and your father have been good to me and even my Skaggs." Sighing, Modi relented, saying, "Perhaps the city will see better days and the Skaggs will be better off."

As night fell, a full moon shone on the high city, which buzzed with activity. A procession of revelers gathered at the city's eastern portcullis and made their way toward the city's center along its main thoroughfare. The revelers passed by four of the nine arches featured on that road. The fifth arch was opened into the city's center plaza, which featured a circular multilevel loggia of limestone bricks. Here, there were several apartments, hostels and shops, the Golden Hearth among them. The revelers planned a great gathering at the center plaza to sing and dance and drink all through the night. Even as the revelers began their procession, citizens, young and old, had already gathered there around a great bonfire.

A crowd had gathered outside the Golden Hearth in the arcade overlooking the plaza. There was a crush of people and sounds of merrymaking inside of the public house. Tharguld sat at his quartermaster's table, which was heaped with roast fowl, bread, and ewers of ale and mead and wine brought by his guests.

"Welcome friends and guests," Tharguld bellowed.

A hush swept through the room as the guests put down their goblets looked to their host.

"I know that I do not have to say how momentous this occasion is. I promised, when we gathered last – three years ago if I remember-"

Uneasy laughter spread among the gathering as most did not want to encourage the old quartermaster to speak for too long.

"During the last Levying festival, I wagered that my drinking prowess could not be matched by any man then present. I promised to host a feast on the last night of the next Levying festival for any man then present

willing to wager a silver feranx who could best me.
Needless to say, I lost that wager.

Early this morning, I awoke to the sound of what
I thought was a furious rain. What blessings from the
gods I thought. Pilgrims and merchants seek out
lodgings when it rains. Unfortunately the rains had
ceased and the sky cleared even before noon. But I am
still glad. I am glad to see you all here. I am glad to see
your wretched faces glow with ale and mead. A
gathering is a blessed thing and I am glad to be your
host tonight. It should not be surprising anyone here if I
continue this tradition for many more years."

"It's profitable!" a guest shouted. Muffled
laughter could be heard around the room.

"What is profitable can be good in other respects.
Let us who are gathered here together agree to honor a
new tradition in the high city. We will call this new
tradition the feast of the Golden Hearth, and it shall be
dedicated to friendship and merrymaking."

A cheer erupted in the Golden Hearth, which was
mimicked outside by those who heard it. There was no
telling whether those within earshot of the old
quartermaster's speech cheered because he was done
speaking, or because they were excited about the
establishment of a new tradition celebrated with drink.
The cheers were awkward and subsided quickly.
Whatever the crowd's motive, the first night of the feast
of the Golden Hearth began in earnest. After the cheers
subsided, maidens with trays of food and ewers of drink
pranced out into the main hall.

"Well said master Tharguld," the merchant
sitting next to the quartermaster said. "You have
brought much goodwill to so many in these difficult
days."

The old round quartermaster looked at the
merchant. "I am old," he said. "My time in this world
is nearer to its end than to its beginning. Now, I have
heard that there are men, guild masters and so-called

Atenarix, shadowy men, who say that immortality is possible. They even say that it is possible to resurrect the dead. When they die therefore, they have their corpses preserved with oils and spices and wrapped in fine cloth and stored in great sarcophagi like the kings."

Tharguld smiled and then sighed.

"This is folly. These men spend all their lives trying to escape death. But in my opinion, this is simply not possible. Worse, in doing so they overlook all there is in life. I think that death is at least a useful thing. Not the painful writhing death of warriors on battlefields, or the slow death by starvation and disease. But a death that passes gently over your eyes after you have had your day. This death makes you value your day. And I value my day, my family, my son, and my friends. I value these gatherings and the opportunity to meet new friends. That is how I find usefulness and purpose of death; that it is a benchmark for life. Death is all that life is not. Weighed against death, life is worth more than all the wealth in the world. The choice is easy for me. I choose the blue sky, the snow capped mountains, the fresh air, the warm springs, the birds, the sea, and all there is in life. I have learned to choose life and leave solving death to necromancers."

"Well said," the merchant replied. "I cannot argue over the effect your conclusion has on your actions. You are a good man. Your goodwill will surely bring a reprieve for many who suffer in this short and brutal life." The merchant held up a goblet and toasted the quartermaster's goodwill. The men in his entourage mimicked him emotionlessly.

Meanwhile at the royal compound streams of courtiers came through the gate and passed under a decorative canopy hoisted up before the portico of the royal apartments. Courtiers in ceremonial dress, donning ornate masks of serene masks for ladies and animalistic masks for men, made their way to the center courtyard. Each man held a narrow ashen staff and each woman wore a red scarf around their waist. The masks worn by each attendee featured wide holes for the eyes and for the mouth, which resembled a gape. Fastened around the head with a silk string, the masks were made of very thin and rigid leather and coated with a resin which made them gleam and which made the leather odorless. The masks were skillfully formed and painted to resemble the passionless feminine for the women and for the men, birds of prey, lions, bears, and other predators.

The revelers convened in the polished stone center courtyard to dance and to eat at tables arranged for them. The air was filled with the aroma of mutton and fowl roasting on spits and enchanted with sound of flutes and harps. The royal family sat at a table near an archway leading into a narrow portico leading into the royal apartments. The great seal of the Vyrdmar was prominently displayed behind them. There was quite a buzz about the beautiful young woman sitting next to prince Varenhil. Eje was radiant. Her black hair, her lobes, and her neck gleamed with silver and pearls. She wore a webbed silver circlet studded with pearls on her head binding her hair. Gleaming silver hoops hung from her ears and the light of nearby fires flickered on her silver necklace with jade studs.

All the revelers wore white as pure as new snow. They moved about bowing and greeting, and dancing. Their white robes flowed like streams vapor wafting above rivers on moonlit nights. As the night wore on the king gestured to his master of ceremony that he wished to speak and upon subtle motion from him, the heralds blew their trumpets and the crowd turned to look on their king who was resplendent in white. He stood up at the center of the table where his children, Varenhil, Ylia, Hovin, Jaïem and his newest daughter Eje. The revelers were now silent.

The king was not known to be a man of many words. He was also not one to find much pleasure in frolicking and merrymaking. And so it was expected that he would be brief and that he would soon be retiring to his royal apartments.

"Princes of Maspeidon, courtiers, and citizens," he said opening his arms. "Let us be thankful for our birthright. Let us be thankful for the bonds of friendship and allegiance. Let us be thankful for the bounty of our fertile land. But our greatest birthright is the light of Yggir, which shines our way through times of shadow.

There are so many things to be thankful for. Maspeidon is united and strong like a great obelisk. We have good harvests and abundant trade with our neighbors across the seas. Let us not forget the devotion and toil of our shepherds and auxiliaries that watch over our plains, farmlands and borders. If you are too full of drink to remember them today then remember them tomorrow. Tonight, let a man take a woman by the hand and a woman bow, and together dance like dragonflies buzzing over the surface streams or like hummingbirds darting and hovering over vibrant flora."

Looking to his side, the king smiled and took his daughter Ylia by the hand. The king took Ylia to the center of the gathering, and together they danced in the traditional manner. Varenhil followed behind the king with his betrothed Eje and danced in the same manner. The revelers all looked on with smiles that could not have been seen from behind their masks. But not all were pleased and full of goodwill. There were also cold stares and gritting of teeth.

After the king and the crown prince had danced for a short while they bowed. The king extended out a hand to welcome the revelers to partake in the dancing. Many slowly took partners and converged around the king. Prince Hovin found his beloved Besia and danced with her as Jaïem looked on for as long as he could bear. It was not long before he withdrew to his chambers to peer over dusty manuscripts. Soon after Jaïem left

Hovin too tore himself away from his beloved to make a final tour of the compound sentries.

Having made his rounds of the royal compound, Hovin summoned Macheleion and three other Harfingals to him. He then rode with them to have a look at the city's sentry posts along the city walls. Hovin did this many times even though his responsibility was primarily over the royal compound, the academies, and the temple. The Harfingals rode out with their captain and surveyed the streams of people going to and from homes and hostels. They rode through the city plaza, and to the northern sector of the city where there was high parapet running east to the eastern gate.

The Harfingals rode up a ramp paved atop a buttress onto the strong northern rampart. They came alongside a guard tower jutting out of the rampart and were saluted by sentries from above. Heading east, the Harfingals reached another guard tower resting above two gated arches below. The two gates opened out into the walled courtyard where the eastern garrison could be seen eating their evening meal.

Satisfied that northern and eastern sectors were secure, Hovin took his men back west along the city's main thoroughfare. He and his men did not get far along their return westward to the Hold, when the city began to erupt in what many thought was awesome pyrotechnics. It was the clairvoyant canines that gave the first warning of trouble. At the royal compound Tngshaz and Faeut growled and barked and scampered along the perimeter of the compound. Then a deafening sound rang out across the city followed by two similar sounds. Flashes could be seen as if a lightening storm had abruptly swept over city. But in that short instance many souls perished along the city's eastern and northern gates, and at the gate into the royal compound. From the shadows, men of the order of the Droa had lit fuses and detonated wagons full of black powder.

At the city's central plaza the Droa casually drew wagons coated with tar and heavily weighed with containers filled with the same substance. The crowd looked curiously as the Droa set the wagons ablaze obstructing passage west to the temple and the royal compound. Now fires erupted all over the city and black smoke wafted up and cast black streaks across the starry sky. Crowds scattered every way they could, screaming, and fleeing from danger. Patrons clamoring within the Golden Hearth leapt from their chairs and fled out into the packed arcade when they heard the explosions and began to inhale the vapors from the fires the Droa had set.

Modi scampered out into the arcade and into the plaza and Farwuld followed helping his old father and mother along. Young Modi looked around and saw black smoke billowing from a roaring fire rising from the ground like a wall of flame. He felt a strange hollow feeling inside; his thoughts echoed in his mind. Then in the distance he saw what appeared to be a man striding toward him. The man wore a plain white tunic like the Harfingals, and seemed to glow. He had flowing black hair resting over firm and shapely shoulders. But when the man spoke, it became apparent to Modi that he was not a man at all.

"Young Modi," the woman called out. "I am Ligia. I am the one who whispered to you while you were confined in that dark pit long ago. I freed you and gave you the whistle you wear around your neck, which is now the heirloom of the Skaggs. Listen to me therefore, Modi, lord of the Skaggs. Blow your whistle, and when your little warriors come to you, take them to Commoners Square to the south and I will meet you there."

Modi had seen this woman before in what he thought was a nightmare, which became a dream. Now she returned to him in a perilous hour, and he felt compelled to obey. Before she left him she whispered words with which he was to rally the Skaggs and the words were seared in his mind. After she withdrew back into the darkness, Modi groped for his whistle and whistled, summoning his Skaggs to him. Even though the call was shrill and could barely be heard over the roaring of the fires and the wild screams of fleeing citizens, the Skaggs heard and came to him.

After Farwuld brought his father some distance from the fire he looked around for Modi. He ran back toward the plaza and saw him standing below one the obelisks in the center of the plaza blowing his whistle over and over.

When the Droa attacked the royal compound, the king and his principal vizir Cerondilus were about to make their way from the courtyard to meet briefly before the king settled in for the night. The Droa had quickly infiltrated the compound's perimeter after destroying its arched gate and guardhouse. The Harfingals burst from their barracks to meet the shadowy enemy. They divided their forces, some rushing to the temple and others into the royal apartments to find their king. Scaling the apartment walls like a black mist, the Droa drifted undetected to the rooftops and took positions overlooking the courtyard. They lit the fuses of their noxious bombs and hurled them into the courtyard. Soon a thick gray smoke spread throughout, overcoming the revelers who had not fled indoors.

The king, his family, and many of his courtiers and guests, lord Dorias, Bojingren the Red, Ahktel and Ixhor among them, were hurried into the king's audience hall on the second level of the royal apartments. Lord Umalein rallied the king's vassals and they rushed through the royal apartments and out into the courtyard to face the enemy. Soon Haldar came to prince Varenhil, bringing him his sword. Taking it from him, he summoned several Harfingals to him.

"Father," he then said. "Remain here and secure these strong doors. I will ferret out this treachery."

King Ylarin took his son by his arm and brought him close. "Bring me my sword," the king called out. Servants scattered to do their king's bidding.

"These men are here to slay kings and princes. Their treachery is clear. They hope that not one son of Wind survives this night. Therefore, curb your fury and your courage and rely on the Harfingals and my counsel. Weak in numbers is an enemy who strikes in the dark. Such an enemy hopes to disorient a stronger foe and neutralize them with concealment, surprise and fear. But such a foe has two very potent enemies; and foremost among them is time. It will not take long for the Harfingals to regain their bearing and solve our enemy's machinations."

The king drew even closer to his son and whispered in his ear. "If you must leave this hall lord of Greingspen, then go down to the catacombs and take my passage to the safety of the temple catacombs."

"He looks to secure his heir," Varenhil thought.

Eje came forward and touched her betrothed. "My lord," she said. "I owe my life to these men you see behind me. Look upon Bojingren the Red, Ahktel son of Tilon and stalwart Ixhor, and know that they will defend what is precious to you."

Ahktel came forward and Eje took him by the hand and translated as he spoke. "The king is right. The purpose of this attack is to slay the king and his heirs. That is transparent. But beware of their lethality and the scope of their treachery. The enemy entered the city in great numbers over many weeks under the guise of merchants. All precautions must be taken to frustrate their ultimate goal."

Hovin and his Harfingals reached the city plaza and were astonished to see the wall of flames the Droa had set.

"Look there," Macheleion remarked. "Look how the city's foundlings have gathered at the plaza. Are they complicit in this?"

The Harfingals drew closer to the gathering of the Skaggs. The lord of the Skaggs, with Farwuld by his side, was rallying the foundlings together with passionate words.

"The gods know no rank among men. Now more than ever, actions will be the measure of even children. If we fight for our city now, we Skaggs will be welcomed and cherished and loved. We will live in the paradise the gods have sown for us even though men may scorn us. And so I do not ask you to fight for men now. I ask you to follow me and defend the city and its hallowed temple for the gods' sake."

After Modi had exhorted them, the Skaggs, over a hundred strong cheered: "For Irilsflir!"

Hovin rode through the gathering of Skaggs with his men.

"Hail lord of the Skaggs," Hovin shouted to his men's surprise. The Skaggs had turned and parted, recognizing the raiment of the Harfingals.

"If you are sworn to defend the city and the temple, as I am, then we are united by a common purpose. Bring your Skaggs with you and follow me to city's northern ramparts since the way west is barred by flames."

Young Modi came forth to meet prince Hovin. He bowed and the prince called him closer.

"My lord," Modi said arching is brow. "We must go south. This is the way chosen by the gods. We must go south to Commoners Square and await instructions from the goddess who summoned the Skaggs together."

Again, to the astonishment of his men, prince Hovin followed the lord of the Skaggs to Commoners Square.

It was not long before the Harfingals and the Skaggs reached Commoners Square, which had an abandoned well as its centerpiece. The prince, the Harfingals, Farwuld and the Skaggs gathered next to a row of kiosks standing next to a cluster of clay huts. There was a strong stone building surrounded by a bronze gate across the square. No sooner than they had gathered to look for a sign, did Ligia appear, resplendent in the distance.

"Down the abandoned well," she called out. "There is not much time."

A Skagg brought a long rope and tethered it on an iron loop. The newly formed company made its way down the abandoned well and into a dark passage with Ligia lighting the way.

The path at the bottom of the well led directly to Aufrey's tower adjacent to the temple, the academies, and the royal compound. Long ago, Aufrey, a benevolent surplicant, would climb the tower and ring its iron bell to call the city's orphans for their evening porridge. This became a tradition for the surplicants. Long after Aufrey had passed from the world, surplicants continued to look after orphaned and destitute children. But as the winters became longer and colder and the harvests less plenty, this practice was abandoned. The tower of the foundlings became a locked storehouse where the surplicants kept excess bookbinding supplies and other sundry supplies.

Now even as the temple gate lay in ruins and many Harfingals lay scattered, broken, and dead, the doors of Aufrey's tower flung open. Out came Ligia and a stream of eager foundlings, some so small that they were barely visible behind the towering woman. But their eyes flashed with fire and their veins flowed with the courage of those accustomed to hardship. Prince Hovin called out to them to gather around him. Standing together, the Vyrdmar prince, Ligia and Modi, all gestured to gather around and listen.

"Find weapons among the dead and follow the Harfingal captain through the quadrangle."

Meanwhile another Vyrdmar prince encountered two masked men with swords like sharp stingers. Varenhil had heeded his father's counsel and made his way to the catacombs. But even before he could begin his descent into that dark place, he and four Harfingals found their way barred by silent men with eyes flashing yellow with malice. These Droa were swift and agile and leapt on the forward Harfingals, slaying them outright. When Varenhil saw the Harfingal's blood oozing down the shaft of his enemies' blade, he became enraged. The Droa could not have known what only those close to the prince knew. Varenhil's fury and bloodlust was like raging fire that only subsided when all was consumed before it. But the Vyrdmar prince was also a skilled and disciplined warrior. He drew his great broadsword and awaited the Droa's attack.

The Droa crept like jackals stalking prey and then leapt into action. The two remaining Harfingals stepped forward and engaged them. One was cut down as he advanced while the other was engaged by the second of the last Harfingals. This cunning Droa dodged the Harfingal's blow, sliding on one thigh and thrusting a dagger into the Harfingal's thigh. Having immobilized the Harfingal, the Droa leapt at the prince with his sword pointed outward. Varenhil gauged the Droa's leap and came forward to cut him down. Then the remaining Harfingals hurried the prince into a dark alcove concealing a stairway to the catacombs. Holding up torches, they made their way down to the catacombs and ran until they came to a hidden passageway.

In the courtyard of the royal compound, blood-curdling shrieks could be heard. There, Bojingren's brave lieutenant Tyeshar and a detachment of Harfingals engaged the enemy, with round shields held high to deflect a volley of arrows. Raining missiles of the compound's defenders, the shadowy enemy had concealed themselves on roofs and trees and along smoldering ruin of the walls that once fortified the royal compound. The Harfingals advanced slowly in ranks holding up their shields walking over the bodies of their fallen comrades. Some charged forward to dislodge the enemy and were cut down. The almost impenetrable darkness slowed their advance and their numbers were fast dwindling. Then they saw a light of hope.

Chapter 13: The Vyrdmar rally

Ligia came from the archway leading to the royal garden with prince Hovin, Macheleion his lieutenant, and two Harfingals. Behind them were Farwuld, Modi, and the raucous Skaggs. Ligia cast beads of light beyond the enemy's position and blinded them. Then the captain of the Harfingals called out to his men and a great blast rang out from a horn. With a thunderous shout, the defenders of Irilsflir swarmed down on the Droa enemy. The Harfingals fell on them with swords and spears, dislodging them from their position along the ruined wall. The cunning and agile Skaggs dislodged the enemy from the trees and along the walls where they were thick like locusts. They leapt onto branches and scaled the walls hurling stones and firing volleys of arrows.

The Droa scattered. Some were struck down, while others scaled back against the rubble along the wall. Hovin ordered Macheleion to pursue the enemy until every one of them were slain. He then summoned a few Harfingals to him and diverted his attention to the royal apartments. Hovin's thoughts were now on his family and his beloved and his heart sank when he saw smoke wafting up over the structure's façade, appearing to billow up from the courtyard. He hurried through the portico and burst through the splintered doors of the vestibule. Hurdling scattered furnishings and the dead, he followed a trail of dead Harfingals, hoping that it would lead to where the king and his court were making their stand.

In the great audience hall, the king and his courtiers armed themselves with swords, spears, and pikes. They piled furnishings against the double doors and Harfingals posted themselves all around the hall, two by every window. Beyond the doors, groans, screams, and shrieks could be heard every now and then. Here and there they could hear the sounds of detonating bombs. The sounds got closer and closer until they were accompanied by ever growing pressure against the doors. Soon the king and his courtiers could hear a commotion just beyond the double doors.

The assault on the audience hall began as Droa crashed through the paneled windows. The Droa crept through the windows like a swarm of insects. The Harfingals leapt on them as they came through the breach. There were too many, however, and soon the Harfingals were being forced back. That was when Bojingren, Ahktel and Ixhor leapt into action. Ixhor hurled a spear, which impaled a Droa, which struck him with so much force that it lifted him, groaning, through a shattered window and down into an outer promenade. Ahktel and Bojingren followed in kind, impaling two others. With a great shout, the entire host defending the king and the royal courtiers encircled the Droa and cut through them.

There was a great cheer and then an uneasy and momentary silence. Now an ominous sound was heard.

There was a thud and then a rolling sound. Ahktel felt a strange tingle behind his ears and the hairs on his neck stood. He saw many Droa beyond the doors and a flash of light. "Move away from the doors," he said inaudibly in the Hekare tongue.

"Move away from the doors," he said – this time louder.

Eje interpreted loudly and the king gestured for the Harfingals to fall back toward the far end of the room parallel to the windows. No sooner than the courtiers and guards retreated to the far wall did a deafening explosion ring out splintering the doors.

Through the smoke and ruin came more Droa brandishing their gleaming stingers. A furious melee ensued with the remaining Harfingals leading the fray. The clash of swords was short lived as the Harfingals cut through the first wave with their broadswords. But more came pouring in. These were larger. They glowered with golden eyes and brandished long swords. This second melee was hard fought and bloody. There were many groans and many came from the brave Harfingals. Bojingren, Ahktel, and Ixhor leapt into action with long spears. The courtiers' defenders pushed the enemy back into the smoky hallway with a frantic and furious onset. Once in the hallway, the Harfingals were seized by a frenzy of bloodlust. Leaving the companions behind, they cut and skewered through the enemy, who fell back in disarray.

On the first level of the royal apartments, Hovin and a few Harfingals heard the din above and bolted up a wide stairway. This contingent of defenders followed the sound of the melee above. Smoke and bodies and debris hampered their way. But then a cool breeze parted the smoke as they scampered into a wide antechamber with two large windows. At first sight, it appeared that this was an entry point for the enemy. Hovin drew close to the shattered window and peered through it and down below saw nothing. Then, as he turned to press on, he saw a throng of retreating Droa.

Hovin heard a shout-"for Irilslflir!"

Hovin and his Harfingals shouted the same and fell on the retreating enemy. Now the Droa were beset from both sides.

Having made his way to the temple, after a brief encounter with many Droa, Prince Varenhil rallied his contingent of Harfingals and led them out into the temple quadrangle. By then Ligia had again withdrawn and hurried off to help others in need.

"The enemy is here to kill your king," he urged them. "Not your gods."

The Harfingal detachment in the temple followed the Vyrdmar prince out to the royal compound where the fight was being waged. As they passed through the royal gardens Varenhil and the temple guards heard a great clamor coming from the courtyard of the royal compound.

When Varenhil and the temple guards came within sight of the rubble that was once the gates into the compound they were amazed to see young commoners and Harfingals engaging an enemy host. Varenhil could see his own brother Jaïem joined in the fray. Jaïem was fiercely cutting down stragglers among the enemy, as the enemy was now fleeing.

"Hail lord Greingspen!" Jaïem shouted when he saw his brother coming.

Varenhil saluted his brother and shouted out orders to the compounds defenders.

"Gather as many horses as can be found and prepare a company to ride out into the city to restore order." His younger brother now joined Varenhil, and along with a party of Harfingals made a determined foray into the royal apartments.

"The rest of you prepare to fall out upon my return." Varenhil called out. "Sound the horns of muster. Rally our brothers to us and move to take back the city."

The horns of muster were blasted and were echoed by other guard posts. The wave of horn blasts could be heard as far as the northern gates and the city plaza. The Harfingals within the royal apartments heard the blasts cheered. But even as the defenders of Irilsflir felt a turning of the tide, the Atenarix hammer fell again. Now the young Skaggs could be heard screaming. Modi and Farwuld scrambled back over the rubble shouting. Along with the shouts, the defenders rallying at the courtyard also heard dull popping sounds. Then small iron balls began to slam against them, searing and tearing through flesh and bone. Varenhil stood tall and motionless to make sense of the building carnage. He could hear the sound of iron balls pelting on surfaces all around and gritted his teeth. Realizing what he was seeing and hearing from his previous campaigns, his heart began to beat wildly. Indeed, the Droa had rallied back with a column wielding long tubes with oaken stock mounted on their shoulders. They bore stout and deadly rifles devised by the most ingenious of the Atenarix metics.

In the main audience hall, the king and his courtiers and defenders looked at each other, wondering if the worst was over. But then they heard more strange sounds and more screams. But every man, including the king was armed and ready for another attack. Now they experienced a vivid sense of dread as if the danger had penetrated the doors and entered the room. Indeed, clouding the senses of those in the audience hall, Promothos had entered the room without being seen or heard. He intended to pass by those encircling the king without being noticed. But Ahktel was aware of him.

Ahktel walked away from the rest of the defenders. He walked slowly and deliberately toward Promothos with his sword resting on his shoulder. Coming face to face with Promothos, he pointed his sword at him and then thrust it suddenly. Promothos was nicked on his side and he swore angrily. Now everyone in the room could see the Amretar master with his black silk robes and a light cloak.

"Fool," he roared. "Be gone." His coarse voice startled all those in the hall, and many moved away toward the doors. Others looked to their king who did not utter a word at first.

Briefly, Ahktel crossed swords with Promothos but could not disarm or injure him. A few Harfingals sprung into action, but with a stern look from Promothos, they were overcome with dread and nausea and fell to their knees.

Finally the king gestured saying, "Go now my children. Your king will stand against this foe alone."

The Harfingals took courage and drew closer still to their king.

"Go," he said. "Go out into the courtyard and lend your skill and courage to the fight there. I fear the enemy has gathered there in force and with potent machinations. I fear that our forces may be in dire need of reinforcements. Now go as I command."

The Harfingals reluctantly obeyed and the courtiers left with them. Bojingren took Eje and gestured for Ahktel and Ixhor to follow. The companions left the room as the king ordered and left the king and Promothos alone. The king now turned to face Promothos who was smiling wryly. His golden eyes gleamed behind the rim of the hood of his cloak.

"Wise king of the Vyrdmar," he sneered. "You dissemble so grotesquely, telling your subjects that your person is inviolable. But now I have come to exact vengeance precisely upon your person for your father's treachery. Shall I devour your children in your stead since your person is sacred?"

"Do not presume to gainsay me in matters of truth and justice," the king answered. "When you last held power under the Pelares you ruled as a tyrant and sowed discord through deceit. You sowed faithlessness, disobedience, and hatred. You promised to erect a new Atlantis on the ruin of the Vyrdmar and bring the light of knowledge and hope to men. Yet all you brought in your time was an unrelenting crucible of hatred, suffering, and death."

Promothos laughed softly. "Very well – I suppose that what you say has merit. I did allow my hatred to cloud my judgment long ago. The Ayimar, my children, suckled on that hatred and became malevolent and hateful. I fault myself for descending into this cycle of petty violence. But who is blameless? Who lives without doing harm? A masterful being should not engage in vengeance. In this, I have behaved poorly. Though, it cannot be doubted that I dream only of man's salvation. But now enough, son of Wind; I know my purpose as you claim to know yours. It is my inexorable purpose to cleanse the world of kings; if not for the salvation of men yet unborn, then for vengeance. Either motive will suffice so long as the objective is secured."

Promothos unsheathed his sword from its black scabbard, and it gleamed, a dull red hue.

"You know of this blade," Promothos said lifting the sword high.

Indeed, the king knew of the anurium blade. He knew that it could kill without striking. He knew that once the anurium blade was unsheathed that its aura would wax stronger and burn his flesh. This was the king's mind when he summoned all of this strength and attacked his enemy.

The king sprung like an old majestic lion, which looks weary when he is at rest, but when he has leapt into action is ferocious and skillful. Promothos flinched and lunged into the fray. Their swords clashed and clanged loudly. It was immediately clear to Promothos that the king's skill with the sword was far superior to his. He knew however that he merely had to hold him at bay until his sword grew glowed so bright and hot that it weakened the king and burned his flesh. The king would have struck him many times, but Promothos pierced the king's mind, dulling his senses and disorienting him.

Searching his mind for memories of a cool soothing place, the king composed himself. He could hear the priestess of Yggir telling him, as she did once, that the Celestial chose Namreddin's line because their warrior hearts were calm like slow moving rivers even in the face of redoubtable chaos and malice.

"Anger and malice breaks like a furious storm on the surface of rocks. Yet courage and unyielding perseverance shapes the world."

Promothos eyed the king curiously and then laughed.

"Where is your god son of Wind? Call out to your god. I assure you he will not come. Do you even know who Yggir is? I know Yggir, that chromatic simian with silvery wings. Yggir lives and breathes like you live and breathe. If mighty Yggir were here, he too would burn. Do you even know that once upon a time, this beast lay by the primordial pool staring into oblivion, its nascent mind reflecting on dark waters? Do you not know that it was the Atenari from beyond the stars that came and awakened the minds of species and made them masterful?"

The king began to feel weak as he stared into the dull red light emanating from Promothos' sword. He drew a deep breath and willed himself to attack with swiftness and precision. He veiled an upward slashing attack with weak lateral slashing attack and a thrust. Coming up almost in one motion he struck Promothos across his left arm. Promothos flinched but he did not give ground. He went to make a thrusting attack but the king parried and grasped his sword arm and they struggled with each other. The king's surprisingly massive shoulders and biceps stiffened and anchored a violent thrust, which sent Promothos sprawling on his back.

Promothos cursed his weakened body. He remembered the strength and speed he possessed long ago. But his strength and speed, the strength and speed of an Amretar, the masterful creation of the Atenari, had wasted away in the catacombs of the temple for over a generation. Even his mind was weakened. His former mental puissance was but a shadow of its former power. Promothos' body clenched and he lifted himself up with vengeance pulsing through his body. He loosed his tentacles, which were hidden under his robes lashing the king who fell back.

The more the anurium blade clashed with the king's sword the brighter it waxed. The brighter it waxed the more its aura enfeebled the king. Some said that the sword's aura had the opposite effect on its Amretar or the Atenari who wielded it. But even if it did not strengthen Promothos, he seemed to draw comfort from it, knowing that soon the king would be overcome. The king rose quickly and resumed his attack. Promothos was nipping with his prehensile tentacles and the king was moving from side to side and getting closer. But he began to tire. The king swung to finish his enemy, but Promothos seemed to nullify the force of his blow, which passed by him harmlessly.

Missing his mark, the king fell to his knees. Now he could feel his flesh burning. His vision blanketed by the crimson light of the anurium blade. Soon he felt a painful heaviness in his chest and began to feel a spreading numbness throughout his body. The king finally slumped over on his knees, supporting himself on his sword. Darkness began to veil his eyes, and he experienced a serene weightlessness. He could hear a familiar voice crying out; it was the king's gallant son, Hovin.

Prince Hovin leapt on Promothos, smote him across his back with his sword tearing through cloth, skin and muscle and severing a tentacle. The Ayimar lord screamed from the deep biting pain. But his disciplined mind did not abandon him at this moment of peril and he whirled around striking on the side with the anurium blade. The blow merely grazed the prince, but he could feel the searing heat of the blade. Using his last tentacle, Promothos lashed the now unbalanced prince. Promothos wrapped the strong member across the prince's neck and began to choke the life from him.

The companions were now standing by the door with several Harfingals who were set to leap into action. But by now the Anurium blade's aura was emanating throughout the hall and was permeating flesh and bone. Even those at the doorway could feel it.

"No" Ahktel said in the common tongue. "Let me face this fire."

Bojingren looked intently into the Ahktel's eyes and saw that it now had its own glow. He thought he saw Ahktel fading like the flickering flame of a candle.

"Go back," Bojingren shouted. With Ixhor's help they cordoned off the entrance to the hall and Ahktel, entering the room, shut its door behind him.

Now Varenhil had rallied the Harfingals in the courtyard of the Hold and Modi and Farwuld had rallied the Skaggs. But they owed the turning of the tide to the Hold's massive canine guardians who dashed into the fray and briefly threw the Droa column into the disorder. All through the night, Tngshaz and Faeut were hunting the Droa intruders. They stalked and crouched and leapt on them and fell on them with their massive paws and tore their flesh and ground their bones. They were cunning too. They retreated before large hosts and only barked and growled. But when they found stragglers they crept out of the darkness and seized them.

Now, prince Varenhil, the Harfingals and the Skaggs were pushing the enemy back as they tried to reload their iron rifles. Then, master Nausterus advanced on a strong mount to rally the Droa. He rode past them, and leapt from his horse, sword in hand to engage the Vyrdmar prince. Nausterus thought to slay the prince to rekindle the Droa's courage. Nausterus and Varenhil were soon tangled in a fierce sword fight. Nausterus towered over Varenhil, who was himself, of great stature among the Vyrdmar. There was a great shout from both sides and a frantic reengagement.

Nausterus swung his great sword wildly and Varenhil moved back and to the side to disorient his lumbering enemy. Varenhil gleaned from his enemy's attack that he was not a skilled soldier. Indeed, whereas Nausterus had great prescience and power over the scattered bakiren that shimmered over pools and streams, he was no soldier. His purpose however was not merely to duel the Vyrdmar prince, it was to hearten his men. And they were now heartened and fully engaged with the Harfingals and the Skaggs. But Varenhil knew Nausterus' purpose and he envisioned a swift and brutal death for his foe. He wanted to gloriously cut the head from the Droa body.

Indeed, Varenhil's attack was swift and precise. In a blur, Nausterus' sword arm was hacked off below the humerus and his side was opened with brutal slashing attack. Nausterus hunched over in shock and pain, and looked up with his mouth gaping open. Yet just as Varenhil was to come down with the final stroke, he was grazed on his thigh with an iron ball from a rifle. Wincing in pain, the Vyrdmar prince fell to a knee. The Droa advanced with a great uproar to claim Nausterus. Many surrounded the fallen Vehe-ta, while others tried to seize their fleeting victory by advancing on Varenhil. But many Harfingals came to his aid, and many more Droa were slain, while the others fled, leaping onto nearby horses and wagons. Undeterred, Varenhil struggled to his feet and called for horses and ordered that the enemy be pursued and the compound secured.

In the audience hall, Promothos turned his attention to Ahktel who was striding toward him. Promothos let Hovin lie and turned his tentacles on the young Hekare. But Ahktel hurled a spear at him before the Amretar master could get close enough to bind him. Promothos leapt aside and stumbled. On one knee he clutched his bleeding torso and let his sword fall away from him. Before he could rise to his feet, Ahktel was upon him with a strong arm wrapped around his throat. Cursing, Promothos rose to his feet while bearing Ahktel's full weight. Livid, Promothos whirled this way and that way, thinking to hurl the Hekare from off of him.

Promothos whirled around until he flung the young Hekare from him. Ahktel landed deftly and positioned himself between his fallen comrades and the Amretar master. Promothos let his sword lie and cast a stern look at Ahktel. Yet the Hekare seemed undeterred and at peace. Now Promothos laughed mockingly.

"The world has such richness of life," he sneered. "I wonder what manner of specie you are. No matter. You will not withstand me. You may be quite deft, but my power is greater than you can imagine. I will let my anurium blade lie for it is a relic of a lost time. The Amretar master does not need a sword. His mind is his sword. Behold the sword of heaven."

The Amretar master lifted himself up and shut his eyes. Gathering his arms together with fingers barely touching, Promothos fell into a deep trance. He then fused the air around him into fine swath. Then he made the swath of air burn red and then yellow and then white and, opening his eyes, he unleashed it, his sword of heaven, against Ahktel with speed and ferocity.

Picking up an abandoned sword, Ahktel evaded the attacks and moved skillfully this way and that. He was amazed at how dense and hot Promothos' astonishing weapon of heated air was. He tried to parry an attack with his sword and was blinded by sparks the clash of weapons emitted. Standing back, Promothos sneered as he navigated his weapon toward the young Hekare, anticipating an imminent fatal strike.

Realizing that he could not defend himself against Promothos' attacks with a sword, Ahktel began to contemplate an astonishing maneuver of his own. Suddenly Promothos lost sight of the young Hekare. Promothos cursed his weakened body. He could feel blood trickling down his nostrils. He thought that his eyes were failing him and that he was beginning to succumb to fatigue. But this was not so. Ahktel was becoming intermittently transparent. The glow of both Promothos' sword of heaven and his abandoned anurium blade was fading as the young Hekare began to emanate his own blue aura. Promothos redoubled the intensity of his attacks. Soon however, his sword of heaven had dissipated into thin air and his anurium blade turned black. Promothos looked on in disbelief.

"You..." he murmured. "You are like the darkness of the primordial pool that contained me long ago."

As Promothos thought to utter another word, he was suddenly overcome with spasm of biting pain. The Amretar master whirled around grasping the hilt of a sword protruding from a penetrating wound. He fell to his knees and looked up to see none other than Jaïem looking back at him. Promothos looked to the ground and then up again tilting his head to the side in a curious way. He smiled menacingly and fell forward convulsing for a while and then becoming still. His shaven and elongated head was now partially revealed from the hood of his cloak. It seemed to glow. And as Jaïem looked down on Promothos' body he felt a sudden tingling delight and a warm sensation at first on his face and then throughout his body. The sensation waxed stronger and stronger and he closed his eyes and welcomed it.

Wondering if this was the thrill of battle, Jaïem felt suddenly faint. He fell to his knees, momentarily losing his bearings. Meanwhile Ahktel leapt up and sheathed Promothos' sword. He passed his hand over the smooth black scabbard and wondered what he should do with the mysterious weapon. Then Jaïem spoke.

"Bring the sword to me," the young prince whispered faintly. Jaïem's voice was barely audible but strangely commanding. Ahktel warily brought the sword to the young prince and helped him to the audience chamber door. As soon as the young Hekare opened the door, those waiting outside mobbed him and the weary prince.

"Where is the king?" "Where is our Harfingal captain?"

The Harfingals rushed forth to give aid. They tended to them as best as they could. Hovin's skin was only flushed, but the king's skin was beginning to blister. Thinking him dead, the Harfingals wrapped their king in silk tapestry hanging on the walls. The Harfingals hurriedly brought the king and his son to a nearby chamber where they had secured the courtiers. Ylia, Eje, and Besia were there huddled in a corner. When they saw the Harfingals bringing bodies into the room, Ylia and Besia broke out in a loud wail. They rushed to the men, whose faces were weary and grave. The princesses threw themselves onto the bodies and wept bitterly.

Meanwhile, Varenhil was leading a company of Harfingals and Skaggs through the city. Many were on horseback while others followed behind calling the people of the city to come out and to bring water to the fires burning in the plaza and at the city's eastern and northern gates. When the people saw mighty Varenhil riding on a strong mount leading a cadre of Harfingals, they came out into the streets and rejoiced. Some followed the prince while others organized to fight the fires. Soon the whole city was abuzz about the defeat of the Ayimar. Many were saying that the Ayimar thought to sack the high city and throw its citizens into bondage in their mines.

Prince Varenhil and his men scoured the city for the Droa but found none. They had vanished into the darkness, leaving the city strewn with heaps of carcasses and smoldering debris. Certain that the Hold was secure, and that the city was no longer under threat of fires, Varenhil rallied the people at the city plaza and exhorted them against the Ayimar and the Atenarix whom he accused of conspiring to sack the city. By then the people had armed themselves with sticks, stones, pikes and whatever weapons they could find.

"To the merchant sector," Varenhil shouted.

The people shouted and cheered again. When the people's fury and purpose had fully ruminated, Varenhil led them to the merchant sector to ferret out the Atenarix.

When the mob arrived at the merchant center, Varenhil gathered them together and spoke to them.

"In this fateful hour," he began. "Remember your proud heritage and cast not your nobility aside. Those who would follow me now must be of one mind with me. Do not burn your city. Rather, go into these halls teeming with treachery and treason and drive them out. Bring them out into the square and bind them to posts. Wait until the morning, and at first light mete out the king's full measure of justice."

At once, the people became grave and purposeful and set out to do the prince's bidding. For the rest of the night, the city and its people belonged to Varenhil, Vyrdmar prince of Greingspen.

The assault on the high city of Chamiahce was repelled and order was restored. South of the city, the scattered remnants of the Droa force were retreating with their grievously wounded master, Nausterus, in tow in a wagon. They rode long into the night and joined with a small force at a lonely glen off the main caravan road. Together the Droa and their master rode wearily south.   To the west, lord Umalein, who had earlier feigned to lead the defense of the Hold in the courtyard of the royal apartments, was well on his way to an awaiting ship on the coast with his chief vizir Alfaisten. Many other disloyal lords, who were not, however, privy to any knowledge of the secret attack, also fled for fear of brutal retribution.   Others stayed hoping to conceal their faithlessness, but were quickly seized or impaled out of hand by the Harfingals.   Meanwhile Jaïem disappeared into his bedchambers.   Overcome with weariness, he fell into a deep sleep that was like death.   The night was dark and the city was infected with foreboding. Now that the Vyrdmar had reclaimed the city, all knew that at first light there would be a great bloodletting.

Chapter 14: The Harfingals' retribution

The Vyrdmar quickly realized that the assault on the high city was to be the beginning of a long struggle with the Atenarix and their benefactors. If the king lived, the disloyal would not be spared, but the bloodletting would be measured and judicious. Yet if the king succumbed to death, Varenhil would be king, and he was vengeful. If Varenhil became master of the high city, his retribution would be protracted, indiscriminate, and brutal. At least this was Umalein's thinking.

Sailing away just before dawn, before the tide receded, lord Umalein mulled over his well laid plans. He knew that his army was already mustered and moving west from Kuthgelon. His plan had always been to lead his army to Chamiahce by spring's end whether or not Nausterus' Droa could sack the city. If Nausterus had been successful, his army would march on the city to secure it. Since Nausterus failed, he now had to proceed with his contingency plan. His fast lupeider was now sailing to Ursol, a coastal town near Beonon, where he would unite with his army, which would then march on Chamiahce and sack it before summer.

Lord Umalein doubted all along that Nausterus' assault would succeed. Nausterus could simply not bring enough Droa into the city. Outnumbered, not even their dreaded rifles could overcome the city's contingent of skilled sentries and Harfingals. He saw some advantage if Nausterus and his Droa could slay the king. If the king were slain, matters of succession would distract the city's inhabitants for some time. Varenhil was unpredictable, but Umalein was sure the city would be vulnerable for as long as these matters occupied the hearts and minds of the king's court.

The high city only had a thousand warriors and sentries defending it, and many of them were on the plains manning the posts along the trade routes. There were of course three hundred Harfingals guarding the Hold, the temple, and the academies. Umalein was pleased that Nausterus and his Droa destroyed the city's eastern gate. All things considered, if the Vyrdmar were slack in their efforts to refortify, he could march quickly to the high city with his army, ten thousand strong, and sack it.

Lord Umalein also wondered about Promothos' fate. The Kuthgelonian lord was steadfastly against Nausterus' ploy to free the Amretar master. This ploy, he thought, put the success of the assault and the larger offensive in jeopardy because it involved the surplicant Owidobel, who was not a sworn principal. Who could be sure of the surplicant's true loyalties or his motives? The surplicant could expose, what he was led to believe, was the Atenarix's plan to release Promothos, and draw the king's retribution even before the assault could begin.

But none of this really intrigue mattered to lord Umalein. He strongly believed that only a war matching the men, machines, and strategy of his army would ultimately unseat the Vyrdmar. He was optimistic about the role Promothos could play in a war against the Vyrdmar. Umalein knew that Promothos possessed knowledge that could sway the tide of a war overwhelmingly to his advantage. He knew that only Promothos possessed the knowledge to restore the fabled Atlantis he and Atenarix pined for. But this promise was also frightening to Umalein. As he searched within himself, he realized that he was not certain he wanted a new Atlantis. He was not certain he wanted to serve a council of enlightened men and the one Amretar master. He was also wary of the Ayimar, the so-called children of Promothos, who were deemed superior to men. What would they do to men when Atlantis was restored?

All the possibilities troubled the Kuthgelonian lord, but he realized that Promothos could very well be dead and Nausterus too. The king, if he were alive, and most certainly Varenhil, would move on the Pelares and ferret out the last of the Ayimar. This would be a fortuitous distraction for Umalein. While the Vyrdmar moved against the Ayimar, he could reunite with his army, move on the Vyrdmar, and achieve what he wanted most.

Umalein realized that he wanted to rule a united Maspeidon and establish his own dynasty on the continent. He now realized that in spite of his pretenses to contrary, he had turned his back on high ideals long ago. He found the idea of possessing supreme power seductive, but not for its own sake. He was curious about the kind of world he could shape. He wondered what kind of a legacy he would build. He wondered if he was the strong and wise ruler he and his Atenarix brothers believed the fractious continent and even the world needed. In all the confusion, he thought, he could reach Ursol in three days, sack the coastal city of Bonthc and march north to Chamiahce while securing a supply line from Bonthc. If all went well, he could be high king of Maspeidon before winter.

At first light, the tenuous silence blanketing the city was broken by shrieks coming from Commoners Square. By that time, Farwuld had left the Skaggs to find his father, who had returned to the Golden Hearth. But all through the night, the Skaggs scoured the city for merchants and brought them to the square and bound them. Armed with an assortment of weapons pilfered from the dead Droa, the Skaggs seized the merchants from their lodgings and dragged them pleading and screaming to the square. By early light, the Skaggs were stirring again, querying their prisoners about their purpose in the city and poking and prodding them with daggers, swords, and pikes.

As the morning wore on, a company of Harfingals came into Commoners Square. The Skaggs greeted them with salutes and eagerly brought them to the prisoners they had gathered throughout the night. The prisoners were quickly loaded into wagons and taken away with the Skaggs running behind jeering them and pelting them with rocks and rotten fruit.

Meanwhile, at the royal apartments, the king's children and chief vizir, Cerondilus had spent the night at the king's side where he was resting in his private chambers. Ylia was slumped over on the king's bed clinging to his hand. The king's face was flushed and contorted in pain. She whispered to him now and again but his answers were strained and incoherent. Also by the king's side was his chief physician, Sadrek, who had mixed a golden colored ointment, which he dabbed on the king's face and hands. Sadrek's face was grave. He shook his head many times as he wrote on a parchment after applying a treatment or noticing a physical reaction.

Across the large atrium of the royal chambers, in a large alcove, Varenhil sat quietly with his brothers Hovin and Jaïem. They had rested there for the night, but with the exception of Jaïem who slept soundly, they were thoughtful and restless. Varenhil and Hovin went to and from to see their father a few times during the night when he could be heard groaning, straining to speak. The king never said anything they could understand. He could only open his eyes and groan and mumble. Only his eyes could clearly express that he was in pain, but that his spirit was strong still.

Now as the new day had fully risen, Varenhil, wincing slightly from his injury, finally made up his mind to speak.

"Brothers," he began. "Our father is gravely wounded, but I am certain that holding his kingdom together is within our abilities. To do this we must be of one mind and one purpose."

Hovin nodded. "You are right brother. But we must look to Cerondilus and the vizir council for guidance in these matters."

Varenhil paused and rubbed his sparse beard.

"That cannot be the best course of action," he replied. "There is not enough time to convene on matters, which by their nature is apparent to all reasonable men and which require swift and purposeful action. Besides, not all among our father's vizirs can be trusted. There may have been vizirs involved in this treasonous assault against the king."

"How do you know this?" Hovin asked.

"This was revealed to our father by one of the Ausremen among the company from Bonthc. This Ausremen is apparently a sage of some kind. He is clairvoyant like the priestess of Yggir."

Varenhil called a servant to him and sent him to summon Ahktel to the king's chambers.

"Brothers," Varenhil urged. "You must acclimate yourselves with the harsh realities of the world. Here you live a life of ceremony and cloistered order. But that order has been torn like a maiden's supple and diaphanous robe before the rapture. Open your eyes and see our enemies at our doors and defend what is yours and mine. Our titles, traditions, and laws will no longer protect us from our enemies. We must take up our swords and beat them back. We must overwhelm them and make them retreat. Like the king our father, we who succeed him will not rule because the gods have decreed this or because men are by nature obedient. Subjects, while they may bow and salute the king, do not so much revere the king. They fear him or their belief that their good fortune lies with the king compels them to suffer him. And so, when they lift their sword up to strike the king, he must show force and reestablish himself as the source of all good fortune. As a master should break a stick across a dog's back should it flash its fangs in disobedience, so must a king smite down his disobedient and disloyal subjects. That is the way of the world my brothers."

"There is yet another world," Hovin then said. "The world of the hidden is real brother. Our father was more than a warlord. He was concerned about more than industry and commerce. He also had a divine mission. Order cannot be maintained in the world through arms and wealth alone. Nothing we do will matter without divine purpose. My Harfingals draw great inspiration from this truth. We serve the king. But the king serves mighty Yggir. And so, through our service to him, we serve a higher purpose."

"You speak like a cadet captain of the Harfingal." Varenhil retorted. "The Harfingals are just as other men. Their fealty has a price. In fact theirs is even greater than others. They want salvation in the afterlife in Yieryos. Others merely want remuneration or to save their hides. Perhaps the Harfingals are lesser men who are born to follow and to graze on familiar pastures. Yet you are a prince among men. You were born to lead and not to follow. As princes, we must find purpose and meaning within ourselves. We must examine the world as men apart from all others."

"I agree with our brother Varenhil," Jaïem added. "I am the youngest among you, and I must defer to the judgment of my elders. The lord Greingspen is the eldest and besides what he says has the ring of truth. I am a prince born to lead. We must find purpose within ourselves even when everything falls down around us. We must always be there to reassure others. We must be firm and resolute now and punish all traitors that men will remember the price of treachery. In these times, we cannot put our trust in even long established traditions and institutions less our father awaken a pauper or worse. We must consolidate power in those who are of the king's own flesh. For, even if neither of us, who are his children were faithful to the laws of our father, it can still be said that a scion of Ylarin, king of men, rules the high city."

Varenhil smiled and looked at Jaïem curiously.

"I cannot gainsay you brother," he almost seemed to marvel.

"Hovin, son of Ylarin, and captain of the Harfingals, you must rise up and muster your men and proclaim martial law in the city, while I call for my warriors from my warlike city Greingspen and bring my warriors here to defend the city against any further attacks."

Hovin sighed and rose to his feet. "What of the laws of our father?"

"The law-" Varenhil interrupted. "As I have heard old men say, law is the stick that wags the dog, and like the stick, it does not impart to the dog the reason the dog heeds its master. The law is for subjects and for times of peace. We must rely on our judgment above all because judgment sired the law."

Hovin stared blankly at his brother.

"We are now engaged in a struggle for survival," Varenhil insisted. "We must have life or law is useless."

Now the servant returned with Ahktel and Eje who both looked weary. Varenhil gestured for them to take seats and sent the servants fruit, bread, and wine.

"We have called for the Ausremen, whether he is a sage or seer, to discuss what his mind's eye has seen that bears on the king's fate. Lovely Eje, my betrothed, will you translate for us?"

Eje agreed and she turned to Ahktel to tell him what the princes wanted from him.

"I am not a sage or a seer," Ahktel began. "But I have come to know myself and the world around me and beyond. What is it that you wish to know princes of the Vyrdmar?"

Varenhil asked about the courtiers' involvement in the assault the previous night.

"Your enemies are many. They can even be found in my own land. I know this. Not from a dream. But as you know things you have experienced. It is only now that I realize the extent of your enemy's plot. I am certain now that these men desire power over the known world west of the gates of Taldur. The men who attacked the city are only one column in a larger force hidden throughout Maspeidon and Cadera, all poised to attack at the opportune moment.

Your enemies are many indeed, and they are men of many pursuits and vocation. I have seen many faces in your city and in your compound that I have seen holding audience with the one you called Promothos who was slain this past night. I do not know their names, though I can recognize their faces."

"Brothers," Hovin interjected. "I am astonished that you are willing to accept what this Ausremen says without scrutiny. Do we know how he knows all of this? And why do we not go to the temple and seek audience with the priestess of Yggir to determine who our enemies are?"

Jaïem agreed. "How does our Ausremen guest know such things?"

"I know what I have seen and heard," Ahktel replied. "A falcon can see clearly to the horizon and detect its prey, while men look up at it and wonder where it is flying to so purposefully. I can no more explain how my eyes see and my ears hear things that are far away than a falcon can."

Eje now interjected her own account saying, "I do not claim to know how Ahktel knows these things. But I can tell you that you disregard his counsel at your own peril. His awareness and his counsel have saved my life and the lives of our companions."

"The Harfingals are faithful to the king," Hovin relented. "But the king is not able to make his wishes known. He chose me as captain of the Harfingal, and so now I must decide in his stead what is to be done. You are my brothers and so I must trust you, and your counsel must weigh heavily in my decision. I admit that all that has happened is not clear to me now. But lord Greingspen is right in that swift action is required. If the king's enemies are among us, we must flush them out. There will be martial law and a cleansing of the city of this infestation of treason and treachery."

A company of Harfingals passed through the ruins of the city with wagons full of merchants and alleged Atenarix. The merchants and the Atenarix were considered by many to be one and the same. But this was not actually so. There were merchants who were initiated into the Atenarix guilds, but many were industrious men who organized trade with other merchants from other lands. Some traded in agricultural goods while others traded in textiles, spices, or anything of value. Some farmers were among them until the nobles were able to prompt the vizir council to require taxes in copper feranxes rather than the traditional tributes in crops and foodstuffs.

The Atenarix, however, was guild trading in secret knowledge. They also provided protection for merchant caravans in exchange for tributes of silver and gold cances. Their members included metics, who were builders and engineers, the Emui, who possessed secret knowledge of Atenari disciplines, the Droa, who were a secret order of men-at-arms, and the Vehe-ta, who were captains among the Ayimar.

Many Maspeidonian nobles, courtiers, and even regents were Atenarix. The matter of their divided loyalties was a matter of concern, but the Vyrdmar kings needed the Atenarix knowledge to build cities, monuments, and machines of war. They also needed physicians, scribes, and artisans taught by the Emui or those who were Emui themselves.

Promothos wanted to break this stalemate. He wanted to actualize Atlantis now and accelerate the evolution of men into the super beings he envisioned they could be. Umalein wanted to break the stalemate because he thought that he was fit to rule. Most in the Atenarix orders wanted to maintain the status quo and incrementally increase their influence over the king of the high city. But now the stalemate has been broken forever and Maspeidon. Now the continent dangles on the precipice shadow and internecine conflict. Without the Atenarix, the aspirations of the Maspeidon's people lacked practical means. Varenhil, if he became king, would seek to utterly destroy the Atenarix and secure absolute power and authority for him and his descendants.

"Was this not what Wind fought for under the Pelares?" Varenhil asked a gathering of hastily mustered vizirs.

"Wind cannot be reborn, but his vision for his house lives in the faithful. Maspeidon cannot have two masters as a man cannot have gods or two souls. One will surely destroy what the other has labored to create. The continent will be mired in a damning cycle of attrition if we do not assert the absolute authority of the Vyrdmar king. For those who think that our world will fall into ruin without metics, I say this to you: where is your faith in that which is most actual and familiar to you? Where is your faith in yourself? Where is your faith in your gods? No, I say. Our genius will not wither and die without the Atenarix. We will overcome their tyranny and superimpose them for a better future. For the Vyrdmar to survive this day, and for the future to be saved, the Vyrdmar must project strength and impose martial law. You must decree this and give the king's great captains the power we need. You must give the captain of the Harfingal the power to find and destroy the enemy wherever he may be found."

The king's vizirs stood motionless in the king's audience hall. None dared to speak except for Cerondilus.

"My lord Greingspen," he began. "We must adhere to the king's laws, which were decreed after due deliberation, with even dire times like these in mind. The laws state that the vizir council should administer the state until the king expires. At such a time as when the king has been incapacitated, the vizir council will issue commissions to the king's vassals on all matters necessary for the conduct of the state. Here, since the city has been assailed, the captain of the Harfingals and the lord Greingspen himself should act in accordance with specific commissions from the vizir council. The power, which you now demand, is easily given. But once given, it is not so easily returned to the council. If the council relinquishes what power it has under the king's laws, it will likely lose that most provident and onerous authority and duty it has in times of succession, to issue the king's decree of who should succeed him."

"But there may not be a kingdom left to bequeath," a shrill voice shouted. Ylia now entered the hall.

"The king and the kingdom are one. The kingdom is one with the king because the gods have enshrined their purpose and their laws in the person of the king. It is not by chance that the Vyrdmar kings have all inherited the kingdom from their fathers. The Celestial has willed it so. The Celestial have tethered their purpose to the men of this noble line. That power cedes from the father to the crown prince without deliberation. No action is required by the council – the crown prince does not need the council's permission to succeed his father unless his father has decreed that another should rule. My father intended that Varenhil should rule. And Gaalden should have a king, not a council.

Therefore, you stand now in the presence of a Vyrdmar king. Do not feign to believe that the instrument and ceremony that announces the regent's ascendancy is actually the source of the regent's power. Varenhil will succeed to the throne because his father was king. I trust him and obey him now as I will on that day, and so should all of you who claim to be subjects. If the king's heir says to you now, as their father lies gravely injured, that there shall be martial law, so be it. Do not pretend to have the actual power to deny him this under the guise of reason and law. You know master Cerondilus that I love you and that I love your daughter, my kinswoman. Now return this love and the trust that attend it and grant what my brothers ask of you."

The vizirs bowed as the princess passed by them to stand by her brothers, Varenhil, Hovin and Jaïem, who were seated on chairs placed on a dais. Jaïem rose to seat his sister and when she had taken her seat, Cerondilus came forth to respond.

"There is no doubt that those before us are the chosen of Irilsflir and the heirs of Wind's line. There is no doubt that the vizir council exists to serve you. But how can we shirk our duty to the king, your father and grant what you wish?"

"Masters," said the old vizir Bereion. "Perhaps this is all a false impasse. After all we have the interest of kingdom in common. There is no need for this council to accede to, or refuse the princes' request. The princes can act on their own accord while the council deals with ministerial matters. Sally out and defend the kingdom, as you all deem necessary. Now, is that not the extent of martial law? Prince Hovin has a duty to defend the Hold. Let him do this as he sees fit. Prince Varenhil has a duty to defend the city. Let him do this as he sees fit. For as the princess has astutely alluded, the princes have the actual power to prosecute the defense of the city in any reasonable manner they wish. What the princes do not have power to do however is to abrogate the law. The law is clear that the vizir council cannot grant you the authority you ask for. Only the king can decree martial law. But the princes would do well to dispatch from this hall and be done with this melee of semantics, and defend the city against all enemies by any reasonable means at their disposal."

A tentative buzz of agreement filled the room and the majority of the vizirs agreed that Bereion's counsel should be followed. Hovin and Ylia also voiced agreement with Bereion. Varenhil was circumspect however. He was not certain that his father intended for him to succeed. If he was rash and the unthinkable happened and power passed to Hovin, the council could successfully conspire to punish him for violating Vyrdmar law. He needed to persuade or coerce the vizir council to grant him the exclusive power he needed to eradicate the Atenarix'. That authority would protect him against any revisionists in the future. Besides, if martial law were decreed, the crown prince would act in the king's stead in all matters under the canon the viziers called presumptive dominion.

But under Bereion's approach, the captain of the Harfingals would be the principal authority in the city, if for no other reason than his men were the only significant martial force there. Varenhil reluctantly agreed with Bereion, however, because he surmised that this cunning vizir intended this proposal as a trap. He hated him for this now, but he wondered if he should not have him as an ally in the future. In the end, these maneuvers were inconsequential. If his father did not recover, he could take the city with his own men from Greingspen. He had already sent his squire Haldar to rally his army there and bring them to the high city.

"Bereion's approach is well reasoned and practical," Varenhil said laconically. "We will dispatch now and look to our duties with urgency, skill, and resoluteness."

Hovin of course knew little of the laws of succession. He was none the wiser that he had almost helped his brother strengthen his hand in what would ultimately be a gratuitous and moot jostle for authority. After all, Varenhil would ultimately be king and not Hovin – the king had intimated this to Hovin. But if martial law were decreed, Varenhil would have become the de facto king of Gaalden even while his father still lived.

What Hovin did not realize was that Varenhil's desire for power was not merely power lust; Varenhil simply had profound confidence in his ability to lead. He had yet another motivation. The crown prince despised the pretension that a king ruled for some idealistic or divine purpose. For him, rule was a fact of life not requiring legitimacy or purpose, but only obedience and loyalty. Varenhil wanted to use the power of the Vyrdmar regent to smash these pretensions.

With Bereion's approach winning the day, prince Hovin mustered his Harfingal guard and gave them orders to move against all Atenarix holdings, to seize their members under the name of the king, and to place their inhabitants on house arrest until they were subjected to an inquiry. There were already prisoners held in the Harfingal garrison adjacent to the royal compound, and Hovin ordered that they be interrogated.

Accordingly and forthwith, the prisoners were mustered in the garrison courtyard in rows of three. Two Harfingals sat behind a wooden table and had each row of prisoners, one after the other, and stand before them to answer to an inquiry. The Harfingal guards asked many questions such as whether they had ever sacrificed to the Celestial and when, what were their vocation, and who were their parents, wives, and children. Any hesitation or incongruous statements resulted in immediate removal to a simple scaffold nearby and within the sight of the others, where they were summarily impaled. Any man who had the peculiar characteristics of the hateful Ayimar with their brown or golden eyes, were taken out to the courtyard and summarily impaled.

Soon many of the prisoners began to fall to their knees, shuddering and weeping in fear. Some pleaded for their lives calling out oaths of loyalty to the king and to the Celestial. Varenhil ordered that these men be immediately impaled unless they were or had been members of the city militia or had served in a Gaaldenian campaign. The inquiry continued and many more were impaled. By mid afternoon, on this particularly warm day, the Harfingals had completed their bloody task as flies began to gather. But then more prisoners were brought into the courtyard from the city. Soon there were two other tables placed for inquiries, which were conducted well into the late afternoon.

All three of the king's sons soon met at the royal apartments after the Harfingals were ordered to bring master Idram and all the academies' schoolmasters to them in the great audience hall. The Harfingals secured a couple of wagons and set out on their task. They found master Idram in his home with his young wife and they seized him, bound him, and dragged him back to the wagons. They went through the western sector of the city, where the schoolmasters and many courtiers had homes and apartments, and seized all the schoolmasters they could find, including the young schoolmaster Ceresmin and brought them before the princes by the early evening afternoon.

Varenhil ordered that there be thick blankets placed in the center of the audience hall. He also ordered that the schoolmasters be bound, gagged and blindfolded, and brought in for an inquiry.

"Certain death awaits all who are less than forthcoming about what they know," Varenhil greeted them rudely. "Now who among you know have sworn a secret oath to the orders of the Atenarix? We already know who some of you are. You may play the game of chance or you may come forward now. If you do not come forward and we know you to be an Atenarix, your life will be forfeit. Now those who wish to come forward, simply bow and you will be taken away and questioned. If you disclose all you know and repudiate the Atenarix, you will lose all privileges of your standing until further notice."

There was a brief moment of stillness and silence, but only one man came bowed. That man was taken away under guard, but not roughly.

"Those among you who have shunned your lord Ylarin's goodwill will rue the day," Varenhil said coldly.

Hovin gestured and two Harfingals armed with long pikes came forth and impaled two hapless schoolmasters. Their muffled groans made the others cringe.

"Come forth now, men of Chamiahce," Hovin urged. "You will be welcomed back into the fold, and not be subject to any further retribution. But you must divulge your dealings with the Atenarix who are now enemies of your true lord."

A few other schoolmasters bowed and were taken away. Two more were impaled and fell writhing until they expired on the floor. Hovin again urged the rest to make their peace with their king. Then all began to bow save one who stood firm. The men were taken away, as were the remains of those impaled. Hovin had the last man unbound. The last man standing was none other than master Idram who had taught them at the academies when they were young men. The old schoolmaster squinted and stumbled at first and then he looked sternly at the two princes.

"Master Idram," Varenhil said sardonically. "Why do you stand there almost beside yourself with apparent indignation? Have you no shame? You have betrayed your lord and have abetted internecine sedition."

"Why do you not submit yourself to your lord's mercy?" Hovin asked. "You were dear to us as few others in the king's court. You taught us the virtues we now defend against a godless enemy. But now we find that you are a hypocrite and that you are in league with our godless enemy."

"My lord princes," Idram said. "If I may speak-" Hovin nodded.

"I submit to my fate, which I know is death, coming sooner than I had expected, but coming nonetheless. Now I have served your father and Irilsflir for a generation. I know your father as my king. As my king, I owed him my loyalty against other lords. I also came to know him and his children. I came to love him and his children as one loves his family. But friendship is freely given and rarely alters the nature of those who give it. Your father never had, and never will have dominion over my beliefs and convictions. It is common among those who have dominion over land and species life, to deal in the absolute that a man may not serve two masters. But I have served my king well for years, and have served the Atenarix all the while. The truth is that a man can serve two or more masters, so long as neither is at odds over fundamental aspects of belief and convictions.

Unfortunately for me, this conflict has come to pass. I had a choice to make and I made that choice. My power, and my right to make that choice, is exclusive to me, and not even the gods could deny me in this. Gods and kings can reward as well as coerce and kill, but they cannot diminish that precious power, which even wretches have, to choose their beliefs and their convictions. I believe in a world where men are free to rise as high as their aspirations and their ability. Now I love my king as a man loves a father, but I love my beliefs as a man loves himself. Rest assured though, I did not advocate rebellion against the king. But I accept the consequences of my beliefs and my convictions.

All that I ask is that you are just in passing judgment. Do not take retribution against innocents. Do not harm my family. Know that the schoolmasters you have seized have no association with the Atenarix. Your ruse was cunning, but in the end, your conclusions have been too sweeping, and paradoxically too narrow. You have duly examined your enemy's motives, but you do not understand their ideas. Worse for you, you have not examined your own motives. In the final analysis, my expectations have been too high, and my faith in the possibility of perfection misguided. There is no exalted law or civilization because all species are perfectly flawed. All that can be expected is that men will desire even what is beyond their understanding. Men will use power to obtain what they desire and will heap elaborate justifications to assuage the haunting sense of alienation we feel as we lose ourselves in our object."

The old schoolmaster looked down and sighed.

"Now I am so weary. I have grown weary of men misapplying principles to justify their own selfish desires. I eschew their cant and machinations. I am disheartened by how far men have fallen in my eyes. Now I have no allegiances."

A weary Jaïem drew near the old schoolmaster, who was overcome with a sudden sense of unease.

"I can appreciate your predicament master Idram. But it would seem wrongheaded for you to take comfort in your disavowal of both the king and the Atenarix. I think it a despicable display of cowardice for you to stand here and say to us that you have forsaken the king and the Atenarix and have withdrawn into an inscrutable place that is beyond the reach of scrutiny."

Hovin came forward and interceded. "No," he said. "I understand master Idram. Do you not remember his lectures on the sovereign individual? Master Idram has never sworn off of his lordship over his beliefs and his convictions. While the king's conduct was acceptable to him, he agreed with the king, but now he stands alone."

"Well then," Varenhil added as if to conclude the matter. "After consorting with the king's enemies, our schoolmaster has withdrawn his precious soul into a place that is beyond the reach of even the king. But his body stands here before us within the king's dominion. Since we have the body, we will exact retribution on that body and leave his cloistered being to the judgment of the Celestial. Now brother, captain of the Harfingal, since there is no question as to where the schoolmaster's loyalty does not lie, what is your final judgment in this matter?"

Prince Hovin paused and gestured for two Harfingals to take the schoolmaster.

"Since you were highly esteemed in my father's court, I order poisoning with a mixture of the mandrake root in lieu of impalement. Take him away and seize all parchments and uncommon objects from his home and deliver them to the Urdar for examination. Do not disturb any other of his possessions."

With the matter of the schoolmasters concluded, the princes adjourned their inquiries for a while and returned to their father's bedside.

Ylia had scarcely left her father's side since he had been bedridden. Sadrek, the king's physician had reported that the king seemed to have been exposed to fire and had been poisoned. He was suffering from a frightful chill and ran a fever. The princes returned to their father's side and begged Ylia to eat and return to try to rest, but she refused. Sitting on chairs nearby, the brothers spoke together for a while. Varenhil queried Jaïem about the dread weapon the guards said Promothos wielded.

"I see that you wear this terrible weapon, which smote our father," Varenhil remarked.

"I wear it-" Jaïem replied, "Because it belonged to the first enemy I have slain."

"Indeed," Varenhil agreed. "But to hear others speak of this weapon, I would think that it should be destroyed."

Hovin nodded in agreement. "This weapon strikes a foe even if it is wielded without skill. It strikes all indiscriminately. Surely it will kill its wielder less he be an immortal or a sorcerer like Promothos."

Jaïem thought for a while and then agreed. "Perhaps you are right. I cannot wield this weapon. I will take it to the high priestess so that she may dispose of it however she pleases."

Varenhil shook his head. "No brother. Not the priestess of Yggir. If, as is apparent, the sword's sheathe can contain its awful power, we should give it to the Harfingal master-at-arms to hold until our father recovers and has decided its fate for himself."

The brothers agreed that the anurium blade would be placed in the custody of the Harfingal master-at-arms. But Jaïem roiled within at his brother's encroachment into what he perceived was his affair.

As the brothers spoke nearby, the king's eyes fluttered and then opened. His mouth gaped as if to say something. Ylia called out to him and then ordered servants to call the king's physician to his side. The princes leapt up and rushed to their father's bedside.

"Beloved," the king whispered. "How I have dreamed of you…"

He coughed and blood trickled from his mouth. Ylia wiped his mouth with a handkerchief, weeping all the while, and with the help of a servant, propped the king up.

"Do not speak father," she pleaded. "Conserve your energy." The old king seemed to laugh softly.

The old king asked that his chief vizir be called in. He was nearby and he rushed into the king's bedchamber to attend the king.

He bowed, saying solemnly, "My liege…" "My children," he struggled to speak. "Your father has looked into the countenance of the Celestial and has realized a familiar face. I have been at ease therefore about my passing from this world. I wept before the Celestial, that he has vouchsafed me this pleasant passing. I wept also because I would not walk with you in your life and come to you when you called out to me. But I now know that there is nothing in the cosmos that ever was that will be bereft of any part of itself at the reckoning."

The king paused to catch his breath and asked for a sip of water.

"I love you all so much," he began again. "That love is our path to each other, even across the inscrutable beyond."

The king paused again. His breathing was visibly labored. "My beloved," he whispered, "when my spirit has returned to the Celestial, give over my body to the priestess to lay in repose deep in the catacombs of the temple in the traditional manner."

The king reached out for each of his children and whispered to them. "Jaïem, know that you walk close to the Celestial, and so do not look far away to find your purpose. Hovin the faithful, never doubt that your courage will be a beacon to your beloved in the shadow that must come. Ylia, when my eyes look back to this world, I will find you because I cherished you the most. Varenhil, I leave you my kingdom because you are the strongest."

Chapter 15: Immortality

Never in the fabled city's history had so many citizens gathered together as they did on that fateful day. The crowds had been gathering since late afternoon, filing in under the watchful eye of the Harfingal guards posted all around the temple quadrangle and the parapets. The day was eerily pleasant. It was a good day for whatever one could make of it. But like the air on that the day, the people's thoughts were still. Along with gray eagles circling above, a vivid sense of quietude and emptiness hovered over everything and every person in the city. Indeed, the silence was unnatural. Down among the crowd, only the wailing of women broke the silence.

That day was an eternity to some. It was as if the reckoning had come and the entire world was awaiting passage into Yieryos, the house of souls. But it finally waned and made many very thoughtful. Some courtiers tearfully whispered that it was a pleasant evening for a walk in a fine garden. They vividly remembered their king taking long walks in the royal garden with his children when they were young. Later in life he took his walks with his beautiful daughter Ylia or with little Jaïem. But no one walked in the royal garden on that fateful day. Forlorn were the narrow trails. The songbirds were silent. The day was a day of sorrow and reflection, and hope.

The people's sorrow and despair was unshakable for at least that day. The people barely noticed the light of day as they were cast in a dark, and deep and frictionless pit of gloom. The world was forgotten. Heaven and earth became inverted and appurtenant to the people's pain and loss. Throbbing over the firmament, their collective hearts bled streaks of crimson over its blue canvas; the day was surreal. Yet the people assembled together to lend their spent hearts to a great apotheosis. It seemed as if every citizen gathered, grave, weeping and wailing, in the temple quadrangle and out into the main thoroughfare. Under the twilight sky, the people melted into a dark mass resembling a gentle stream that twinkled and glistened under the cool silvery light of the young moon.

Most who were present could not see the platform erected at the temple's gates. It was covered with a white canopy and adorned with the standards of the Vyrdmar. The king's principal courtiers and heirs, all dressed in white robes, sat with somber faces, his noble sons with white tunics bearing the insignia of the eagle clasping the cross-staff. At the base of the platform were many Harfingal dressed in ceremonial regalia, standing tall and grave like lonely poplars. They wore white tunics and bronze breastplates, and donned rounded helmets.

According to the Vyrdmar, the souls of men passed into the dreaded void to wait for the day of reckoning. As shepherds of the people, kings were welcomed into the Hall of Yggir after a long and peaceful rest. When the day of reckoning came, the kings were to be united with their bodies, which were preserved in massive sarcophagi, and would return to the world and gather their flock and entreat the Celestial to claim their souls into Yieryos. Then, after their final duty was completed, the kings would live out another life in the fields of Edassir beyond the hall of the Celestial until they passed on into Yieryos themselves.

To ensure that a king had a restful sleep and completed his voyage through the afterlife was the most important duty for the surplicants and the priestesses of Yggir. The salvation of the Vyrdmar's souls depended on this rite. All the kings would be needed at the reckoning to gather the countless Vyrdmar souls. If even one king was missing, the kings would be compelled to search him out, and the day of reckoning would be delayed or lost, and the kings would wander the world until they themselves passed into the dreaded void and the salvation of the Vyrdmar with them.

Three days earlier, Varenhil was wed to Eje in a secret ceremony in the courtyard of the royal apartments. Only the royal family and a few courtiers and vizirs were in attendance. The next day Varenhil was anointed the one hundred and fourteenth Vyrdmar king, defender of Irilsflir, and his wife crowned as his royal consort and Vyrdmar queen. On that day, Varenhil became lord of the Hold, king of Gaalden and high king of Maspeidon. He did not decree martial law, as many thought he would. Rather, he immediately called together his vizir council and commanded that preparations for war against the Ayimar and all disloyal lords be made.

Early the next day, prince Jaïem came before an assembly of courtiers and spoke eloquently of the meaning and gravity of the king's passing. Jaïem the beautiful lived up to his moniker, not only because of his countenance and stature, but also because of his words. He evoked a divine understanding of his father's passing, saying, "When I looked upon my king, I saw him gazing into tomorrow through me. He was forlorn because he knew that he was embarking on a journey on which his flock, like his shadow could not go. I looked upon him. Our eyes met as my presence intersected the space between his eyes and the long tomorrow, and with a heavy heart I thought I heard him whispering: 'remember me.'"

The young prince wept, as did his siblings, and many who had gathered to view the great gold sarcophagi, adorned with geometric relief, and capped with an ivory faceplate. Jaïem composed himself and looked out into the gathering with teary eyes.

"As it does now, the king's words set off a fit of emotion that rumbled and gushed like a storm until tears had overflowed, and soothed and brought a peace of still winter mornings. But we must take courage. I took courage as I looked upon him and replied: 'you are as a glorious day ascending to flourish, and with serenity to drift into the dreaded void for a time, but not so to oblivion; but to live on to bring everlasting life to the faithful and to live in the hearts and minds of men forever.'"

After the dead king's family and courtiers had gathered for the ceremonial viewing, the great sarcophagi bearing his body was carried into the temple quadrangle and placed before the citizens of Chamiahce. A great horn blast bellowed through the still air. The lonely sound echoed into the heavens and then the priestess of Yggir appeared from the temple, followed by an entourage of priestesses in white ceremonial vestments with gold trimming – the first carrying a dangling censer. The priestess carried a great staff ensconced with a symbol of infinity, which she used to perform three incantations. A priestess behind her carried a small clay jar.

"A peaceful sleep," the priestess of Yggir whispered. "A sublime traversal to the halls of Yggir," she added. "And a glorious return to us at the reckoning."

After the incantations were performed, the entourage of priestesses bowed solemnly.

"Harfingal," the priestess called out. Hovin turned to face her and came forward.

Following behind him were six strong Harfingal guards. After the prince and the Harfingals were purified with oil from the clay jar, the priestess uttered a fourth incantation. When the seven men were properly purified, they, led by Hovin, solemnly carried the great sarcophagi into the temple. After they had passed through, the doors were closed behind them and the gathering looked on with profound grief and sadness. Tears flowed abundantly as the last rays of the sun disappeared beyond the western horizon.

"It was all so sudden," Farwuld said shaking his head. His father nodded in agreement and took a draught of mead. "All along we lived under the threat of Atenarix treachery. Many of the merchants and the artisans who walked among us were Atenarix. Some even ate and drank with us. They were indeed the best among us. Historians say that their skill rivaled the ancients who were said to have built the old site upon which this new city was founded.

The old quartermaster, Tharguld scoffed. "My son, I never trusted these men."
Farwuld smiled. "Yet you broke bread and drank with them."

"My dearest son," Tharguld replied. "I have two lives, as do many of our good citizens. We have our family life and our livelihood. We do all we can rightfully and even wrongfully to bring the bounty of our toil to our family, who are dear to us. In doing so, we sometimes dine with wolves."

Tharguld spoke in this way with his son, in the main hall of the Golden Hearth for a while on the night king Ylarin was interred in the catacombs of the temple.

They did not expect any guests that night. But to their surprise Modi, lord of the Skaggs appeared through their doors.

"Greetings friends," young Modi called out. Farwuld and his father greeted the young Skagg. Now Modi was dressed in a clean gray tunic, but was still wearing his flute. He wore a cloak of fine wool over his shoulders. Walking over to where the quartermaster was sitting with his son, he stood briefly and bowed.

"Please take a seat," Tharguld said. Modi smiled and sat next to his good friend Farwuld.

"Did you go to the king's interment?" Farwuld asked.

"No," Modi replied. "I wished that I could have. I cannot think of a good man who did not love the king. But these last few days have been prosperous for the Skaggs."

"The fortunes of the mendicant Skaggs have changed for the better," Farwuld remarked.

"Your Skaggs thrive in the recent lawlessness."

"Yet good and honorable men have lost their livelihood," Tharguld snorted. "I am glad that some order has been restored."

"Order is good," Modi agreed.

"But what the Skaggs were due us. There were many disloyal merchant hoarders in the city. Many served the guilds. They were in league with the Atenarix guild masters. The guilds plotted the king's overthrow and would have enslaved us all."

"Spectacular rumors," Tharguld remarked.

"Lies," he snorted. "These Inventive stories have been strewn together from threads of truth. The Atenarix are learned men to whom we owe much. Those among them who plotted against the king were justly punished. But, I am sure that most belonging to this order were good men and not the monsters many of our citizens now believe them to be. As for the Ayimar, they are strange men indeed. But I can see no reason to

say that the Ayimar were not created by the same
Creator who created all living things. To say that they
are unnatural is a worse charge than even treason. Even
a condemned dissident can take comfort in the truth that
his creator, who is perfectly just, will determine his fate
in the afterlife. Yet certainly, a man who is created by
another man cannot look to the Celestial for passage
into Yieryos. I suppose that all that is left for him after
his passing is oblivion."

"Maybe you are right," Modi replied. "Some say
that the Skaggs are not children at all. To ease their
guilt at our suffering, they say we do not have mothers
and fathers. They say that we come from wayward
bakiren and whores. But we are children. We are
orphans. Most of us lost our parents in the mines. Like
the Skaggs, the Ayimar steal and raid. We filch
foodstuff and scraps. The Ayimar terrorize the
farmlands to the south. Like the Skaggs, the Ayimar are
flesh and blood. But unlike the Skaggs, the Ayimar hate
the Vyrdmar. All we want is the Vyrdmar's love. The
Ayimar want to destroy the Vyrdmar."

The old quartermaster sighed and took a draught
of mead. He thought to himself for a while as Farwuld
and Modi spoke. Then he leaned back in his chair as if
talking to himself.

"All will be well. Good friends of mine who saw
the king's stalwart son Hovin said when he rode west
through the city that fateful night when the enemy
struck, the air seemed to crackle around him. The mere
sight of him was inspiring. A very old man said that
prince Hovin reminded him of mighty Wind when he
was young long ago. It seems that Namreddin's line
will always renew itself. The nobility of this line does
not seem to wane as others in the world have. No
matter the peril, the masters of the high city have always
risen above it all, and we citizens have always reaped
better days."

Many in the high city echoed old Tharguld's hopes. The people's hopes rested on king Varenhil and the new king was determined to bring order to his city and his kingdom. His warriors began arriving into the city from Greingspen just a few days after the old king's interment. The new king sacked his father's council and appointed a new one. However, his sister Ylia persuaded him to keep master Cerondilus as his chief vizir, and retain master Bereion as well. King Varenhil decreed that order was to be restored. The new vizir council commissioned the captain of the Harfingals to cast a great eye over the city and stamp out all rabblerousing and treachery. The Urdar were everywhere and even the slightest sign of trouble and heresy was to be marked and purged.

The king commissioned his brother Jaïem to muster as many young men from the academies, as were fit, and create a company of men-at-arms. The young prince moved quickly to do this, naming his good friend Csem as his lieutenant. When he had mustered them, calling them the Patuloi guard, prince Jaïem at once began patrolling the plains south of the city for Atenarix and Ayimar spies. The city militia was conscripted into a ready infantry under the command of the king's old squire, Haldar. All mines and foundries were seized and their machines were commanded to produce only the weapons of war.

Meanwhile lord Umalein had arrived in Ursol with his chief vizir Alfaisten. He entered the city under guise of a merchant and traveled to the home of his distant cousin Gilthein, who was a wealthy farmer in that region, and with whom he had constant dealings. Gilthein had a large house in the hills overlooking the town. Gilthein knew very well why lord Umalein came. He sent his servants to the town's busy market to purchase provisions and also summoned eight strong young men who served on his farm.

After a short night's rest, Gilthein led the Kuthgelonian lord and his vizir, along with his men on a couple of days' march to the north and east. Hidden there in the valley was Umalein's forward army, some two thousand strong. When the lord from Parilos in Kuthgelon rode into the camp, his men cheered loudly and banged shields and pots and whatever they could find. The sound was deafening and menacing, but lord Umalein reveled in it. Soon, he thought, he would send for the rest of his army perched on the Kuthgelonian border. But while he waited for their arrival, he would not lay idle. Lord Umalein determined to move on the coastal city of Bonthc where lord Dorias ruled, and Bojingren the Red called home.

Now that the new king in the high city began to fully secure his seat of power, he turned his attention to his new bride. Not known for his appreciation for niceties and long walks, as his father was, he could now and then be seen stoically walking in the royal gardens with his queen Eje. Even in the shadow of war, he tried to conduct himself like his father in many ways. He visited the temple and entertained courtiers, but always his face was stern, his lips wound tightly, and his gaze piercing. But when he was alone with his young bride, he smiled and laughed softly. He was frightening to her, and she was intriguing to him. Her brown eyes were warm and her skin gleamed like amber that is held up to the sun.

"We do our duty because we love our fathers who command them," he told her as they sat together in their bedchambers. "But could you learn to love me as a woman truly loves a man? If this is something that is real and not the stuff of fables, I would like to learn this love with you."

She was still loath to look into the prince's piercing blue eyes.

"You are noble and strong," she replied. "You are my king and I respect you. You are unlike the men in my homeland, but you are handsome nonetheless. If you are kind and good in my eyes, then I would be foolish and wicked if I did not come to love you. But in the meantime, if we must do our duty, I would think it not so onerous, if it be with you."

The days were fast approaching when lord Dorias was to return to his city by sea with his captain Bojingren the Red. The young Hekare would make that voyage with them. The king bade them stay a week longer so that the Hekare could teach the mounted Harfingals Xedun horsemanship and tactics. The Hekare agreed and lord Dorias also agreed to remain in the city a while longer.

For three days, Ahktel and Ixhor displayed the formations used by the Xedun who patrolled the Eptarean plains, and the Vyrdmar were awed and attentive. For those three days, the Hekare lived like the Harfingals, eating and drinking with them and living in their barracks. They took part in their morning exercises and in their afternoon exercises. They bathed with them after the afternoon exercises, but ate with the king.

Most attentive among the Vyrdmar were Hovin and Jaïem; surprisingly Jaïem most of all. He was eager to learn the Hekare's mounted formations and javelin attacks. He was fascinated by the Hekare's technique with their curved swords. From their mounts, the Hekare's sword attacks were blindingly swift and deadly to light infantry. According to Ixhor's account, engagements with the sword should not be protracted to avoid dulling the blade. He encouraged maintaining balance, positioning, and using superior footwork and speed to expose an enemy's vulnerability. He urged that a swordsman use killing attacks sparingly and only when the enemy was exposed.

On the day before the Hekare left the city, a riveting exhibition between Ixhor and Bojingren ensued with the Vyrdmar weapon of choice; the broadsword.

When the king, Varenhil, suggested it, the two companions were at once eager and anxious to cross swords. This was a welcomed opportunity for both men. They had developed so much respect and admiration for each other since their adventure began.

There were many quips and much repartee between the men as Bojingren the Red and the Ixhor prepared to cross swords in full armor. Ahktel worried that Ixhor would not wear the Maspeidonian's armor well. But when he appeared out of the armory, his armor glistening in the sun, Ixhor looked like a very formidable Harfingal warrior. He strode out looking determined and menacing. Bojingren the red followed him into a circle of Vyrdmar, including the king, princes Hovin and Jaïem, and many Harfingals.

Later that day, striking Ylia, and lovely Eje and Besia, walked together in the royal garden. They held hands in a manner typical of maidens in the high city, Ylia stopping once, as if to pick flowers. But she moved on with a heavy heart after realizing that there was no longer a king for whom to pick flowers. Besia held her close to comfort her. Finally, the three ladies of Irilsflir sat on a bench facing a small fountain. They were speaking at length, Ylia, trying to divert her grief, spoke about Gaaldenian customs, when a woman, with her face hidden by a shawl over her head approached them.

The woman removed her shawl to reveal that she was none other than the high priestess of Yggir.

"Royal ladies of Irilsflir," she greeted them. The three young women seemed mildly startled. "Be at ease, for I have come here only to see the garden my old friend was so fond of."

"The king loved this garden," Ylia agreed. "But after he had a private garden built and cultivated, that garden soon became his favorite. He was fond of looking down at the garden from his balcony overlooking it. He passed through this garden every now and then though, to take brisker walks with his hounds…"

Ylia stopped to wipe the tears welling in her eyes. Besia dried her cheek with a handkerchief and Eje held her hand tight.

"Take heart my sister," Besia said.

"Indeed," the priestess added. "Your father, our sleeping king, and my good friend, was a great king and wise shepherd of his people. He has gone now to the Hall of Yggir to await the passing of the five hundred and seventy seven day Siechil…"

The four women paused as they heard someone approaching. It was Ahktel, taking the opportunity to view the garden, a day before his departure from the city. He saw the women and walked slowly, as if not wanting to disturb them. But Eje saw him and called him over to share their moment. She thought just then that Ahktel would have some insight to ease the princess' loss. And so, Ahktel came to sit with the women, kneeling next to Eje where she sat on a stone bench.

When Ahktel had taken his place next to Eje, the priestess looked at him, and smiling, continued to speak.

"Master Ahktel should well know," the priestess resumed. "Being a Hekare, that the passing of men from this world is not like a final chapter in a book. The king will return. He will return to his body, which we have preserved. When he returns, along with his royal forebears, together they will gather the souls of the Vyrdmar and entreat the Celestial to suffer them to enter into Yieryos, the house of souls. Together with his mighty fathers and sons, our beloved king will live out another life in fields of Edassir, until they all pass on into Yieryos for an eternity."

"Your words are beautiful," Ahktel said in the common tongue. To Eje's surprise, he spoke well, although with a heavy accent.

"My sister and countrywoman," Eje said softly, holding Ylia close. "Surely this is an actual and good destiny. Even among my people, and Ahktel's people, it is believed that those who have passed do not perish, but rise to a hallowed place."

"Who knows these things," the sobbing princess countered. "We do not actually know where we come from or why we are here. We live and experience a myriad of things; pleasure and pain, and know these are real. Then we die, and pass into an inscrutable and imperceptible place, or perhaps no place at all. All I know for certain is that my king has died. Alas for him. I weep for him because, even if he will live again, he will never be again as I once knew him. He will never be again as he once was, after this coming of eclipse, this end we all know is coming, but is always a lifetime away."

The women and Ahktel looked at each other and then looked up at the darkening sky.

"Your majesties," Ahktel said.

"The princess is right. We do not know what awaits us at our passing. Who knows what one has not experienced? But there are many kinds of experiences. In this life and in this place where things come to die, we experience pain, pleasure, and the fear of one, and of the loss of the other. But I know there is more. Among the Hekare, fire is believed to be the eternal sword of the Spirit the Elihe call Eizierh, destroying and causing pain and loss to the faithless and the wicked. But this is lore. Fire is of this world. The flame that some fear and yet others want to harness is merely an expression of the strain of life and death in this world. Eizierh is a god of love and the author of life. He sends the wind and the rain. The wind is the eternal harbinger of change and with the rain brings forth renewal and rebirth, which sweeps away the ruin that fires have left behind, and blows seeds of new life to new lands."

Clinging on to Ylia, Eje looked deeply into Ahktel's eyes. So did Besia and the priestess, all listening intently to the young Hekare.

"What will happen to us? What will happen to our world?" Eje asked.

"When you ask me this, I recall a dream. I once dreamed that I was drifting in a luminous space. I heard sounds of whispers of a time unending. I heard voices saying that this world we cling to and hold so dear will decay and die. I heard voices say that species will wane like ripples moving across a black pool, becoming a smooth surface. I heard voices say that species have embarked on a cycle of death and will extend too far from the locus of its original cause and will become bereft of purpose."

Listening closely to Ahktel, the women heaved a collective and weary sigh. Ahktel paused and then looked up at the sky.

"Do not fear," Ahktel said reassuringly. "For as certain as the good gardener sows new ground before abandoning the old, so too will the Spirit sow seeds in a new world for species to tread. But this is not the good news. This is not the prophecy of seasons. The good news is that life is eternal. The good news is that species imprints itself on the consciousness of the Spirit, which caused ripples in still waters, when it passed in the dawn of time.

Everything that is, is the Spirit, but also conceals the Spirit. Look closely and you may see who you truly are looking back at you. Look into each other's eyes and see the Spirit looking back at itself. As you are in your beholding of the Spirit, so will you be in life everlasting. This transcendent experience is species' connection to the Spirit. Only through this connection will species truly live. Only through this connection will species realize it's oneness with the fabric of infinity and ascend to knowledge of eternal life.

Therefore, do not weep for those that have passed from this world. For they have always been and will always be one with the Spirit if they ever truly lived. That is the good news and our only comfort; that the purpose of life is the coming together of all expressions of the Spirit - the coming together of all things for all time."

Chapter 16: Pride of men

Two men huddled together by a gentle stream nestled among tall poplars. It was early morning, but the sky was gray and foreboding. Spring's eclectic symphony was silent except for the hollow sound of flowing water gently passing over and splashing on stones. One of the men, the old schoolmaster Idram as it were, was recognizable by his strange patches of thin gray hair dotting his freckled head. He sat on a leather satchel.

The other man, gray-eyed prince Hovin, sat before him with his legs crossed as he might have done long ago when the old schoolmaster taught him at the academies. Both men were wrapped in thick gray cloaks even though the morning air was rather temperate. Master Idram watched from the side of his eye, as a small slithery creature crawled from the ground onto the hem of Hovin's cloak and all the way up to Hovin's lap. It was only then that Hovin saw the animal. It was a serpent with a colorful membrane flowing from its crown. Men called this serpent a pydra and were fearful of its painful and deadly venom. Yet knowledgeable men knew that the pydra was reluctant to bite and use its venom. But all who encountered pydras either retreated or slew the animal to avoid any possibility of poisoning.

"You do not flinch…" master Idram remarked.

"Harfingals are not immune to the pydra's toxins. It could bite you now through your cloak with its powerful fangs and inject you with its venom."

Hovin snapped his cloak and flung the serpent aside and watched it gather itself and slither away.

"I have been at ease of late," the prince answered.

Hovin was not master Idram's most promising student at the academies. Master Idram opined that of all of king Ylarin's children, Hovin seemed to lack the intensity of the others. Even Jaïem, who was strange and aloof, had a great passion about whatever vocation that caught his fancy. It was only when Hovin engaged in martial exercises that he seemed purposeful. When once, master Idram brought this fact to Hovin's attention, the young prince paused and thought for a while.

The young prince stared blankly at the old schoolmaster and said nothing for a while.

"I understand a sword's purpose. A sword's purpose is to kill. I am certain of that. It is not a creative instrument. I can learn to wield it, and of course defend others – but only by killing the wicked."

Though now as master Idram looked into Hovin's eyes, he began to see the young prince in another light.

"You have changed," Idram remarked. "Yet you are so young. You are young, like the Vyrdmar were young once."

"What do you mean?" Hovin asked.

"You look at the world like a child looks at the world. You realize that you know so very little and you look to others to teach you."

"I must agree with you in that," Hovin said almost inaudibly. "There is so much to know."

"Indeed," Idram agreed. "Though to know this, is to know much. If only your brethren could realize this as you have."

"How would that have saved us from the treachery of the Atenarix?"

"I am not certain. Perhaps all of this was unavoidable. But your perspective may help us avoid a bitter future yet to come. Like children, the Vyrdmar began their passage through history with wide-eyed wonderment and hope. Awed by the world around them and the glorious future not yet realized, they combed the landscape in search of meaning and fulfillment of purpose. Their wonderment blossomed into humility and vigilance as they began to realize their place in the world. Their awareness was sharpened. They realized an inner power. But then something dreadful and pernicious happened."

The schoolmaster paused and thought to himself for a while.

"What happened to us who began so with so much promise?" Hovin interjected.

"Vanity, fear, and lust for power..." Idram exclaimed. "A sapling of fear began to grow. We became afraid of losing the possibilities we gathered in our minds. We became fearful of loss and death. We struggled to find solace from our fears but soon found comfort in the belief that we could bend the world to our will. We superimposed our likeness onto divinity. We became haughty and honored our own image – that is why the Celestial does not suffer any human likeness in His temple. The Celestial knows our frailty. He eschews our intrinsic vanity and fear.

But this is not only the Vyrdmar's story. The whole world suffers this fate. Every creed either believes that they are chosen by divinity or nature to wield power over the world. Some of us look to the priestess of Yggir to cultivate our belief. Others look to the Atenarix to ostensibly guide us on our search for purpose. But what are we really looking for? Not divine purpose. The Celestial's flock looks for solace from famine, cruelty, and eternal oblivion. The Atenarix aspire to power over life and death – a clear overreaction to frailty. Who actually lives up to his creed? We Atenarix have turned our backs on the Atlantean creed. We embrace ourselves like orphans huddled together during an endless cold night. We are lost, yet we fancy ourselves masters - masters of frailty and fear.

This web of frailty and delusion is surely a sign of decline. For when we retreat into ourselves out of fear and no longer search for more perfect knowledge of transcendent being because we believe we have found it in ourselves, we begin to die. In truth, we have found nothing and have realized nothing. We are merely setting the stage for the gradual erosion of divine values and law, and the ascendancy of the capricious will."

"Alas for the Vyrdmar if we allow ourselves to be swept up by the tide of hubris," Hovin remarked. "When you intimated that you were disloyal to our king and my father, I was at first blinded with anger. But that was even before our king passed from this world. Yet when he died I was sad but not angry. In my heart, I knew from what I had seen with my own eyes that the time had come for answers and not slaughter. I realized that of all the men at court, I could look to you for answers. Seeing you that fateful day when we put so many to the pike, I was sad. I was sad to lose an uncommon source wisdom and temperance. Even though you admitted to being an Atenarix, I could not bear to lose you. Even when your life hung in the balance you were perceptive and truthful. I decided that day, that I would not suffer you to die."

Master Idram smiled. "I am glad for that my prince. I have said this to you before..." Master Idram's eyes began to well with tears. "I have never taken up arms against your father. He was a good man and a good king. But I was loyal to the man and not the crown. I regarded him as any man who was good in my eyes. My loyalty to him grew out of friendship and admiration. But then I saw him swept up in the whirlwind of orthodoxy and ignorance, I turned from him to find a new way. But I know now that the Vyrdmar and the Atenarix are more alike than they are different. Men of both beliefs are afraid. Their fear has led them to betray their creed and become tyrannical.

"What are you saying, master Idram? My father was ever faithful to the Celestial and to the laws of our fathers. He was kind and humble and loved his people."

"I believe that he was as you say. I know that he was a good man. But the virtues of one man, not even a king's, can atone for the frailties of an entire people. Our good king could not even diagnose the Vyrdmar's disease. He could not detect our endemic fear. He could not see how this fear has driven us away from the Celestial. He believed our adherence to our fathers' traditions would bind us to divine purpose. But he was wrong.

Our fathers taught us what to believe and to do. They taught us the consequences of disobedience, the capital sin. But they did not teach us why we should believe and obey. When men are strong, they are loath to believe without proof or reason. The rewards of the afterlife soon become abstractions and unfathomable and fade under the glare of the living sun.

The virtue of obedience needs to be demonstrated and not declared by kings. And most of all, we need to know why we must believe and obey. Only then can we discern whether Vyrdmar law is an expression of divine law. It is not surprising then, that our laws and our beliefs now crumble around us. As soon as the enemy sprung, you and your brothers sought to abrogate the law. You did not have faith that your laws and your gods would protect you.

That outcome is not surprising. Our laws are fast becoming useless because our fathers, who set them down, ignored man's fundamental nature. Men do not adhere to laws because laws are perfect and just, but because adherence to laws results in useful outcomes. Our fidelity to law changes as our desires change-all we are left with is our very capricious and pernicious will to decide what is right and what is wrong and what is to be the fate of all we survey.

Our only hope is to be touched by the Celestial Himself. Our only hope is to be imbued with his love, which is the only talisman against the sickness of fear. Know this. When you are no longer afraid you become masterful. When you become masterful you become compassionate because you no longer evaluate others in relation to your fear of loss, but in relation to their state of fear and need. You are no longer focused on yourself but on others. You become an instrument of love and divine purpose. I sense this love in you. You have been saved. You have been saved from your brethren's fate. Your heart is tranquil. You are not afraid. You are still as destiny poised on the tip of the Celestial's finger."

Later that day, king Varenhil met with his brothers Hovin and Jaïem. The great audience hall was dimly lit and cluttered with chairs surrounding a large wooden table. The king sat at the head of the table, slouched with his chin resting on a closed hand and his elbow on an armrest.

"My lord," Hovin said softly. "What is your mind now that your forces are mustered? Should we call your vassals to a war council?"

The king motioned for a Harfingal guard. The guard came close and bent over as the king motioned for him to lend him his ear. Some words were whispered and the guard bowed and proceeded out of the hall.

"We have twelve thousand warriors camped within and beyond the walls of the city. According to my generals, we have almost two thousand conscripts being trained as we speak. Yet you would have me call my treacherous vassals to a war council and wait. That is unacceptable."

"My lord" Hovin insisted. "It is true that war is upon us and cannot be avoided. But it would not be wise to miscalculate so early on in the looming conflict. As we speak, your armies will have to deal with three fronts. Your mind is fixed on punishing the Ayimar below the Pelares, but we must also deal with your disloyal vassals, Umalein of Kuthgelon, Iagais of Tarpedon, and Eruilhin of Caphus. To be victorious against all our enemies, we must first engender unity among our allies."

"I agree with our brother," Jaïem chimed in. "But I must add that we should devise a more comprehensive plan for victory at sea as well as land. We must make use of lord Dorias' fast ships and attack our enemies' coastline cities. Caphus, for example is a coastal city with no walls. If we succeed in a naval attack, we could take that city and move on nearby Agodon from the south and the west. If we send a force north to harass Parilos, lord Umalein's city, we should be able to take Agodon and control the entire southern region of Kuthgelon. From there, we can send ships south to Cadera and assert ourselves on two fronts while using only one supply line along the coast."

"Princes of Gaalden," Varenhil replied coldly. "I have heard nothing to dissuade me from my plan. An attack on the Ayimar to secure our south is the best course for now. After we have dealt with the Ayimar, we can move on Parilos and sack that city and raze it to the ground. We will undoubtedly face Iagais and

Eruilhin in the heartland of Maspeidon. They will come to face us, and we will deal with them accordingly."

"Lord Dorias is our kin," Hovin said insisted. "He secures our south. We have lord Elesias' sword, but we are not certain about the others. Should we not first determine who our allies are?"

Hovin paused to compose himself. "We do not know the extent of the Ayimar threat. While their exact numbers are unknown to us, most agree that they do not have an army. We assume that your disloyal vassals are in league with the Atenarix. If that is so, the way to Parilos will be treacherous indeed. The Atenarix are crafty and your vassal's armies are well trained and equipped, and can move on the high city and threaten your subjects. If we are to defend the city and ensure success in our future advances, we must muster an army of some thirty thousand men with supply lines to sustain that force for a campaign lasting well beyond the summer and the coming winter."

"Hovin is right to urge caution," Jaïem nodded. "We must move cautiously to preserve the kingdom as well as to punish our enemies."

"The power of the Vyrdmar king is indivisible from his inviolability," Varenhil insisted. "That is the issue here. Securing the perception that the Vyrdmar king is inviolable is more important than any military objective. That inviolability may be a myth, but it must be assiduously preserved, or else the Vyrdmar king will not rule for long. Our father, my father, was slain by the Ayimar enemy and the myth of the Vyrdmar king's inviolability was smashed like a porcelain statue. Now men whisper in the shadows that the Vyrdmar are not godlings as was once thought; that they are as other men."

The king inhaled deeply and exhaled fire. He paused, his face becoming flushed and then returning to a paler hue just before he continued.

"That is all well. The gods have chosen such an end for our father. Now what can I do as king? I cannot restore that which was broken. But I can take my vengeance such that men will shudder to look upon the Vyrdmar. Like fierce Wind before me, I will take bold action. But men will not say that king Varenhil blows through the field. I will anoint my glorious rule with rampant blood and fire, and ruthlessly stamp out disloyalty wherever it may be found. My enemies will rue the day they ever showed disdain for the nobility of the Vyrdmar. Alas for them now, the Vyrdmar will rule by fear when once they ruled by divine right."

A hush passed over the hall. The two Vyrdmar princes looked at each other blankly, but with a glint of concern.

"Brothers," Varenhil continued. "The fate of our father, the late king deeply grieves me. His passing from us greatly displeases me. Perhaps now my emotions cloud my judgment. There is anger in me so potent. It began like a tremor from deep within me, rising up from my soul and surging to the crown of my head. Now my hands shake and my mouth is parched. Like a beast I hanker for blood. I shudder to think that I will act rashly and bring ruin to all that our father and his father before him have wrought. But then I think that perhaps my anger is the will of the gods. Perhaps I am the instrument of our father's vengeance that will punish our enemies and return the Vyrdmar to their lofty place in the world. That is why I cannot be dissuaded from the fierce and direct course I have settled on. In a fortnight, I will set out with my army for the Pelares to sever the Ayimar from the tree of species. Then I will go east to Parilos, and sack that city. I will not be merciful; I will fully satisfy my bloodlust. So far will I descend into depths of cruelty that when I return to the high city, I will have to be purified and kept aloof from others as a feral king."

Varenhil paused and glared at his brothers. "Countrymen," he said, sighing wearily. "I will have my vengeance as I see fit. It is only the last few days, weeks since my father's interment that I have come to terms with the dishonor and loss that was permitted to visit his house."

With eyes welling with tears, the king began to rub his eyes but then passed his hands over chin to unsuccessfully conceal his pain and anguish.

"I am bereft of him," he said through clenched teeth. "My enemies have taken my king from me. They have taken my youth and my dream of eternity; for as passes the father, so passes the son. I can see my own end now."

Hovin looked as if he would speak, reaching out a hand to his brother and king.

"No," the king said coldly. "When next I face my enemies, I will greet them with fire and sword. Their kin, countrymen, young and old, and servants alike, will all suffer the same fate. From branch to root, I will wrest all from the earth to atone for the sins of their treasonous lords. I will remain steadfast in prosecuting this duty, whether for justice, vengeance, or for pride, even if our entire world must be thrown into the pits of Nur's fiery tomb."

Night fell over the city and another chapter in its fabled history was written. Ruin had not come – at least not yet. The darkening sky was foreboding though. Far away, fire was churning beneath the earth and there were rumblings sounding ever louder. In the east, the earth had cracked opened and fissures appeared where there were once none. Golden eyes, not all-seeing, but sharp, surveyed from high above and saw the spectacles.

Later, the high priestess was once again holding vigil with her lantern sitting in a rectangular hall. The familiar wavering light shining eerily across her gentle face and gray hair gathered over her shoulders and bound with silk tassels. But a new season had taken hold, and the nights were not as crisp. The air was still and solemn as her gentle face. She sat on a bench with robes folded around her and placed her lantern on an adjacent bench, and then she bowed her head to await her expectant visitor.

Soon her head lifted at the sound of a gentle breeze whistling in from beyond the partially opened panel doors of a large window at the far side of the hall. Then a gust blew and the panel doors swung back on their hinges and once again the old woman reached for her lantern and reflexively cupped her hand around its thin metal panes to shield its fragile flame. The air quieted abruptly and was still, and the winged silhouette of the Celestial appeared at the window. The Celestial sprung inside the room and effortlessly made His way over to the dais at the center of the hall and crouched.

"The Deceiver has been set free from his mortal bondage," the Celestial began. "He is hidden from me now just as before, when in the dawn of time we were hidden from each other."

"Is this his doing?" the priestess asked.

"No," the Celestial replied. "This is nature's law; that species and symbiotes should be hidden from each other. It is the primordial law that binds even immortals. Yet he will surely find another host and be revealed. He spurns the symbiotes' nebulous realm. He yearns for the sensual existence of species. He yearns to live among men and to rule them all."

"But why?" the priestess asked.

"Promothos is driven by a yearning borne out of the souls of the Atenari who are not from this world. The Atenari were Promothos' first hosts and they rued their mortal frailty. They perished long ago believing they could bend all of nature's laws to their purpose. But time was too long and they passed from this world with bitterness. The Atenari's fear and condemnation of death became a maculate on the symbiotes' immortal being – and so through the ages, Promothos and his hosts have rallied men under the banner Atlantis, the Atenari ideal, and unleashed their evolutionary machinations to command the world and defeat death."

"The possibility of defeating death gives men hope," the priestess remarked.

"Alas," the Celestial sighed. "The Atenari way is seductive to species. Promothos has always shown men marvels they have found comforting and useful; marvels to veil their fear of frailty and death. To escape death, men have even embraced monstrous things."

"Indeed." The priestess nodded and then bowed her head.

"You have always been faithful, the Celestial added. But there is not much merit in that for you. You see me as men see the marvels of the Atenari. To you I am real, and not an abstraction. Yet men do not know me as you do. That is why they will reject me in the end. The traditions we offer them are based on an abstraction. Worse, the traditions we offer them alienate them from the sensual comforts they desire most. Promothos however promises them more of what they see every day; he promises them satisfaction. They may continue to erect temples in my name, but they will give their hearts to the Deceiver."

"There is hope," the Priestess pleaded. "As god-head, you are a path to the transcendent being binding all. You are a path to everlasting life. This truth has been revealed to some and they embrace it. I recently encountered a young man from the Austral land, and he seemed to have realized this truth. If this truth has been revealed to him, then surely it will be revealed to many others when the time is right. As long as there are those who realize the truth, Promothos will not be victorious."

"I hope you are right. I hope that in unraveling the benign, yet false traditions we have offered men, that they will not become embittered and distrustful. I hope that we do not lose them forever to the Atenari way and the famine of life and purpose that will ensue."

Meanwhile, Jaïem was looking out into torch-lit paths leading from the royal compound to the temple beyond from a window in his chambers. His mind was an oscillating scale of thoughts and potential. Now a dialogue was convening in his mind.

"What can be wrong with a conversation," he thought. "Men are curious and expressive. A conversation seems a foregone conclusion."

"But why are men so curious?" he countered himself. "That answer is clear," he answered.

"Men are here to find what is hidden even from the author of life. Our purpose is to search and to find the secrets of species and life. Men are purposed to reveal the mysteries of the past and to shape the future. But some believe that we are not meant to be the beneficiaries of our own purpose – that our expression serves a higher power. If this is the path chosen for us, we refuse it. We reject this tyranny. We want a destiny of our own making. We will search to find the means to our own ascension to the pinnacle of knowledge and power over life and death for our own satisfaction. Better to perish seeking to superimpose a destiny thrust upon us by the incidental dance of particle and motion within space, and the frailties of lesser species. Let us be free. Let us live and die in a manner of our own choosing. Let us not die at all, but rather simplify the manifold, and devour, and be sustained."

"Verily," Jaïem continued, "that is the way. That is the way of those anointed by the primordial flame."